MERCILESS

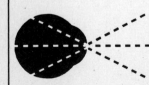

This Large Print Book carries the
Seal of Approval of N.A.V.H.

MERCILESS

MARY BURTON

THORNDIKE PRESS
A part of Gale, Cengage Learning

GALE
CENGAGE Learning™

Detroit • New York • San Francisco • New Haven, Conn • Waterville, Maine • London

GALE
CENGAGE Learning

Copyright © 2011 by Mary Burton.
Thorndike Press, a part of Gale, Cengage Learning.

ALL RIGHTS RESERVED
Thorndike Press® Large Print Core.
The text of this Large Print edition is unabridged.
Other aspects of the book may vary from the original edition.
Set in 16 pt. Plantin.

LIBRARY OF CONGRESS CATALOGING-IN-PUBLICATION DATA

Burton, Mary (Mary T.)
    Merciless / by Mary Burton.
      p. cm. — (Thorndike Press large print core)
    ISBN-13: 978-1-4104-3647-4 (hardcover)
    ISBN-10: 1-4104-3647-0 (hardcover)
    1. Serial murder investigation—Fiction. 2. Women
lawyers—Fiction. 3. Psychopaths—Fiction. 4. Large type books.
  I. Title.
  PS3602.U7699M47 2011
  813'.6—dc22   2011001252

Published in 2011 by arrangement with Zebra Books, an imprint of
Kensington Publishing Corp.

Printed in the United States of America
1 2 3 4 5 6 7 15 14 13 12 11

Merciless

PROLOGUE

The foul odor of decaying flesh roused the woman from her drugged haze, burning her nostrils and lungs like a freshly snapped ammonia capsule.

She blinked, clawed toward consciousness, searching the pitch-blackness for a landmark to anchor time or place. However, there was nothing except the stench that grew more potent with each hitching breath. She coughed and gagged. The contents of her stomach churned and rose up in her throat.

She lifted a trembling hand to her mouth but discovered the slight movement drove a cutting pain through her muscles and ribs. She froze, didn't want to move, fearing more agony, but nausea overruled everything and had her rolling to her side. Tears burned her eyes as she gripped the edge of the metal table and vomited until her throat burned.

When the worst of the vomiting had

stopped, she collapsed on her back, allowing only small shallow breaths as she stared into the darkness. She closed watery eyes and gently swiped her fingertips across her lips. The odors still hovered, but the worst of the nausea had passed.

With the sickness satisfied, there was only the pain. *Only.* Every square inch of her flesh pulsated. Throbbed. Burned.

Fear rose up, but she quickly wrestled it down. Now was not the time to crumble.

She blinked. Once. Twice. But the fetid darkness didn't diminish. It could have been the middle of the day or night, winter or summer. She couldn't tell.

She tried to rise again, but her insides screamed. Again, she collapsed.

Where was she? What had happened? She had to get free.

Think back.

In the last few weeks, she'd sensed that she was being watched. At first she'd chalked up the feelings to an overactive imagination. But as much as she denied the feelings, they grew stronger whenever she'd stepped out of her apartment, whenever she arrived at work, or whenever she took a Pilates class. Soon she'd thought twice before she went anywhere. She'd stopped going to the gym and her favorite nightclubs. Her world shrank to the small path between home and work.

And then the notes arrived. *I love you. Together always. You are never out of my mind.*

The notes had been a relief. In fact, she'd laughed when she'd received the first. *Of course!* Her ex had been her stalker. It had been three weeks since they'd shared a bed or seen each other, but she knew he was the one watching. He enjoyed dark, erotic games. He liked scaring her. Keeping her off balance.

Knowing he was watching, she'd worn tighter skirts and sweaters, proudly strutting and hoping she tortured him with jealousy. She met a younger man and took pleasure kissing him, knowing her ex was lurking in the shadows.

When she'd found the red velvet box with the ivory pendant nestled inside, she'd known she'd won. She'd been energized by her power over him, knowing soon he'd beg for forgiveness. Men were so easy. So weak.

"Oh, God," she whispered.

Someone had been stalking her. Watching. Planning. But it had not been her lover.

Pushing through pain and sickness, she sat up. "I'm alive. And that counts for something." She repeated the words like a mantra.

She blinked again and again, willing the blackness to fade and the stench and pain to vanish. But no lights magically flicked on. It hurt to breathe, and her thoughts moved like thick muddy waters.

Where had she been last? The theater? Her apartment? The club?

And then she remembered. She'd been at the Duke Street Café. There'd been an impromptu party. Someone had decided to celebrate another large donation to the theater. The donation ensured that the theater would be able to make its payroll and mount a grander, more expensive production in the spring.

The party had been a glittering, exciting affair, and she'd been happy. There'd been lots of champagne — so much so, that she'd lost count of how many times the waiter had refilled her glass. Of course her ex had not come. He never met up with her at public events. But another old boyfriend had hit on her, and because she'd felt so good she'd flirted back. It had been fun. Intoxicating.

How had she gone from such magical moments to this cave of horrors?

She ticked through the evening's events.

Wine. Music. Singing. A bite or two of food. Some guy, one of her ex-boyfriend's buddies, had offered her cocaine, but she'd turned him down, knowing the drug would keep her wired most of the night and make her look too puffy for tomorrow's photo call.

Had the actor and his friend slipped her something anyway?

Thoughts blurred in her mind. She couldn't cut through the misty mosaic to access the right memories. All she had was the party and then this dark, dank hole that smelled of death. The middle had vanished.

It didn't matter how she got here. What was important was escaping. And if she was good at anything, it was cutting her losses.

As much as she strained to see, she couldn't make out the room's details. The place was as still as a grave, and then suddenly she heard a tap turn on and water trickle.

She cocked her head. "Is someone there?"

Water gurgled and bubbled, but no one answered.

Struggling with a choking fear, she swung her legs over the side of the metal table. Her head spun, pain slammed her, and her stomach threatened another revolt. She hesitated and waited for her body to calm.

Gingerly, she set bare feet on a floor made

of cold, wet stone. Her toes curled. She hated the slimy surface, so much like a lake bottom.

Wobbly limbs screamed under the protest of her weight as she stood. Every muscle ached. Her dress felt damp, but she had no idea of the cause.

The soothing *drip, drip* of water remained her only reference. It sounded as if it was off to her right. At least now she had a direction.

Get to the water, and she'd figure out her next move.

She took a tentative step away from the table. Sweat dampened her body. Her dress clung to her breasts, hugging her nipples in an intimate way that left her feeling exposed. But as tempting as it was to cover up with her arms, her outstretched hands were all that kept her balanced.

With each step, the stench grew worse, and the urge to turn away increased. Still, she kept shuffling toward the water. Without warning, her knee bumped painfully into the side of what must have been a giant metal tub. Bolts of pain shot out and reverberated up and down her leg. She gasped, and the smells nearly overpowered her.

Instinct had her turning from the tub. "Shit."

She didn't have the strength to retrace her steps to the table now swallowed up in shadowy obscurity.

Tears filled her eyes and rolled down her cheeks. It would be so easy to surrender. But she'd never been a quitter. Ever.

Summoning her most imperious tone, she said, "I demand to know if anyone is there."

The shadows hovered around her, mutinously silent, still, and unmoved by her practiced sternness. Her only answer was the steady, quiet trickle of water dripping into the tub.

"I shouldn't be here," she said. "This is a terrible mistake. People are expecting me to show up at work. They'll call the cops if I don't show."

She shoved a shaky hand through feathered curls and righted her hunched shoulders. Body and bones creaked as if she'd just passed her ninetieth birthday and not her twenty-sixth. What had happened to her? "I demand to know where I am."

This time a shadow in a corner shifted. "You demand? If I were you, I wouldn't demand. I'd beg."

The rough, clipped voice had her head jerking around. "Why should I beg?" Even as she asked the question, she saw the absurdity. She'd beg or do whatever was asked of her to get out of here. "What do I need to beg for?"

"Your life would be a good start." His voice was so silky and gentle. And for a moment, it sounded very familiar. Had he been at the party? Where had she heard his voice before?

She leaned against the tub, fearing her legs would give way and she'd fall to her knees. "I am not afraid."

A soft chuckle snaked through the gloom, unsettling her more than if the shadow man had hurled threats. "You should be afraid."

Tears streamed down her cheeks, but she raised her chin. "What is that smell?"

"Rotting flesh."

This time her knees did crumble. She dropped to the ground, digging long fingers into the stone. "Why?"

"Why? Why are you here? Why is there rotting flesh in the room? Why what?"

His voice sent fear knifing into her. "Why me?"

She heard the clip of his shoes on the stone floor as he moved away. For a panicked second she thought he'd leave her alone in this room of horrors. Instead, he flipped on a light.

In a blink, overhead fluorescents clicked on, flooding the room with light and forcing

14

her to wince and shield her eyes from the burning glare. Carefully, she cracked her lids, letting the light leak into her pupils.

When her gaze finally focused on her jailer she saw he stood directly in front of her. He wore crisp jeans, a dark sweater, and rubber gloves. He looked so normal. Handsome even.

"Do I know you?"

"Doesn't matter." He clapped his hands. "Want to have a good look around before we get to work?"

The source of the smell had her turning back toward the tub. It was a vile, putrid concoction of greasy, black water. Loose fatty deposits floated on the surface. Oh shit! Was it flesh clinging to bone?

She screamed and lurched back. "What is that?"

"It's where the polishing process begins. Flesh must be stripped from the bones before I can polish them." The lightness in his voice told her he was truly enjoying this moment. "Now, we better get moving. We've got work to do."

"Work? Where is this place?"

"Far enough from anyone that can help you."

Tremors started to move through her limbs. "Where *am* I?"

"It's where I do my work. My art."

"What kind of art?"

"Look behind you."

She turned and saw a workbench. Equipped with saws, carving knives, and buffing pads. It reminded her of a jeweler's workstation. Until she saw it — the polished white femur.

"That's not art!"

"You seemed to like the cameo I gave you."

Her hand rose to her throat where the brooch had rested just days ago. "That was bone?"

He winked. "I love the way the light glistens on the bones, don't you? Human bone carves like sandstone."

"You are demented."

Blue eyes sparked. "To each his own."

"Please, don't do this to me."

"No going back now."

"Of course there is. I won't tell."

And then as if she hadn't spoken, he said, "If we get started now, we'll be done by this time next week." He hooked a steady, gloved hand under her elbow and pulled her to a standing position. "Let's get you back on the table."

Her legs wobbled, and her insides ached with fire. When she glanced down, she saw

16

that blood stained her skirt and legs. Crimson droplets covered the ground around her feet. "What have you done to me?"

He guided her toward the table. "I haven't done anything. Now up you go."

"My body hurts." She'd been invaded, assaulted. Flickers of what had happened flashed: an attacker shoving into her with such force she'd screamed. He'd laughed, pushed harder, and then he'd leaned down and bitten her shoulder until her blood had spilled. He'd taken pictures. "You did this to me! You did this!"

"Not me. Him."

Her head spun, and her pain paralyzed her muscles. "There are two of you?"

He ignored the question. "You know you have the most perfect bone structure. Your cheekbones are symmetrically perfect. It's as if an artist sculpted them."

"Please," she whispered.

"Mother Nature can be so haphazard and fickle, but with you she really outdid herself."

She lay back against the cold metal, her body collapsing with exhaustion. Whatever reserves she'd possessed had vanished. She was empty. "What are you going to do?"

Out from the shadows stepped another man. She knew this man. She'd run her

17

fingers through his hair. She'd kissed his face. Gotten to know the feel of his broad shoulder blades under her hands. "You did this to me."

Smiling, he snapped another picture. "I'm finished with her. She's yours now."

"No, please," she said.

He didn't answer but simply turned. He left her alone with The Other, who grinned as he selected a knife from a table.

"Don't leave me here with him!" she screamed.

A door closed.

The Other picked up a knife. Light glinted from the steel. "I'm going to make the pain go away."

As much as the pain scorched through her body and stole her breath, it was proof of life. Without the pain, she feared, she'd be lost. "I want to leave."

Gently, he smoothed his fingertips over her forehead. "Shh. We can't do that."

The gentle touch detonated shivers. And then he dragged the razor sharp blade over the tender flesh of her neck. The pain was sudden and searing. Warm blood drained so quickly from the wound.

She inhaled, but her lungs didn't respond. She tried to pull in a second breath. Nothing. Panic exploded as she directed her energy toward her lungs.

Breathe! Air!

A gurgling sound rose in her chest as the air already in her lungs seeped out through the wound. More blood pooled around her shoulders. She gripped the table, clinging to her final hold on life.

He kept smoothing gentle fingers over her head. "Don't fight it. Fighting only makes it worse. It will just be a few more seconds, it will all be over, and I can get you in that tub with the others."

Her vision blurred. Her lungs and flesh howled for air. Gentle fingers stroked her hair and cheeks.

"So pretty."

Delight danced in his eyes. The more she struggled to breathe the greater his enjoyment. In these last moments of her life she realized bliss for him was watching her die.

The blackness returned to the edges of her vision, and with each second her constricting pupils squeezed out more light.

She had no breath to scream.

And then, like the final curtain call in the theater, the blackness dropped.

He stared down at her. It was a miracle that she'd gotten up off the table. After what the First One had done, it was a wonder she was alive. But he'd have been furious if she'd died. The killing was his treat. His well deserved reward.

He'd not expected she'd be such a fighter. She was a beautiful woman accustomed to using her beauty to get what she wanted. She'd never tasted the harshness that life really could offer.

But she'd faced him with a haughty arrogance that he found a bit charming. It was always more fun to bring the bossy ones down a peg.

He clicked on an overhead light and studied her face. Her flesh had been torn and bruised. If anyone saw her now, they'd be appalled by the damage. He didn't like it when skin was mauled and ruined.

But thankfully, her injuries were only skin-deep. Flesh may have been torn, but her bones were sure and strong.

She would make a fine addition to his collection.

Chapter 1

Tuesday, October 4, 9 p.m.

The flashing lights of the cop cars at the entrance to Angel Park grated Detective Malcolm Kier's nerves as he pulled his badge out from his glove box and strung it around his neck. He'd been in the mountains for the last three days, taking a much-needed vacation in the small cabin he owned. Nestled on a lake in the Shenandoah Valley, his cabin was set on thirty acres connected to the main highway by a dirt road that snaked up the mountain. The closest store was twenty miles away.

The log cabin that he'd built had small, shuttered windows that kept the bugs out in the summer and the cold at bay in the winter. There was a front porch that overlooked a lake, but it was only wide enough for two chairs. A generator fed electricity to a small refrigerator, and a propane tank supplied a crude kitchen stove with gas. Indoor plumbing was limited to cold water only in the kitchen, and until he paid down the loan on the land, a full-scale bathroom was the dream and an outhouse the reality.

Most would look at the cabin and wonder what kind of sane man would bother. But from the moment he'd laid eyes on the land, he'd felt at home. At peace.

No, the place wasn't comfortable or easy, but that's what he liked about it. He liked that not just anyone could saunter through the front door and call the place home. He liked that he didn't smell the grit of the streets; that he didn't hear the blare of sirens or the sobs of victims.

Most of the cops he worked with considered the utter silence a curse, but he loved it. No cell phone service meant that when he took a few days off from the demands of being an Alexandria homicide detective, he was truly off.

His girlfriend, Olivia, had been after him to take her to the cabin for weeks. He'd relented, hoping she'd see beyond the obstacles and grow to love the place. However, on her first and only visit, she'd been using the outhouse when a black snake had slithered past her feet. Her scream could have shattered glass. And when she burst out of the outhouse, tugging up her pants and trying not to trip, he'd had the good sense not to laugh. He'd found the snake and told her it wasn't poisonous. Olivia had recovered enough and announced in a calm voice that she didn't care. She wasn't returning. She still loved him, but this was a part of his life she'd not share.

A smile curved the edge of Malcolm's lips as he thought about her traipsing toward his car and mumbling.

Over the last few days, he'd missed his gal and had been half tempted to drive down the mountain and call from town. But the lure of calm and silence had been stronger than his need to talk, and in the end he'd never called her.

Kier had been twenty miles outside of Alexandria, Virginia when his cell had rung. The sound, which he'd not heard in seventy-two hours, had him straightening. A glance at the caller ID told him the call came from dispatch and that his vacation had officially ended.

He grabbed his holster and revolver from under the seat and got out of the car. He slipped the holster over his black flannel shirt and then shrugged on a jean jacket.

Angel Park was an eleven-acre recreation area sandwiched between Duke and King Streets. By the looks there were picnic areas, ball fields, and lots of places for kids to run and hide.

On a warm day, this place would have been swarming with kids and parents. There'd be the peal of laughter. The squeak of swing sets.

It pissed him off that a killer had breached a place reserved for kids. Places like this shouldn't allow death or evil. But he'd learned long ago that killers violated any rule that suited.

Malcolm glanced toward the yellow crime-scene tape and saw his partner, Detective Deacon Garrison. A tall man, Garrison stood a good head above most of the other officers. Malcolm's shoulders were as broad, perhaps more muscular, but at five-foot-ten, he had to tip his head back to make eye contact with his partner.

Garrison had a thousand-watt smile that he used with laser precision to disarm witnesses, cajole judges, and piss off defense attorneys. Kier had often quipped his partner could sell ice to an Eskimo with that smile.

Malcolm strode past the uniforms, nodded, and ducked under the tape. He moved beside his partner, who stared at an empty patch of dirt. "Not the kind of welcome back I'd hoped for."

A humorless smile tipped the edge of Garrison's lips. "You have a nice vacation?"

"Yeah. The woods always bring me back to life."

Garrison shook his head as he slid a hand into his pocket. "If your place is only half as bad as you've said, I don't know how it could. Seems to me the primitive setup would do the opposite."

Malcolm shrugged. "Hey, if you ever want me to suffer, lock me in that airplane hangar of yours and make me work on that pile of junk you call an airplane."

Garrison's smile warmed a fraction. "It is a classic '38 Beechcraft. Beyond the rust is great beauty."

"Whatever you say, boss." Malcolm and his partner were opposites in so many ways. When faced with a pile of shit, Garrison could smile and appear as if nothing bothered him at all. However, Malcolm, a self-described powder keg, blew up fast and wore his anger on his sleeve.

Malcolm nodded his head toward an area lit up with floodlights and roped off with yellow crime-scene tape. No doubt they'd be hearing from the park's residential neighbors complaining about the light. "Body's over there?"

"Wait until you see this." Displeasure

deepened the lines on Garrison's face as they strode toward the shelter closest to the woods.

Malcolm braced, wondering what horror waited.

In the middle of a picnic table sat a pile of bones stacked neatly in a square. Resting in the center of the bone square was the skull, which stared sightlessly at him.

The bones weren't bleached white, as if they had been lying in the sun, nor were they dark and molded as if long buried under layers of dirt. Light beige, they were oddly clean, stripped completely of flesh.

"The killer took his time arranging the bones."

Garrison nodded his head. "Yes."

"Time that would have exposed him to potential witnesses." Malcolm rested his hands on his hips and leaned in for a closer view. "He's meticulous. Detail oriented. Likes order in his life. Takes pride in his work."

"Maybe. Whoever did this wanted to get someone's attention."

Malcolm tried to imagine the killer arranging the bones and then standing back for a moment to admire his handiwork. The homicide detective had a talent for slipping into the skins of the men he tracked. The trait made him a good cop and at times a bad boyfriend, son, or brother. "Arranging the bones generates fear and creates one hell of a puzzle for the cops."

"Plausible."

"The average killer does not do this."

"No, he does not." Garrison shoved out a sigh. They'd had a very extraordinary killer stalk Alexandria last year. Dubbed the Sorority House Killer by the press, the killer had not only displayed the victims, but had set a fire at the first murder scene to draw attention. However, the Sorority House Killer had been convicted of murder and now resided on death row.

"Where is forensics?" Malcolm searched the half dozen cop cars. Normally the forensics unit beat the detectives to the crime scene.

"They're on the way. They've been overwhelmed by the string of robberies. They're running in circles right now."

"Who found the bones?"

"Three boys were staring and pointing fingers when an off-duty cop spotted them. He'd just gotten off his shift and was walking his dog. When he called out to them, they bolted. However, the cop's dog is retired from our K-9 unit."

Malcolm grinned. "They didn't get far."

"No."

"Where are they?"

"Cooling their heels by the squad cars," Garrison said.

Malcolm saw three teen boys leaning against a marked car. Arms folded over their chests, they did their best to look tough despite downcast gazes messaging worry. Low-slung jeans, white T-shirts, and matching leather jackets with yellow bandanas tied to their right forearms suggested a gang.

"This could be gang related," Garrison said. "The placement of the bones could be some kind of initiation. Leaving bones would send a clear message."

Malcolm studied the boys. "They don't look like the types who have the know-how or patience to stack bones."

"People never stop surprising me."

Malcolm glanced toward the yellow crime-scene tape and spotted a slim man, slightly balding and wearing glasses that reflected the floodlight's glare. Paulie Sommers. Forensic technician. Efficient. Brusque to the point of rudeness.

"What do we have?" Paulie ducked under the tape and approached.

Malcolm eased out of Paulie's way. He liked razzing the guy. "Not as quick on the draw as you used to be."

"Tell the boys in robbery to catch the son of a bitch who's breaking into every jewelry store in town. Once they do that I can have time for *better* crimes like your murders." Sarcasm dripped from the words.

"I'll be sure to send a memo."

"Do that."

Most didn't understand that cops could be so casual in the face of death. But it was that very distance mingled with dark humor that kept the horrors they witnessed at bay. "We've got bones stacked. Neatly arranged. I need anything you can find around the area that might help."

Paulie squinted. "There should be foot-prints. The ground is soft from yesterday's rain." He glanced at the crowd around the scene's perimeter. "But God only knows how many of them traipsed around here and contaminated the area."

"That's why you were called, my friend," Garrison said. "You are the miracle worker."

"Don't blow smoke up my ass." Paulie raised his digital camera and snapped photos of the area. "Now get out of my crime scene."

"Charming as always," Malcolm said.

"Bite me."

Garrison laughed. "So what's got you more pissed off than usual, Paulie?"

"It's fucking freezing out here. And because of those damn robberies and because Lorraine Marcus is still on maternity leave, I had to leave a hot dinner, which is now likely cold."

Malcolm laid his palm over his heart. "Stop, you're going to make me cry."

Paulie muttered something under his breath as Malcolm stepped aside to let the man shoot pictures of the bone collection.

Rubbing the back of his neck, Malcolm wished now he'd grabbed an energy bar from the trunk of his car. It had been about three hours since he'd eaten, and it was going to be a long night.

As Paulie continued to snap pictures, Malcolm pulled his notebook from his back pocket and flipped it open. Paulie would document the scene in great detail, but Malcolm always kept his own maps of a crime scene. And he took notes constantly, knowing one day a detail could come back to bite him when some courtroom defense attorney was chewing on his ass. "I'm going to talk to the cop first so he can get out of here. The kids can wait."

"Take your time," Garrison said. "It'll be a while before Paulie is finished doing his thing."

Malcolm pushed through the uniforms

and found the cop and his dog, a German shepherd, sitting on the tailgate of a red truck. The cop was dressed in jeans and a worn hunting jacket. He had short hair and a thick mustache. He smoked a cigarette. The dog lay in the bed of the truck on a blanket, sleeping, as if crime scenes held no interest.

When the off-duty cop saw Malcolm coming he took one last pull on the butt, and then ground it into the tailgate of his truck. "So you got questions?"

Malcolm extended his hand. "More than I can count. I'm Malcolm Kier."

He shook his hand. "From Richmond."

"Nice to see I'm noticed."

"It's a big small town in Alexandria. I'm Grant McCabe. I work narcotics."

"Hell of a way to end an evening."

"Tell me about it." The cop's shoulders slumped as if carrying the heavy weight of fatigue. "Shoot."

"Give me the basics."

"Arrived about seven p.m. I'd been on the job since seven a.m. but couldn't break away until after six. Had to babysit a teen drug addict at the emergency room. Picked her up near a crack house I had staked out. Anyway, got home, changed fast, and took Striker out for a run. He's a good guy, and

31

I can take him off the lead most nights. Tonight, he paused just as we entered the park: then he bolted past the play equipment. Figured it was a squirrel. Since he's old and retired, there's something about October that makes Striker a little nuts. It was the kids hovering around the shelter."

"Were they looking at the table or arranging bones on the table?"

"Looking. Their arms were folded over their chests. They sounded excited. Agitated. Scared even."

That could or could not mean something. Killers often got scared when the reality of their act settled. "Keep going."

"So, I call out and ask what's what. They don't answer but take off. I go bolting after them, cussing like a sailor. Striker raced past me. He stopped them. When I catch up, the kids are about to piss in their pants. I tell Striker to heel. The old dog looked mighty proud of himself. Long story short I show them my badge and drag them back to the shelter. Striker starts barking like a crazy dog."

The shepherd glanced up at McCabe, his head cocked. McCabe scratched him between the ears. "So, I shine my flashlight on the table. That's when I saw your victim."

His victim. In less than a half hour he'd

gone from vacation to taking charge of a dead body. "You called it in."

"Right away."

"See anything?"

"Your partner already ran through the checklist. No, I didn't see anything. No cars in the lot. No one hanging around the woods. No creepy sounds or smells. It was business as usual until Striker got a whiff of the bones."

"Thanks, McCabe." He wrote down the officer's contact information. "Why don't you take off? If I need you, I know where to find you."

McCabe rose gingerly to his feet as if his body ached. "Swear to God, my bones are telling me it's going to be an early winter."

"Man, you're too young to be creaking."

McCabe laughed. "Rugby in high school and in college. Beat the piss out of me."

Striker jumped down from the bed and trotted to the driver's side of the truck.

"See you around, Kier."

"Sure thing, McCabe."

While Malcolm waited for Sommers to finish up his work at the scene, he moved to the trunk of his car and got a few energy bars. They could hardly be considered cuisine, but they'd stave off the hunger until he could get a real meal.

■ ■ ■ ■

It was past one in the morning when Sommers declared that the bones could be removed from the table and transferred to a bag. He'd photographed the entire area, noted the location of the bones, and taken impressions of shoe imprints in the dirt.

Paulie moved toward them, his thin shoulders stooped. "I called the medical examiner and ran this one past her. She should be here any minute."

Malcolm raised a brow. The medical examiner, Dr. Amanda Henson, rarely came to crime scenes. It didn't make sense for her to visit each and every murder scene when she had so much to tackle in the autopsy room.

But this case had to rank high on her odd-o-meter, and she would be curious. And frankly he didn't mind the arrival of the big guns because he never said no to help on a murder investigation.

Dr. Henson's black SUV pulled up behind the police cars. She slid out from behind the driver's seat. Her red hair was tucked up under a Nationals ball cap, and she wore a large peacoat over jeans. Worn sneakers covered her feet.

She moved quickly, efficiently with a burst of energy that didn't seem right at this time of night. She ducked under the yellow crime-scene tape and held out her hand to Garrison, Malcolm, and Paulie. Her handshake was firm and quick. Her hands were small, delicate even, and her nails neatly trimmed. Malcolm had seen those nimble fingers play guitar at the lab's Christmas party last year and grip bolt cutters as she snapped rib cages apart during autopsies.

"Gentlemen. Paulie tells me you have an unusual case here." She never raised her voice, but that didn't diminish the authority.

"All we got right now are bones," Malcolm said.

"Have a look at the pictures." Paulie pulled the camera strap from around his neck and switched his digital camera to VIEW.

She squinted, clicked through several images, and then handed the camera back to Paulie. "Bones in the body bag now?"

"That they are," Malcolm said.

She nodded, moved past him, and as she pulled on gloves she glanced into the body bag. Gently, she picked up a bone and under the glare of the floodlight studied it. A frown wrinkled her brow.

"So what are you thinking, Doc?" Malcolm asked.

"How long were the bones exposed to the elements?" she asked.

"The kids said they came through the park yesterday. Seems this shelter is their favorite meeting spot," Garrison said. "This is where they exchange drugs and money. Anyway, no bones yesterday."

Dr. Henson frowned. "So we can assume the bones were positioned very late yesterday or early this morning."

"Arranged like Lincoln Logs."

She cocked a brow. "Only you could equate bones to a child's toy, Detective Kier. Jung would have a field day with your childhood."

Unfazed, Malcolm held her gaze. "The childhood was normal. But I wasn't a normal kid."

"Who was?" Garrison said. "Sane people don't stare at bones at one a.m."

Dr. Henson nodded, seeing the greater truth behind the words. "So they weren't exposed to the elements?"

"Not here," Malcolm said.

"Interesting." She glanced into the bag and picked up the skull. "Your victim is female."

Malcolm's interest peaked. "How can you tell?"

"The narrow brow line and the high cheekbones are both characteristics consistent with a female. I'd also guess that she was Caucasian and around thirty."

He scribbled down what she'd just said. "Because why?"

Dr. Henson traced her finger down the center of the skull. "Narrow nasal passage is consistent with the Caucasoid race, and see these lines in the top of the skull?"

"Right."

"That doesn't happen until mid-twenties."

"Really?"

"Bones will tell you a story if you know how to read them." Carefully, she replaced the skull in the bag. "The bones aren't brittle or old as a body long dead would be."

"Any guess on time of death?"

She raised a trim brow, and for the first time he saw amusement dance in her eyes. "Sorry, that will take a little more work."

"Worth a try."

"I would suggest you contact Missing Persons and ask them to search for Caucasian women between the ages of twenty-five and thirty-five."

Malcolm unclipped his cell phone from

the holster on his hip. "Doc, they were first on my call list."

CHAPTER 2

Wednesday, October 5, 6:01 a.m.

Missing Persons had four possible Jane Does that could have matched Malcolm's victim. The first two were hookers, the third a drug addict, and the fourth an actress. Malcolm tried to contact the people who'd issued the reports on the hookers and drug addict, but no one answered the numbers provided in the report. Not surprising. Hookers and drug addicts lived on the fringe, and associations and friendships were tentative at best. It also made them easy prey for killers.

Last on his list was the actress. Sierra Day. The man who'd called in the report, Terry Burgess, was the manager of the West End Theater, and he was also directing Sierra's latest play.

When he dialed Burgess's number, he was surprised to hear an alert, if not angry, "What!"

39

"This is Detective Malcolm Kier with Alexandria Police."

"Okay." His tone bordered on brittle.

Malcolm's hackles rose, but he kept his voice even. "I'm calling about a missing persons report you filed."

"Right. Yeah. Sure. Sierra Day. Did you find her?"

"That's what I'd like to talk to you about. Can we meet?"

"It's really not a good time. I'm at the theater and up to my ass in work. We open in nine days."

"We need to meet now." His steely tone was the verbal equivalent to him baring teeth.

"Sure. I'm at the theater." Burgess sighed and gave the address.

Malcolm jotted the address down, hung up his phone, and glanced at Garrison. "Another charming citizen who believes he's doing us a favor."

"Let it roll off your back, man."

"Easier said than done."

Garrison shrugged. He gave good advice, but they both knew he also took the job too personally at times.

"According to Burgess's missing persons report, Sierra Day, the lead actress in his upcoming play *The Taming of the Shrew,* failed to show up for play practice."

"When was that?"

"Ten days ago. When she missed an important photo call, Burgess called the cops."

"She's been missing a week and a half? The bones had no traces of flesh. With the cool weather a body wouldn't decompose that fast. Doesn't seem to fit."

"No, but she's our only lead now."

By the time Malcolm and Garrison arrived at the West End Theater in Old Town it was just after six-thirty in the morning. They'd woven down side streets skirting the morning commuter traffic that clogged the Washington Beltway.

Parking in Old Town Alexandria, the historic section of the city, was challenging at midday but just after dawn fairly easy. The cobblestone streets and centuries-old town houses housed trendy shops, restaurants, and museums that were a magnet for tourists who streamed into the area.

At this hour the historic district remained asleep except for a few coffee shops that catered to the locals working in the area's service industries, hotels, and diners.

Garrison pulled down a side street and parked right in front of the old brick building that was home to the West End Theater. Located on a corner, the theater building was freestanding. A wrought-iron fence bordered a backyard featuring a simple stone stage surrounded by seats made of the same stone, reminiscent of an old Greek theater. In the summertime the trees would be lush and full, the grass green, and the random planters filled with brightly colored flowers. But now fall had stripped the trees, leaving their branches nearly barren and the ground covered with brown leaves.

Malcolm glanced at the laptop computer screen mounted between their seats in the front of their Crown Vic. "According to the theater's website they've been here since 1934." He shook his head as he stared at the building. "I've passed this place enough times but never stopped. Olivia has been after me to attend a play with her, but I keep dodging."

"Can't say I'm a theater person, either. Mom and my sister dragged me to a play a couple of months ago. I dozed off."

"They catch you?"

"My sister Carrie did, but she didn't narc to Mom." Carrie, adopted by Garrison's parents from foster care when she was five was now fifteen. She was a precocious child whose brown eyes reflected the losses she'd suffered. As Garrison liked to say, she was fifteen going on fifty.

"Not much gets past teenagers. Or kinder-garten teachers."

"Olivia bust you for something?"

He shrugged. "She dropped the M word right before I went out of town. I knew the steaks and homemade bread were too good to be true."

"She wants to get married."

"Yeah. But she did say that I don't have to marry her right now. She's just looking for some kind of timetable."

Garrison looked amused. "A deadline."

"She likes to have all the facts."

"So what did you say?"

Malcolm opened his car door and got out. "I kept smiling and saying how great the food tasted and how great she is." Why he couldn't just say *yes* worried him. Good or bad, he made his decisions quickly and with no regrets. Except this time.

Garrison followed and closed his door. "You've been seeing a lot of her. She seems to fit your profile."

"Profile?"

"Pretty. Great cook. Easy going. Wants kids."

"I like her. She's easy to be around."

"So do I hear wedding bells?"

Malcolm slammed his car door and locked it. "I should be asking you that question.

You and Eva have had a thing for well over a year."

"Hey man, Eva and I are opposites. Draw charts and grids to analyze us, and you'd figure us for failures."

"And yet you keep seeing each other."

Garrison shook his head. "The woman drives me crazy."

"That good or bad?"

"Both. We got into it at King's last night." Eva worked at King's as a waitress/bartender and office manager. At twenty-eight, she'd just started her junior year in college. She made no attempt to hide the fact that she'd first entered college at seventeen but a decade in prison for a murder she'd not committed had delayed her education. The real killer had been caught, Eva's conviction had been overturned last year, and she rarely looked back. Fiercely independent, she didn't shy away from conflict and had an IQ that was off the charts.

"She's still volunteering at that halfway house for ex-cons?"

"Yeah." Garrison shook his head. "Damn dangerous. They had a knifing there last week."

"Eva in the middle of it?"

"Oh, she broke it up. I only found out about it yesterday. The uniform that had been on scene told me." The darkening of Garrison's gaze testified to his frustrations.

"Eva's a little too fearless."

"Must run in the family." Eva's older sister was Angie Carlson, Esquire. Defense attorney. Brilliant, hardworking, and tenacious, many in the department called her "The Barracuda." Malcolm had only crossed swords with her a few times, and the encounters confirmed she would do whatever it took to defend her client.

"They are as different as night and day," Garrison said.

"Maybe in looks, but under the skin . . . there's no mistaking the genetic link."

Garrison frowned. None of the cops in the area were fond of Carlson's tenacity. "You trying to piss me off?"

"Stay out of my love life, and I'll stay out of yours."

"Agreed."

They strode up to the theater's double red front doors. Brass knockers, tarnished by weather and neglect, hung in the center of each. To the right of the door was a list of the upcoming season's plays, which was to kick off next week with *The Taming of the Shrew.* Spring brought two plays unfamiliar to him: a comedy, *Noises Off,* and the drama *Terra Nova. A Christmas Carol* was their

December production.

"According to the theater's website, the place used to be a warehouse when the city was a thriving port. The building was about to be condemned when a bunch of rich ladies bought the place in the thirties and founded the theater. It was their way of creating jobs and entertainment during the depression."

Garrison pounded on the front door. "Well, let's see what we can find out about Sierra Day."

Heavy footsteps sounded on the other side of the door, and seconds later it opened.

A short man with red-rimmed eyes, a neatly trimmed beard, and wire-rimmed glasses glared up at them. He wore jeans, a Stones black T-shirt, and polished black cowboy boots. "You Kier?"

Malcolm nodded. "That's right. You Terry Burgess?"

"Yeah."

"This is my partner, Detective Deacon Garrison. Thanks for meeting with us."

"Didn't sound like I had a choice." Burgess stepped aside so that they could enter the building.

The hallway was lined with hundreds of framed photos taken during countless plays. An overhead bulb didn't spit out enough light to fully illuminate the hall, but Malcolm guessed that was intentional. In full light the place likely would show more age and wear. Stacked along the wall were dozens of brown boxes imprinted with the logo A&A PRINTING.

"You always get in early?" Malcolm asked.

"It's late for me. I've been here for thirty-six hours straight." Brittleness crackled in the guy's tone.

Malcolm held on to his patience, as he remembered he was also sleep deprived. "That's rough."

Terry pinched the bridge of his nose. "It's been a very long night. My understudy for Sierra Day is a disaster, and at the rate she is going reviewers will hammer us when we open next week. Can we just talk about the missing persons report on Sierra?"

"You've already replaced her?"

"I waited two days, but I had to move forward. Too many people are working on this show, which is costing me a fortune."

"Could she have just taken off?" Malcolm asked.

"Sierra is temperamental, a bitch, demanding, but she never misses play practice or photo calls. She's too vain and too ambitious."

"What about a man or drugs?" Garrison asked.

"Doubtful. I mean she's been through her share of men. But nothing stood between her and the stage. She loved it. And she never did drugs."

"Was she angry about something? Did you two have a fight?"

"Her last day here we got into it about the lighting. The new public relations manager commented that the lighting looked hot, and then Sierra got all worried that she'd start to sweat on stage, and her audience would see it."

"It was a big fight?"

"We yelled. And we called each other a few choice names. But that's how we do things. When I call her a bitch it's only in the nicest way."

"So she left angry," Malcolm said. "She's not hiding out somewhere and cooling her heels just to make you sweat?"

"She better not be. Or I just might strangle her with my own two hands." Burgess delivered the line with enough flourish to undercut the words' meaning. He sounded like an actor on stage.

Malcolm raised a brow. "Why's that?"

"I chose this play for the season because she agreed to do it. Sierra was the perfect

Katherine. She was made for the part, and I was hoping for great reviews. Now she's gone."

"Do you have a picture of Ms. Day?"

He nodded and reached into an A&A Printing box. "Just delivered. Now we'll need to print a correction." Inside were Playbills for *The Taming of the Shrew*. Burgess flipped to page three and showed them the picture of a bright-eyed blonde with a smile that would make any man stop and notice.

Malcolm didn't know if this woman was his victim. But it sickened him to think someone so young and vibrant had been stripped of her identity.

"Have you found Sierra or not?" Terry asked.

"We've found a body," Malcolm said, choosing his words carefully. "But we've not made an identification."

Terry's face paled. "You can't compare the picture to the body?"

"Not in this case." And without giving too many details he added, "The killer didn't leave us much."

Burgess looked sick. "How did she die?"

"Can't say. Right now we are just trying to determine our victim's identity. Sierra Day's missing persons report matches what we know about our victim. Is there anyone who would want to hurt Sierra?"

"The better question is who didn't."

Malcolm raised a brow and pulled out a notebook. "Start at the top of the list."

Terry glanced down at Malcolm's pen poised to write on his notepad. "Hey, and when I said I could kill Sierra, I didn't mean in the literal sense."

"Duly noted," Malcolm said. "Who hated Sierra?"

"Her soon-to-be ex-husband for one. His name is Brian Humphrey, and he acts in plays here from time to time. He was never as good an actor as Sierra, and I think that didn't help their marriage. And then toss in the fact that Sierra is a bit of a whore, and well, you get my point."

"Sierra slept around?"

"According to Brian she started an affair with another actor here two months after they got back from their honeymoon."

Garrison raised a brow. "Two months. Who was the guy?"

"I don't know. You'd have to ask Brian. But I can tell you that Brian was one angry dude. He came by the theater several times during rehearsal, and he and Sierra got into some knock-down, drag out fights. The last time she slapped him."

"When was that?" Kier asked.

"Three weeks, give or take."

"What can you tell me about Sierra?"

"She was stunning and very talented. She could slip into a role like you or I put on a coat. She had the *it* factor."

"Did she know she was good?"

"Oh, yes, she did. She was a smart one. She knew she had the talent to go far. And she wasn't afraid to do whatever she needed to get what she wanted."

"Can you explain that?"

"Two years ago she was the understudy in a play. The night of opening, the lead actress, who was healthy as a horse, got sick as a dog. Threw up so much she had to be taken to the hospital for IVs. Sierra stepped into her place. The lead recovered, but it was two weeks before she could work again. By then Sierra had gotten all the opening-night reviews and notices. That gig quickly led to another bigger role. She had her sights on Broadway and Hollywood."

"Who was the actress who got sick?" Malcolm asked.

"Zoe Morgan."

"Where can I find her?"

"Works at the ballet now. I don't know where she lives." Burgess sighed. "Box-office sales were strong because of Sierra. She was a local favorite. I hate to think of the refunds we'll have to process when word leaks out she won't be in the play."

"You said she had her sights on Hollywood and Broadway?"

"This was her last season with us. She planned to leave at Christmas after her surgery."

"Surgery?"

"She was planning on getting a boob job."

Malcolm shook his head. "She told you this?"

"Oh, yes. She was quite open about her plans. She understood the bigger the boobs the better the roles down the line. She was pushing along her divorce so that she could get her financial settlement. Needed the money for the surgical work." He scratched the back of his head. "She was on the phone with her attorney last week, yelling for a court date."

"Who was her attorney?" Garrison asked.

"I'll never forget the name. I heard Sierra yell it out enough. Angie Carlson."

Eva's sister. The Barracuda.

Garrison stiffened.

Malcolm muttered an oath. "Figures."

"You know the woman?" Terry prompted.

"Yeah." Last spring she defended local plastic surgeon James Dixon, who'd been accused of attempted murder of a prostitute. Malcolm and the other cops in homicide suspected that James might be linked to the disappearance of several other prostitutes, but they'd not been able to prove it. DNA had linked him to some of the women, but at the time each had vanished, he'd had an alibi.

However, the last hooker who'd survived her time with Dixon had run from their motel room after enduring several hours of his sadistic tastes. Bleeding, she'd run down a dark street screaming until an undercover vice cop had stopped her. She blurted out her story, and the cop put out an APB on Dixon. Officers stopped him six blocks away.

Dixon had been arrested for attempted murder. He'd hired Carlson, who had shredded the prostitute's testimony on the stand. She proved the woman was a drug addict and an admitted liar. The jury accepted all of Carlson's explanations and ignored the prostitute's testimony. They found Dixon not guilty.

Malcolm didn't believe Dixon was innocent for a minute. He might have been a model citizen this past year, but he was like a spider nestled in a web. He was waiting for the right victim to come along before he pounced.

"Did she ever mention the name of her plastic surgeon?" Malcolm asked.

"Yeah. Talked about him a lot. James Dixon."

"Say that again," Malcolm said.

"Her doctor was James Dixon." Burgess nodded. "I know who he is, and I even told her to stay clear of him. But she liked the fact that Dixon was surrounded by his own drama. Sierra liked drama."

Malcolm ground his teeth as he glanced at Garrison. "Carlson and Dixon. The Dynamic Duo."

"With those two," Garrison said, "Sierra Day would have gotten her fill of drama."

Malcolm tried not to let his mind run wild with scenarios. "Did Sierra Day have a dentist?"

"I suppose. Her husband would know. Why?"

"Because we're going to need dental records to identify this victim."

CHAPTER 3

Wednesday, October 5, 7:05 a.m.

Angie Carlson lived and died by her routine.

Rise at five, arrive at the gym by six, swim laps in lane four for thirty minutes, and then shower. Breakfast was a bagel at Bill's, and then she was at the office by seven-thirty.

As a defense attorney her days were jampacked with meetings, briefs, motions, and court dates, and there was little time to do more than swim, work, and maybe catch dinner with her sister, Eva.

Her days were painfully predictable, and she liked it that way.

And the fact that she was an hour behind schedule irritated her. She'd not slept well last night. She'd hit snooze on her alarm one too many times.

Last week, she'd had her annual CT scan, blood work, and chest x-rays to see if her cancer had returned. Results were due in this morning. Though she'd been clear since her surgery a little over seven years ago, she never lost the fear that the disease that had killed her mother had returned.

So to walk out of the ladies' changing room and see that someone had taken lane four in the swimming pool only deepened her foul mood. Even as frustration and anger bubbled, she knew she was being silly. A lane was a lane and hardly life threatening. Her body didn't care where she swam as long as she swam. But it was safer to fret over a lane than cancer so she allowed herself to sulk.

Angie tucked her shoulder-length blond hair under her cap and pulled her goggles up on top of her head. She scanned the pool and saw that the other lanes were full. Damn.

The swimmer in four paused at the edge of the pool and glanced up. He had a tanned, muscled body and dark, thick hair that he flicked away from blue eyes with the jerk of his head. He tossed her a boyish grin. "Want to share the lane?"

She returned the smile. "Yes, that would be great."

"I'll stay to the right."

"I'll go to the left."

The guy shoved off from the wall and moved down the lane, effortlessly cutting through the water with cool, lean strokes. With a touch of annoyance, she noted he was a fine swimmer. Heck, a fine-looking man. The shimmer of desire surprised her. It had been almost a year and a half since she'd dated, enjoyed a man's touch, and learned the painful lesson that she was better off alone.

Angie lowered into the pool, biting back an oath as icy waters shocked her system. She hated the cold; hated the first few chilly laps that bit.

Anxious to get moving, she set the timer on her waterproof watch, pulled her goggles down over her eyes, and pushed off from the wall. Her first few strokes were choppy and stiff, but soon she settled into the rhythm: *reach, pull, breathe, reach, pull, and breathe.*

She and the other swimmer passed each other without effort, and soon she forgot about him. Her body warmed and her thoughts drifted.

Swimming was Angie's daily therapy. It kept her sane.

Almost eighteen months ago when her sister, Eva, returned to Alexandria, Angie's life had been on the verge of sinking. She was haunted by the fact that she'd defended and helped free a sadist like Dr. James

Dixon. From the moment Dixon had sauntered into her office and declared his innocence, she'd sensed something that was off about him. It was the kind of feeling that had her perching on the edge of her seat and glancing toward the exit. But Dixon had sworn he was innocent and he was wealthy, ready to pay top dollar, and as the newest attorney at Wellington and James, she'd been anxious to make her mark. She'd shoved aside her gut reactions and focused on the facts, which in the right light proved his innocence.

In the courtroom, she'd jabbed at the prosecution's case and shredded the testimony of the prostitute Lulu Sweet. By the time Angie had finished, the young girl's story was in shreds and Lulu in tears. When the acquittal had been announced, the cops who'd made the arrest had grunted their displeasure as Dixon had thrust his arms in the air. She'd left the courtroom, the congratulations of peers buzzing in her ears and the press swarming for a quote. After that case, she'd not lacked for business. In fact, she'd had to turn some away. Overnight, she'd gone from an unknown, idealistic defense attorney to "The Barracuda."

That's about the time she'd started having a few glasses of wine before dinner.

She'd fought so hard to stay alive just a few years before, and suddenly she needed wine to make life more bearable. Soon a couple of glasses didn't do the trick, so she drank four or five. Before she realized it, she had a full-on drinking problem. A disastrous affair with a reporter, coupled with the fact that her sister had almost been murdered, had shaken something free in Angie.

Humiliation and fear had shoved her toward an AA meeting, where she confessed her fears. She'd never consider herself fixed, but she could now proudly say she had been sober four hundred and seventy days.

Her limbs pushed through the water. The water now caressed her skin. *Three pulls. A breath. Three pulls. A breath.* When the other swimmer finished his laps and got out of the pool, she glided to the lane's center and picked up her pace.

When her watch beeped and signaled she'd swam thirty minutes she glided to the wall, breathless but totally relaxed. She pushed out of the water and crossed to the bank of chairs where she'd draped her towel. She'd barely dried her eyes and hair when she heard a deep voice call out her name.

Angie stiffened. She recognized the gruff baritone. Detective Malcolm Kier. The cop made no effort to hide his contempt for her and her work. Instantly, she wished she had on her business suit and high heels. She straightened her shoulders and faced him. "Detective Kier. What a lovely surprise."

He possessed a powerful build. Not more than an inch taller than her, he radiated a raw energy and a don't-fuck-with-me demeanor that intimidated most everyone. He rattled her as well, but she'd decided long ago that she'd eat dirt before she ever let him know it.

"Counselor. Good to see you stay in shape." He wore denims with muddied hems, a faded flannel shirt, a jean jacket, and scuffed work boots. A leather gun holster peeked out from under his jacket.

"I try. You just roll in from the mountains?"

"Just about."

"You're a regular Grizzly Adams."

His grin did not reach his eyes. "That's right."

Water dripped from her suit. Drying herself off in front of Kier felt awkward. But the cooling air and her refusal to be intimidated motivated her to slowly begin drying her arms and legs as if she didn't have a worry in the world. "So what brings you to the gym, Detective? Looking into membership?"

His gaze didn't waver. "No, I'm here on official business."

She wrapped the towel around her waist, tucked it in place, and scooted her feet into waiting flip-flops. How had he found her? And then she remembered that she'd once told Kier's partner, her sister's boyfriend, that she swam daily here. "Need an attorney?" she goaded. "I'd be happy to see you in my office. Feel free to call my secretary for an appointment."

"I don't need your services."

"Then why are you here? Bored? Here to rattle my cage a little more?" Kier had been a constant shadow presence since the Dixon trial. It seemed he never missed an opportunity to annoy her.

"I don't rattle your cage." The smugness didn't support the words. "I could care less about you."

"That why I see you at King's several nights a week?"

He shrugged. "I like the food. Plus you know I took an apartment across the street."

"Right. So why is it you always make a point to hold me up in the courthouse when I'm late?"

"Just making conversation."

"How about the four parking tickets I've

gotten in the last year?"

"The city marks its no-parking zones clearly. You're being paranoid." He reached in his jacket pocket and pulled out a theater program. "I'd like you to look at this."

Annoyance crept up her back, bunching the muscles she'd worked so hard to relax. "This is not the best time for me to discuss the arts, Detective."

As if she hadn't spoken he turned a program toward her. "Do you know this woman?"

She held his gaze, not wanting to look and give him the satisfaction that he'd won this little standoff. "Like I said, call my secretary."

His stare darkened like an angry storm on the horizon, but it didn't waiver, nor did the picture in his hand. "Look here, or look at the station. Makes no difference to me."

"You wouldn't."

"Nothing would give me more pleasure than to steal a few billable hours from you."

Asshole. He'd do it. She blinked and lowered her gaze to the program. The young woman's pale face and blond hair accentuated a high slash of cheekbones. Bright green eyes sparked and her lips curved upward as if she knew a secret.

Angie knew her. "Her name is listed in

the program. You can read, can't you?"

He held the picture out an extra beat, then slowly tucked it back in his jacket pocket. "How long has Sierra Day been your client?"

Staring down angry cops and prosecutors was part of any defense attorney's turf. "I don't discuss my clients. You remember attorney–client privilege, don't you, Detective?"

"Why did she hire you?"

"I can't tell you that."

"Tell me about the divorce. Was it nasty?"

"Seeing as you have all the answers, why are you here?"

"Word is she and her soon-to-be ex-husband mixed it up a few times."

"Talk to him."

"I'm asking you."

And then she cut through her own indignation and really thought about why he was here. Kier was a homicide detective, and he wasn't making a social call. What had happened? She thought about the last time she'd seen Sierra. The woman had breezed into her office unannounced and demanded that Angie settle her divorce immediately. Sierra needed cash and wasn't ashamed to admit it.

"Do you know where she might be?" Kier asked.

Sierra could be reckless. "Why the interest in Sierra Day? Is she in trouble?"

"She was reported missing by the West End Theater manager ten days ago."

"You don't work missing persons."

He shifted his stance. "Did her husband ever threaten her?"

"Has something happened to Sierra?"

"Like I said, she is missing."

"And like I said, you don't work missing persons. What aren't you telling me, Detective?"

He studied her. "Sierra's stats match the characteristics of a body we found late last night."

"Characteristics?"

"Female. Mid-twenties. Five-foot-six to five-foot-eight."

"That fits Sierra and a lot of other women." Her skin chilled. "What else do you know about your victim?"

"Not much."

"Meaning?"

He studied her, as if wondering how much to give for maximum return. "All we have are bones."

"Bones." For a moment her heart softened for the unknown young woman who'd died.

"It can't be Sierra. I just saw her about ten days ago. It's been so cool the last few weeks. A body wouldn't decompose that quickly."

"Like I said, her missing persons report matches the medical examiner's preliminary examination."

"So you've not made a positive identification?"

"We're in the process."

"The link between A and B sounds slim."

"It's a start."

Her gaze narrowed. "We don't have anything to say to each other until you have a positive identification on your Jane Doe."

His lips flattened, signaling frustration. "Do you still represent Dr. Dixon?"

Mention of Dixon's name caught her off guard. She tightened her grip on the towel and jerked it up. "What does Dixon have to do with this?"

"He was Sierra's plastic surgeon."

Sierra was vain and never satisfied with anything. Plastic surgery made sense. But to use Dixon . . . what woman would allow him to cut into her flesh? "Dixon has a lot of patients."

"When is the last time you saw him?"

She frowned, annoyed. "It's been a couple of years. He's not my client anymore."

"Did Sierra ever mention Dixon?"

Until she spoke to Sierra she had to walk a fine line and not breach her attorney–client relationship. "Do you believe Dixon is linked to your Jane Doe?"

"Let's just say when Dixon's name comes up, I pay attention."

"So there is no evidence connecting Dixon and your Jane Doe? And your links between Jane Doe and Sierra Day are slim."

He frowned.

"You don't have squat."

"I will soon."

"Don't let me stop you."

Kier tensed. "I'll be in touch."

It took effort not to take a step back. "I can't wait." She moved to leave.

He blocked her path, and for a split second she glimpsed his gnawing anger and frustration. "Do you even give a shit that your client is missing?"

A burst of air from a vent above hit her skin puckering it with gooseflesh. "I'm not the bad guy here, Detective."

"So you say."

The jab was intended to piss her off and make her say something she shouldn't. She'd used the technique herself. "Call me when you have proof."

Angie moved around Kier, walking toward

the ladies' shower room with careful assured steps.

When she was able to strip off her bathing suit and duck under the hot spray of the shower, she was trembling. Sierra was missing. Was this just another Sierra stunt? Did the connection to Dixon matter? Both bits of evidence could be totally unrelated. Likely they were not linked.

Still, she decided to make a few phone calls when she got back to the office and see if she could find Sierra.

Malcolm got into the waiting gray unmarked car parked in front of the gym and glanced over at Garrison, who sat behind the wheel. His body was relaxed back against the seat, and his wrist rested easily on the top of the steering wheel. He'd kept the car running and the heater blasting. "How did it go?"

"How do you think? She gave me nothing."

Garrison sighed. "I should have talked to her. It's no secret you two don't care for each other."

"Yeah." Kier wondered that himself as he'd left the gym and strode across the parking lot. He'd been too anxious to drop the bad news on Carlson to see her reaction.

He'd wanted to see her tossed off balance and upset.

"She might have been more polite if you'd asked the questions, but the bottom line doesn't change. Carlson is one smart attorney and she won't give away shit until she's looked at all the angles." Kier glanced at his notes. "We need to find Sierra Day's husband."

"I made a few calls while you were inside. Brian Humphrey works at a nonprofit in Arlington."

"I thought he was an actor."

"Only on nights and weekends. Computer technical work pays the bills."

Malcolm checked his watch. "Yeah, I want to get to him before Burgess or one of his friends tips the guy off, and he lawyers up." He shook his head. "Damn, I hate lawyers."

CHAPTER 4

Wednesday, October 5, 9 a.m.

Malcolm and Garrison arrived at Humphrey's office building near Van Dorn Street. The square building had a smooth façade made of pressed uniform brick. Tinted windows, which likely did not even open, lined each of the five floors. The boxy structure was so nondescript Malcolm would have missed it if not looking at it. "9901. This is the place. The Parker Pest Control Building."

The detectives got out of the car and crossed the parking lot. The bright sun had taken the edge off the morning chill, but the air still had a bite. They moved to the lobby, checked the floor for Computer Science Arts, and took the elevator to the fifth floor.

A receptionist sat behind a gray desk, a phone cradled under her ear as she maneuvered through a series of calls. Her mousy brown hair was pulled into a ponytail, and her beige sweater-blouse barely covered the folds of her belly. She was as unforgettable as the building where she worked.

When she reached a stopping point, she glanced up at the officers. "Yes?"

Malcolm pulled out his badge. "Detective Malcolm Kier. This is my partner, Detective Garrison. We'd like to see Brian Humphrey."

Brown eyes widened. "Is Brian in some kind of trouble?"

"Why would he be in trouble?" Garrison said. His relaxed demeanor drained the challenge from the question.

"Oh, he wouldn't be in trouble. But I wouldn't doubt that his soon-to-be ex called the cops on him."

"Really?"

"It's no secret that his divorce has been a mess. When he blocked his soon-to-be ex from his cell phone she started calling the front desk. She is very clever and can change her voice so I'd send the calls through. She's an actress."

"Really?" Garrison grinned.

Malcolm marveled at the way his partner could cajole with that smile. His own grin, he'd been told, was more akin to a snarl.

"The last time I let her call through, they

got into a huge fight, and when Brian came out his face was so red. He told me to hold all calls until he could get her to stop bugging him."

"What did she want?" Malcolm asked.

The woman's gaze shifted to Malcolm and lost what little warmth it had gained. "Money."

"They fight about anything else?"

"If the weather changed, they fought." The phone rang, and she answered it. When she'd forwarded the call she glanced up. "Why don't I get Brian up here?"

"That would be great."

Minutes after being paged, Brian Humphrey appeared. Malcolm had expected him to be bland and lifeless like the building, but instead he was surprised to see a tall man with broad shoulders and a lean build. He had dark hair, complete with a wave in the front, chiseled features, and tanned skin. He reminded Malcolm of a Disney hero. He'd glimpsed a few when his nephew and niece watched cartoons at his parents' place. What was that guy's name in the last video the kids had been playing over Christmas? *Beauty and the Beast.* Brian Humphrey looked like Gaston.

Malcolm held up his badge. "Mr. Humphrey?"

"Yes." His voice was a deep baritone, and no doubt the guy had a singing voice as smooth as Gaston's.

"We'd like to talk to you about your wife, Sierra Day."

Humphrey's face grew contemptuous. "She will officially be my ex-wife as soon as I can get her to sign the papers. And I prefer to think of her as my ex."

"Is there some place we can chat in private?" Garrison said. "Maybe your office."

Humphrey didn't need to glance at the receptionist to know she gawked at them. "Sure. It's small, but it's private."

They wove down a hallway created by the configurations of twenty or so gray cubicles. Throughout the central room, the voices of office workers mingled with the tap of fingertips on keyboards and the whir of a copy machine. All conversation ceased as they passed. They reached a small office in the back corner.

Humphrey shut the door behind them. "Delores, she's the receptionist, has put the word out on the jungle beat that you are here."

"We have that effect," Malcolm said. People got nervous around cops.

He glanced around the guy's office. There

72

was a large window behind Humphrey's desk, but tinted glass and mini-blinds filtered out most of the sunlight. Pictures taken of Humphrey in various plays covered the walls. Humphrey as Hamlet. Humphrey as a clown. Humphrey as Sherlock Holmes. In a few spots, only a nail and a shadow imprint of a frame remained. It didn't take much of a leap to guess Sierra had been in those pictures.

On the desk were a half-eaten bagel, a diet soda, and a well-worn script.

"So what do you do for Computer Science Arts?"

"I manage databases for nonprofits and other marketing entities. It's all very dry and boring, and as you can see from the walls, I have greater aspirations."

Garrison nodded. "Just paying the light bill."

"We've all got to eat." Humphrey stood behind his desk, his posture erect, his fingertips pressed to the desk as if addressing a great crowd. "So what does Sierra want from me now? Has she trumped up more lies about me?"

"What kind of lies did she tell about you?" Malcolm asked.

"That I tried to dupe her out of money. That I cheated on her. That I would have loved to see her dead. You name it, Sierra made it up."

"Did you want her dead?" Malcolm asked.

"Believe me there were times when I could have cheerfully strangled her. She did nothing but break my heart from the moment we said our *I dos.* But I never would have hurt her. It wasn't worth the effort."

"How long have you two been married?" Malcolm asked.

"Six months. We've been separated for most of that time."

"Why?"

"Because Sierra took up with another actor. When I found out I tossed her out."

"So why is she giving you so much trouble with the divorce?"

"Because two weeks after she left, my grandfather died and left me a nice bit of money. Sierra believes she is entitled to half of it. But I can promise you she won't get a dime. She didn't even know my grandfather."

Is. Believes. He spoke of her in present tense. "When is the last time you saw her?" Malcolm asked.

"A couple of weeks. She stormed in here making more of her dramatic threats. I threatened to call the cops, and she left."

"When was that exactly?"

He flipped through the pages of his calendar. "Thirteen days ago. It was a Friday. So tell me, what is this all about? What has Sierra done?"

Malcolm never enjoyed this part of the investigation. "We have a body that we are trying to identify. The description of our victim matches a missing persons report filed by Terry Burgess of the West End Theater."

Some anger seeped from Humphrey's features. "Terry filed a missing persons report on Sierra?"

"Ten days ago."

Humphrey frowned. "That means Sierra missed play practice."

"Burgess thinks she'd not miss practice for anything in the world."

"She would if there was a better opportunity. But it would have to be a huge opportunity."

"Such as?"

"That I don't know. Her attorney might know. Her name is Angie Carlson." He coated Carlson's name with disgust. "But then again, you might have better luck getting blood from a stone." He rubbed the back of his neck. "Do you think Sierra is dead?"

"That's what we're trying to determine.

Do you have the name of her dentist?"

Humphrey sat down as if the air had been siphoned right out of him. "You need dental records to identify the body? My God, what happened?"

"That's what we're trying to figure out."

Humphrey blew out a breath. "Sierra's dentist is Scott Marcus. He's in Arlington and in the book. She saw him right before we got married. Veneers. Which *I* paid for."

"You said Sierra was having an affair. Do you have a name?"

He dug long fingers through his thick black hair. "Sure. Marty Gold. I don't know where he lives, but he's in a play at the Springfield Theatre now."

"Did Sierra live with him?"

"She did for a while, but they broke up. I hear she's renting space from a friend. Zoe Morgan. A dancer. In Alexandria." He looked up at them. "I didn't kill her."

The line sounded clear and perfect, as if Humphrey played to an audience of hundreds.

"We didn't say that you did."

"But I am the husband, and cops always blame the husband."

"Not always," Malcolm said. Though Humphrey was right. When a woman was killed, statistics proved an acquaintance did the deed.

"What can you tell us about Sierra? Her likes, habits, friends. Anything so we can piece together the last couple of weeks."

"There's not much to Sierra. If she wasn't on the stage she was trying to get on the stage. She'd walk over broken glass barefoot to get the right part. She wanted Broadway, and she wanted Hollywood. She craved fame like a drug." He shook his head. "I knew that about her, even sensed that I was a temporary fix, and I still married her."

"Those blank spots in the wall have her picture in them?"

"I just took those down about a month ago. I guess until then I was holding on to something. But she drove the final nail in the coffin so I threw them in the trash."

"What was that nail?"

"She called my dad and told him she'd been pregnant with our child and that I'd forced her to have an abortion."

"Any truth?"

"Hell, no. It was hard for Dad to hear it. I always knew she was selfish but never evil."

"Did she hit the bars?"

"Not a lot. She didn't drink or smoke for fear it would ruin her figure and face. Vain could have been her middle name. And she didn't go out unless it benefited her career."

"Family?"

"None to speak of. Distant cousins. Parents dead and no siblings."

Malcolm pulled a card from his pocket and laid it on Humphrey's desk. "If you think of anything else, you'll call me?"

"Sure." He picked up the card and flicked the edge with his fingertip. "When do you think you'll know if the body is Sierra?"

"Day or two."

"I'd lay odds it's her."

"Why?"

"I've not heard from her since Thursday a week ago. She takes great pride in driving me nuts with her calls and notes."

"We'll let you know."

"Figures I'd be left holding the bag."

"What's that mean?"

"If she'd had the decency to sign the damn divorce papers, the state would have had to bury her. Now I'll have to do it."

Minutes later in the car, Malcolm started the engine. "You have to wonder what those two saw in each other."

Garrison settled in the passenger's side as he checked his phone for messages or missed calls. "It doesn't take a genius. They both are lookers. Made a handsome couple."

"Oh, I bet the wedding album was a work of art."

Garrison flipped open his phone and hit three on his speed dial. It was the number for the Alexandria Homicide department.

"This is Sinclair." Detective Jennifer Sinclair was a member of the city's four-person homicide team. Standing at five-foot-eleven with brown hair and a toned body, Jennifer conjured images of Amazons.

The other member of the team was Detective Daniel Rokov. His dark hair and olive skin testified to his Russian gypsy roots.

Kier had put both Rokov and Sinclair on notice this morning when they'd found the body. This case would hit the media sooner than later, and the fact that the body had been reduced to bones would garner big headlines. He wanted answers for the press and the community as soon as possible.

"It's Garrison. I have the name of a dentist I need for you and Rokov to visit. He should have dental records on our possible Jane Doe." He rattled off the name.

"Will do. I also plugged this case into the ViCAP system." ViCAP was a national database dedicated to tracking violent crimes. Not all cases made it into the system, but it was always worth a try.

"Great. Maybe we'll get lucky."

The Other listened to the police scanner,

tapping his fingers against his thigh, waiting for any mention of the bones. There'd been none. But he knew the cops had found his precious gift because he'd driven by Angel Park and seen the police activity.

The cops had been careful to keep their chatter off the radios, no doubt because they were worried about the media. His bones would make a great story.

Now as he sat in the dimly lighted room and stared down at the delicate white carving, he had an unexpected moment of panic so acute, it sent adrenaline slicing through his body. He set down the carving and flexed his fingers, working the ache and stiffness from his joints.

"It's okay. It's okay," he whispered. "This is what you wanted."

In a moment of boldness and bravado, he'd decided to leave the bones where they could be found. After all, games were always more fun when you had a playmate. And what was the point of greatness if it went unrecognized?

So he'd left the bones out. And they had been found.

So why was he afraid? Why was he suddenly worried that cops would storm his stronghold and drag him to a small gray cell?

Breathe. Relax.

He'd lived in the shadows for a very long time, and he'd grown so tired of hiding. He'd grown tired of wanting things and not being able to have them. He'd grown weary of denying his true self.

He'd wanted the cops to know what he could do. He wanted to be feared. He wanted to be that terrifying bedtime story that kids told each other when they needed to stir dread.

And now they would know.

For a few panic-stricken moments, he'd considered leaving town. Maybe it had been foolish to poke a stick at the cops. He'd been killing quietly for three years. He'd been creating his carvings, taking pleasure in polishing them and displaying them. Why the need for attention now?

Should he leave town? That's what he'd always done when things didn't go well. He ran and hid.

The Other paced the workroom, even considered running upstairs and packing a bag. What would he pack? How long should he hide this time?

But as the seconds ticked past and the rush of fear abated, he discovered a small kernel of excitement taking root. As he paced and moved about the small room, anticipation grew and grew until it over-

81

whelmed the fear completely.

The cops had found the bones. So what? He'd been careful. There was no trace of him on the bones. No evidence to link him to what he'd done.

His nerves calmed as he ticked through the steps that were to come.

Eventually, the cops would put a name and a face to the bones. They'd learn what they could about her. They'd ask her family and friends who could have done such a horrible thing. But in the end . . . they'd come up empty-handed.

No one could link him to her. No one had seen them together. There were no e-mails, faxes, or texts that they'd exchanged. His very silent partner, who would never talk to anyone about anything, had arranged the meeting.

He thought about the cops running around in circles like crazed dogs, trying to figure out what end was up. They'd growl and beat their breasts, but in the end they'd find nothing.

The notion that Detectives Kier and Garrison would be left with an unsolved case — a blot on their records — had its appeal. In fact, it gave him great pleasure.

He thought about the last minutes with the woman. Her eyes brimmed with fear.

Save me. Please spare me. Please!

But of course he had not. The thrill had been watching the life seep from her eyes. With each delicious second, death had drained the color from her face until it was a pale lifeless mask.

He glanced down at the white femur bone on his desk. So smooth and white. Like polished ivory. Later tonight when the house was quiet, he would begin carving the next pawn in his chess set.

CHAPTER 5

Thoughts of Sierra tugged at Angie as she pressed her cell phone to her ear and waited in traffic. On hold she was forced to listen to the elevator music her doctor's office played while they held their patients hostage.

"Sierra, where are you?" she muttered as she tapped the steering wheel with her index finger. "Tell me you've not done something really stupid."

She watched the light in the intersection turn green, and she eased forward with traffic. The elevator music droned as she inched along.

Angie ticked through the details of her last meeting with Sierra. It had been about money. Sierra wanted more from her divorce. She'd been angry. But Angie had sensed the young woman played a role. Outraged victim. The orphan. The world

84

had once again dumped on Sierra Day, Sierra had repeated. Angie remembered how her own impatience had thinned as she'd listened to the young actress's rants.

"He's made you a fair offer," Angie said. "I suggest you take it."

With the dramatic flick of her fingers, Sierra tossed the edges of her blond hair over her shoulder. "I will not settle. It is not fair. It is an outrage."

A headache thumped behind Angie's eyes. "It's a good offer. Take it, and get on with your life."

Green eyes narrowed. "Are you on his side?"

Annoyed, Angie sat back in her office chair. "Save the drama for everyone else. I don't care."

The hysteria melted from her demeanor. "Fine. No drama. But I want more money."

Angie put on her blinker. Just as she made a sharp right turn into the parking deck a block from her Old Town law offices, the on-hold music stopped.

"Miss Carlson. You still with me?" The nurse's pert tone clipped at each word.

Angie cradled the phone under her ear as she downshifted the gears on her BMW and rounded another sharp turn. "Still here,

Mrs. Davis. Did you find my test results?"

"Sure did. They are all negative, except for the blood work. We are going to run that a second time."

Angie's anxiety level, which on a good day hovered in the high range, shot past stressed to panic. "What's wrong with the blood work?"

"The markers are slightly elevated. Likely, it's nothing to be worried about, but we need to be sure."

"Do I need to come in and have more blood drawn? I can be there in fifteen minutes."

"No. Like I said, we can rerun what we have. If it's high then I'll have you come back in."

"So basically you don't think the cancer is back."

"That's my guess." The brittleness had vanished from the nurse's voice. "But no one can say definitively until the tests give us the all clear."

"When will you call?"

"Tomorrow. Friday at the latest."

"You'll call as soon as you know?"

"We will."

"Thanks." She hung up the phone and let it drop to her black wool skirt.

■ ■ ■ ■

Angie had awoken from the surgery, her body numb and heavy with anesthesia. Tubes ran out of her arms and nose. She opened her eyes, knowing what the doctors had done to her so that her life could be spared. Through the haze she made out the shape of her father. He sat at her bedside, reading one of his precious books.

"Dad?"

He closed the book and pulled off his glasses. "Angelina."

"What are you doing here?"

"I couldn't let you do this alone."

She'd only told him about the surgery yesterday. She'd not wanted to worry him and told him she'd handle it alone.

His presence stirred something in her, and the emotions she'd held on to so strongly broke free. She let the tears roll down her cheeks. "Did they do the surgery?"

"Yes. The doctor said it went very well."

A lump in her throat nearly choked her. "I'll never have children."

"No."

She wept.

He patted her hand. "Maybe it's all for the best."

She opened her eyes and looked at him. "How can you say that?"

His eyes telegraphed sadness and pain. "Now you'll never be vulnerable."

With as much care as she could muster, she pulled into the tight spot marked RESERVED: A. CARLSON. She turned off the engine, set the parking brake, and released the clutch.

For a moment, she simply sat in her seat, hands resting on the wheel. "Shit."

The old fears returned, and for a moment made it impossible for her to move forward. Sheer will kept her from driving to the nearest grocery, buying a bottle of wine, and driving home to polish it off. "Don't do this to yourself."

Those that called her The Barracuda would laugh if they saw her now. God, Kier would have a field day.

It was the flash of his face that had her straightening. He would never see her afraid, not as long as she had breath in her body.

Keys in hand, she grabbed her briefcase and got out of the car. Wasting no time, she hustled across the lot and punched the elevator button. She glanced at the numbers above and cursed the fact that the elevator was at ground floor. It would have to travel three floors to reach her. Twenty seconds if no one on the other floors lingered. But this time of day someone always dawdled.

Angie stroked her thumb over the worn handle of her briefcase, which had belonged to her father. She pressed the button a few more times.

In a distant corner of the garage, a car door opened and closed. She turned to see if she saw anyone. No one emerged from the shadows, but careful footsteps paced back and forth. She leaned forward, trying to see into the darkness, but she couldn't make out anyone.

Someone was there, but why not come out? Why just stand in the shadows and watch her? Her heart jumped. The elevator dinged. One floor down. The footsteps clicked back and forth, back and forth.

"Come on, damn it." Perspiration trickled down her back. The elevator dinged once again and again. Two floors to go.

She searched the shadows, wondering why whoever was out there didn't emerge. It was almost as if he or she didn't want to be seen.

Ding. Ding. Ding.

And then the doors opened. A rush of relief washed over her so swift and hot that she nearly tripped into the car. She punched the ground floor button six times as she stared into the shadows.

As the doors were about to close, a man appeared on the lip of the darkness. She couldn't make out his features, but she had the deep bone-chilling sense he stared at her.

The feeling that she'd been followed and watched chased her as the elevator rose to street level and down the block-long walk to Wellington and James.

Relief washed over her as she climbed the brick steps of the mid-nineteenth-century building. The large black lacquer front door was flanked by a set of windows made of double-pane glass. Window boxes brimming with red geraniums that had so far survived the chilly weather added a pop of color.

The exterior look was traditional, all very much in keeping with the colonial feel of Old Town Alexandria. However, her boss, Charlotte Wellington, was a stickler for security. That meant the front door that looked so traditional had a state-of-the-art locking system that was always secure. You either had the pass code to punch into the keypad by the front door or you were buzzed into the reception area. No one just walked into Wellington and James.

Angie punched in the code, waited to hear

the click of the lock, and quickly pulled open the door to find her sister, Eva, sitting in the lobby.

Eva was twenty-eight, four years younger than Angie, but Eva could have passed for a teenager. Straight black hair framed a heart-shaped face, and her petite frame usually clad in jeans and a dark T-shirt often had people dismissing her as an airhead kid. That was always a mistake.

Eva's intelligence scored off the charts. She'd all but breezed through the college courses she'd taken this past year. She was expected to graduate by next summer with degrees in English and social work.

Eva had endured so much darkness in her life, and it would have been easy for her to be bitter, but Eva had never succumbed to anger. Her motto was "Eyes forward."

As Angie entered, Eva rose, shouldering her knapsack. "Hey!"

Angie crossed the room and hugged Eva. They'd been separated for so long Angie had vowed never to let simple moments like greetings be ignored.

Eva hugged her back. "Your receptionist, Iris, let me in. She just had to run down the street for coffee. Said she'd be right back."

"Iris without her coffee is a bad thing." She glanced at Eva's pale skin and the hint of darkness under both eyes. "You feeling all right?"

"Just burning the candle at both ends. Too much life to make up, I suppose."

"So what brings you here this morning?" Angie said.

"A woman at the halfway house where I volunteer. She's in trouble. I need a favor."

In the last year, Eva had never asked for one favor. "Come back to my office."

Angie led them down a hallway painted in a hunter green and decorated with expensive-looking landscapes. Charlotte was very into the Old Virginia, traditional look, which she said her clients preferred. Angie would have opted for sleek modern, but until she made partner such decisions were beyond her.

The furnishings in Angie's office were in keeping with the firm's look, but her bookshelves weren't crammed with leather-bound volumes. Instead they featured bits of artifacts from her father's museum and family pictures of Eva and their mother and some of her father, Frank Carlson. Angie had her icy Nordic look from Frank whereas Eva had gotten her dark gypsy looks from her father, Blue Rayburn.

Angie shrugged off her coat, hung it on the back door hanger, and held out a hand for Eva to sit in one of the leather chairs in front of her desk.

Angie took the seat next to Eva. "So tell me about this person."

Eva smoothed her hands over her jeans. "You know her, as a matter of fact."

"Do I?"

"Her name is Lulu Sweet."

Angie sat back in her chair. She knew Lulu Sweet very well. Lulu had been the prime witness for the prosecution in the Dixon case. She'd been the prostitute whom Dixon had hired and brutalized.

After nearly two hours of abuse, he'd told a half-conscious Lulu that he had to stop. He didn't want her to die yet.

She panicked and somehow managed to grab the light on the nightstand and hit him on the side of the head. He'd been stunned long enough for her to run naked into the streets, screaming for help.

"What does Lulu want?"

"She wants you to represent her."

"Really? I would think I would be the last person she'd want as an attorney."

Eva's lips curled into a half smile. "She said, and I quote, 'I want your sister to represent me because there is no meaner bitch alive.' "

Instead of being insulted, Angie laughed.

"She said that?"

"Word for word."

As a woman, Angie had pitied Lulu. But as an attorney she'd been forced to look beyond her youth and bruises. She'd focused on Lulu's arrest record and her meth addiction. The woman had had a string of arrests under her belt, and she'd been known to perjure herself. Angie had used all those facts against Lulu and torn her apart on the witness stand.

"Lulu made it very clear what she thought about me the day she testified. She called me more than a few names as she was leaving the courthouse."

"So she told me."

Angie shifted in her seat. "So what is Lulu up to these days?"

"She moved out of the halfway house a few weeks ago and into her own place. Before the house, she did ninety days for possession. But she swears she's clean now."

"They all do."

Eva shrugged. "I'm not a wide-eyed innocent. I've seen enough. I know when someone is using."

"I'll trust you on that. So if she's not using and she's out of jail, where do I fit into the picture?"

"Lulu has a son."

Angie frowned. "I had her completely investigated. There was never a mention of a child."

"She got pregnant shortly after the trial."

It shouldn't have mattered that Lulu wasn't pregnant when she'd gone after her. But it did.

"She lost custody?"

Eva shrugged, seemingly unsurprised by Angie's guess. "When the boy was born, Lulu was living with her mother. She'd been clean during her pregnancy, but when the baby was a month old Lulu took a hit of meth. Her mother found her sitting in a stupor with the baby crying in his crib. Her mother kept the baby and threw her out. And she really went downhill from there."

"Okay."

"That's how she landed in jail. But she's clean now."

Angie's thoughts jumped to the baby, who would be about nine months now. Unreasonable outrage burned through Angie as she thought about the baby. "You know my history, Eva. You know I can't have children. I can't defend a woman who is so careless with her child."

"Her mistakes haunt her, Angie. She is truly upset by what has happened."

"Upset doesn't feed and clothe a baby,

Eva. The kid sounds like he's better off where he is, which I'm assuming is with the grandmother."

"Lulu really wants her boy back. She wants to be a good mother to him."

Angie couldn't jettison the anger and opted to remain silent.

Eva hurried to say, "There is a custody hearing tomorrow."

"Tomorrow?"

"I know. Her last attorney didn't tell her about it until yesterday."

"Okay."

"Lulu and her mother are to meet before the judge who is deciding which one will get the boy."

"There are plenty of other attorneys out there."

"Yeah, I know. But she came to me and asked me about you. She wants you." Eva pulled out a picture and handed it to Angie.

It was a photo of a boy, maybe six months old. He had bright blue eyes, a sloppy drooling grin that made Angie's heart wince.

"The kid really loves his mother," Eva said in a quiet voice. "Lulu has visitation, and she went to see him last week. He misses her."

She handed the picture back to Eva. "I'm sure he does love her."

"Lulu's mom is great. But she's not well."

"What's wrong with her?"

"I don't know for sure. But she has that sick, pale look like Mom had before she was diagnosed."

After Frank had divorced Angie's mother, Marian, he'd sued for and won custody. The agreement dictated that Angie only saw her mother one Saturday a month. She'd not been around her mother and Eva much, and by the time her mother had gotten sick she'd already left for college. Her father had not told Angie about her mother's illness until she was dying.

As a kid, she'd wanted her mother so much at times. Too many nights, she'd cried herself to sleep.

Angie cleared her throat. "I'm not making any promises, Eva. I can't make any decision until I see Lulu."

Eva's eyes brightened. "But you will see her."

Angie rose, moved to her briefcase, and pulled out a black leather-bound calendar. She flipped a couple of pages. "You said the hearing is tomorrow?"

Eva rose. "Yes. Thursday. Twelve noon."

"We don't have much time."

"No."

"I've got time today at one p.m. Have her

97

come by the office. And tell her not to be late, Eva. Because at this point I'm looking for an excuse to say no to her."

Eva nodded. "I will tell her." She hoisted her backpack on her shoulder. "Thanks, Angie. I know you're doing this for me."

"I am."

"I appreciate it."

Satisfaction elbowed its way through the nagging mixed feelings. "You are welcome."

"I better get going. I've got an early class and then the lunch shift at King's."

"Why do you still work at King's? With your brains you could work anywhere."

Eva shrugged, no hint of doubt in her gaze. "I like King and his kid, Bobby. Feels like family there. And that's worth more to me than anything."

Angie understood. "What about that boyfriend of yours, Garrison?"

"What about Deacon?"

No need to mention that Garrison had helped Kier track Angie down this morning. He'd been doing his job. "He's got to feel like family."

"Sure, when we're together. But there is a lot to keep us apart. School. His work. My work. And we fought last night."

What wasn't she saying? "Trouble?"

"No." She hesitated. "Just busy."

98

Angie didn't press. She wasn't crazy about the fact that her sister had jumped into a serious relationship. Eva should be focused solely on herself. But as much as she wanted to share her more candid opinions, the time and distance they'd spent apart had created a chasm they'd not fully bridged. Some moments she just didn't feel like she had the right to push.

"You'll let me know if I can help?"

"Always."

CHAPTER 6

Malcolm and Garrison arrived at the Commonwealth's Northern District medical examiner's office. Though the center was located in the neighboring county, the office served the entire Northern Virginia area, which included Alexandria.

They pushed through the metal doors on Dr. Henson's floor. Immediately, the strong scent of bleach greeted them as they moved down the tiled hallway. Fluorescent bulbs cast a bright, if not antiseptic light on the entire floor.

Malcolm hated this place. He hated the smell, the gray tones, and the feel of death that hovered here. This place was a necessary evil that he would endure for the case.

He checked his watch. "Henson has had the bones seven hours. She said she'd get right on them."

Autopsies often required a twenty-four to

forty-eight hour turnaround at best, but if Henson said a case rose to the top of her list, it did.

They reached the last set of doors and pushed through. They found Dr. Henson in Examining Room Three. She wore green scrubs, a mask with an eye guard, and a cap. She leaned over a stainless-steel exam table that now held the bones laid out in anatomical order. Her assistant Bruce, also dressed in scrubs, stood with a clipboard in hand.

"Dr. Henson," Malcolm said.

She glanced up. "Detectives."

"Thought we'd swing by and see if you've made progress."

"I only just received the dental records from Ms. Day's dentist and was preparing to compare them to the teeth in Jane Doe's mouth. It might take me another few hours before I can get to it."

"Anything you can tell us so far?"

"My earlier assumptions were correct. Female. Mid-twenties. She had healthy bones. Didn't suffer from malnutrition, and she did have good dental care. She had veneers put in fairly recently."

"Sierra's husband said he paid for his wife's veneers," Malcolm said.

She cocked a brow. "Really?"

Moving to a desk, she picked up a manila

file, pulled x-rays, and stuck them on a light box. "Might as well have a look now."

Henson leaned into the film. "Sierra did have veneers. And also she had two fillings. Both in the back right molar."

She turned to the skull and examined the teeth. "Veneers and right back molar with two fillings."

Malcolm leaned in. "So you're saying this is Sierra Day?"

"I'll run DNA on the marrow to be one hundred percent certain."

"You and I both know that will take weeks or months."

"She has very distinctive teeth. If I had to call it now, I'd say this was Sierra Day."

"Sierra Day has only been missing ten days. That's not enough time for Mother Nature to strip the bones."

Henson nodded. "Not given the current climate. Too cold." She picked up a bone. "No trauma to the bones at all. In fact, I see no signs of saw marks or ax marks that would suggest she'd been hacked apart."

"She didn't just fall apart, Doc."

Wisps of red hair peeked out from the edges of Henson's cap. "Well, if you strip the flesh and tendons from the bones, then there is nothing to hold them together, and they do fall apart."

"How do you do something like that? Acid?"

"I don't think acid was used. Acid would have left marks on the bones. If I had to guess I'd say the flesh was soaked off."

"Soaked?"

"It's a common process."

Malcolm rested his hands on his hips. "For who?"

"Companies that process animal bones for museums. You ever been to an exhibit and seen a display with an animal skeleton?"

"Sure."

"Well, I can promise you that those bones did not arrive from nature all clean, white, and odor free."

Garrison glanced at the bones on the table, which had a yellowish hue. There was no stench or sign of flesh. "These are not pristine by any stretch of the imagination."

"Well, there are a few more steps. Next is the beetle tank. The bones are laid in a tank full of flesh-eating beetles, which eat remaining traces of flesh from the bones. These bones are clean of flesh so likely made it through step two. Then there is the whitening and bleaching process. These bones have a dull cast, so I'd say they haven't been bleached."

Malcolm shook his head. "How do you

know this?"

"I worked a summer in a bone-processing plant out west. We handled thousands of bones just like this. Of course they were animal bones." She lifted a forearm bone. "Whoever did this, I think, did not finish the job."

The process had soured Malcolm's stomach, but Garrison stared at the bones with a vague curiosity sparking in his eyes. "Got any theories why the killer didn't finish?"

"Maybe the only goal was to strip evidence. I don't pretend to understand why anyone would do this." She adjusted her eye gear. "I can tell you that the victim's right femur is missing."

"His idea of a souvenir?" Malcolm said.

Henson shrugged. "You're the detective, not me."

Malcolm laughed. "Yep, that's why they pay us the big bucks. Call us when you've thoroughly checked those dental records."

At one minute to one, Angie glanced at the small gold ivory-framed clock on her desk. It had belonged to her father, and it was one of the few things of his she'd kept. She thought about her promise to represent Lulu Sweet as she tapped her pencil on her desk and watched the seconds tick. Regret nagged her.

A part of Angie hoped Lulu wouldn't show, or would be terribly late or even would show up high. Any one of those reasons would be excuse enough to banish Lulu from her thoughts and confirm that Angie's courtroom character assassination of the woman had been just.

Angie had left the courtroom that day satisfied that she'd shattered the prosecution's case. She'd not expected Lulu to be waiting outside the courthouse. She'd not expected the girl's outrage or anger.

You twisted my words well enough, but that man you are defending is evil.

The memory had Angie straightening. That day in the courtroom Angie had been defending the justice system and a defendant's right to representation. She needed to be the one who believed in the system and what it represented. She needed to provide Dixon the defense that Eva had been denied so many years ago.

Her phone buzzed.

She pressed intercom. "Yes?"

"There is a Ms. Lulu Sweet to see you." The voice belonged to Iris Stanford. Iris had run the offices of Wellington and James since the days the doors had opened — six years ago. A paralegal/administrator/mom, she kept Charlotte and Angie organized. The other named partner was overseeing a murder defense trial in Texas now and had been out of the office for two months. She wasn't expected back until the first of November.

The clock chimed once, signaling Lulu's punctual arrival. "Bring her back."

Rising, she smoothed the wrinkles from her skirt and pulled the jacket off her chair. She slipped it on and fastened the middle button just as Iris appeared.

Iris had short, neatly trimmed hair with a subtle black headband. Her blue preppy dress and patent leather flats always gave Angie the sense that the woman had been plucked from the 1950s.

Right on her heels was Lulu Sweet. To Angie's amazement the young woman had lost the pink spiked tips on her blond hair, the nose ring, and dark black eye shadow. A long-sleeved turtleneck covered her tattooed arms and chest. New jeans hugged her figure, which had filled out to a healthy weight. Even her scent had changed from dark and spicy to a clean soapy aroma. Without the hooker getup, Lulu looked a decade younger, reminding Angie that she couldn't be more than twenty-one.

Angie extended a hand and a cool smile.

"Lulu, you look great."

The young girl's grip was firm and her gaze direct. "That was the plan. I need to look the part if I'm going to get my son back."

Iris slipped away, vanishing down the hallway.

Angie released Lulu's grip. "So is this just an act for the court? Because I can tell you right now, I won't represent you if you aren't completely serious."

Lulu's fingers tightened around the strap of her purse, but her gaze didn't waver. "I'm very serious. I want my kid back."

"Kids are a lot of work, Lulu. And you're young. From what Eva tells me you barely have gotten your life back on track."

"I know I'm not the perfect anything. I know I've made more mistakes than I should have. But I love my kid, and I want to be his mother. He is the only really great thing I've ever done."

Whatever Lulu's motivations were in the past or whatever they'd be in the future she couldn't see. What she could see was that right now Lulu was willing to move heaven and earth for her son.

Angie held out a hand toward an empty chair in front of her desk. "Have a seat."

Lulu moved toward it but didn't sit.

"You've got to be wondering why I chose you."

Angie arched a brow. "Eva told me you needed a mean bitch like me."

Lulu didn't flinch or appear remotely embarrassed. "That is true. My mom's got a good attorney, and I need a better one. I know you're good. But I know it's more than just that."

"I don't understand."

"I wouldn't even have my son if it weren't for you. The path I was headed on when I took that witness stand was a bad one. I was using a lot. David would have been messed up good even before he was born if you hadn't torn me apart on that stand."

"I don't follow."

"I was so pissed."

"I remember."

"So pissed that I could have been made to feel so low. Even when I was with a john, I always felt in control. Even when Dixon did his worst I thought I'd find a way out of the fix. But with you there was no escape. You brought me down lower than anyone ever had."

Angie raised her chin. She'd done her job. She hadn't seen Lulu as a person. She'd been an obstacle to be overcome. Now, she

108

couldn't dismiss the woman so easily. "Okay."

"If I hadn't hit rock bottom that day, I'd have stayed on the same path. I was so mad at you I wanted to show you I could be a better person."

Angie knitted her fingers in front of her, not sure why she didn't trust her voice at that point.

Lulu dug a picture out of her purse and set it on Angie's desk. "That's the last picture I took of David. It was taken last week. Mom only let me visit for a half hour with him."

Angie picked up the picture. The boy was staring up at Lulu. His smile and eyes were bright in his mother's presence. Angie suffered a twinge of jealousy for the girl who had given birth to such a perfect child. She wanted to trace the curls framing his face. Instead, she laid the picture down. "Why did your mother limit the visit?"

"The court said I only get a half hour at a time. Mom plays by the rules."

"She's trying to protect this child — your son."

"I know. I see that."

Angie picked up a Montblanc pen and pushed a legal pad in front of her. "I'll help you, but I need to know if you are using."

"I am not."

"So I could drug test you right now."

Lulu lifted her chin. "Sure. Bring it on."

Angie stared at her a long moment. Instinct whispered Lulu was on the level. "I've got a list of things I'm going to need you to do."

Lulu scooted forward in her seat, her eyes anxious and ready. "I'll do whatever you say."

"First, if you're still hanging with people who are using you need to dump them. They can drag you into trouble in the blink of an eye, and if that happens your case will be damaged."

"Sure."

"You do have a place to live?"

"Yes. An apartment. It's small, but there's room for a crib." Lulu rattled off the address.

"And a job?"

"I work for a cleaning service by day. And I waitress at night."

"Who is going to watch the baby when you work?"

"My neighbor. She said he could sleep at her place at night while I work."

"What about during the day?"

"I've just got the day gig to make extra money now. When David comes to live with me, I'll quit."

Lulu had thought through the details, but Angie still worried. So much could go wrong.

"What if the baby gets sick?"

"I've got other friends. They have kids. I've helped them. They will help me."

"They're responsible?"

"Yes."

Angie's gaze narrowed. "And if you get sick?"

"Those friends will help me too." Lulu leaned forward. "Why are you grilling me?"

"I'm asking all the questions the judge is going to ask."

"You sound mad."

"I'm not."

Lulu rubbed her hand over her arm. "You don't like me."

"I never said that."

"A good hooker learns to read people well."

Angie leaned forward. "My job is to prepare you for court, to press any weakness and see if you will break. Because if you break here and now, the chances are good you'll break in the courtroom."

"I doubt any judge can dish out anything worse than what you did during the Dixon trial."

"Don't bet on it."

Lulu's fingers tightened on the chair arms. "What else could the judge ask?"

"Dixon paid you extra so he could brutalize you. What kind of decent mother does that?"

Her gaze thinned. "I needed a hit and the money to buy it. The drugs made me desperate. No more drugs. No more desperation."

"You're sure?" Her own struggles had shown her that sobriety could be as fragile as crystal. One slip and it all shattered. "Raising a kid can be stressful."

"I'll manage."

"You sound glib."

"Just determined." She sat back in her chair and ran fingers through blond, spiked hair. "You're hoping to find a flaw."

"It's my job to find and fix the flaws."

"Yeah, but you're really hoping you can find some reason to ditch me."

The observation hit near to the truth. "I told Eva I'd help and I will."

The mention of Eva's name softened Lulu's anger a fraction. "She's good people."

"Yeah." Angie shoved out a sigh. She had told Eva she'd help Lulu. "I have a friend who owns a dress shop. I want you to stop by. I'll call her and let her know you are coming to borrow a dress."

Lulu frowned and glanced down at what she was wearing. "I thought this was the kind of outfit the judge would want to see."

"It's a real improvement," Angie conceded. "I can see you've done a lot of work on yourself. But the right dress will just take it up another notch." She scribbled the address on a pad. "I'm also writing down the name of my hairdresser. Again, use my name. She'll know what to do."

"My hair is wrong?"

"Wrong for the kind of impression I want to make for the judge. Perception is everything, Lulu." She tore the paper off and handed it to her.

Lulu frowned and glanced at the addresses. "These are in the nice part of town."

"I know."

"A dress shop in this area is going to be expensive," she said without shame.

"The owner, Molly, owes me. Like I said, she'll let you borrow a dress."

"Will she even let me through her front door?"

"I'll let her know you're coming. She'll take care of you."

Lulu folded the piece of paper and creased the fold with her fingernails. "Okay."

"I called the courthouse this morning to double-check the time of your hearing. It's Thursday at noon."

"Yes, I know."

"Tomorrow."

"I'm not stupid."

"You miss that day, and it's over."

"I know."

"I want you at the courthouse at eleven."

"Why?"

"I want us to have time to review some of the questions your mother's attorney will ask. Normally, I take more time with my clients, but we are in a time crunch so we'll do the best we can."

"Can I get my boy back?"

Angie offered a tentative smile. "You do your part, Lulu, and I'll do mine."

Lulu stood and held out her hand. "I promise, Ms. Carlson. I won't let you down."

"It's not me who's counting on you. It's David."

With the information supplied by the medical examiner, Malcolm and Garrison wanted to talk to Dixon. His priors plus his association with the victim made him a suspect in their minds.

Malcolm had to double-check his address

for Dixon. The office space he'd had two years ago had been huge. Glittering glass, polished chrome in a high-rise on Duke Street. He remembered the view from the reception area. It had looked out over the Potomac past the Wilson Bridge toward the meandering landscape that had once been home to centuries-old plantations like Mount Vernon and Gunston Hall.

However, Dixon's newer offices were more than a few steps down. The small suite off of Van Dorn Street had a cramped reception area furnished with bamboo furniture that looked as if it belonged on a patio. Even his receptionist had changed. Gone was the tall, sleek blonde with the perky breasts and tight rear end. In her place sat a fifty something woman with graying hair and a sour expression. There were no patients in the waiting room.

The publicity from Dixon's murder trial had taken a toll. Clearly, it had chased off the Washington elite searching for a private nip or tuck. Malcolm should have gotten some satisfaction knowing the doctor had been knocked off his lofty pedestal, but he didn't. Dixon belonged behind bars.

Shoving aside frustration, Malcolm strode up to the glass window and held up his badge. The receptionist's blank gaze didn't waver as she pushed open the window. "What can I do for you, officers?"

"Is the doctor in?"

"He's in his office."

"Let him know Detectives Kier and Garrison are here."

"Is he expecting you?"

"He'll want to see us."

"All right." The receptionist rose, moving down a short hallway and vanishing.

Through the entire trial, Malcolm had sensed that Dixon loved their cat-and-mouse game. The doctor's ego had fed on the attention. As negative and destructive as it had been, the doctor had maintained a smirk, as if he knew a secret no one else would ever discover. The expression had irritated Garrison, but it had chipped away at Malcolm's temper. There'd been times in the courtroom Malcolm had mustered all his control to keep from leaping forward and throttling the monster that pretended to be human.

And when Dixon had walked, he'd risen from the defendant's chair, tugged the vest of his expensive dark suit down, and strode out of the courtroom. The doctor had all but glowed when he'd talked to the press. He'd spoken of justice winning out, of returning to his life and the devoted friends and patients that meant so much to him. He planned, in fact, to hold office hours that very afternoon.

As Malcolm glanced at the faded green carpet satisfaction did flicker. "How far the mighty do fall."

Garrison smiled, but his eyes shone with anger. "Not far enough."

"It's only a matter of time."

"You're optimistic."

"Shit, no. I'm determined. He'll end up in jail. That's a promise."

Garrison shrugged. "Don't drive yourself insane over what can't always be controlled."

"There is a lot in this world I can't control, but putting Dixon behind bars is one thing I can."

The receptionist reappeared. Her sour expression held a hint of worry. "The doctor will see you."

Malcolm and Garrison moved down a narrow hallway lined with photos of Dixon at many different black-tie events. Senators, congressmen, and lobbyists all stood by him, their smiles as frozen as ice.

There were also framed diplomas. He'd graduated top of his class from top-fleet medical schools. Not bad for a guy who'd come from a poor family. They'd never determined how he'd gotten the money for medical school.

If you talked to any of his patients as Malcolm and Garrison had done two years ago, you'd hear nothing but praise. *A genius. Masterful skills. An artist.* No one doubted that Dixon was a skilled surgeon. It was his after-hours hobbies that Malcolm found vile.

When they reached the threshold they found Dixon sitting behind his hand-carved mahogany desk. The desk was a holdover from his old life. Judging by the small room, it was about all that remained of the old life.

The doctor's dark hair was slicked back, and he had a tan that suggested a recent holiday or visit to a tanning bed. His red tie was fastened in his trademark Windsor knot, and he still took extra starch in his shirts.

The office was small but as impeccably neat as the fancy uptown space he'd vacated. Every paper on his desk was in a neat stack. His pencils lined the top right corner like soldiers, and the books on the bookshelves were still kept in alphabetical order.

Malcolm refused to knock or clear his throat. Instead he waited for the doctor to raise his gaze from the paper in front of him. The doctor appeared in no rush, and their silent war raged for several seconds until Dixon looked up.

He didn't appear shocked or troubled by the visit. Instead, his eyes danced with the excitement of a child ready to play a new game. He stood, tugged his vest over his narrow belly, and nodded. "Detectives Kier and Garrison. What's it been, a year or two since we last spoke? Time does fly."

A primitive urge demanded Malcolm grab the doctor by the lapels and smack his head against the desk. Not only would that kind of stunt bring Internal Affairs and a lawsuit down on him, but also it wouldn't find Sierra Day's murderer.

"It does," Malcolm said. The natural rasp of his voice made anything he said sound harsh so he tossed in a smile to give the doctor a relaxed impression.

"So what do I owe the honor of this visit, gentlemen?"

"Official business," Garrison said. "Concerning one of your patients."

Dixon frowned. "That sounds ominous. Please have a seat." He motioned to the two club chairs in front of his desk and waited until the detectives had sat before he retook his seat. He closed the file on his desk and laid the folder on a neat pile to his right. "Which one of my patients?"

The low, too-soft chair tried to swallow up Malcolm. He pulled a notebook from his pocket and flipped it open. If his dad could see him now he'd have a good laugh. How many years had his old man begged him to pay attention to the details? *The devil is in the details, boy. He'll hang your ass if you miss the wrong one.*

"Sierra Day's body was found yesterday in a local park," Malcolm said.

Dixon's raised dark eyebrows showed real anguish. "Are you sure it's Sierra?"

"We are."

Dixon shoved out a breath and for a moment seemed lost in thought. "That's just awful. I am so sorry to hear that. I just saw her about two weeks ago."

The son of a bitch had managed just the right blend of surprise and remorse. "Can you tell us about your routine for the last few days?"

"Why?" He raised a hand. "Never mind. I know why. Our unfortunate history. I wonder when I will finally escape it."

"We must do our due diligence," Garrison said easily.

"I should be offended, but I know you are trying to find Sierra's killer. Damn, but she was such a sweet girl."

Malcolm tried to put himself in Dixon's

120

place. If he'd been falsely accused of attempted murder and acquitted, he'd be damned pissed if the cops showed up on his doorstep. "When exactly is the last time you saw Ms. Day?"

He turned to his appointment book and flipped slowly through several pages. "Ah, here it is. I saw Ms. Day eleven days ago. She had a nine a.m. appointment."

"Did you see her often?"

"That was her second appointment." Carefully, he closed the book. "That was our last consultation before surgery."

"What was she planning to have done?"

He hesitated. "She's dead, so I suppose there is no doctor–patient relationship to violate. She was going to have breast augmentation. Like many young women she wanted larger breasts. She'd planned to go from a B to a double D. And she wanted me to liposuction her buttocks and abdomen. She was looking for a model-perfect body, as most actresses today want. She'd planned on having her surgery next week. She was very excited."

"That was the last time you spoke to her?"

"Yes." Dixon sat back in his chair. "I still can't believe she is dead. I just can't believe it."

"Really?"

Dixon was a master liar and manipulator. "You do believe me, don't you, Detective?"

Malcolm met the doctor's earnest eyes with a deadpanned expression. "Do I have reason not to?"

"As I mentioned, we do have a history, Detective."

"I'm here with no agenda, Dr. Dixon, other than to recreate Ms. Day's last days."

"Do you always interview your victim's doctors?"

"I interview anyone and everyone when I'm investigating a murder." He flipped a page in his notebook. "What can you tell me about Ms. Day?"

Dr. Dixon hesitated. "She was a very excitable young woman. Prone to drama, you know? But it fit her vocation. Who would want to watch an actress who didn't have a flair for drama?"

"Did you ever see her in a play?"

"I did, as a matter of fact. I went to see her over the summer when she was in *Twelfth Night.* I'm a contributor to the West End Theater, and the actors awarded us with a special viewing of their summer show. I met her afterwards. She pulled me aside during the party and told me of her desire for plastic surgery. I gave her my card and left it at that."

"And you didn't see her during the summer?"

"No. I did not."

When he questioned friends and family, he'd be sure to bring up Dixon's name. It had been his experience that no matter how careful people could be, someone somewhere had seen them or heard about them. "Is there anyone who might like to hurt Ms. Day?"

"All I know is that I did not kill this woman, Detective. I liked Ms. Day. She was a stunning woman whom I'd planned to make even more beautiful."

"Like Lulu Sweet?" Malcolm tossed her name out to Dixon like bait on a hook. He wasn't sure what he'd catch, but he was willing to take a chance.

Dixon twisted his cuff link. "So this is related to the old charges you could never prove?"

"Your attorney won your acquittal fair and square." Carlson might be a bloodsucker, but she had followed the law to a T.

"Oh, come on. This visit is about getting a pound of my flesh. It wasn't enough that you shattered my reputation — now you are going to try and pin a murder on me."

Malcolm felt the tug on his fishing line

and gave it a little slack. "No, sir, not at all."

Dixon leaned forward. "I've been practicing in this hovel for nearly two years, barely scraping by with patients like Sierra Day who can't afford a top-of-the-line surgeon."

The line had grown tight, and Malcolm reeled it in. "It made you angry that you weren't serving the cream of the crop anymore."

"Of course it bothered me. I resent the fact that a penny whore I hired freaked out on drugs and nearly ruined my reputation. I resent that my partners dropped me from the practice, and I resent that my patients abandoned me. But that doesn't mean that I killed Ms. Day."

"I never said you did."

"But I'll bet money that you'll do your best to pin it on me."

"I'm looking for a killer, not a pound of flesh."

"Humans search for the information that supports their opinion. And we are more likely to reject what doesn't fit our world-view. And your tiny worldview paints me as a villain."

"Did you kill her?" Garrison asked.

"I can't believe you asked me that question."

"Did you murder Sierra Day?" Garrison's voice had more force.

"I should call your supervisor and demand you be reprimanded."

"Did you kill her?"

Dixon faced Malcolm directly. "No."

For a long, tense moment Malcolm stared at Dixon. He knew in his bones that the doctor was connected to this. And he feared it was only a matter of time before another woman fell prey to him. "Thank you for your time."

Dixon rose. "That's it?"

"For now, yes."

"Should I get an attorney?"

"That is totally up to you."

The detectives left the office, moving carefully and slowly as if it were business as usual. But when they got in the car, Malcolm gripped the steering wheel, wishing he could snap it. "That son of a bitch is evil. I know he's connected to Sierra Day's death."

"Knowing and proving are two different things."

Malcolm was silent for a moment. "It's a gut feeling."

"Let's dig into his recent activities. We need more than your gut."

Malcolm fired up the engine. "I want to put a tail on him."

"As much as I'd like to, we don't have just cause."

Malcolm backed out of the parking spot and punched the gas. "Then we better find it."

CHAPTER 7

Wednesday, October 5, 5 p.m.

Malcolm and Garrison arrived at the Springfield Theatre in Annandale just after five in search of Marty Gold, Sierra's ex-lover. They'd called ahead and discovered today's play practice focused on their upcoming production of *Hamlet*. Marty was expected.

This theater was markedly different than the West End Theater. It was smaller, housed in the end space of a strip mall, and its main entrance was just yards from a drug store. Still, the owners had gone to lengths to blacken the windows and display posters of upcoming productions.

The detectives pushed through the glass doors and entered a small lobbylike area created by a black curtain that partitioned off the front section from the back. A tented opening connected the two. A display counter exhibited a collection of *Springfield*

Theatre! T-shirts that were for sale.

A slim, tall woman with black hair slicked back into a bun stood behind the counter. She had pale skin and wore the leotard of a dancer under a black skirt. "May I help you?"

"We're here to see Marty Gold."

A slim, neatly plucked eyebrow raised in judgment. "He's in practice."

Malcolm did his best to smile, but found his patience wearing thin. He'd been up nearly twenty-four hours, and a dull headache throbbed in the back of his head. He pulled out his badge. "Police."

The woman didn't bother to glance at the badge. "You can find him on stage now. He's the one holding the skull."

"Skull?"

"It's a prop. He's Hamlet. The skull is supposed to belong to his dead father."

"Charming."

They pushed through the curtains and entered the theater section. The floor, ceiling, and walls were painted black with silver flecks. Dark metal chairs created a semicircle around a simple wooden stage that rose up a foot off the ground. "Not as fancy as the West End."

"Everybody's got to start somewhere," Garrison said.

"Yeah." Malcolm held up his badge and in a loud voice said, "We're with Alexandria Police. We're here to see Marty Gold." His gaze settled on the guy with the skull, who glanced at them with a deer-in-the-headlights look. He was short with thinning blond hair. Dark tights and a tunic accentuated a stocky build. "You Marty?"

"Yeah, I'm Marty."

Malcolm crooked his finger. "Got a minute?"

The guy grinned as if to say he had no idea what was going on and crossed the stage. He hopped down and moved toward them. "What can I do for you?"

Gold wasn't a handsome guy like Humphrey. His nose hooked to the left slightly as if it had been broken a few times, and his dark eyes were wide set. His build was more muscular and his hands large as if accustomed to manual labor. He was definitely rougher around the edges than Humphrey.

"Sierra Day. We want to ask you about her."

His gaze turned guarded. "What is she saying about me? I did not take her car if that's what she's saying. She said that I could use it. And I did not put the ding in the back bumper. She did that herself." He still held the skull in his hand, but his grip

129

tightened considerably.

"She's not complaining about you, Mr. Gold."

He relaxed a fraction. "What did she do?"

"When was the last time you saw her?"

"A week ago. We hooked up."

"We'd heard you two broke up," Malcolm said.

"We did, but that didn't get in the way of some good clean fun."

"A week ago would be last Wednesday?"

"Yeah. We were at an impromptu cast party. We had a great time." His eyes narrowed. "I can promise you that the sex was consensual."

"No doubt."

"If she's not complaining, then why the visit?"

Instead of answering, Malcolm countered with another question. "What do you do for a living?"

"I work construction," Gold said.

"Where?"

"The job site is out in Fairfax."

"Missed any work lately?"

"No. You can ask my boss. I've been working overtime for the last couple of weeks so I could have time off for play practice." He supplied his boss's name and number.

Malcolm wrote it down. "And you come

here right after work?"

Gold's frown deepened. "Ask anyone. I just about live here. What's this about?"

"We've found Sierra's body. We're trying to retrace her steps," Malcolm said.

That undercut Gold's bravado. "Oh. That's rough."

"Yeah. Rough. So the last time you saw her was at the party?"

"Yeah, and she was alive and kicking. After we did our thing, she said she had a better dude waiting for her. He was rich. She took off to see him."

"This dude got a name?"

"Don't know."

"Anyone show great interest in her that you were aware of?"

"Sierra attracted attention like honey does bees. She knew how to work a room, and when she wanted to she'd light it up. If you could get Sierra at your party, she made it fun. And for the record, I didn't send her those notes."

"What notes?"

"The ones that said she was pretty."

"Where did she find these notes?"

"Front door. Car. Dressing table. The guy even gave her an ivory pendant."

"Who would have the notes and jewelry?"

"Zoe, I guess."

131

"That Zoe Morgan her roommate?" Garrison said.

"Yeah."

They'd put calls into Ms. Morgan but hadn't connected with her.

"Go see Zoe," Gold said. "Knowing Sierra, all her crap is still piled high in Zoe's spare room."

Zoe Morgan's third-floor walk-up was located in Old Town over a dress shop that had GOING OUT OF BUSINESS SALE signs in the front window. The racks in the store looked picked over, and only a few half-interested women milled around inside.

They climbed the stairs. On the second floor the distinct scent of roasting chicken wafted out from one of the apartments. The sound of a television and a woman talking loudly leaked out from behind another door.

Police work was hardly the glamorous stuff he saw on television. It was a lot of mundane legwork that produced too much information that had to be sorted through for the few nuggets of gold. But to give in to the mundane was dangerous. In a blink the routine could explode in violence.

The stairs that led to the third floor narrowed. They found her apartment and knocked. Zoe answered her door on the third knock.

Dressed in a dark suit and a white silk shirt, the woman who greeted them looked as if she'd just gotten home from the office. A tight ponytail held back brown hair and accentuated a high slash of cheekbones and a peaches-and-cream complexion that needed no makeup.

"Can I help you?" the woman said.

Garrison pulled out his badge. "We're with Alexandria Police. Are you Zoe Morgan?"

Her shoulders edged back just a fraction. "That's right. What's the problem?"

"May we come in?" Malcolm prompted.

"First tell me what this is about."

"Your roommate," Malcolm said. "Her body was found yesterday."

Zoe's lips parted in surprise, and the muscles in her face tightened. She stepped aside. "Come in."

The place was neatly arranged. A floral couch, two chairs, a flat-screen television, a built-in shelf loaded with books, and a large window that allowed the fading afternoon light to flood into the apartment. On several walls were framed posters of ballet productions: *Giselle, Swan Lake,* and *The Nutcracker.*

Malcolm made no effort to disguise his

appraisal of the room. He'd discovered living spaces said a great deal about people. "How long was Sierra Day your roommate?"

She folded her arms over her chest. "About a month. It was only supposed to be for a few days, but I should have known better with Sierra. Once she's in a place it's hard to get rid of her."

"You two were friends?"

"I wouldn't say friends. We were acquaintances. I'm the marketing director for the Washington Ballet. She worked at most of the theaters in the metro area. We ran in the same circles. When she asked me if she could stay for a few nights it seemed the nice thing to do."

"How did you two meet?"

"She was my understudy in a play a few years ago."

"You the actress that suddenly got sick just before opening night?"

Dark brows creased. "How did you know?"

"Grapevine says that Sierra gave you a little something that made you sick so she could step into your role."

Zoe frowned. "That's not true."

"What was wrong with you?"

She hesitated. "Food poisoning."

"That's a bad break."

Zoe was cool, controlled. "Not really. I was trying to act when I could no longer dance. Acting was not a good fit for me. I landed the ballet marketing job a few weeks after that play shut down."

"Why'd you let Sierra move into your place?"

"She needed a place to crash. That play stuff was water under the bridge."

"Okay."

Zoe folded her arms over her chest. "So where did you find her?"

"She was found at Angel Park."

She arched a brow. "Really?"

"That means something?" Malcolm said.

"Her last reviewer called her an 'angel on stage.' She liked the description and repeated it a lot."

"A lot of people heard it?" Garrison said.

"Knowing Sierra, yes. She was no shrinking violet. How did she die?"

Malcolm would bet that Zoe was no shrinking violet either. "We're still trying to figure all that out. Did she pay you rent?"

A smile tipped the edge of Zoe's lips. "Not a dime. But then it was just supposed to be a few days."

"How long has it been since you last saw her?"

A crease formed on her smooth forehead. "Ten or eleven days. A Wednesday, I think."

"It didn't surprise you that she didn't come home for so long?" Garrison said.

"No. She's been coming and going like that since day one. Last Friday night I paused and wondered if she'd come home. I peeked in her room, but couldn't tell if she'd been through or not. It's always a wreck. I left early on Saturday for a seminar and just got back today."

"Where was the seminar?"

"New York. It was a medical convention focused on healing injuries."

"You want to dance again?" Malcolm said.

Her fingers tightened very slightly around her forearms. "Yes, I do. I used to be a very talented dancer. A car accident changed all that. I'd hoped the seminar would show me new healing techniques to strengthen my right ankle."

"Did it?"

"No." The clipped word hinted to her disappointment.

"So you just lost track of your room-mate?"

"Yes." She sighed. "I had a lot of hopes pinned on this trip and was distracted. I wasn't going to deal with Sierra until I got back."

136

"Can we see her room?" Malcolm asked.

"Be my guest."

She crossed the living room and opened the door to a guest room. The contrast between the living room and Sierra's room was stark. Clothes covered Sierra's floor either in discarded piles or in stacks piled in green plastic garbage bags. There was a pizza box on the middle of an unmade bed. Cups lined the floor by a dresser piled high with all kinds of makeup. Layers of jewelry hung from the mirror.

"As you can see, it's hard to tell when she comes or goes. The room's been like this since the first night she arrived." Zoe shook her head. "She was an irritating woman, but I am sorry."

"What else can you tell me about her?" Malcolm asked. He moved to the dresser and picked up a lipstick. He opened it and studied the bright, bright red.

"Nothing anyone else wouldn't tell you. Ambitious. Driven. She'd have done anything to be a success."

"Anything?"

"Just about."

Malcolm stared at the makeup, wondering how she even picked out what she needed on any given day. Mixed among the makeup were a box of diet pills, a sleeve of condoms, and a wad of black panty hose. He glanced at a pair of high heels, black with red soles, on the floor. He picked them up and studied them. Expensive.

As he turned back toward Zoe, his gaze caught sight of a business card tucked in the bottom corner of the mirror. Dr. James Dixon.

"I guess you all know Dixon's past," Zoe said, catching his line of sight. "I told Sierra to stay clear of him. I read about what he did to that prostitute."

"Do you know how the two met?"

"Through me, as a matter of fact. I invited her to a ballet fundraiser over the summer. He was there. And they hit it off." She shook her head. "The guy always gave me the creeps, and I told her so a few times, but she didn't seem to care."

"Did he ever give Sierra reason to worry?" Malcolm asked.

"No. In fact, she said he was the gentlest of souls. That he made her feel completely comfortable."

Lulu Sweet had testified that he'd been gracious and polite, and it was only when they were alone in the motel room that his mood turned violent.

On the bed among the rumpled bed covers was a script, *The Taming of the Shrew.*

The spine had been creased, pages dog-eared, lines highlighted and annotated. "Looks like she was studying hard."

"Sierra was totally dedicated to whatever play she was in. She never missed a mark and always showed up knowing her lines. That's one of the reasons she got so much work in the area. Pretty helps, but it's only a foot in the door. If you don't deliver in this area, word gets around fast, and you don't work."

"You ever help her with her lines?" The script smelled faintly of perfume.

"Sure, a few times. And it was kind of amazing to see her transform from a woman I didn't really like into a character that totally captivated me. She was a gifted actress."

Garrison walked to the lone window in the room and stared out. "Where does the alley below lead?"

"To a small parking lot. Tenants of the building have access to it."

"Marty Gold said Sierra received notes."

"She mentioned that. She thought they were from her ex."

"Which ex?"

"Your guess is as good as mine."

"Do you know where the notes are?"

"Likely buried in here somewhere."

He pulled a card from his jacket pocket and handed it to Zoe. "Will you call me if you hear of anything?"

She glanced at the card. "Sure. Should I clean out her room, or do you want me to wait?"

"I'd like to send my forensics guy here and have him go over the room."

Zoe stared at the mess as if it made her skin crawl. Zoe Morgan was a woman who liked control. The disarray in this room, as well as her leg injury, had to be eating at her.

"Did it bother you to see her succeeding?"

Zoe's lips flattened. "She broke all the rules. I followed all the rules. In the end her star rose and mine didn't."

"Until she was murdered."

She shook her head. "I'll never dance again. Period. Sierra's death does not change that."

"Might make it a little more palatable."

Annoyance snapped in her eyes. "So is this what you cops do? You drop ridiculous statements like that hoping you catch a big fish?"

Malcolm leaned forward a fraction so that he breached some of her personal space. "Never know when I'll catch a whopper."

CHAPTER 8

Wednesday, October 5, 6:30 p.m.

Iris appeared in Angie's doorway. She wore her overcoat and held her neat square pillbox purse. "We have a last-minute visitor."

A dull headache pounded behind Angie's left eye. "Who?"

The fine lines around Iris's mouth deepened. "Dr. James Dixon."

Angie set her pen down carefully on a brief she was proofing. "Say that again?"

"He's out front, and he wants to see you."

She pinched the bridge of her nose. The last time he'd visited her it had been after his trial, and he'd suggested they go on a date. "I don't have time for him. I'll be here until midnight as it is."

"He's not going to leave without seeing you." She tugged at the sleeve of her jacket. "My first inclination was to call the cops and have him dragged out of here. But sometimes I overreact so I thought I'd check first."

Iris had never liked Dixon or even tried to hide her feelings toward the man.

As much as Angie didn't care for Dixon she tried to see the situation with greater perspective. "The last thing I need is for it to get around that Angie Carlson, The Barracuda, had to call the cops to contain James Dixon." News of a police intervention would spread throughout the department like wildfire. She'd be a laughing stock.

"You wouldn't be calling. I would be."

She rose. "Better not."

Displeasure darkened her gaze. "You'll see him then?"

"Give me a minute and then send him back."

Iris shook her head. "I'll stay until he leaves."

"That won't be necessary. If anything, Dixon is dedicated to good manners and public perception. He doesn't want trouble any more than I do. Besides, Charlotte is here, and you have your ballet class tonight."

Iris pulled her cell from her coat pocket. "I'll keep my cell phone turned up."

Angie smiled. "Won't be necessary, but thanks."

She smoothed her hand over her hair to flatten any strands that might have escaped her twist. She shrugged on her jacket and fastened the middle button just as Dixon appeared.

He looked so mild mannered — a proper, staid man who appeared more suited for books and libraries than plastic surgery. He nodded to older people when he passed them in the street; he opened doors for women; and he always rose when a lady stood. And according to the drug-addicted Lulu Sweet, he had nearly choked her to death as he'd rammed his body inside her and called her a whore.

"Dr. Dixon." She remained behind her desk, not feeling the need to venture around and offer a handshake.

He grinned and seemed genuinely glad to see her. "Ms. Carlson. It's been far too long. How long has it been?"

"Over a year."

"Far too long." He approached the desk and extended his hand to her.

She took his hand, allowing his smooth, long fingers to wrap around her hand and squeeze gently. In a flash, she pictured those hands wrapped around Lulu's neck.

She tugged her hand away. "What can I do for you, Dr. Dixon?"

Dark eyes flickered to her hands and then back to her face. "I'd like to retain your services. The police came by my office this afternoon to ask me about the death of one of my patients. Sierra Day. She was an actress, and apparently they found her body this morning."

"As I said when we saw each other last, I will not represent you again. Our business is concluded."

"I was hoping you might have changed your mind." He adjusted his tie. Hearing *no* had never suited him.

"I have not."

He pressed the tips of his fingers onto her desk, like a spider searching for an anchor from which to spin his web. "I never understood why you dropped me. I was proven innocent. I paid on time. I was a good client."

And you gave me nightmares for months. "All you need to know is that I won't represent you again."

He leaned forward a fraction, and the soft scent of his aftershave drifted toward her. "Do you believe I'm guilty?"

A shiver tingled up her spine. "You told me several times that you were not guilty, and I have to take you at your word."

"But you don't believe me."

"I never said that."

"You don't have to. Your actions speak volumes."

He liked games. And the longer he kept her talking the longer she played whatever sick game he had planned. "Doctor . . ."

"Ask me."

"Ask you what?"

"Ask me if I killed the prostitutes that vanished. They tried to use that poor delusional Lulu Sweet against me. They thought if I was convicted of her assault I'd somehow crack and confess to the other killings."

Dixon hadn't forgotten about Lulu.

Cold fear hardened in the pit of Angie's stomach. She remembered the police photos of Lulu. Dark bruises and cuts covered her face and body. "We've already had this discussion, Doctor."

"I haven't killed anyone."

Having him this near sent a chill down her spine. He may not have been guilty of murder, but the things he'd done to Lulu . . . just remembering them made her ill. "It's time for you to leave."

"I make you nervous."

"Not at all."

He grinned. "I do."

Suddenly, her mindset about the cops changed. She'd call them to get this man out of her office, even if it meant dealing with their snickers and jokes for the rest of her life. "It's time for you to leave."

"We're not finished."

"Leave or I call the cops."

A hint of bravado vanished. "You wouldn't."

She reached for her telephone. "If you learned anything about me during that trial, I never make a threat I won't carry out." She dialed a nine and a one. "Leave or I finish dialing."

He raised his fingertips from the desk and straightened. "I don't understand you."

She didn't ask for clarification. He was stringing the conversation along as he searched for something else to prolong this visit. She dialed the final one, listened as the phone rang, and held out the phone so they both could hear. *"911, state your emergency."*

Angie's gaze remained locked on Dixon. As much as he liked playing games with her, he didn't want or need trouble with the cops. He backed out of the office, saluting her as he did.

She watched the door carefully in case he doubled back.

"911. State your emergency."

"I'm sorry. I dialed the wrong number."

"And whom am I speaking with?" the operator said.

"This is Angie Carlson. I just made a mistake."

"Everything is all right?"

She heard the front door close. "Yes. It's fine. I'm sorry."

Angie hung up the phone and walked out into the lobby. From the front window she could see Dixon striding toward his dark sedan. Her hands shook as she smoothed a hand over her hair.

She moved back to her office and wrestled off her jacket. She'd just sat down and tried to refocus her thoughts when Charlotte appeared in her doorway with a printout in her hands. Angie pulled her spine a little straighter as she always did when Charlotte approached. Her boss was only a couple of years older, but Charlotte radiated a stern energy that aged her beyond her thirty-four years. Angie considered herself disciplined and hardworking, but when she compared herself to Charlotte she felt like a slacker.

"I have the billable hours breakdown for the month of September," Charlotte said. She rarely wasted time with simple day-to-day pleasantries. In fact, they never spoke of private matters. Angie knew as much about Charlotte Wellington today as she did the first day they met.

Angie often wondered if a time clock, not a heart, fueled Charlotte's body. "I had a strong month."

"It was good. Not great."

Angie set her pen down carefully and arched a brow. "I disagree. By my own calculations I was up ten percent last month alone."

"I'd like to see that kind of growth again this month if not more."

Angie shook her head. "There are only so many hours in a day, Charlotte. There's not much more time I can squeeze."

"Then perhaps you should consider cutting back on the pro bono work. You've been doing more and more of that lately."

"That was the deal we struck when you hired me. You know that's something that's important to me."

"It's noble. And I appreciate your efforts, but pro bono doesn't pay the light bill. I saw that young woman today. Lulu Sweet is her name? I don't imagine she will be paying you."

Anger had Angie's jaw tightening. "No, she will not."

Charlotte smiled. She was good at using the carrot-and-stick approach when managing people. "I know you work hard, and I remember and will honor our deal. But there are times when you've got to fully focus your attentions on the paying clients. It's the only way we will grow, and let's face it, in this economy no one can turn down paying clients."

"I've not turned away one paying client."

"Dixon just left here, and he looked angry."

"He's not the kind of client we want."

Charlotte folded the billing statement and creased the edge sharply with her manicured fingers. "Why?"

Angie rose. "I'm not representing Dixon, Charlotte, and if you have an issue with my decision I will pack my briefcase now, and we can part ways."

Her brows rose. "Angie, why are you so touchy about this?"

"I'm not touchy, Charlotte. But I know what I know. If Dixon needs an attorney he'll have to shop elsewhere. Now if that is an issue for you, then you'd best say it now."

Charlotte studied her for a long moment. Angie had never driven such a solid line in the sand before, and Charlotte understood if she crossed it, she'd lose a very talented attorney. "All right. I will respect your wishes on that. But I do need you to limit the Lulu Sweets of the world for the time being."

"What's going on, Charlotte? Are we in financial trouble?"

Charlotte kept her expression neutral. "You know as well as I do that cash is always up and down with small businesses. Accounts receivable is lagging this month, and the bank is not extending the bridge loans like it once did. The more we can bill for the short term the better off we will be."

"Duly noted."

"And on that note, I do have a paying client that could bring a great deal of money into this firm. We had lunch yesterday." Charlotte had a talent for drumming up the business. She could move in any circle and find something to talk to anyone about.

"Great. Who is it?"

"Micah Cross."

"Micah? You know my sister's history with his family."

"It's been my understanding that Micah Cross had nothing to do with the misdeeds of his mother and late brother, Josiah."

"Misdeeds are a nice way of putting it. As you may remember his brother raped my sister."

"But Micah did not rape your sister. And there was never a link discovered between

150

him and the Sorority House Murders. From all that I've been able to learn he is a good man with an unfortunate pedigree. In fact, he wants to hire us because he's interested in setting up a charitable foundation. I thought you'd be all over the charitable angle." Charlotte enunciated the last few words to add challenge to the statement.

"I just can't help worry about the potential for conflicts of interest."

"What conflicts? The man is a pillar of the community. And we would be representing him on a civil matter, not a criminal matter. And if we do a good job, this work could lead to more. I'd like nothing better than to be the go-to firm for Cross Industries." She sighed. "If we represented only the people we liked we'd go out of business in a month."

Angie nodded. "You're right." Micah had done nothing wrong. "Seems odd he'd choose us knowing my sister's connection to his family."

"Maybe he wants to make amends. Maybe this is a peace offering."

"Maybe."

"We've scheduled a morning meeting here."

"Will do."

Only after Charlotte left did Angie release

her breath. She rubbed the back of her neck. "Out of the frying pan and into the fire."

He sat in the straight-back wooden chair and clicked the power button on the television. It was just after six-thirty, and he did not want to miss the local evening news. Elation gripped him the more he thought about the cops carrying away his discarded trophy and the media swarming around the park, now designated a crime scene.

The newscaster opened with a house fire in Fairfax. Discussed a car accident involving a local businessman. A story on traffic improvements followed. And still no mention of his bones by the commercial break.

The Other rose and paced the room, realizing his annoyance was growing. His work deserved attention. "How often is a pile of bones found in a park for Christ's sake?"

He moved to a display case and clicked on the interior light that illuminated the specimens inside. The bones of the women had been cleaned, bleached to perfection, and carved into dozens of chess pieces. He had all the pawns he needed to complete his set. Now it was time to turn his attention to creating the more powerful pieces:

the bishops, the knights, and, of course, the queen.

He picked up a delicately carved white pawn. He'd used a femur for this piece. The woman had been tall and lean; she'd had a high slash of cheekbones reminiscent of her Nordic ancestors. She'd worn far too much makeup, and her hair had been dyed a brilliant red that looked cheap. Tattoos had marred her skin, and she'd had a belly ring. She'd done tacky, horrible things to the flesh God had given her.

But the damage she'd done had only been skin deep. Surface. Cosmetic.

When she'd lain on his table and he'd been ready to slice her neck, she'd shouted obscenities at him and called him terrible names.

But under the anger, he'd seen the glint of fear. When he cut her throat, he'd savored the way it had grown and overtaken her body as blood and life seeped from her.

And when he'd lowered her lifeless form into the vat, anticipation had made his skin tingle. Soon, the damage would be stripped away, and soon, he would see the bones that he suspected were perfect.

In death, with the damage of life stripped from her frame, he had found perfection so pure that he'd been humbled. She'd been a diamond in the rough, and he'd been the one to reveal her real beauty.

His mind turned to Sierra. So perfect on the outside. Such a lovely graceful face. And hands that had been long and expressive. She had a dark soul, but he didn't care about the soul. He only thought about bones. Perfection. And his chess set.

Sierra was a perfect addition to his collection.

But taking Sierra had been a bold move. She wasn't like the others. She would be missed. But then what was the fun in playing if there was no risk?

He stroked his pawn. So cool and smooth in his hands.

It made good sense to wait. Let Sierra's case turn cold. But his body had hummed since her killing.

The added danger had given him a thrilling boost that enhanced the killing experience. And he did not want to lose it.

"You should wait," he whispered. "You should wait."

But as he smoothed his hand over the display case he knew he'd not wait.

In fact, he had already selected his next victim.

CHAPTER 9

Wednesday, October 5, 7 p.m.

Voices on the police scanner crackled in the background as Connor Donovan sipped his scotch and stared at the blank computer screen. The scanner was the constant companion of a crime reporter. And at his best Donovan could write on deadline while listening simultaneously to the crackle of police chatter.

However, nothing of great interest had crossed the scanner in days, weeks, and months. Not to say there was no crime, but it held no real interest to him since he'd covered the Sorority House Murders.

Out of boredom he typed his name into the Internet search engine. The cursor blinked as he waited for the search to finish. A year ago, he'd have been able to search his name and see dozens of references associated with his true crime book, *The Sorority House Murders*. However, in the

155

last few months his name had appeared less and less.

The Sorority House Murders had dragged up the details of a story he'd covered over a decade ago. Four young coeds, sorority sisters, had been celebrating the end of the school year. It had been their last night in the house before summer break. Three of the girls had made a run to the grocery store for more wine. The youngest, Eva Rayburn had been at the house alone. By night's end, Eva had been raped and brutalized and her attacker Josiah Cross was dead. Eva spent the next ten years in jail for a murder she did not commit.

What no one had realized was that a killer, bent on revenge, had been awakened when Eva was released from prison. Three of the sorority sisters had been cruelly murdered and Eva had nearly died.

Connor himself had almost died at the hands of this killer, who had seared and mutilated his gut with four-star brands. Even to this day, he could conjure the stench of his own flesh burning. The pain had been crippling. He'd been humiliated when he'd cried and begged for his life.

The killer had spared Connor so that he could tell the story to the world. *The Sorority House Murders* had been the pinnacle of

156

his career. It had given him all that he'd dreamed of and more. Fame. Fortune.

The book and experience had also stripped him of something deep inside him. It was the something that made him a writer. Since he'd penned that book he'd not been able to write a word.

His fifteen minutes of fame had officially ended. He flopped back in his chair and winched at the sudden movement.

Even after a year and a half the scars on his chest remained sensitive. The doctors had told him time would fade the pain, but it remained a constant during his days. And at night, sleep brought some relief, but then the nightmares came. Often in the darkest hours he awoke in a sweat, shaking and expecting to see the killer standing over him.

Nearly dying had changed him. He'd been stripped of boldness and left with impudence.

"Fuck." He turned up the scanner.

Over a month ago, he'd put out feelers with his old contacts. He'd visited morgues, police stations, and back alleys, spreading money and letting it be known that if you tipped Connor Donovan with a great story there would be good money in it for you.

So far, the calls he'd received had been disappointing. The murders had been mundane, mostly drug related or domestic. Arson reports had been run of the mill, profit motivated, or petty revenge. Nothing that had crossed his desk would ever be a headline grabber.

And frankly, he'd been relieved. No story meant he didn't have to stick his neck out.

His phone beeped, signaling a text. When he picked it up, he was just drunk enough not to worry if he had the stones to write a really good story. He glanced at the message.

Bones found. Call.

Bones found. Connor set the phone down and finished off the dregs of his scotch. He poured another glass and swallowed it before he set the tumbler down hard on his desk.

"Now or never, sport," he muttered. He punched the reply button and waited as the phone rang once. Twice. His texter picked up on the third ring.

"Melanie Wright." She worked in the medical examiner's office. A low-level clerk, she'd only been at the facility a few months, but she still saw what came and went through the doors.

"Connor Donovan."

"Word is you are willing to pay for a story?" Her voice dropped to the hushed whisper of a conspirator.

Connor glanced at the piles of papers and periodicals on his desk. He'd been a stickler for neatness a couple of years ago, but he'd not worried so much about tidiness since the attack. A lot had changed in him since that night. "Depends. What's the deal with the bones?"

"How much?"

"Details. Then money."

A heavy pause hung between them, and then Wright sighed into the receiver. "Cops brought in a bag of bones today. Word is they belonged to a woman."

"That's the kind of headline that comes and goes in forty-eight hours." He reached for the half-full bottle of scotch on his desk and refilled his glass.

Again another pause followed. "The cops think she was killed only a week or two ago. That the killer found a way to strip the flesh from her bones."

"Really?" His heart kicked up a notch. "What's the jurisdiction?"

"Alexandria."

"Garrison and Kier or Rokov and Sinclair?"

"Garrison and Kier."

The cops had saved his life on that dark day a year ago when they'd burst into the killer's home and found him bleeding and burned in a side room. He remembered hearing gunshots and deep voices calling for EMTs. But after that he'd had minimal contact with the cops. They'd come to interview him in the hospital, but he'd been very careful only to speak to them when his attorney was present. There'd been some talk of hauling Connor up on obstruction-of-justice charges, but his attorney had gotten that thrown out in exchange for his testimony against the killer.

When he'd tried to interview Eva Rayburn for his book it had been Garrison, her new lover/boyfriend, who'd blocked him at every turn. But he kept writing and had brokered a sweet deal for it. He'd worked around the clock to get the book done quickly so it could capitalize on the still-fresh headlines.

He'd thought his troubles were over.

And then Angie Carlson had filed a few injunctions that had delayed his book. Legal fees had chewed up his advance, and he'd been on the brink during those months.

Bitch. She'd clearly been bitter when he'd broken off their relationship. She was only interested in hurting him.

His anger for Angie energized him.

160

He found himself growing stronger by the second. He quickly brokered a deal with Wright, and the two agreed to meet in one hour.

Connor would supply the cash, and Wright would give him a few more key details.

King's pub was crowded when Angie pushed through the front door just after eight. She was starving, and since her cupboards were bare it made sense to eat at King's. The food was good, and it gave her time to visit with Eva. In fact, Angie now ate here several times a week. She and Eva didn't always have a lot to say to each other, but it was nice just knowing she was near. Made Angie feel a little less alone.

Angie settled at the corner barstool. It had quickly become her spot. She'd also stopped reading the menu because she'd soon discovered the salmon cakes were delicious. They'd become her new favorite food. Her creature-of-habit ways made her so predictable.

Eva stood at the other end of the bar. Her black hair skimmed the middle of her back and was tied back with a rubber band. She rarely wore makeup, but she had a clear complexion that even makeup couldn't improve upon.

She leaned in as an older customer spoke to her, laughed at some joke he must have been telling, and then refilled his beer from the tap.

Eva and Angie shared the same mother but had different fathers. Their mother, Marian, had been married to Angie's dad, Frank Carlson, when she'd met Eva's dad, Blue Rayburn. Frank and Blue had both worked together at the same museum — the Talbot Foundation, a small, pristine collection of antiquities and eclectic collections associated with the Talbot family.

But the men were as different as night and day. Frank was the staid intellectual who was more worried about his collections than his wife, and Blue had been the dark gypsy who'd been reckless and dangerous and had charmed his way into a security job at the museum. Their mother, after yet another cancelled lunch appointment with her husband, had stalked out of Frank's office onto an elevator where Blue stood. It hadn't taken long for Blue to strike up a conversation. Sparks quickly ignited an affair.

When Marian Carlson, pregnant with Eva, had left Frank, he'd filed for custody of four-year-old Angie. His connections had earned him full custody. Marian had only been allowed to see Angie one weekend a month.

Angie remembered the visits to the small house that her mother shared with Blue. She always looked forward to the visits. As the days and hours grew closer for her mother to arrive she'd found it impossible to concentrate. And for a few years, Marian and Blue had shown up with baby Eva without fail.

Then one Friday her mother had called and canceled and had not shown up until late on Saturday. On this visit, Eva had been in her car seat, but Blue had been absent. Angie had never seen Blue again.

The humble house that her mother had shared with her husband and half sister decayed over the next decade. But Angie still looked forward to her visits, savoring the time she spent with her mother and sister.

When her mother had died, Angie had begged her father to allow Eva into his home, but he'd refused.

"She's better off in foster care, Angelina."

"Dad, she's fifteen."

"She's not my child."

"But she is my sister. I'll fly home and take care of her. I'll make a home for her."

"You're barely nineteen. You can't, and I won't let you throw your life away." His tone softened. "She's better off with a real family. They have good people in foster care. You'll see."

To Angie's great shame, she'd listened to her father.

Eva had gone into foster care, been awarded an early scholarship to college, and then spent the next ten years in prison.

Angie shoved out a breath, trying not to dwell on the loss. She and Eva had found each other. Their family might not be whole and perfect, but it was their family and it was enough.

Lately, lingering questions about Blue had nagged Angie. She wasn't sure why she cared about Blue's fate, but she did. He'd blown up so many lives and just walked away. A month ago she'd hired a private detective to find out what she could about the man. She wasn't sure what she'd do if they found him, but she'd cross that bridge when she came to it.

Eva spotted Angie, smiled, and moved toward her. She paused to fill an iced glass with a diet soda and set it in front of her. "You're running a little late tonight."

Angie sipped her soda. "Slammed at work."

Eva punched in Angie's order for salmon cakes. "So how'd it go with Lulu?"

"Your pal seems to be eager to make good. I heard from my dress shop friend that she stopped by today and picked up a nice outfit."

Eva nodded. "Good. She might be one of the few who could pull herself out."

"Let's hope."

"Her court date is still tomorrow?"

"Twelve noon. She's promised to meet me at the courthouse an hour early so we can review the testimony."

"Great. I knew you'd take care of business."

Angie set her glass down carefully, tracing a path through the beads of condensation. "Charlotte has taken on another new client today."

"Really?" Eva studied her sister, clearly sensing a shift in energy.

"Micah Cross. He wants us to handle the legal work associated with his new charitable foundation."

Eva shrugged. "Why are you worried about it?"

"I'm not."

Eva grinned. "You are, Angie. You look

like you could explode."

"Your history with the Cross family was fairly dark. I don't want to dig into old wounds." And yet she searched for Blue.

Eva arched a brow. "So you're telling me you'd walk away from a big client like Micah Cross just so you wouldn't hurt my feelings."

Angie didn't have to process all the variables. "Yes. It would mean leaving the firm because Charlotte would have a meltdown, but I'd walk away."

Eva stared at her a long moment. The softening in her gaze churned emotions in Angie. "Thanks. That means a lot."

"Are you okay with this?"

Eva picked up a rag and absently wiped the bar. "Look, Micah wasn't like his family. He was always kind to me, and when the police investigated his family last year he went out of his way to be helpful. He may have been Josiah's twin, but he was not evil like his brother."

"So, you're okay with me working for him?"

She waved her hand as if brushing away a pesky fly. "Represent away."

"Thanks."

Eva retrieved Angie's appetizer, and just as she set it in front of her, the door to the pub opened. Eva glanced toward the door, and immediately her gaze turned super soft. Angie didn't need to turn to know that Eva's boyfriend Deacon Garrison had arrived.

Angie didn't have a beef with Garrison. Though they'd been on opposite sides of the courtroom, they'd always found a way to be professional and polite. And with him in Eva's life now, they'd even been friendly on occasion.

However, Deacon's partner, Malcolm Kier, was a different matter. The detective carried an angry chip on his shoulder when it came to anything associated with Angie. Kier had made his thoughts clear when she'd represented Dixon. And even though she'd gone out of her way to help them with their murder investigation last year, Kier's opinion of her had been unchanged.

Eva came around the bar and greeted Garrison, hugging him warmly and kissing him on the lips. "You made it," she said. He stood nearly a foot taller than her, and she looked so small in his embrace.

Garrison traced a strand off her cheek with his thumb. "I can't stay long. Just a quick bite."

Eva squeezed Garrison's arm. "Then have a seat and I'll punch your orders in."

Angie's heart softened when she saw the two. It kind of gave her hope that people could find love, a fact she'd seriously doubted after her relationship with The Worm, a.k.a. Connor Donovan.

A man settled next to her, and the wide breadth of his shoulders coupled with a familiar scent identified him immediately. Her insides tightened.

"Detective Kier."

He plucked a French fry from her plate. "Counselor. I hear your kind doesn't eat real food."

"My kind?"

"Vampires. I thought you just consumed blood."

Carefully, she laid her napkin in her lap and picked up her fork. "Sometimes it's just easier to order a sandwich than scramble for a pint."

"I heard the politically correct term for vampires was 'children of the night.' That right?"

"Since when have you ever worried about political correctness?"

"Since never." He watched Eva and Garrison walk away. "I was just trying to be nice for Eva's sake."

"Don't change your ways on my account, Detective. I'd hate to overtax you."

She spared him a glance this time. Dark stubble now covered his square jaw, giving him a rugged-mountain-man kind of vibe that was not wholly unattractive. He still wore the same clothes he had on this morning when he'd visited her at the gym, which told her he and Garrison had been going nonstop. That was standard procedure in a murder case, which were more likely solved in the first forty-eight hours when leads were the hottest.

She pushed the food around her plate but didn't take a bite.

Eva sat burgers in front of Malcolm and Garrison, who had rejoined them. The men ate immediately. No doubt they'd not had time for much food today, and this meal would have to hold them for some time.

Her salmon cakes arrived, and for several minutes the three ate in silence as Eva served other clients at the bar, tallied bills from other waitresses, and restocked glasses. When Garrison had finished he excused himself and found Eva.

Angie's thoughts turned to Sierra and the dozens of fruitless calls she'd made today on the woman's behalf. "Did you ever get an identification on your murder victim? Was it Sierra?"

"Funny you should bring that up." Kier

carefully set down his burger. "Dental records confirm our Jane Doe was Sierra Day."

She reached for the coffee Eva had just set in front of her. She didn't want the brew so much as she needed to do something with her hands. "I'm sorry to hear that."

"Well, you are the first, Counselor," Kier said. "The woman did not have a huge fan club."

Sadness chewed at her. "She could be a challenge."

"That's not the word I've heard bandied about," Kier said.

"She was ambitious. And driven. I've been accused of both and called a few bad names for it."

Challenge sparked in Kier's eyes. "Have you ever been called a liar or manipulator?"

Directness was her blessing and curse. "Yes. And as I remember you've used a few extra choice descriptions: Countess of Evil, Wicked Witch of the East and what was the other one? Oh, Bride of Satan."

No trace of apology altered his features.

Angie's loyalty to her clients hadn't been severed by death. "Sierra had her faults, but she didn't deserve to be murdered or to have her flesh stripped from her bones."

"No argument here, Counselor."

Kier and Garrison were good at what they did. They would put aside personal feelings and move heaven and earth to find Sierra's killer.

"Got any suspects?"

"You know I do. But I'm dealing with airtight alibis around the time the victim vanished."

"Dixon visited me today."

He tensed. "Really?"

"I refused to represent him."

Kier's lips tightened. "Why?"

"You don't need the specifics. You just need to know I'm not his lawyer."

He crumbled his napkin into a tight ball and tossed it on the bar. "Did he tell you anything of interest?"

"Only that he feels like you tried to railroad him with Lulu Sweet."

"He mentioned her by name?"

"Yes."

Malcolm traced the edge of his plate with his thumb. "Too bad."

"I assumed you've checked his alibi."

He nodded. "Dixon was at a convention in New York until Saturday morning. Turns out he's got hundreds of alibis of people at the convention. Plus surveillance cameras at Dulles Airport show him passing through security."

She cradled her cup. "Sierra never once mentioned Dixon or plastic surgery during our visits."

"Maybe he suggested she keep it to herself."

"Why?"

"You tell me. You have got insights into the man few have. Maybe he didn't want her to know too much about him."

She no longer had secrets or privacy to protect when it came to Dixon. She'd been very clear she wanted nothing to do with him. "He didn't look rattled. Miffed that I wouldn't take his case but cool and controlled. In fact, he reminded me of a child playing a game. I was just a piece he wanted, and when he couldn't get what he wanted, he left."

Kier tossed his uneaten fry down. "So he left without a problem?"

"For the most part. It was nothing I couldn't handle."

"Be careful, Counselor — he is not a nice man." No missing the worry in his voice.

"I can take care of myself."

For a brief moment, an odd sense of kinship drew her toward him. As if for the first time they were on the same side. It felt good. "So with his airtight alibi, he is off your suspect list?"

Kier shook his head, his expression dark and brooding. "That son of a bitch is into something. I know it. Can feel it in my bones. His request for representation makes me more certain than ever."

"That's not proof, Detective."

"No, it is not. But I will get it."

CHAPTER 10

Wednesday, October 5, 10 p.m.
Lulu Sweet felt like shit. She'd been late for her shift at the nightclub because she'd had to go by that stupid fancy shop and get herself a dress for court tomorrow.

The lady running the shop had given her The Evil Eye when she'd walked into the shop. She'd felt so small and dirty and the *May I help you?* had sounded like a *Get the hell out of my shop!*

But Lulu had held her shit together, reminding herself that David was more important than a dress shop clerk. So she'd jutted out her chin and told her that Angie had sent her.

The woman's hard eyes had warmed immediately, and she'd said she'd been expecting her. That had helped thaw some of the ice coiling around her spine, but she'd never really warmed up to the whole idea of a makeover. She wasn't interested in looking

174

like one of the bitch-snob mothers who lived in the Old Town. She was who she was, faults and all, and she knew she could be a good mother to David regardless of the color of her hair or the patches on her jeans.

But she'd played the game, thanked the lady for the nice, ugly dress, and headed to the hair salon. However, when she'd gone to the salon, she'd balked when the hairdresser wanted to dye her hair back to her natural black. Not a super-dark, bitching black but an old-lady, mousy black. She thanked the lady as nicely as she could and left the salon.

Now, dressed in a mini and halter, the uniform of the club, her hair still blond, she felt like herself. Hot. Bitching. Smart. In this bar, this area of town, she was in her element. She understood the rules and how to swim with the sharks.

But that familiarity, instead of calming her nerves, stoked her worry. This dark world was no place for a kid. What if she couldn't make it in the real world?

It had been a smart move to get Angie Carlson's help. The woman would sell her case to the judge. Shit, Carlson could sell sand in the desert.

So what if Carlson got the judge to give her David? What if she won and got every-

175

thing she'd ever wanted? And what if Lulu fucked up the kid?

Sure, she wanted him, just like she'd wanted to go to that dress shop and hair salon. But in the end she'd not seen it all the way through. What if full-time motherhood felt as awkward as that damn dress and hair color? David wasn't a hunk of fabric that could be tossed aside or a style to be changed. He was *forever.* And what if she couldn't do forever. She sure as hell had never managed long-term anything before.

Jitters knotted her stomach. Her hands trembled as she tied her apron around her narrow waist. In the old days she'd run to the booze or meth. Both dulled the sting of nerves and the you're-not-good-enough thoughts.

But that was before. And this was now. And now was different. Right?

Six months ago when she'd sat in a jail cell holding David's picture, she'd sworn she'd never, ever use again. And she'd been good to her word.

So why now when she was so close to winning did she want to drink so badly that her hands shook? "Fuck."

Lulu started taking orders, trying to just focus on work. But time did not ease the fear or the tremble in her fingers when she keyed in orders.

"So what did that machine ever do to you?" The husky voice came from a blond waitress by the bar.

Lulu glanced up at Marcia — or was it Maureen? She was in no mood to make nice. "The damn thing is just slow."

Marcia or Maureen shrugged. "Works fine for me."

"Great." The dull ache behind her right eye really pounded, and the fragile hold on her temper slipped.

"Maybe if you didn't punch it so hard?" the girl offered.

"Right."

"You need to relax."

"I don't need to relax. I just need to get this damn order rung up!"

The girl raised a knowing brow. "Tony is out back if you need something to help you relax."

Tony. He dealt drugs. Pot. Coke. Pills. Not the meth she'd learned to love so much but other stuff that could take the edge off.

Lulu took her first real good look at Marcia/Maureen. The girl was skinny, had spiked hair and a nose ring. Tattoos covered her chest and arms, and she had a spark in her eyes that hinted to the drugs in her system. Flash back a couple of years, and

Lulu could have been her.

That time hadn't been all darkness. The tricks weren't always bad, and the drugs took so much of the pain and worry away. And Lulu wanted so badly just to take a break from the anxiety and the fear. Just a break. She loved David, and she'd fight to the death to get him back, but right now she just needed a break.

Lulu sniffed. "You said Tony is out back?"

"Yeah. And he asked about you."

"Did he?"

"He misses you."

The logical part of her brain told her that he didn't miss her. He missed her money and body. But the primitive emotional side of her that was so needy and hungry for love, warmed. For just a few minutes, she wanted to fit in and not worry. Just a few minutes . . .

Lulu smiled, knowing if she could soften a little she could coax a favor out of this chick. "Can you cover my tables for about ten minutes? I'll owe you."

The chick nodded. "Yeah, sure. Hey, and I'm working this party late tonight. If you want to come, well the more the merrier."

Lulu knew what the girl meant. She was turning tricks tonight. Lulu hadn't turned a trick in six months, and as bad as it was,

178

like the drugs it was familiar and resided in the world she understood. "Maybe."

Maureen/Marcia nodded. "It will be fun."

"Sure." Lulu pulled off her apron and pushed through the crowded bar, through the kitchen, and out the metal door that connected to the alley. The cold night air hit her as the door slammed behind her. Even out here, the pulse of the music throbbed in her gut.

Lulu hugged her arms around her chest. She stood under a lightbulb that spit out enough light to illuminate the back stoop but not enough to light the alley. Darkness surrounded her, but she knew Tony was out there. She could feel his gaze on her. She could almost see him reaching out from the darkness, taking her by the hand, and gently pulling her toward him.

But she knew Tony well enough. He would want her to come to him. Especially after her dramatic speech the last time he'd tried to tempt her with drugs and his bed. "I'm giving that shit up for good." She'd been so full of strength and will then.

Lulu shoved out a breath. "Tony."

Cars passed on the street at the alley's lip. A horn honked. A couple argued on the street. But no Tony.

Bitterness tightened her chest. He was go-

179

ing to make her work for this. He'd been pissed by her last rejection, and he wanted her to beg.

She'd done enough begging over the years. It was part of life. A tool to get what she wanted from her mother, drug dealers, or even johns. The only time begging really hadn't worked had been the night she'd been with Dr. Dixon. She could still remember looking up at him as he'd tied her to the bed. But when he'd pulled out the scalpel and tracked it over her breast, she'd shivered with terror. That time when she'd begged him not to cut her, she'd meant it. She hadn't liked the rough sex but had survived it. The one thing she'd not banked on was getting cut or dying.

"Don't, please," she whispered. Tears stung her eyes.

His Mr. Rogers grin telegraphed his enjoyment. He liked the way her breasts quivered when she struggled. "I can make you perfect."

And then he sliced his scalpel over her breast, splitting the skin.

"Leave me the fuck alone!"

Blood trailed down her pale skin. "I want to keep going, but I don't get to kill. The Other one kills."

Pain scrambled clear thinking. "Who the hell

is that? Is that you?"

He didn't answer, but the streets had been buzzing about the three missing girls.

She didn't know who the girls were, but she'd heard whispers. When the first had vanished, there'd been no real alarm sounded. Girls disappeared from the streets. It was a part of this world. But when the second didn't show, other girls had whispered about a killer on the hunt. By the time the third had gone, fear snapped like electricity on the streets. The girls had wanted to pull back and stick with just the regulars, but their pimps pushed them to work and so they did.

Lulu screamed loud and long, and the noise startled Dixon. He glanced around, suddenly afraid that even in this seedy motel her screams would attract unwanted attention. He rose off the bed and went to his briefcase where he kept his little toys. He was getting a gag.

But there was a dark, dangerous look in his eyes. He'd kill her to survive.

She'd never know how she squirmed free of her bindings, but she had.

When he turned to face her, she had the lamp in her hand and hit him as hard as she could. He stumbled back and hit the floor. She scooped her clothes off the floor and ran out of the room into the street naked. She ran a half block before she stopped to pull on her T-shirt and shorts.

There'd been a female cop working the corner that night. A tall redhead, she was talking to one of the girls and had spotted Lulu the instant she'd paused by the front stoop of a bar.

"You okay?"

Her clear voice startled Lulu. Instinct told her the new girl was a cop so she clutched her hand over her breast to hide her injury, which had bled through her shirt. She didn't want more trouble. "Fine. I'm fine."

"You don't look fine." The words were wrapped in a genuine gentleness that had sent her defenses crashing.

Lulu had wept. "Some john got a little rough."

The cop pulled out her phone. "You're bleeding badly."

"I'll heal."

"Not without help." She called for an ambulance.

Lulu's head spun. She'd have fallen if the cop hadn't cupped her elbow and guided her to the curb. Again, she was gentle. "My name is Officer Julian."

Tears welled in Lulu's eyes.

"Who did this to you?" Julian asked.

Lulu sensed the other girls on the corner were watching like wolves ready to destroy the weakest member of the pack. "He's a regular. His name is Dixon."

Officer Julian squatted next to her, radiating a strength that made her feel safe. "He cut you."

She glanced into Julian's eyes for the first time. To her surprise there was no judgment. No disgust. "I think he was talking about the girls that went missing. I think he killed them."

And from that moment, her life had changed. She'd gone to the hospital, been stitched up, and the cops had asked her all kinds of questions. She'd identified Dixon in a lineup and soon found herself the key witness in a murder trial.

Lulu shut her eyes. She did not want to remember that part of her life. "Tony! Where are you?"

The shuffle of feet followed, as if he pushed out of the lawn chair he always brought with him. Tony was a big guy and hated standing for long stretches. "I'm here, baby."

The cold made her nose run. She swiped the back of her hand across it. "I need just a taste. Not much. Just a taste."

"Baby, I got all the taste you need." He stepped into the fragile ring of light, his black face blending with the darkness. He

183

grinned, his gold and diamond grill catching the light. "What kind of taste do you want?"

"Nothing harsh. Just a little to get me through."

He chuckled. "Thought you didn't want no more parts of me."

How could she have been so sure then and so unsure now? "Yeah, we all say stuff."

"Sure, baby."

"I just want a taste." She played a dangerous game. He'd give her a sample, knowing she'd want more. And when she came begging for more, he'd start making demands. But she wouldn't want more.

She wouldn't!

He slid his big, black hand into his pocket and pulled out a baggy full of tissue-paper wads. "I can give you a few hits."

She glanced around the alley, worried for the first time that someone would see her. "Just one will do." She dug a twenty out of her pants pocket and handed it to him.

He took it and happily handed her a little tissue wad loaded with coke. "I tossed in a little extra."

Lulu stared at the wad in her hand, hating and craving it all at once.

"I'll be here for a few more hours if you need me again, baby."

Her fingers tightened around her little lump of happiness. "I won't be back."

Genuine laughter rolled out of his chest. "Right." Brown eyes glistened and danced as Tony stared down at her. The hunter stared at his prey.

Unable to bear his gaze on her any longer, she turned and moved toward the other edge of the light. Her heart hammered in her chest as she slowly unfurled her fingers.

Just a taste.

I won't be back.

With a trembling hand she untwisted the top of the wad and found the little lump of white powder. Just a sniff and she knew how good she was going to feel.

Just a sniff.

Just one.

She raised her palm to her nose, and in a blink Angie Carlson's face flashed in her mind. The attorney had stared at her this afternoon, clearly expecting her to be a fuckup. The gaze had raised Lulu's ire, and she'd been determined to prove to the snotty bitch that she was worthwhile.

For several moments sitting in that fancy office, she'd felt as low as she had on the witness stand. And that had pissed her off. But she'd held her tongue because she'd wanted her son more than she'd wanted to tell Carlson to fuck off.

And staying in control had served her well. By the end of their meeting, there'd been the faintest hint of hope in Angie's eyes.

I want my son.

This little bit of white powder would not only destroy Angie's flicker of hope, but also if the judge ordered a random drug test tomorrow, she'd be fucked for good. She'd never get David back, and Angie would drop her.

Tears burned in Lulu's eyes as she stared at her shaking palm. She wanted the hit so bad that her muscles quivered.

But did she want the drugs more than David?

"Fuck!"

Before she had time to second-guess she brushed her hands together and sent the white powder flying into the night.

Her hands trembled. "Am I stupid or what?" She'd just tossed away a sure escape from trouble. But as she breathed in and out, a real sense of triumph seeped into her limbs. Today, she'd fought and resisted the junk.

But what about tomorrow?

"I only got now." For several seconds she just stood there breathing in air. She didn't want to go back in the bar, but she needed this job. She needed to work. Good mothers had jobs.

Lulu turned, ready to go back inside, when she heard the shuffle of feet behind her. "I don't want any more, Tony." There was some strength behind the words now, and she sensed she could make it to tomorrow. Beyond that she would worry when the time came.

A strong hand landed on her shoulder, and she shrugged it off. "I said no, Tony."

"No is not an option."

The unfamiliar voice sent a tremor down her spine, and as she turned, a needle pricked the side of her neck. Before fear could take root, her knees buckled, and the alley's gravel asphalt dug into her bare knees.

Her world spun. Rough hands hooked under her armpits, and the stranger dragged her down the alley. One of her high heels caught on a pothole and flipped off. Her last conscious thought was of the bar door fading away.

CHAPTER 11

Thursday, October 6, 5 a.m.

Angie spent a restless night. She dreamed
of holding her own son. In the dream, Angie held the baby close, savoring the scent
of milk and baby powder that clung to but-
ter soft skin. She stroked his blond hair and
stared at his tiny fist as he chewed and
drooled over it. She was amazed that he was
so perfect and fit so well in her arms.

At four a.m., she woke and sat up in bed.
She stared at her empty arms and endured
a knife of sadness and loneliness.

It was at these times that she'd have risen
and gone into the kitchen for a glass of
wine. Even now, she imagined the sweet,
cool liquid sliding down her throat and
warming her body.

Angie swung her legs over the side of the
bed. She'd tossed out the bottles of wine
well over a year ago and most days she
didn't miss it. It was just moments like

this. . . .

She glanced at the clock. The gym would open in a half hour. She'd not planned to work out until six, but what the hell. She could get there early, beat the guy who had taken over her lane, and squeeze in a few extra laps.

Angie slipped into her bathing suit, sweat suit, and flip-flops and grabbed the clothes she'd laid out last night.

In her car, she turned on the engine and flipped on the radio, waiting as the heater defrosted the icy mist on her windshield. The morning news rumbled in the background, and she was half paying attention until she heard a very familiar voice: Connor Donovan.

Her fingers gripped the wheel as she thought about the guy who had befriended her, wormed his way into her bed, and made her feel alive — all to gain access to Eva. He'd been working on a story and had expected she would lead him to Eva. As much as she tried she couldn't forget the moment after they'd made love, and he'd been in the shower. She was curious about the man who had invaded her life and felt too good to be true. So she'd dug into his briefcase. It wasn't cool, but she'd been driven to know more. Her instincts had been right. She'd found a file on Eva. When she'd confronted him, he'd not shown the least bit of remorse. In fact, he'd asked her for a quote.

"Ass."

She shoved aside the anger and listened. She'd heard he'd gotten a radio gig that tied into some television deal.

Police discovered the bones of a woman at Angel Park two days ago. Sources close to the investigation report that the victim was local actress Sierra Day. . . .

The jerk was good at digging up the details. No doubt he'd charmed or bribed his way into some back office. She dropped her head against the leather headrest. Kier was going to be one pissed hombre.

A smile played on her lips. Every cloud had a silver lining. But as much as she'd like to have enjoyed Kier's frustration, he was trying to solve the murder of her client.

Connor's voice drew her back. It wouldn't take much digging for him to figure out that she'd represented Sierra. That would bring Connor to her doorstep sooner or later.

"So how did the son of a bitch find out our victim's name?" Malcolm glanced at the cash register receipt in his hand before shoving it in his pocket. They'd heard the morning radio report minutes before arriving at the diner for breakfast. "He spits out a few facts and then proceeds to spin a bunch of crap. *Her husband, Brian Humphrey, believes she is the victim of a violent serial killer.*"

Garrison accepted the egg bagel and coffee from the cashier and handed her a ten. He pocketed the change and followed Malcolm to a corner table. The two took a seat in a corner booth. Both had their backs to the wall and had a clear view of whoever entered or left the shop. "I'd like to know who the hell he paid off to get Sierra Day's name."

"I'd like to know why Humphrey has changed his tune with Donovan. Yesterday he was certain one of her exes killed her," Malcolm said.

"Serial killer is dramatic. And Humphrey is getting face time in front of the television cameras. What better ad for an actor?"

"I've got to be in court this morning for that Latimer case. Could you get to the theater restaurant today and talk to whoever was working there the night Sierra vanished? Maybe you can find somebody who was sober enough who can remember who she left with."

Garrison pulled out his notebook. "I'm a step ahead. The place is called Duke Street

Café. From what I've heard it's a real theater-people hangout. They host a lot of cast parties."

Malcolm bit into his bagel, barely tasting it. "We've hit a lot of damn brick walls in this case. No forensics. No witnesses. It's like we're dealing with a damn ghost."

"Or someone that was caught before and doesn't want to be arrested again."

"Dixon."

Garrison shrugged. "It can't be him. We have hotel security camera footage showing him in New York the night Sierra vanished."

"It is a bit odd that he's got so many damn alibis. It's as if he really needed to prove he was out of town the night Sierra vanished."

"Saying that was true, that would mean he's working with someone else."

"The appetites that got him into trouble before have not vanished."

Garrison shrugged.

"Dixon has a few favorite places. I might check a few out this evening."

"I'll go too."

"No. Together we don't blend in so well."

Garrison grinned and nodded.

The front door to the bagel shop opened, and Malcolm, out of habit, glanced toward it. He did a double take when he saw Angie Carlson stroll into the shop. She reminded

him of a queen, all ice and frost, so but-
toned up that he wondered if she ever took
a full breath. Her blond hair was back in a
tight bun and still damp, no doubt from a
morning swim. A memory of her standing
dripping wet in her red bathing suit flashed
in his mind, and he grew hard as a pike.

Shit. Times were hard if the prim Ms.
Carlson was doing it for him. It had been a
couple of weeks since he and Olivia had gotten together, and he really needed some
alone time with her.

"Wicked Witch at five o'clock," he said.

Garrison had already noticed her. "What
brings her here?"

Carlson spotted them and crossed the
room in quick efficient strides. The click of
her heels had Malcolm's gaze lowering
down the long length of well-formed legs to
three-inch heels. He'd have figured old Angie would wear the practical grandma shoes
rather than the do-me kind of pumps.

Garrison rose. "Angie. What brings you
here? Eva all right?"

She smiled at him. "She's fine. This is
business."

Garrison slid to the side, giving her room
in the booth.

Malcolm took another bite of his bagel,
not really tasting it. He was determined to

prove The Barracuda hadn't tipped his senses off balance. "I thought you people didn't come out in the daylight."

"I got a special blessing from a priest. But I avoid direct sunlight."

No matter what he hurled at her, it rolled off her back. She had a tough skin, and he admired that. "What kind of business do you want with us?"

"I have Sierra Day's client file."

"Why?"

"She's dead, which frees me to discuss her case with you. We only met a handful of times, but I wanted to share with you my impressions. It might help."

Malcolm glanced to the file, and her neat, manicured fingers resting casually on top. "I was expecting a fight."

"No fight, Detective. She is dead so I am no longer bound to keep her secrets."

He sat back in his booth. A soft scent wafted from her. Spicy. Slightly erotic. He'd have expected a different kind of scent. Soap maybe. Or deodorant. Olivia smelled of soap. Sometimes crayons or paint. But not perfume.

"What do you have?" he asked.

She opened the file and pulled a pair of reading glasses from her purse. The glasses gave her a naughty librarian look that stoked his libido all the more. Shit. He had to exorcise this chick from his senses and concentrate.

"Sierra came to me about six months ago. She'd not left her husband but was considering her options. She'd only been married a couple of weeks. At that point she was seeking an annulment. She soon changed her mind when her husband inherited money. She expected a healthy settlement."

"She saw Marty Gold about that time?"

"Him among others," Angie said. "She didn't share with me all her boyfriends, but I know there was another guy. He was rich. He bought her a lovely ivory necklace. Heart shaped."

Malcolm leaned forward. "We never heard about this guy."

"She kept him very secret. No one knew about him because she said he insisted on it."

"She never told you the name?" Malcolm said.

"No. But he did fly her to Florida a couple of times. He keeps a boat down there. And they always met in a private condo."

"You know where?"

"No. Again, she didn't tell me." She pulled off her glasses. "She told me just about everything in her life. In fact the details got to be a bit much at times. But this guy she never talked about. She liked him, but she was a little afraid of him as well."

"You said she also never mentioned Dixon."

"That is correct."

"Could they be one and the same?"

"I don't know."

"Would this mystery man have been at the cast party week before last?" Garrison said.

Angie shook her head. "I doubt it. It would have been too public for him. But that doesn't mean he wouldn't have been waiting for her nearby. Or maybe she went to see him after the party."

"Maybe he was pissed she hooked up with Gold at the party."

Angie shrugged. "That's for you to determine."

Garrison sipped his coffee. "Can you give us anything else?"

"She had a weakness for lingerie. And this guy liked to give it to her. She often commented that he bought her nice things."

"That it?" Garrison said.

"If anything else comes to mind, I'll call." For the first time the ice dropped, and he glimpsed a caring woman. Angie once told her sister that Eva's false conviction had driven her into the law. She'd been determined to help those who had the system against them. A noble cause that Malcolm guessed had been tainted by money.

Malcolm could see that she wanted this killer caught as much as he did. "Have you heard any more from Dixon?"

For the first time he saw disgust tighten her lips. "No. As I said, I made it clear that I didn't want any more to do with him."

Malcolm leaned forward, narrowing the safety zone that she liked to keep around her. "Did he ever work with anyone else?"

"What do you mean?"

"Anyone who might have shared his darker tastes?"

She didn't retreat. "I don't know."

"You don't know or won't tell?" Malcolm said.

"I don't know." She sat back, and he noticed the pulse at the base of her neck throbbed faster.

"You never asked, did you, Counselor? You never asked him about his dark fantasies."

"I asked him if he was guilty, and he said no."

"But you didn't push."

"If a client confessed truly horrific details, I could not represent them."

Malcolm's gaze narrowed. "But you don't

demand that they tell you everything."

She didn't answer.

"So you could have been representing an animal?" He wasn't sure why he was dumping his anger on her. She'd come to help.

Angie rose. "I'll call if I discover anything else that would be relevant."

"Great." Malcolm watched her walk toward the door.

"So why did you go out of your way to piss her off?" Garrison asked.

The reason was so complicated he couldn't have condensed it into a short answer even if he could. "I don't know."

"You rattled her for a reason."

He sat back in the booth, tearing his gaze from the door she'd just vacated. "She didn't look rattled."

"Defense mechanism."

"She covered it well."

"She's an attorney."

Angie wasn't looking forward to her meeting with Charlotte and Micah Cross.

She'd have preferred to have spent the morning reading over Lulu's case file because she didn't want to go into the court hearing cold. Especially considering that Judge Odom would be on the family court bench this morning. He was very conservative by nature and wasn't afraid to terminate parental rights in favor of protecting a child.

As she glanced at the digital clock on her desk she realized she'd have to use that hour before court and just cram in as much information as she could. As long as Lulu showed up, was sober and dressed for the part, she might be able to get Judge Odom to grant some form of visitation for the young mother. He was a tough nut but not uncaring by any stretch.

The bottom line was that no amount of legal tricks or prep work would combat a drugged-out mother. If Lulu didn't do her part, not much else mattered.

A soft rap on her door had her looking up to find Iris. "Mr. Cross is here. I've settled him in the conference room and notified Charlotte."

"Where is Charlotte?"

"Wrapping up a call."

"And wanting me to make nice." Angie rose and smoothed her hands over her pencil skirt. She didn't need a babysitter to handle Cross. She'd swum with enough sharks to know how to maneuver. "Thanks."

She grabbed her leather-bound notepad and moved with calm efficiency toward the conference room. She found Mr. Cross standing alone, facing the door, his hands clasped behind his back. Behind him stood bookshelves filled with the gold and red spines of the law casebooks. He wore a dark, hand-tailored suit, a crisp white shirt, and a red tie made of fine silk. Dark hair was slicked back off his angular face.

He had a jaw that was freshly shaved and likely would remain smooth most of the day unlike Kier, who sported a five o'clock shadow by early afternoon. Cross's body was lean, well toned, and fit, no doubt whipped into shape by a personal trainer. Kier's percentage of body fat was just as low, but his body was broad and more muscular. She hesitated, wondering why she'd bothered to make the comparison.

Angie smiled broadly and extended her hand as she moved across the room toward her new client. "Mr. Cross, it is a great pleasure to have you in the office."

He wrapped warm, soft hands around hers. His gaze projected intensity so much like his father's. She'd only met Darius Cross once. It had been at Eva's trial. The old man's eyes had bored into her as he'd stared at her across the courtroom. She'd been caught in a hunter's sights. Young and inexperienced, she'd been afraid.

"Ms. Carlson. It is indeed a pleasure," Micah said.

She refused to acknowledge any fear now. "I understand we are going to represent you with regard to a charitable foundation."

He held her hand an extra beat, and then released it. "You are. And before Ms. Wellington arrives I wanted us to have a moment to talk about the connection between our families."

"I promise you I will give you the very best representation. I do not hold you responsible for the actions of your family."

He nodded. "I appreciate that. But let's face it, those connections were dark and rather brutal."

"Eva has told me you have been nothing but kind to her. That is enough for me."

"I appreciate that."

He had an easy charm about him that had her relaxing. "Let us move forward, Mr. Cross, so that our professional relationship thrives."

"You are an open-minded woman."

Charlotte appeared in the doorway. She'd swept her red hair up into a chignon and applied a discreet but effective amount of makeup to a porcelain complexion. She'd chosen a hunter-green suit and an off-white silk blouse. Both accentuated her figure but not so much that she bent any professional standards. Charlotte understood where the "line" was and could dance right on it without crossing it.

"Mr. Cross," Charlotte said. "I am so glad you could join us. It was so kind of you to come to our offices. We'd have been glad to meet you at yours."

Cross stared at her, a gleam of appreciation in his eyes. "It was important to see your offices for myself. A person's space tells me so much about them."

Charlotte arched a brow. "And what do our humble offices tell you about us?"

"That you are going to do an excellent job for me. I have chosen wisely."

Angie had to hustle to make it to the courthouse by eleven. Her meeting with Cross had gone longer than she'd expected. However, the meeting, which could have been an awkward mess, had been oddly relaxed. Cross gave off an easy vibe that had her dismissing initial concerns about him. She'd worked hard not to be like her father, and it seemed Cross had done the same.

Hauling her overstuffed briefcase, she dashed up the front steps, her high heels clicking on the brick steps as she hurried through the front door. A quick pass through the metal detector and she was hustling toward the domestic court. The hallways were crowded today, full of lawyers in dark suits, and clients in all manner of dress from ragged jeans to their Sunday best.

Angie hoped it would be the latter for her and Lulu today. It would be nice to see her legal training help out the "little guy" for once.

She searched the hallways hoping that Lulu would be waiting for her in the lobby. Her initial sweep did not reveal Lulu's blond spiky hair. Annoyance took root, and on reflex she checked her watch. Two minutes past eleven. Lulu could be running a little late, just as she had been.

Too much nervous energy raced through Angie, making it impossible for her just to sit and wait. Her fingers tightened around her briefcase, and her toe tapped the marble floor. Minutes passed as her gaze swept the hallway again.

This time she searched more closely, remembering she'd told Lulu to change her hair. But a second and third search did not reveal the young woman. Angie called Lulu's cell number and was annoyed when it went straight to voice mail. She left a curt message and snapped the phone closed.

Angie checked her watch at eleven-fifteen and again at eleven-thirty. Their hearing was scheduled for twelve, and their critical prep time was vanishing. Another call to Lulu's phone landed her again in voice mail.

"Damn it," she muttered.

Angie moved through the crowds to the elevator, hoping now that Lulu had somehow gotten mixed up and had gone to the courtroom on the second floor. As she rode the elevator up, her blood pressure rose. "This should not be so complicated. This should be easy."

But people like Lulu often made simple events complicated. They missed appointments, took drugs knowing a court-ordered test was imminent, or shouted out the wrong statement to the judge.

Angie pressed a trembling hand to her forehead, willing the impending headache away. When the doors dinged open she stepped out into a less-crowded hallway and searched for her wayward client. Again, no Lulu.

This time Angie took a seat outside the domestic courtroom so that she could glance through the files. At least she could be familiar with the case.

However, the case file did not give her much hope. Lulu had been arrested for drug possession not once as she'd said but three times since the birth of her son. She'd

<hr />

also been picked up for solicitation six months ago, and she'd missed two visitations with her son.

Angie called Eva, but the call went to voice mail. She was about to curse the recording but remembered Eva had advanced calculus and wouldn't be out of class until after two. "Why do I do this to myself?"

Angie sighed and let her head tip back against the cold wall. Even if Lulu waltzed in here right now, looking like a saint, the facts in the file would be hard to overcome.

She checked her watch. Five minutes to twelve. Anger knotted her stomach, and she would dearly have loved just to get up and walk out of here.

And she would have if Eva hadn't asked this favor of her. Instead she dashed down the stairs hoping that Lulu had arrived. She hadn't.

Angie had to sprint back up the stairs to reach the courtroom by twelve sharp. Breathless, she moved into the courtroom and took her place on the plaintiff's side. To her right she glanced at an older-looking woman who shared Lulu's sharp features and expressive eyes. The woman had to be Lulu's mother. Instead of staring ahead, the woman searched the room, her eyes expectant, not angry.

"The next case on the docket is Sweet versus Sweet." The bailiff's voice cut through the courtroom.

Lulu's mother rose, as did a young man in a dark suit who sat beside her.

The judge peered over his glasses, glaring down at the mother. Immediately, his gaze swept the room in search of Lulu. "Where is the plaintiff?" He glanced at his paperwork. "Lulu Sweet."

Angie stood.

The judge was going to chew her ass out for her client's absence. She'd been chewed out before and had developed a thick skin. But it irritated her that she was now defending a woman who had duped her.

"Does Ms. Sweet have representation?"

Angie rose. "Angie Carlson here, sir, representing Ms. Sweet."

Judge Odom cocked a bushy brow. "This isn't your usual turf is it, Ms. Carlson?"

"No, Your Honor." Her voice was clear and strong. "But I am the counsel for Ms. Sweet."

He shrugged. "So where is your client, Ms. Carlson?"

"She has not yet arrived at the courthouse."

"She's a no-show?"

Angie's gaze remained on the judge. The

last thing she wanted to do was show him any ounce of disrespect. "So far, she has not arrived."

The other attorney cleared his throat. "We all knew this was a critical hearing, Your Honor. The fact that Ms. Sweet is late speaks volumes about her commitment to her son. I move that you award full custody to my client."

Angie straightened. "Your Honor, I move for a continuance so that I can find out what has befallen my client. She understood the importance of this court date and was anxious to be present."

"And yet she is not here," the other counselor said. "She has a history of drug use and arrest."

"We haven't proved either is behind today's absence," Angie countered. She shared the counselor's fears, but she couldn't let her own concerns sway the fact that she was here to argue for Lulu. Later, when she got her hands on the girl, she'd sort out this mess, but for now she was about damage control.

"Do you know where your client is, Ms. Carlson?" Judge Odom said.

"I'm sure if you just give her a little more time." Angie hoped for a miracle now. *Come on, Lulu, drag your butt through those doors and give the judge a valid explanation.*

But no Lulu appeared, and the seconds ticked as Angie stared at the judge.

"Where is your client, Ms. Carlson?" Impatience nipped at the words.

"I don't know."

"When did you last speak with her?"

"Yesterday. She was quite anxious to be here."

The judge sighed. "The road to hell is paved with good intentions." He glanced at the other attorney. "You have Ms. Sweet's mother here today."

"Right at my side, Your Honor."

"And she is willing to take the child?"

"Yes, sir. She is most anxious to give the child a stable home."

Angie glanced at the woman, and this time really looked at her. Her frame was fragile, and her shoulders stooped. She was older than Angie would have expected — perhaps in her mid-sixties, suggesting that Lulu had been a late-in-life baby. Mrs. Sweet's skin was pale, and her bony hands were riddled with blue veins. She hardly looked strong enough to lift the baby, let alone raise him. Eva had hinted that she was sick.

"Mrs. Sweet, are you willing to take the minor child, David?" the judge asked.

"Yes, sir." Her voice held a surprising

strength and clearness that Angie had to admire. The woman might not have wanted this curveball life had tossed her, but she was doing her best to handle it.

The judge glanced again at Angie. "Give me something, Ms. Carlson."

She'd have talked her way through this if it was a corporate client. She possessed dozens of tricks up her sleeve to drag out a hearing. But this wasn't a merger or an acquisition. It was a child. And the mother had missed her chance to parent him. "I can't."

He nodded. "Let the record show that Ms. Lulu Sweet did not appear in court and that I award custody to Mrs. Vivian Sweet." He pounded his gavel on the bench. "Next case."

Angie turned and left the courtroom, her stomach churning with anger. What an utter waste of time and energy.

She'd just reached the elevator when she heard her name. Mrs. Sweet moved toward her. Her attorney remained by the courtroom door, watching but not approaching.

"Ms. Carlson, may I have a moment of your time?" Vivian Sweet's voice had lost the power and now sounded weak and defeated.

"Mrs. Sweet."

"Thank you for trying to help my Lulu."

Angie had expected an attack, not thanks. She nodded stiffly, not sure what to say.

"Lulu wants to straighten out, and I really hoped this last go-around she would. The last few weeks have felt so hopeful. I hoped she'd win today."

"That seems surprising."

"I don't want to be in this battle with my daughter. I want her to get her act together and raise David. But though there have been glimmers of success, even weeks of it, a baby needs more. He needs his mother all the time, not just when she feels like being a mother."

Angie leaned toward the woman. "Yesterday she seemed very determined to be here. I believed her."

"And she believed herself. She wants to do it right, but every time she gets close she stumbles."

Genuine regret coated the words. "I'm sorry."

Mrs. Sweet raised her chin as if pity was the last thing she wanted. "If you see Lulu, tell her that I love her. And that David is doing fine."

"Are you doing fine?" It was an inappropriate question, and one Mrs. Sweet shouldn't have answered.

Her eyes darkened with worry before she seemed to brush it aside. "I'm fine. I have to be for David."

"Mrs. Sweet." The other attorney was clearly unhappy that his client had chosen to talk to opposing counsel.

Mrs. Sweet glanced toward him and smiled. "I'll be right there." She looked at Angie one last time. "Thank you."

The woman vanished into the crowd, leaving Angie angry with her client and her sister for putting her in such a situation. She punched the down button, and when the elevator didn't instantly open, she pressed it several more times as if the machine would sense her frustration and hurry.

"So, it's Angie Carlson." The smooth voice had her spine stiffening so sharply that she thought it might snap. Connor Donovan.

"Mr. Donovan, what rock did you crawl out from?"

CHAPTER 12

Thursday, October 6, 12:30 p.m.

Donovan moved beside Angie, so close she could feel the heat of his shoulder as it nearly brushed hers. "*Mr. Donovan?* Angie, after all we shared . . . call me Connor."

When she'd discovered he'd used her so badly, she'd tried to brush the rejection off and tell herself it didn't matter. But the wound he'd inflicted had been slow to heal. And there were still days when she feared she'd never really open up to a man again.

"I could call you asshole. Dickhead? How do they sound?" She met his gaze as if leveling the barrel of a shotgun.

His stare didn't waver. "You have a right to be pissed. I get that. I was a dick."

"So we can agree on something."

His grin waned. "Look, Angie, I saw you here today, and I wanted to come over and apologize. I've had a chance to rethink a lot of things in the last year, and what I did to

212

you, well, was wrong."

She'd done things she regretted, and those regrets were part of the reason she was here today. But she suspected Donovan didn't care about right and wrong. "Beat it."

"Ah, come on, Angie. Can't we get a drink?"

The elevator dinged, but a quick glance told her it was stuck on the floor above, forcing her to stand and wait with him. She considered the steps but refused to run from this jerk. "Go away, Donovan. Find another rock to crawl under."

His easy veneer melted, and something harder and colder appeared. "You can't cry foul. You are a user just like me. You do what you need to do to win. I'm no different."

She cleared her throat. "This is not the time or the place."

"It's as good as any."

"Drop dead."

His eyes narrowed. "You've been perched on your self-made pedestal for so long you've forgotten you are a muckraker just like me. Let's face it, sweetie — your talent for nasty is as honed as mine."

Color rose in her cheeks. "Do you have a point to make, Mr. Donovan? I've got work to do."

"Don't we all."

The elevator doors dinged open. To her dismay it was packed. The doors closed.

"Why are you here?" she asked. "Don't you have something more entertaining to do like pulling the wings off of flies?"

"I'm here about your client."

"I don't talk about my clients."

He leaned toward her. His aftershave reached out to her . . . it was the same brand. Armani. When he'd first touched her, she'd savored the scent like an aphrodisiac. Now it made her sick. "Not even the dead ones?"

A bitter taste settled in her mouth. "Ah, you are here to use me again."

"I came to ask questions."

"Wrapped in sweet apologies."

"So?"

"No comment."

"You have no idea who would want to kill such a lovely young woman?"

She glanced at the elevator buttons above the door. It held on the floor above for what seemed like forever. Forget it. She pushed past Donovan with as much force as she could muster and headed down the hallway through the crowds toward the stairs. She'd just reached the door to the stairwell when long fingers wrapped around her arm.

"Don't walk away from me." The anger in

Donovan's voice had her readying for a fight as she turned.

"Get your hands off me." She tried to jerk free, but he held firm.

"Not until you tell me about Sierra Day. What do you know about her?"

Again, she tried to wrench free. "Let me go or I will scream so loud that every deputy in this building will come running. And then you can explain why you were roughing up an officer of the court." She drew in a breath, fully intending to scream.

He dropped his hand but didn't move away. He whitewashed his anger with a grin. "Ah, come on for old time's sake. Tell me what you got on Sierra?"

"Prick."

The brutally delivered words hit their mark, and the normally iron-skinned Donovan flinched. "Bitch."

The lame comeback made her laugh. "If that is the best you've got then I am not impressed."

He leaned toward her and said in a voice only she could hear, "The only reason I fucked you was because you were so god-dammed pathetic. Like throwing a bone to a starving dog."

The words pierced the shell she so carefully nurtured and sliced into her heart.

Emotion welled up so fast and furious in her throat that it left her breathless.

"There a problem here?" The deep male voice cut through the tension.

Angie glanced over to see Detective Kier. She had never been happier to see the man.

Kier wore a blue sport coat, red tie, and white shirt that could have used an iron. Clean-shaven with his hair neatly combed, he could have passed for civilized if not for the menacing expression on his face.

As much as she didn't want help from Kier, getting rid of Donovan ranked higher on the priority list. "Donovan doesn't understand that no means no."

Donovan muttered something under his breath and stepped back. Though he stood a little taller than the detective, Kier, with his muscular build, looked as if he could make quick work of any challenge that Donovan offered.

"I was just asking her a few questions about Sierra Day."

Kier rested his hand on his hip, letting his gun peek out from the folds of his jacket. "From what I heard she declined to answer."

Donovan masked any outward annoyance with a shrug. "I wouldn't be doing my job if I didn't push her for an answer."

Kier grinned. "And I wouldn't be doing mine if I didn't tell you to back off." His gaze never wavered from Donovan. "Frankly, nothing would give me greater pleasure than to arrest you."

"On what charge?"

The moment's diversion gave Angie the time she needed to recover her breath and footing. "Harassment. Battery. Unlawful detention. I'm sure if you gave me a few more minutes I could come up with more charges."

Donovan glared at her. "That would never stick."

"Maybe. Maybe, not. But I could create a hell of a legal mess."

Donovan's lips flattened. "We'll catch up later, Angie."

"I don't think so."

He winked at her. "Count on it."

She tightened her hand on her briefcase handle. "Then count on charges being filed against you."

"We'll see." The reporter darted down the staircase.

For several heartbeats she stood rigid, unmoving, waiting for Donovan to return. Then, certain he'd truly left, she faced Kier. Now he was looking at her with a gaze not so consumed with fury but worry.

Her cheeks flushed. "If you say one comforting word to me, Detective, I'll sock you."

His throaty chuckle caught her off guard. "Wouldn't dream of it. Besides, what would be the point? I've heard vampires can't be hurt. No heart."

Without missing a beat she said, "With no blood to pump through our veins, a heart is just extra baggage."

Whatever concern had been in Kier's gaze thankfully vanished. "I'll keep that in mind."

He could have just turned and vanished into the crowd, but he lingered a beat.

It was enough time for her to drop her guard for just an instant and say, "Thanks. Donovan was more persistent than I'd imagined."

"Give me a reason, Carlson, and I'll haul him to jail."

She lifted an eyebrow. "Why, Detective, that's the nicest thing you've ever said to me."

"I mean it." There was no hint of humor now. He would arrest Donovan if she gave the word. "He's a real creep, and I'd love nothing better than to bring him down a peg."

The banter felt right and good. Her world came back into balance. "I can take care of myself. But thanks."

"An extra hand never killed anyone."

"Like my dad used to say, if it doesn't kill you it makes you stronger. I'm still standing, so I guess I can thank Donovan for making me stronger."

"Stronger or more cautious?"

"Both." She didn't want to talk about herself. "Any news on the Sierra Day case?"

He shoved hands into his pockets and rattled the change. "No. A lot of people would have liked to have killed her, but they all have alibis."

Her mind clicked into defense-attorney mode. "Alibis are easy."

"Finding this mystery boyfriend is not."

"He's out there. Somewhere."

He hesitated as if struggling for words. "By the way, thanks for the tip."

"Sure."

Angie turned, and as she moved away she noted she and Kier had been quite civil to each other. She suspected she'd just witnessed a minor miracle.

Malcolm watched Angie Carlson walk away. She moved slowly, shoulders back as if she were queen of the world. He'd never seen her guard down until he'd seen her with Donovan. For just a second, when Donovan had been venting nastiness, Malcolm had glimpsed pain behind the ice. Whatever Donovan had fired her way had struck a nerve.

To her credit, Angie had rebounded and rallied. He believed if he'd not arrived when he did, she'd have landed a punch or two of her own. Frankly, nothing would have given Malcolm greater satisfaction than to see the counselor hit Donovan.

During last year's investigation into the Sorority House Murders and Donovan's near-death experience, Angie's relationship with the reporter had come to light. Instead of hedging or trying to hide a very embarrassing episode in her life, she'd been honest and straightforward when questioned by Garrison. She'd plainly admitted that Donovan, who'd only been after information on Eva Rayburn, had made a fool out of her when he'd coaxed her into his bed and tried to elicit information.

Carlson could have lied about the whole episode. But she hadn't. She'd put protecting her sister above her own feelings.

In fact, as he thought back, he couldn't point to one time when she'd lied to him. She'd grilled him in court, mocked him to his face, and directly denied him information, but she'd never lied.

Cops called her The Barracuda for a

reason. Not only could she take care of herself, but also when she latched on to a witness she didn't let go until she tasted blood.

But she'd never pretended to be otherwise. She was who she was.

So, why should this matter? And why had he had the urge to protect her when Donovan had had her cornered?

Malcolm blew out a breath as he rubbed the back of his neck. "Because I'm a god-dammed idiot."

Donovan had never considered it wise to give in to hate. It was a pointless, vain emotion that often blinded the unwise to opportunity. But as he watched Angie leave the courthouse his hate for her would not be denied.

He released the reins and let the emotion free. He let his imagination go to its darkest places and pictured himself destroying her, word by word.

After all he'd been through last year — the trauma, the surgery, and the rehab — he had every right to every bit of success he could grab. She had no right to deny him.

She'd stood in front of him like a righteous Puritan today, but the heart of a hot little whore beat under that silk suit. She'd liked all the nasty things he'd done to her. Hell, she'd loved it all. She simply didn't want the world to know that she was a freak.

A client of hers had been murdered, and he intended to play that detail to the hilt. He'd drag her sweet ass through every bit of mud he could find.

CHAPTER 13

Thursday, October 6, 7:15 p.m.

Angie wasn't mad at Eva because Lulu hadn't shown up in court today. Okay, maybe put out, but not mad. People misjudged people all the time. And though Eva had an off-the-charts IQ she was susceptible to liars just like the rest of the regular folks.

But she was now officially annoyed with Eva because her sister had not answered her cell phone. Eva had spent ten years in jail for a crime she didn't commit. The confinement had been during the cell phone explosion, and when Eva was finally released, she'd become so accustomed to not needing the gadget she often forgot to charge her phone or even bring it along with her.

Angie had given Eva a phone for security reasons. No matter how many times Angie spoke to Eva about the phone, and no matter how many times Eva swore she'd do a better job in the future, they always found themselves right back in the same boat.

She took her seat at the bar at King's and waited for Eva to see her. Eva looked pale and tired. She didn't have the usual zest. All Angie's recriminations lost steam. "What's going on with you?"

Eva set the soda down in front of Angie. "Why do you say that?"

"You look like shit."

Eva arched a brow. "I love you too."

Angie shrugged. "You never look sick. You now look sick. What gives?"

Eva shrugged. "Flu, I suppose. Bound to happen sooner or later. I'm in the public every day."

"How's school?"

"Good. How did Lulu do today?"

Angie traced the rim of her glass. "Funny you should mention Lulu. I tried to call you from court."

"In a test. Had to turn The Thing off."

"Did you turn the phone back on?"

A half smile tugged at the edge of Eva's mouth. "Judging by your expression I'd say no. And I'd say if I turned The Thing on right now I would have three or four missed calls."

"Three."

A hint of amusement sparked in her eyes.

"You're getting better. Not the full-out panic when I don't answer."

"You did almost die last year."

"That was last year."

Angie shook her head. "It's beyond me how you can just let the past go."

"What's the sense in hanging on?" Eva punched in Angie's dinner order. "I assume the usual."

"Yeah."

Eva shrugged. "So did Lulu do a great job? I know she was thrilled you were helping."

A heavy silence hung for a moment or two. "Lulu never showed in court."

Eva leaned forward. "You are kidding me."

"Nope. I waited outside the courtroom until the last possible second, then dashed into court to get my ass reamed by the judge."

"Shit."

"Tell me about it."

Eva shook her head. "That's not like Lulu. She was very committed to getting David back."

"She is also a drug addict who has only been clean six months. You know the stats on addicts. They can lapse so easily."

"Not Lulu. I've seen her walk away from temptation too many times. She wouldn't screw this up for anything."

Angie hated to see Eva upset. "I don't know what to tell you, Eva. She messed up big time. The judge awarded custody to her mother. And her chances of getting it back now are slim to none for the foreseeable future."

Eva's lips flattened. "I don't buy this. Something is wrong."

"Eva. Nothing is wrong other than Lulu can't stay away from the drugs."

Eva leaned forward, a spark of anger refreshing the paleness in her face. "I've been on the wrong side before. I know what it's like to have the whole damn world against you and to have no one to call a friend."

When Eva had been on trial, Angie had gone against her father and flown back to Virginia from college to see Eva. She'd been prepared to help. But she hadn't been prepared for Eva's anger or her demands that Angie leave her alone.

"Just get the fuck out of my life!" Eva had shouted in the visitors' room.

To this day, Angie deeply regretted that she'd not looked beyond her own feelings of hurt and rejection and seen that Josiah's father, Darius, had threatened Eva if she accepted any help.

"You are not Lulu," Angie said. "This is not your murder trial."

"She *is* on trial. Her whole future is at stake." Eva shook her head. "She's not much older than I was when it all went wrong. She's alone." The last words held so much emotion and sadness that for a moment it took Angie's breath away.

"She wasn't alone. She had you, and she had me. She had people in her corner. She was the one who chose not to play by the rules."

Eva's fingers gripped the edge of the bar. "Who knows who or what kept her from that courtroom today."

"Lulu kept Lulu from that courtroom today."

"I don't buy it." Eva checked her watch. "But I intend to find out what happened."

"What are you going to do?"

"I know where she keeps a small apartment, and I know where she works. I am going to see both."

"You're working."

"The night is slow. King won't mind."

Angie sat forward. "Yeah, well, I mind you snooping around in God-only-knows-what back alley for someone who might not want to be found or worse is strung out on drugs and would hurt you."

"You sound like an old lady. Stop worrying so much."

The *old lady* jab dug a little deeper than it should have. "I'm not old. I'm just careful."

"Super careful, if you ask me."

"What's that mean?"

"Come on, that crap with Donovan did a number on you. You're wrapped tighter than an old nun."

"I am not. I take chances."

"When?"

"Hell, I don't keep a diary." She wagged her finger. "But I am not an old nun."

Eva's gaze trailed over Angie. "Right. Well, I don't have time to argue. I'm going to Lulu's apartment and then to her bar. I want to know if anyone has seen her."

"You're going now?"

"Yes." Eva smiled. "Look, I'll be fine. Don't worry. And I'll turn on my cell phone so you can call me any time you want." To prove the point, she pulled the phone from her back hip pocket and made a show of turning it on.

Angie wasn't old. She wasn't a nun. She took chances. Sure, she was cautious. Sane people were careful. Shit. "I'm going with you."

"What?"

"I'm going with you. Right now. I'm going with you to wherever Lulu worked."

"When the people in that bar see you they'll think the cops or the FBI have arrived. You're too buttoned-up."

Angie glanced down at her dark pencil skirt, matching tailored jacket, white shirt, and single strand of pearls. "I was in court today."

"You still look stiff. Hell, you're wearing a bun, Angie."

Angie gently touched the chignon, which she'd carefully twisted up this morning. She'd been pleased that it had gone up so easily, and the single comb had secured it on the first attempt. But without hesitation, she pulled the comb free and let her thick blond hair fall and skim the top of her shoulders.

She shook her head and ran her fingers through the mane to comb out the kinks. "Okay, lend me some clothes. I can fit into your jeans, and I know you have a million T-shirts."

"You're kidding."

"No, I am not. Where you go, I go."

Eva studied her sister. "You're going to need some makeup to tart you up a bit."

"Great. Have at it."

"Okay. Let's get going."

Within a half hour, Eva had spoken to

229

King. Angie had changed into faded jeans that hugged her hips a bit too tightly for her tastes and a red T-shirt that said *Back Off.* Eva had applied too much mascara to Angie's pale lashes and caked on eye makeup and rouge.

Angie stared into the rearview mirror of her car as she waited for traffic to clear. "I look awful."

"And now you just might fit. The only trick will be to remove the metal pole that seems lodged in your spine."

"I'm proud of my good posture." She sighed. "But I get the drift. Slump."

"Yeah. Forget all the polite stuff your dad taught you. Embrace the dark side."

Angie laughed and pulled into traffic. "Great."

"We'll stop at Lulu's apartment first. Then hit the bar."

"I'm game."

The drive to Lulu's apartment took twenty minutes. It was in a seedy, run-down building that smelled of cabbage and garbage. The halls were dimly lit, and the sounds of a couple arguing and a baby crying drifted through paper-thin walls.

Eva rose on tiptoes and ran her fingers along the top edge of Lulu's front door. She found the key, unlocked the door, and opened it. She flipped on the light inside the apartment. "Lulu. Are you here?"

It was a one-room apartment with a Murphy bed and a kitchen with a microwave, sink, and very small refrigerator. There was a small round table, equipped with four mismatched chairs, a ten-inch television with rabbit ears, and a single window covered with a white sheet.

The Murphy bed was neatly turned down. The sheets were crisp and clean. In the corner was a crib. It had worn edges and clearly was older, but it was clean and filled with stuffed animals.

"Looks like she expected to come back last night. But didn't," Eva said.

"Yeah."

Angie walked to the kitchen table where she found a framed picture. It was a photo of Lulu and her son just hours after he was born. Lulu's face was freshly scrubbed, and though she looked exhausted she was beaming. Carefully, she set the picture down. "Any sign of her in the bathroom?"

"No," Eva said. "No mail. Nothing weird. It doesn't look like she was here last night."

"What about signs of drugs?"

"Nothing. Not even a drop of alcohol or a fleck of tobacco."

"She could be in a back alley or with a john."

"She's not. I know it."

"Okay." Angie smoothed her hand over the table's surface and discovered it was clean. "So we head to the place where she worked?"

"Yeah. ZZ's."

"Let's go."

The ten-minute drive to ZZ's took them deeper into a dark world, a universe away from the historic streets of Old Town Alexandria. The area had a hard, industrial feel, with traffic lights and lots of traffic congestion.

Angie parked in an all-night diner's lot as Eva instructed.

"We'll walk the rest of the way."

"In this neighborhood?"

"Just keep your eyes forward and try to look pissed, like you might sock someone if they get too close."

"A lesson from prison?"

"One of many."

The night air was cool and quickly cut through the soft fabric of the T-shirt. They moved down semi-lighted streets past hookers and a couple of shady guys. However, Eva didn't quicken her pace until she spotted a beat cop.

When they were a safe distance, Angie said, "So are you still afraid of cops, or are you afraid of being recognized and word getting back to Garrison?"

"Both, I guess. I still clench when I see a uniform. I have too many bad memories of being led away in handcuffs. And Garrison knows just about every cop on the beat. Word can very easily get back to him. He worries, and I don't want him to worry."

"So you care about him?"

Eva shoved long fingers in her jeans pocket. "I like him well enough."

"That's why you see him almost every night."

"We do all right together. I just wonder if we can make the long haul."

"Why couldn't you? I see the way he looks at you. He's insane for you."

"I don't have a history of long-term anything except prison. So I try not to plan too far ahead."

When a couple of girls came bursting out of a bar, music mingled with a rush of smoky, warm air.

"You are the one that's always preaching 'eyes forward.' "

"Yeah, well, we all worry." She nodded to the block ahead. "That's where she works. ZZ's."

Angie glanced up to the red neon sign that blinked. The front window was lit up with a beer sign, and she could see inside that the place was crowded. "What kind of people come here?"

"Rough people."

"Like how rough?" She'd dealt with her share of rough clients, but it had always been in the courtroom or a jail visitors' room. She was always in control . . . in her element. Now as she descended into their world, she wanted to ask Eva again if this was a good idea. She wanted to preach caution, but the steel in Eva's features told her the words would hit deaf ears.

And to be honest, she wanted to know where Lulu worked. She wanted to find the girl and give her crap for leaving her in the lurch. "So what do we do?"

"You stay by the front door. Keep an eye out. I'll talk to the bartender. I kind of know her, and she might talk to me."

"How do you know her?"

"We were cellmates." Her tone was casual.

"Okay."

Inside the bar the music was so loud she could feel the beat pounding in her breastbone. The smoke was so thick, despite the recent ban on smoking in bars. She guessed cigarettes were the least of the vices in a place like this. Eva moved through the crowd, her shoulders back and her chin lifted. By all appearances she wasn't afraid, but Angie could tell by the way Eva's fingers tapped the side of her leg that she was nervous.

A couple of big burly guys came into the bar, and one bumped into Angie. She stumbled and almost tripped over a small round table that hosted several girls in tight dresses. They glared at her.

"Oh, sorry."

Angie righted herself and searched for a safe place to stand. The cigarette smoke burned her eyes even as the music assailed her eardrums. The floor felt gummy under her borrowed boots. She glanced back to an open space of wall, noting it was covered in graffiti. *Death. Wolf Pack. #18.* Great. They were in the heart of a gang hangout.

A tall Hispanic man approached a guy who was talking to a young dark-haired girl. The Hispanic man wore a sleeveless T-shirt, his black hair slicked back and a dark mustache on a pockmarked face. Tattoos covered his arms, and all the images incorporated the number 18.

The man shoved the second guy, who quickly rallied with a punch. In seconds they were on the floor fighting. The crowd in the bar cheered. A giant of a man came out of nowhere and split them apart. Blood smeared the Hispanic man's T-shirt, and the other guy had a deep gouge above his temple. The crowd booed, disappointed the show was now over. The bouncer tossed the guys out of the bar.

Angie glanced back toward the bar and realized she'd lost sight of Eva. She searched the crowd but saw no sign of her. So what was she supposed to do now? Just wait and see if Eva came out? Call Garrison?

Angie shoved her hair away from her face. She'd go to the bar, buy herself a drink, and search for Eva. If she didn't find her in five minutes, she was calling in the big guns.

Lulu woke to the sound of water and then to a stench that made her stomach topple. She was lightheaded, and for a moment she wondered what she'd done to herself. Shit. She'd used. She'd fucked up her chances to get David.

But as the recriminations pounded her brain, a sliver of reason cut through the din. She'd not used. She'd been tempted. So tempted. But in the end she'd walked away from her deal, shaky but determined.

So where the hell was she?

She pushed herself up into a sitting position and searched the basement room for anything that looked vaguely familiar. The floor was made of brick, as were the walls. A wooden staircase snaked up the far wall toward a closed door. Behind her there was a workbench and a tub.

Pressing her hand to her mouth and nose, she took small, even breaths, hoping to stave off the stench. "God, I've landed in an outhouse."

But shit wouldn't have been the right term for this place.

Not shit.

Death.

Rotting flesh.

She swung her legs over the side of a metal table, searching her memory for what had happened. She'd been in the alley. She'd said no. She'd been headed back to work. And then she'd felt the long fingers on her arm and the sharp prick of a needle. Her world had gone black.

Hugging her arms, her thoughts immediately went from her current situation to the courthouse. What time was it? Had her court date come and gone, or was it still tomorrow?

Her heart pounded hard and fast. "I need to get out of here. I need to go to court."

The words echoed off the walls, and as

237

they bounced back at her they sounded so tiny and pathetic.

"Hey, I mean it. I've got to get out of here. I have a child. A baby boy. I have a court date."

Tears welled in her eyes as she pushed off the table, and her bare feet touched cold, wet stone. She had to get out of here. She had to find out what time it was and get to court.

Stumbling forward toward the stairs, she tripped on the uneven stone and fell hard on the floor. "Let me out of here! You don't understand. I've turned my life around. I don't do the nasty stuff no more."

A soft chuckle rumbled from one of the darkened corners. A chill snaked down her spine, teasing cold fear to life.

"This is not funny! I have to get to court. I have a lawyer. I have a chance. I don't do this kinky shit no more."

"Maybe you could do it just one more time for me. For old time's sake."

CHAPTER 14

Thursday, October 6, 11 p.m.

Malcolm had stood in the back of the bar watching the two Hispanic dudes fighting. One fellow had stumbled backwards and nearly knocked a table over. The crowd had roared with laughter. He hadn't wanted to identify himself as police but would if pressed.

He'd come to the bar because it had been a favorite haunt of Dixon's. Since Dixon had dodged his attempted murder conviction, Malcolm had taken to keeping tabs on the doctor. He paid attention to where the doctor drank, when he cruised for a hooker, and when he was out of town at one of his conferences. For the last eighteen months the doctor had been a very good boy. Too good. He'd learned long ago that appearances could be so deceiving. And the cleaner the doctor appeared, the more convinced Malcolm was Dixon was hiding something.

The dudes yelled a few choice words in Spanish to each other. Malcolm knew enough Spanish to know one wanted to cut the other for looking at his girl. And when he saw the glint of a knife, he knew he'd have to intervene if the bouncers didn't. He pushed away from the bar just as a couple of bouncers raced toward the fight.

The bouncers were big burly guys, with big guns and tattoos on their arms and necks. It took a few well-placed shoves and holds to break up the fight.

Malcolm settled back against the bar when one of the guys broke free and stumbled back. He banged into a woman and this time sent her teetering. The slash of thick blond hair caught his gaze, which quickly slid down her slim body and then back up to her face.

He stopped short. *Angie Carlson?*

Malcolm did a double take. The thought that the prim lawyer would come to a place like this did not make sense.

His gaze narrowed as he watched Angie right herself. Immediately her gaze searched the room for someone. He'd have bet a paycheck that The Barracuda wouldn't come to a place like this, but there she stood.

Curious, he sipped his beer, amused that

the attorney hid a darker side. The jeans and tight T-shirt she wore were far cries from the buttoned-up schoolteacher look. And the thick tumble of hair down her shoulders was a surprise as well. She kept the mane plastered so tightly in a bun he'd never thought of her as even having hair.

As he studied her face, he could see that her eyes didn't possess the usual sheet of ice. In fact, they telegraphed worry. She chewed her bottom lip, and her hands slid in and out of her pockets as if she wasn't sure what to do with them.

What the hell are you doing here?

Did she know something about Dixon? As Dixon's attorney, she'd have been privy to all kinds of information about him. Did she know this was where he liked to relax?

It didn't surprise him that she hadn't told him about this place. She always played her cards close to her vest.

She seemed to grow restless. Finally, she pulled her hands from her pockets and pushed through the crowd toward the bar. She was still searching. When the bartender asked for her order she seemed flustered but recovered and ordered a beer, which she made no move to drink. In fact, when the bartender looked away she set the icy mug down untouched.

241

He followed her line of sight and spotted Eva talking to another bartender.

Angie and Eva. Eva's presence explained Angie's make-under. Eva would know how to dress and move through a place like this.

Thelma and Louise. What the hell were they up to?

Angie spotted Eva talking to a tall woman with short black hair. The woman frowned down at Eva, shaking her head no. She tried to turn away from Eva, but her sister grabbed the woman's arm. Eva's gaze matched the taller woman's intensity. Finally, the woman pulled her arm free and moved away.

Eva shoved long, shaky hands through her hair. Angie wasn't a lip reader but easily picked up on the few choice words Eva now muttered.

Angie cut through the crowd and came up beside Eva. "Did you learn anything?"

Eva glanced at her. "I thought you were going to stay by the door."

"I did until a couple of guys got into it, someone pulled a blade, and then I lost sight of you. Eva, this is not a safe place."

Eva's jaw set into a grim line. "No, it is not. And I didn't make us any friends."

"What happened?"

"The bartender did not appreciate my questions."

"I thought you guys were buddies or something."

"No one is ever your friend in prison, Angie. There are alliances, but they end as soon as they are no longer beneficial."

She glanced around the room, sweeping the space for new threats. "So the bartender has no reason to help."

"No, she doesn't. And toss in the fact that I'm dating a cop means she really wants nothing to do with me."

"Did she say anything about Lulu?"

"She said she showed up for work last night. She took a break and never came back. One of the waitresses went looking for her but only found her shoe in the alley."

"What time?"

"About ten."

"What about her purse? She carried a purse yesterday."

"If she left it behind it's long gone."

Angie glanced toward the bar. "I've got some strong interview skills. Let me talk to her."

"No. This is not your world, Angie."

"No kidding. But I can still handle myself." Angie glanced toward the bar and saw that Eva's friend was now chatting with the guy who'd served Angie the beer she hadn't touched. When they glanced over and saw her staring at them, their dark expressions turned murderous.

"We should get out of here," Angie said.

Eva's line of sight trailed her sister's in time to see the female bartender pull a bat from behind the bar. Angie and Eva turned and shoved through the crowd.

The music grew louder as her heart kicked up a notch. She glanced over her shoulder, hoping the bartenders remained in place. She spotted the woman coming after them. Adrenaline shot through her limbs. What the hell can of worms had they opened?

The crowd thickened and surged. Though the front door was twenty feet away, it seemed miles away.

This woman was going to beat the crap out of them.

Malcolm realized quickly what was happening. He shoved away from the bar on an intercept course for the bartender. He managed to get a step ahead of her and block her path.

She glared at him, ready to fight when he shook his head. "Let her go."

"You're blocking my path, asshole."

"She's mine. Let her go."

"She's an undercover cop."

That made him laugh. "Not on her best day."

Angie and Eva pushed through the front door of ZZ's. It slammed behind them, cutting off the rock music, the loud hum of conversation, and the thick stale air that smelled of smoke and sweat.

They hustled down the street and didn't stop until they reached her car. Angie's hands trembled as she fished the key from her pocket and shoved it in the lock. The click of locks releasing had them sliding into their seats. Angie fired up the engine and drove.

Three blocks away from the bar she released a breath. "Shit. What the hell happened in there?"

"Margo didn't like my questions." Eva shook her head. "She never did like questions."

"All you did was ask about Lulu."

"That appeared to be enough."

"Why?"

"Because of Garrison. Margo thought he sent me in to ask questions."

"That's one hell of a place to work. How did Lulu land there?"

"I got her the job. I knew Margo and knew she needed a waitress."

"That's not the best place."

"It beats the streets. Lulu got a steady paycheck, and she didn't have to turn tricks."

"Yeah, but that place is one of the worst."

Eva looked at Angie as if she were a child. "It's hard to get a job when you've got a record. I was real lucky that King was looking out for me. If he hadn't I'd have been in a place like that."

"You weren't guilty."

"Does the general population care? I lived in a prison with bad people. That makes me tainted."

"You're not tainted, Eva."

"Don't be a Pollyanna, Angie. A decade in prison changed me and like it or not will always shadow my future. There is no changing that, no matter how many times I try to pretend otherwise."

Angie glanced at Eva, surprised by the bitterness that edged her voice. "What's this all about? You never worry about the past."

"I worry about it a lot." Eva settled back into her seat and folded her arms over her chest. Angie wasn't sure what caught her eyes first: Eva's fuller cheeks, the new ruddiness in her complexion, or the sudden

246

fullness of her breasts.

Angie recognized the signs because she'd read about them and obsessed over the fact she'd never experience them. "You're pregnant."

Eva hurled a sharp glare at her. "I am not."

Angie may have been out of her element in the bar, but she was back on solid ground now. "Did you know you still furrow your brows when you lie? It's just like when you were a kid, and you got into my makeup and lied about it."

Eva closed her eyes. "I don't want to talk about this."

"If you're holding back to spare my feelings, don't. My lack of childbearing ability shouldn't enter into this." When Eva didn't answer, Angie pressed on, unwilling to let the subject drop. "Have you told Garrison?"

A long heavy silence followed. "No."

The simple word confirmed the pregnancy, and as it did a torrent of emotions assailed Angie: happiness for her sister and then quickly on its heels bitter sadness. For a moment she drove down the streets, winding in and out of traffic. And only when she thought her emotions had been duly subdued did she speak. "Why haven't you told him? He's crazy about you."

"A baby wasn't exactly in the plan."

"All the more reason to talk to him."

"Yeah." She muttered an oath as she picked at a stray thread on her cuff. "He told me he didn't want kids. He watched his sister die of CF, and he doesn't want to pass the disease on to his own kid."

"A hypothetical baby and a real one are very different."

She pressed her palms together. "Yeah, well, what if the baby is sick, and I don't have what it takes to take care of the kid. Both my parents abandoned their child. Mom left you. Dad left me."

Angie cleared her throat. "Mom saw me as much as my father would allow. And she told me she wanted to take me with her."

"But in the end she chose to leave you and be with Blue. And then Blue chose to leave me."

Angie cut through the bitterness that rose inside her. "You are different from Mom and Blue. You won't leave this baby, sick or not."

Eva laid her palms on her still very flat stomach. "I am afraid I could really screw this up. I've only just figured out myself. And now toss in a baby, a husband, and a potential medical problem. It could all get messed up so easily."

"Eyes forward, Eva. That's what you

always say. What our parents did has no bearing on us. And I know you. You are very loving. You would never leave your kid, no matter how bad things go."

"Yeah, maybe."

She thought about the secret investigation she'd launched into Blue's past. "Have you ever heard from Blue? I mean all the publicity last year. It had to have caught his attention."

She stiffened. "I never heard a word from him."

She kept her tone even. "Did he contact you when Mom was still alive?"

"Once a postcard from Colorado. *Happy Birthday, kiddo.* That was all he said. I was seven."

Angie knew the bare stats on Blue Rayburn. He'd been hired by Angie's father to work in the museum as the head of security. Angie's father had been the museum's director. They'd worked together for a few months without incident, and then Blue and her mother had begun their affair. Soon after Frank had discovered his wife's deception, the marriage had collapsed.

She'd asked her dad once about her mother's leaving, but he'd refused to say more than, "Life changes people."

What had happened almost thirty years

ago to change her parents so much? She doubted she'd ever know.

"Have you seen a doctor?" Angie asked.

"Yes. Last week. She confirmed it. The baby is due in seven months."

Spring. Intuition whispered the baby was going to be a girl. Easter bonnets, lace dresses, and tiny, tiny booties flashed in her head. Eva would be holding a baby in her arms by spring. Angie's insides tightened. "And all is well?"

"Healthy as a horse."

"That's perfect."

Eva faced her. "I'm sorry."

"Why would you be sorry?"

"Because you want kids. And you can't have them."

"Hey, my life is super full. And this isn't about me. It's about you and your baby. You've got to tell Garrison."

Eva let her head fall back against the plush leather of the BMW's seats. She seemed lost in thought. Her phone vibrated, she sat forward and pulled it from her pocket. "It's Garrison."

"Talk to him."

She held the phone until it stopped ringing. "When I see him face to face."

"Once Garrison stops freaking, he is going to go nuts," Angie said. "He's going to spoil this kid rotten." She lightened her tone as much as she could. "And he'll have to get in line. I'm going to be one bitching aunt."

Eva's expression remained serious. "Don't tell him I was at the bar. Knowing we had to run for it won't sit well on a good day. But toss in pregnant and he'd have a kitten."

Angie laughed. "That I'd like to see."

"You won't tell?"

"My lips are sealed."

Malcolm found his partner at King's, nursing a cup of coffee and checking his watch.

He sat on the seat beside Garrison. "Where is Eva?"

"King said she had an errand. I've been waiting a half hour."

"And she's not answering her cell?"

"No." No missing the worry. "How did it go at ZZ's?"

"Enlightening." Malcolm snagged a handful of nuts from the jar in front of him.

"How so?"

"I spotted two familiar faces." He waited a beat. "Angie Carlson and Eva."

Garrison cocked his head. "Say that again?"

"Eva and Angie were at ZZ's. And I'll bet

they come busting through the front door of King's any minute."

"Did something happen?"

"There was a bar fight. Nothing out of the ordinary." He opted to skip the Margo-with-the-baseball-bat chapter. "They were there asking questions."

"About?"

"That's what I'd like to know."

"Any sign of Dixon?"

"No."

The front door of the bar opened, and Angie and Eva hustled inside. They had red cheeks and a hint of wildness in their eyes. They seemed no worse for the wear.

Garrison rose. "You talk to Carlson. I need to have a chat with Eva."

"Sure."

Angie glanced between Eva and Garrison. Normally, Angie had something to say, but this time she kept her mouth shut. She watched as Eva and Garrison kissed and vanished upstairs.

"That looks like trouble," Malcolm said. "What am I missing?"

Angie sat at the bar. "I'm sure they'll tell us sooner or later."

King approached them. He was a short guy with a trim build, and some likened his appearance to a leprechaun. However, he

252

was not a man to be underestimated. "So no hello from Eva?"

"She'll be right back," Angie said. "She needs a minute with Garrison."

King set a soda in front of Angie. "You hungry?"

"Starving. Roast beef on rye."

"What no salmon cakes, babe?"

She grinned. "Living dangerously."

King winked and laughed as he left.

As Angie sipped her soda Malcolm watched her. With her hair down, and a tight T-shirt stretched over pert breasts, she looked . . . sexy. Shit. More attraction to The Barracuda. Not good.

She didn't spare him a glance. "Yeah, I know. Not my usual apparel."

"I'll say. But then if you're going to a place like ZZ's it's best to ditch the suits."

She glared at him. "How did you know?"

"I was there."

"I didn't see you."

"That's the idea. Blend in. Don't piss off the staff."

Her eyes narrowed. "What were you doing there?"

"That's a question better answered by you."

The flush in her cheeks deepened a shade. "We went to ask after a client of mine."

"Sierra Day?"

"No. Lulu Sweet."

He'd heard it all. The key witness in the Dixon trial — the same woman Dixon had referenced in Carlson's office the other day. "You tore her apart. And now you're her lawyer?"

"As of two days ago. Eva asked me for help. Lulu is trying to get custody of her son."

He'd never liked the way the system had torn into Lulu, but it really bothered him to know now she had a son. "How old is the kid?"

"Nine months. And I know what you're thinking. The kid was born after the trial. Anyway, she swears she didn't use for most of her pregnancy, and she was clean until he was a month old. Her mother found her in a stupor and took the kid. Lulu is trying to get him back. She was supposed to meet me in court yesterday but didn't."

"That's when Donovan cornered you."

"Right."

Absently, he traced circles on the table with his thumb. "The grandmother got custody?"

"Yeah."

"Maybe it's for the best."

She shook her head. "Lulu really seemed

254

to want that kid."

Malcolm had to put a few points in Carlson's column. She'd been trying to help Lulu. "You call Lulu?"

"Quite a few times. Eva was sure she had gotten into trouble and wanted to check it out. Lulu worked at ZZ's as a waitress."

"I've seen her there before. She works hard. Seems to keep her nose clean."

"Why were you there?"

"It's a new favorite spot of Dixon's. Just thought I might pick up something."

"Did you?"

"Not after you and your sister's show. Made sense to leave."

"Right." She stared into her cup. "I didn't realize that Dixon liked that place. He never mentioned it before."

"Like I said, it was a new haunt." He frowned. "When did Lulu start working at ZZ's?"

"Six months, give or take."

"That's about the time Dixon started frequenting the place." He'd come to believe that true coincidences were very, very rare. "And no one has seen Lulu?"

"No one. We even visited the room she rented. Nothing out of place."

"When was she last seen?"

"Last night at the bar. Went on a break.

Never came back. Her shoe was found in the alley."

He snorted. "Anyone call it in?"

"No."

He traced the rim of his cup. "Two women who knew Dixon. One is dead. One is missing. And you have links to all three."

A cold sensation settled in her belly. "I only accepted Lulu as a client a few days ago, and I doubt anyone knew it other than Eva or Lulu."

"Lulu could have told someone. She wasn't known for her discretion."

Angie's brows knitted. "I don't think it was her. She was very focused on this case."

"Both women knew Dixon. Both women knew you. That is too odd to dismiss."

"Lulu could still turn up."

"She could. But I'd like to speed the process up and look for her. Something tells me she's a piece of the puzzle."

"What puzzle?"

"That's the million-dollar question, Counselor."

Angie had heeded Kier's warnings to be careful but refused his offer to drive her home. She was just parked across the street.

So when she heard footsteps behind her as she approached her car, she tightened her hold on her keys and tensed.

"Hey, mermaid."

The familiar voice had her raising her head as she opened her car door. The man stood only a few feet away. He had come out of nowhere, and though he was smiling and relaxed, her senses jumped to alert. She glanced back toward King's, hoping to see Malcolm standing watch over her. She didn't see him in the crowd.

She threaded her keys through her fingers. "Do I know you?"

The man grinned. He was young, maybe early twenties, and fit. Long, thick dark hair curled around his face, and his expressive blue eyes made what would have been an ordinary face striking. "You don't recognize me. I'm hurt."

"Who are you?" The vague hint of welcome in her voice vanished.

"I guess you're not used to seeing me with my clothes on." He laughed. "From the gym. I'm the swimmer who shared lane four with you."

Relief rushed over her and eased the tension that had wrapped around her spine. She'd been casual about her safety around Kier but now realized she was anything but safe. She barricaded her body behind the open car door. "Right. Sorry. I guess the

257

dry hair threw me off."

He chuckled. "Swim goggles aren't the most attractive look."

Breathe. "I love the impressions the goggles make around my eyes. I look a bit like a bug when I get out of the water."

He wagged his finger at her. "But you're there almost every day."

"I'm hooked, I guess." She relaxed back against the car frame. "You swim like you're in training."

"Not anymore. But I guess old habits die hard. I used to swim a lot as a teen. Competed some, but now swim just for fun."

"You must have been good. You make me feel like a turtle in the water when you zoom past."

He shrugged. "I did all right." He held out his hand. "My name's Martin."

She accepted the hand and wrapped warm, long fingers around his callused palm. "Angie."

He tightened his grip around hers, momentarily trapping her hand in his. A second clicked by. The hesitation didn't last long enough to set off alarm bells, but it was enough that when he loosened his grip she drew back her hand. "Well, Martin, thanks for saying hi. I've got to be going. Early day tomorrow."

He slid his hands into his front pockets. "You going to hit the water?"

"I'm going to give it a try. Depends on how much work I have to review tonight."

"Work. This late? What do you do?"

"Lawyer."

He nodded. "I figured you for some high-profile professional."

"Why's that?"

"The way you carry yourself. Your discipline. Not many people are as dedicated as you to working out. That generally translates into high-achieving professional."

"Which makes you . . . ?"

"A guy who's just traveling around the country before he settles on a graduate school. I'm trading swim lessons at the gym for pool time. Chances are I'll be moving on soon."

That explained why he'd appeared out of nowhere a few days ago. "Right. Well, Martin, I've got to get going."

She tossed a final smile and slid behind the wheel, slamming the door in place. Inside her car the tensions gripping her body eased. Silly to be so wound up. Must be the lingering nerves from ZZ's.

As she fired up the engine she tossed one more smile at Martin and was a bit surprised to find him staring at her with an intensity that rattled her composure.

She nodded.

He waved.

And she drove off, knowing already that she wouldn't be swimming in the morning.

CHAPTER 15

Friday, October 7, 7 a.m.

"We got a break in the case," Garrison said to Malcolm as he entered his office, two cups of coffee in his hands.

Malcolm sipped his coffee, needing the jolt. "What's that?"

"We found Sierra Day's car."

Malcolm set the second cup on Garrison's desk. "Where?"

"The big outlet mall twenty minutes south of here. Local deputies have roped off the area around it."

"Let's go."

Within minutes, they were on the Washington Beltway headed toward I-95 South. The cold day was clear and bright.

"So why do you look like shit?" Garrison said.

"I could say the same for you. You slept as much as I did."

Garrison grunted. "I'm more interested in

your reason."

"Mine wasn't so interesting. I was reviewing surveillance tapes of ZZ's."

Garrison shot Malcolm a glare. "Why?"

He shrugged. "Did Eva tell you why she and Angie went to the bar?"

"Lulu Sweet."

"Yeah, well, her connection to Dixon and to Angie just bugged the hell out of me. I wanted a look at the surveillance tapes. I wasn't sure how often ZZ taped over them."

"And?" Garrison said.

"Turns out the tapes go back about ten days, and then ZZ re-tapes. The cameras focus mostly on the bartenders. ZZ is worried that they're double hitting the booze or stealing from the till. He doesn't seem to care much about the customers."

"And?"

"There are shots of Lulu working the bar. In fact, she was there two nights ago. The last footage of her was around nine-seventeen, and then she never showed up again."

"What about Dixon?"

"He showed up on the tape nine nights ago," Malcolm said.

"Was Lulu working that night?"

"No." He sipped his coffee. "He sat at the bar for an hour or so and then left. No trouble. In fact, he barely spoke to anyone."

"So Dixon hangs out in the bar where Lulu, the woman who nearly put him behind bars, works."

Malcolm drummed his fingers on his thigh. "But he never spoke to her or approached her."

"Just getting the lay of the land."

"It looks that way. But he did have an airtight alibi for two nights ago. At some reception for the ballet." Malcolm snapped his fingers. "Ballet. Zoe said he met Sierra at a ballet fundraiser."

Garrison shoved out a breath. "He's tied up in this. But I don't see how."

"Yet. If we dig enough, we'll figure it out." Malcolm sipped his coffee. "So why do you look like shit?"

Garrison glanced at him. "Eva broke up with me."

Not much surprised him anymore. That did. "I thought you two were tight."

He shook his head. "I did too."

"Did she say why?"

"Said with her family history it was a matter of time before she screwed things up, and it was better just to end it now versus later."

"I don't see the logic."

Garrison shoved out a breath. "You and

me both, pal."

"So what are you going to do?"

"Give her a day or two to cool off, and then go talk to her. Something is chewing on her, and until I know exactly what it is, I'm not going anywhere."

"Do you think it's another guy?"

Garrison gripped the wheel. "It crossed my mind at about two a.m., but no, I don't. She's running away because she's afraid of something. I'll find out what's going on."

Malcolm shrugged. "You are a detective."

Garrison's grin held no mirth. "So they tell me."

They arrived at the mall a half hour later and drove to the northwest quadrant of the parking lot, located in front of a furniture store. The car had been roped off with yellow crime-scene tape, and a deputy was parked beside it.

When they pulled next to the deputy's car, he glanced toward them and then pushed himself out. He had a barrel chest, a thick mustache, and wire-rimmed glasses that framed dark gray eyes.

He held out a hand to Garrison and then Malcolm. "Deputy Hall. Looks like we found the car you were looking for."

The detectives exchanged pleasantries with Hall and moved toward Sierra Day's car, a bright red Mini with personalized plates that said SPRSTAR. There was a ding in the bumper, as Gold had said. Blue and red prayer beads hung from the rearview mirror and a bumper sticker read: THEATER ROCKS!

It wasn't a plain four-door that just blended into the scenery, seen and forgotten within seconds. No, this car made a statement. People took note of it when it passed. Just as they did with Sierra.

"Car's locked up tight," the deputy said.

"Forensics found a spare key in her room at Zoe Morgan's and passed it on to us." Malcolm pulled rubber gloves from his pocket, and then the key, and unlocked all four doors with two clicks of his wrist. "Have you called your forensics team?"

"We have. Should be here within the hour."

There appeared to be no signs of violence. Her purse was not in the car, and the interior was neat and clean. No stray coffee cups or papers. Her apartment was a mess, yet her car, which was a part of her public persona, was immaculate.

The forensics van arrived just minutes later, and soon Malcolm watched as the tech meticulously photographed the car's exterior and interior. He dusted for prints on the door, the hatchback, and the steering wheel. He lifted dozens of prints, but that didn't mean much. Most likely they all belonged to the victim.

Malcolm's gaze scanned the enormous parking lot, which in the last hour had filled with hundreds of cars. "It's a damn needle in a haystack."

Malcolm stared at the car's open hatchback. All that Sierra had kept in the back was a garment bag from a mall store called Joy! and a small valise filled with makeup. "Any word from mall security?"

"I called them again. They're pulling tapes. Should be soon."

Malcolm rubbed his eyes. He didn't want to look at more tapes. But he would. "You want to stay with the car while I visit that dress shop and security?"

"Sure." Most didn't realize that a crime scene extended to anywhere there was evidence. This car, even though it was in another county, was as much a part of the Sierra Day crime scene as the spot where they found the bones.

Malcolm made his way into the mall, located the directory, and quickly found the store. It was an upscale women's dress shop that carried evening apparel.

He moved to the store's front desk and

waited as a petite blonde, neatly made up, rang out another woman. The sales clerk glanced at Malcolm and frowned. "I'll be with you in a minute."

"Sure."

He didn't fit in a store like this, and she knew it. His presence had set off alarm bells. The customer left, and Malcolm pulled out his badge. "I'm Detective Malcolm Kier. I'm with Alexandria Police."

The woman fiddled with the gold bangles on her wrist as she stared at his badge. "You're kind of far afield, aren't you?"

"Had a question about a customer of yours." He pulled Sierra's picture from his breast pocket. "She would have been in here week before last. Tuesday or Wednesday."

The woman glanced at the photo and immediately nodded. "I remember her. She bought a green satin dress for a party."

Witnesses had said Sierra wore a green dress to the cast party. "We found her car outside. In it was a Joy! bag containing a green satin dress. What day was she in here?"

"Thursday a week ago."

So she'd made it to her party in her new dress and back to the mall to return it before she'd vanished. "Any reason why she'd return here with the dress."

The clerk frowned. "I thought she'd bring the dress back."

"What do you mean?"

"She asked me twice about our return policy. Wanted to know if the dress didn't match shoes or a jacket could she bring it back. I'll bet she went to a party or something, kept the tags, and thought she could return the dress."

"Does that happen a lot?"

"Enough." Full lips frowned.

"She say anything about the party or her plans?"

"She was real excited. Said there was a bigwig who was going to be there. He was going to fund her so that she could make it to Broadway."

"She say anything about this guy?"

"Only that he was well connected and rich."

The list of people from the party had revealed no one matching that description. If she'd met up with him it had been later after the party.

He thanked the clerk and tracked down the mall's security office located at the end of a bland hallway near the food court. It didn't take long to find the head of security's office, produce a badge, and make introductions.

The security guard was a tall, lean man with deep creases ironed into his pants and shirt. A neatly trimmed mustache and a sharp part in the center of thick hair finished off the polished appearance.

The security guard's brown eyes sparked with excitement. "I got a heads-up from your partner. I found something for you. Last Thursday morning. Your victim pulled into her parking space at ten minutes after ten. Here, let me show you."

He turned and clicked a television remote. The screen behind him flicked on, and a grainy black-and-white tape rolled. "This is her spot a minute before she arrives."

Malcolm watched, his nerves jumping. Sierra pulled into the spot, checked her makeup in the rearview mirror, and reached for her purse. She got out of the car and opened her hatchback. Tall and regal, she moved with confidence. She was just reaching for the garment bag when a figure approached her. He wore a dark coat and a hat so his face was obscured from the camera. When she spotted him, her pensive expression brightened.

"Seems she knew whoever approached her," the guard said.

Malcolm nodded. Dixon. But the size didn't seem right. "So it seems."

"And look here. He says something to her, and she closes the car up, locks it, and follows him without a bit of hesitation."

"Do you have footage of where they went?"

"The camera in that section of the mall wasn't working. Someone had shot it out with a gun."

"A gun. Like a rifle?"

"So it seems. Came to my attention last Friday. We had it fixed by Saturday."

"Do you have the old light with the bullet?"

"Maintenance crews didn't save it."

Frustration chewed at him. "What about footage of whoever might have shot the camera out?"

"Nope. He never came into camera range."

"Shit."

"Whoever you're chasing after is one slippery bastard who does not want to be caught."

He didn't want to be caught, and yet he'd left Sierra's bones out for anyone to find. He didn't want to be caught, but he wanted to play a cat-and-mouse game with the cops.

Lulu lost track of time in the shadowy, putrid room. Whoever had spoken to her from the darkness had made no move to approach her.

And so she'd sat in the darkness, breathing in the smell of death as she sat on the stone floor, her back to a cold, damp wall.

Several times she dozed off. But the sleep was not restful or peaceful. Even in her dreams a dark figure chased her and laughed as she struggled to run and get away. But the harder and faster she ran the slower she moved. Her pursuer always caught her, and when his icy hands touched her bare flesh she'd start awake.

Lulu's head rolled from side to side. "I don't know if you can hear me, but please let me go. I won't tell anyone what happened here. I just want to leave. I just want to see my kid."

Each time she'd plead to the darkness there'd been no response, but this time she heard the creak of a door.

"Now why would you want to leave? The party is just about to get rolling."

The deep, familiar voice sent her scrambling to her feet. She wiped her mouth with the back of her hand. Hunger had her swaying. "Please, just let me go."

"I can't let you go. We have yet to play, and I have been looking forward to this for so very long."

The lights flipped on, and she winced at the sudden brightness. When her gaze focused and she looked into the eyes of her captor, she knew she'd never see the outside of this room again.

She screamed.

The hum of conversation drifted around Angie's head as she sat in the metal folding chair. Her chair, like a dozen others, was a part of a circle located in the basement of a local church that hosted AA meetings. She attended meetings regularly because they had been so helpful in the beginning, and she hated to fiddle with success.

Everyone in the room shared a common experience: they all struggled with addiction.

Though Angie had not taken a drink in nearly fifteen months, temptation had been nudging her hard the last day or two. She understood the stress of her pending medical test results had been weighing on her. But it was Sierra's death and Lulu's disappearance that lurked behind the urges. Was there something that linked the women, other than their association with her? Was she missing a key link that would solve these cases? She wracked her brain for answers, but there'd been none. There'd been only an unholy thirst that beckoned surrender.

"Angie." Sara Wayne's soft, soothing voice cut through her thoughts.

Angie uncrossed and crossed her legs as her gaze shifted to the petite woman with ivory skin and a splash of freckles across the bridge of an aquiline nose. Sara couldn't be more than thirty, but behind her warm gaze was wisdom rooted not just in academics but personal experience. "I'm sorry, my mind drifted to the office."

If Sara recognized Angie's white lie, she didn't call her on it. "We're making introductions. It's your turn."

Her gaze shifted around the circle of six. There was Sandi, a sixtyish school bus driver who'd been beaten and raped and drank to forget; Denise, a plump, round-faced girl of twenty who'd lost her parents in an accident; Jason a slim, nervous man who'd only once been able to talk about his near drug overdose; and Winnie, a waifish woman who loved to wear red and struggled with a meth addiction.

There was a new man in the circle who, to her surprise, had taken the seat next to her while she'd been lost in thought. He'd moved so silently that he'd barely disturbed the air around them. Tall, broad shouldered, he wore a blue dress shirt, a sport jacket, and khakis. He looked neat, pulled together, and she couldn't imagine him lost to drugs or alcohol.

Angie straightened, cleared her throat, and recrossed her legs. "I'm Angie. I've not taken a drink in four hundred and seventy-two days." At some meetings she mentioned that her mother had left her when she was four. Other meetings she discussed her bout with cancer. And at others she'd mention her sister's imprisonment. But this time she opted out of the personal details. She couldn't say why. Maybe Kier's warnings had put her senses on high alert. Maybe it was the presence of the new guy. Maybe she just wasn't up to it. It didn't matter. She wasn't sharing today.

Sara waited an extra beat, and then smiled. "Congratulations, Angie. That is no small feat."

And she was proud of it. "Thanks."

"We have a new member," Sara said.

With a boldness Angie didn't feel, she swung her gaze over to the man beside her, as if daring him to ask her a question.

Brilliant blue eyes stared at her with an intensity that warmed and chilled her in an instant. She could see that The New Guy had to be in his late fifties. He had an olive complexion, lines around his eyes, graying hair that dipped slightly below his collar, and a square jaw. He wore no aftershave, but the faintest aroma of soap mingled with his scent.

With ease, he shifted his gaze from Angie to Sara. The brittle blue eyes softened. "My name is Robert. Like Angie, I'm not interested in discussing too many details. But I will say I've not taken a drink in six months, two days."

Robert's voice was steady, deep — the voice of a man in control. That was the thing with people with addiction. It was a sneaky, quiet affliction, and those who suffered with it worked double-time to look normal.

The others had supplied a good many details initially. Even Angie had said more than she'd intended the first day. But Robert ended his statement with a clear control that piqued her interest. He either didn't need the group, or he was here to satisfy someone other than himself. Unless the extreme control masked deep chaos.

Sara offered her warm *Welcome* smile. "I'm glad you could join us, Robert. Feel free to chime in at any time."

Robert nodded to Sara. "Thanks."

Again, the brief answer gave nothing away. Angie found his silence intriguing. Was there someone else in the world who didn't like blathering on and on about their problems?

Sandi discussed a nightmare. Denise mentioned a panic attack in the grocery store. Winnie talked about her dead sister's birthday. She'd wanted to toast her with a can of beer. Through it all Angie and Robert didn't speak, remaining silent witnesses to the carnage.

Finally, when Sara had finished giving Winnie meditations to consider, she shifted her gaze to Angie. "You're quieter than usual today. Everything all right?"

She refused to talk about Sierra or Lulu. The investigations were open and active, and she did not want to say anything that might compromise the police department's work. The information shared here was considered sacred and not to be shared. But after her affair with Connor Donovan, she didn't trust anyone.

Folding manicured hands over her lap, she told of restless nights and the desire to sit on a beach with her toes in the sand. For a moment, everyone in the room stared at her, their expressions reflecting varying degrees of understanding. "My nerves are on edge. I even got a little freaked out in the parking garage the other day. Not like me to worry about shadows."

Robert's gaze remained direct and unmoved by the account. "You've a talent for saying a lot and not saying anything. You a lawyer?"

Angie glared at him. "I am."

Robert folded his arms over his chest. "Thought so."

Sara cleared her voice like the schoolteacher reining in a couple of children. "Robert, I hear judgment."

A half smile tweaked the edge of his lips as he glanced to Sara and then back at Angie. "No judgment intended."

Angie didn't spare Sara a glance. She didn't need a defender. "If you have something to say you are welcome to say it, Robert."

The muscle in his jaw pulsed before it eased, and he smiled. "I know you. I've read about you in the papers. If I were you, I'd drink too."

Sara sat forward. "Robert. That's unnecessary."

Angie held up her hand. "No, Sara. Let Robert say what he needs to say."

"I'm not saying anything that everyone else in the room isn't thinking. You are the attorney that defended that guy Dixon, and now you got that client who was murdered. Body reduced to bones. Kind of an odd coincidence."

"Really?"

"You must think there is a connection."

If law school had taught her anything it was to turn an attack back on the attacker. "You know so much about me, and I know so little about you."

Robert frowned, but if Angie thought he'd trip into some long explanation of the demons that had brought him here she was mistaken. In seconds, he slipped behind a steel veil. "Maybe another day."

She folded her arms over her chest.

Forty minutes later the meeting ended, and Angie found herself grateful to stand. She rarely remained after the group to chitchat with the others.

She'd just reached the top step of the banister leading out of the church basement when she heard steady, purposeful footfalls on the staircase. It didn't take a glance over her shoulder to know who followed. Robert had an energy that radiated and announced his presence.

"Angie," he said.

She exited the staircase and moved to the sunny, wide-open lobby of the church. The warmth of the sun gave her a calming sense of connection. "Yes, Robert."

"I didn't mean to go after you back there."

Sitting he'd been intimidating, but standing he overwhelmed. He stood over six-five, and his shoulders filled the average doorjamb. Her pulse throbbed faster in the base of her neck. "You were just asking questions. No harm, no foul."

"Are you sure?" He dipped his head a fraction as if to whittle off some of his height. She guessed this was a practiced move he'd done a thousand times before.

"No worries, Robert." She checked her watch. "And I don't mean to be rude, but I have a meeting in a half hour."

"Of course."

She tossed him a smile because it seemed the right thing to do and turned.

"Interested in coffee?"

She hesitated. "I have a meeting."

"Yeah, but you'll be here next week won't you? I could tell by the way you sat in that room that you're a regular."

"You could tell that by just looking at me?"

"You act like you're in charge of the group."

"That's Sara's job."

"But people glance to you when they speak. I mean they look at Sara too, but they want your approval just as much."

"You're mistaken. I'm in the same boat as

they are."

"In their eyes, you are the leader."

She cocked an eyebrow. "Nothing like being captain of the *Titanic*."

His grin broadened. "So is that yes or no to the coffee next week?"

Instinct had her shaking her head even as curiosity tempted her to say yes. "I don't think so."

He grinned. "So that's a maybe."

"You're persistent."

"So I've been told."

"If I see you next week, we'll see."

He cocked a brow. "If?"

She didn't like being pushed. "Like I said, if I come to the meeting."

He slid his hands into his pockets and leaned forward. "I bet you almost never miss."

This guy had known her for less than an hour, and already he sensed things about her that few recognized. Not good. And more than a little unsettling. "Take care, Robert."

She turned and left without glancing back, but she felt the steady weight of his gaze on her even after she pushed through the front door and hurried down the street. With each step she resented Robert more and more. Who was he to interlope on her group and read her as if she were a book? Who the hell was he?

And of course, she had no answer.

CHAPTER 16

Friday, October 7, 8:45 a.m.

Angie sat at her desk, grateful to have her meeting behind her, a mug of hot coffee beside her. The papers on her desk remained neatly stacked and piled as she lifted a silver letter opener and sliced open the back of an envelope.

She scanned e-mail, surprised to see a note from Dr. Evans. She clicked it open.

Dear Angie, I am pleased to tell you that the results of your CT scan, chest x-ray, and blood work are NEGATIVE.

Angie stared at the last word: *NEGATIVE.* Her heartbeat pulsed in her chest. She released a deep sigh letting it carry the worry from her body.

NEGATIVE. She smiled.

For this year she'd dodged another bullet. She was cancer free. Evans said that she should have no worries. But the elevated blood levels had added a layer of stress she couldn't shake until now.

Her mother had been dead by forty-eight of the same cancer, and she'd seen firsthand how devastating her death had been. As much as she'd loved her mother, she was in no rush to follow her.

She printed out the e-mail, neatly folded it, and replaced it in an envelope, which she tucked in her desk drawer. She deleted the message from her in-box and recycling bin. She'd told Eva, but Charlotte and Iris didn't know she'd had cancer, and she planned to keep it that way.

Her mind clear, she turned her attention to the mail. It included news from a subpoena company, discovery documents from a North Carolina attorney, and several notices from other clients. It was the last letter that sent a jolt down her spine.

The handwritten envelope was from a private detective, Bill Patterson. She'd done him a few legal favors, and he'd repaid the deeds with investigative work.

Angie had had Bill look into Blue Rayburn's past. Though Eva had never asked Angie to delve into her past, Angie had decided she needed to know more about the man who'd been her father's friend and her mother's seducer.

Angie ripped open the manila envelope and pulled out the typed report. Bill was efficient, and if there'd been facts to dig up about Blue, then he'd find them.

Ms. Carlson,
Per your request, I have investigated one, Elijah "Blue" Rayburn, 57 years of age. Mr. Rayburn was born in North Carolina to low-income parents and joined the Navy when he was seventeen. He was dishonorably discharged three years later. He traveled around a lot in his twenties before settling in Alexandria, Virginia. He took a job in the security department at the Talbot Natural Museum.

Angie sat back in her chair, staring at the typed words. She'd known Blue had worked for the museum but had never known what he'd done before that.

Within a few weeks of his hire, Mr. Rayburn rose to the rank of head of security at the museum, where he remained for a year. Twenty-eight years ago, he married Marian Carlson and the two had a child, Eva. After leaving the museum, there are no employment records for Mr. Rayburn.

After three years of marriage, Mr. Rayburn left his wife and child and moved west. He established a wilderness exploration company and married, though I doubt the marriage was lawful. He fathered a son. Mr. Rayburn was arrested several times for assault, but charges were dropped when witnesses later refused to testify. Mr. Rayburn's home burned to the ground several years ago, and shortly after that he left his second "wife" after twenty years of marriage and vanished. At this point his trail dies out completely. I have been unable to locate Mr. Rayburn.

I have enclosed several photos of Mr. Rayburn.

Angie set the letter aside and opened the smaller envelope marked PHOTOS. She pulled a black-and-white photo of Blue when he was in his early twenties and, judging by his uniform, still in the Navy. He and Eva shared the same dark hair and high slash of cheekbones. He had been a darkly handsome man who looked as if he radiated energy.

He was the mirror opposite of her father, a tall, slender man who avoided the sun and loved his books. Frank Carlson had been steady and focused but not exciting.

The next photo was a group picture that appeared to have been taken in front of one of the museum's collections. There were ten people in the group, her father included. All men and all in their early thirties. They appeared genuinely happy as if the photo had just been snapped during a celebration.

She studied her father's face, alight with a smile that she never remembered seeing. He'd always been so somber, and though he smiled, it wasn't the brilliant explosion of glee that this grin radiated.

Beside her father stood Blue, who had wrapped his arm casually around Frank's shoulders as if they were old, casual friends.

She glanced in the corner and saw that the picture had been taken twenty-eight years ago. Just before Blue had begun his affair with her mother.

The men's smiles looked so true and bright that it seemed unimaginable that treachery lurked down the road. By the end of that year her mother had left her father and Angie's safe world had been shattered. Loving parents had morphed into an emotionally absent father and a mother she saw only once a month.

Angie flipped the picture over and read the inscription.

Celebrating the donation of the new wing to be dedicated to the Darius Cross Foundation.

Darius Cross!

Her face flushed, and her heart raced. She reread the inscription.

Angie had never imagined that her family's ties to the Cross family stretched back beyond the dark night Josiah had raped Eva. She'd assumed Darius's taste for revenge was due to grief. But now it appeared that Darius had known Eva and Angie's history better than they did themselves.

She searched the faces of the men in the photo and realized the man on the far right was Darius Cross. Thirty years ago he'd have been in his forties. He cut a striking figure. His hair was thick and only grayed at the temples. His skin sported a deeply tanned hue, and his teeth flashed bright and even. Micah strongly favored his father's appearance.

The Darius Cross she'd remembered was heavier. His hair had been much thinner, and the rawboned cheeks had softened. At the trial, his eyes had reflected anger and mistrust, not excitement and joy.

She traced Darius's face. Her family had deep ties to the Cross family. That fact stirred unease and scared her for reasons she could not explain.

Angie picked up her phone and dialed Eva's cell. She'd commissioned the report without her sister's knowledge, but she could not sit on the information. Eva had a right to know what had happened to her father.

And perhaps, this new information would jog Eva's earliest memories, and they could learn more about the families' connections.

"This is Eva," the voice mail message said. *"You know me, I never remember my phone but leave a message anyway."*

"I swear to God, Eva, I am going to surgically implant that phone in you. I will just talk to you later." Angie snapped the phone closed.

Whatever she had to say to her sister would have to wait until a return call or dinner tonight when Angie went to King's.

Malcolm arrived at the home of Vivian Sweet just after ten. Her home was a small, one-story rancher located off of Glebe Road. Like the other homes around it, it had been built after World War II, and despite the low square footage, the homes in this area sold quickly when they went on the market. The homes to the right and left

288

of Mrs. Sweet's house looked as if they'd undergone facelifts. No doubt the older owners had sold out to young professionals. Whereas Mrs. Sweet's house looked tired, dated, as if it hadn't seen much TLC in a long time.

He climbed the brick steps and rang the bell. A planter by the door sported a mum with dying orange blossoms, and chipped and rusted black paint covered a cast-iron railing.

Seconds passed and no one answered. He rang the bell again, glancing toward a large picture window to the right of the steps. Drawn curtains blocked his view into the house.

There was no solid connection between Lulu Sweet and Sierra Day. Most would question the time he'd spent this afternoon looking for Lulu when he was knee-deep in an active murder investigation. But they still had no real leads in Sierra's case. And as the hours ticked by and he found no sign of Lulu, he believed there might be a connection between the two cases.

Finally, he heard footsteps on the other side of the door. A chain scraped against a lock and dropped to dangle against the door. A dead bolt slid free, and the door opened.

Standing on the other side of the screen door was a willowy woman. She wore a blue housecoat and slippers. A baby's cry drifted out from another room.

"Can I help you?" the woman said through the screen door.

"Mrs. Vivian Sweet?"

"Yes."

He withdrew his badge from the breast pocket of his jacket. "I'm Detective Kier with Alexandria Police."

The baby's wail grew angrier, more insistent. "Are you here about Lulu?"

"How did you know?"

"You're not the first policeman to show up on my doorstep asking about Lulu. Trouble finds her pretty quick."

"Can I ask you a couple of questions about your daughter?"

Mrs. Sweet glanced back into the house toward the source of the baby's wail. "I have to get my grandson."

Malcolm grinned. "Boy's got some lungs on him."

A ghost of a smile tipped the edge of her lips. "That he does. Come on in and wait in the living room while I get him."

She unlocked the screen door and Malcolm stepped into the house, which smelled of baby powder and Vicks VapoRub. Circumstances had forced together two generations that didn't really fit.

Mrs. Sweet reappeared with a baby resting on her hip. The kid was bald, had big watery blue eyes, and chewed on his meaty fist. The kid's bulk made his grandmother look all the more frail and old.

"What's his name?" Kier said.

"David."

The baby wiggled in his grandmother's arms and then thrust out his hands toward Malcolm. Instinct had Malcolm moving toward the kid, who reminded him of his nephew, Jack, and his niece, Elizabeth. When he was in Richmond, he was always hoisting those two, tossing them in the air or changing a dirty diaper.

Mrs. Sweet hesitated. "He'll drool all over your jacket, and sometimes he spits up."

Malcolm grinned. "I'll chance it."

"Suit yourself."

Malcolm held out his hands to the kid, who tipped his body weight forward and all but plunged into Malcolm's waiting hands. The kid stared up at him, his big eyes searching and curious. David had "handful" written all over him. "He looks like he might walk soon."

Vivian nodded. "You're right. You mind holding on to him while I grab a bottle? It should be warm now."

"Sure." The kid smelled of powder, but judging by the mushy weight of his diaper, he had already filled it up. When Vivian vanished into the kitchen Malcolm looked at the kid. "You're carrying a load, aren't you, pal?"

The boy gurgled and laughed.

"Figured as much."

Vivian reappeared. "I can feed him."

The veins in the woman's hand blazed blue and bright, and he noted her fingers shook very slightly. "Let me. I've got some experience."

They sat on the small sofa and chair in the living room. Vivian released a sigh as she sat down. "You got kids?"

"No. Not yet. My brother has a couple of kids, and I see them often." Malcolm cradled the boy, who greedily grabbed the bottle, tossed his weight back into the crook of his arm, and sucked the nipple. "He's an eater."

"He's going to be a bruiser."

"He seems healthy."

She pushed a wisp of gray hair from her face. "He is, thank God. Lulu was clean when she was pregnant."

"That's good for the kid."

"Yes." She smoothed her palms over thin

thighs. "No matter how hard she tries to climb out, the junk drags her down every time. No matter how much she swears she'll never use again, she does." She picked at a stray thread on her housecoat. "Did the courts send you?"

"I came because Ms. Carlson was worried about your daughter. I promised to ask around."

The scent of illness clung to the woman, and he guessed she wasn't plagued by the flu or a cold but was gravely ill. "I spoke to Ms. Carlson in the courthouse yesterday. She looked frazzled when she came barreling into the courtroom. She'd been waiting on Lulu. She'd been so convinced that Lulu would show." She shook her head. "Funny that Ms. Carlson would help. She all but tore my girl apart on the stand."

"I remember."

"I was so blistering angry with Ms. Carlson. I wrote her a few letters after the trial and told her I thought she was a bloodsucker. Dixon didn't deserve a fair trial. He deserved to be hung. Lulu has her faults, but he hurt her bad."

Malcolm had had similar thoughts regarding Dixon, and still he heard himself defending Angie, saying, "A fair trial is a basic right for everyone."

"I don't care about rights. Dixon was bad. He needed to die."

"Has your daughter seen him at all since the trial?" No one in their right mind would seek out a man who'd brutalized them, but he'd seen a lot of odd behavior since joining the force.

"She said no. And I believed her. But she's lied before. Are you here to tell me she's been seeing that monster?"

"He patronized the bar where she worked. I don't know if she knew that or not." He glanced at the kid. The boy's eyes had drifted to half-mast. "Were you surprised when Lulu didn't show in court?"

She sat back on the couch. "I had hoped she'd make it. I really want my girl to get her act together. David needs a mother."

"You've not heard from your daughter in the last couple of days?"

"Not a word. Each time the phone rings I think it's her. That's her pattern. Mess up and then call and apologize. Not hearing from her has me wondering if she really has screwed up this time."

"She mention anyone that she hung out with much lately?"

"No. We don't talk a lot."

He hesitated. Mrs. Sweet knew Lulu better than anyone. "What do you think has happened to her?"

Tears glistened in her eyes. "She has finally overdosed."

David had completely relaxed back in Malcolm's arms, and his eyes had drifted shut. It pained him to know the kid was in for a rough life thanks to circumstances.

"Do you think she's dead?" He hated to ask the question.

She lifted her chin. "No. I don't feel that. But I fear it's a matter of time."

"I've checked her apartment and spoken to neighbors. No one has seen her."

"I don't know what to say."

He studied the woman's pale features. "Do you mind me asking you about your health issues?"

She hesitated and then released a sigh. "I've got congestive heart failure. I've had it for several years. Medication and rest keep it in check pretty well. But the stress of the last year has made it steadily worse."

"What do you plan to do with the baby?"

"I'd half hoped Lulu would come through, and I could get back to taking care of myself."

"Do you want me to call social services? Do you want help?"

"No. No social services. I can take care of my own. Don't you worry about David. I love him, and I'll see that he's tended to. You can do me a favor and just find my daughter so we can get this mess sorted out."

He glanced at the boy. David had drained his bottle and fallen asleep. Malcolm rose slowly and laid the boy in his grandmother's arms. Shit. The kid didn't belong in a sick house with a fragile woman. He deserved parks and games and swing sets. "I'll let you know when I find your daughter."

"Can you find her?"

He looked at David. "One way or the other, I'll find her."

The four detectives gathered in the meeting room around an old wooden conference table that looked as if it had seen its best days in the seventies. Its matched chairs and credenza also showed thirty years of wear. Gray industrial carpet made the windowless room's white walls look dingy.

Malcolm had a thing against windowless rooms. He understood they were practical for cops. No one could shoot into the room. But his body craved the sunshine almost from the minute he closed the door behind him.

Steam rose from the hot cup of coffee warming Malcolm's hand as he took his seat. When Garrison, Sinclair, and Rokov took a seat, he said, "We're four days into the murder investigation of Sierra Day. Forensics has given us little so far. Sommers is processing dozens of footprints found at the scene, as well as fingerprints pulled from Sierra's room and car. That'll keep him digging for a good while. Do we have anything on Sierra Day's financials or cell phone records?"

Sinclair opened a manila folder. "We've back traced most of her cell phone calls, and all lead to her ex-husband, ex-lover, lawyers, or the theater. She did make calls to Dixon's office, but the time and duration match with a schedule change to an appointment."

"We heard rumors of another boyfriend," Malcolm said.

"If she had a secret guy, she didn't call him from her cell phone," Sinclair said.

"Okay. Financials?" Malcolm said.

"No expenditures that seemed out of the ordinary," Rokov said. "Day carried nearly sixteen thousand in credit card debt. And almost all her expenses were related to clothing, drinking at Duke Street Café, gas, and publicity pictures. No out-of-town trips or hidden hideaways where she might have gone with this mystery lover we've heard about." He tapped his finger on the table. "Sinclair and I also spoke to her neighbors and colleagues, and no one noticed anything out of the ordinary."

"Carlson told us that Sierra's mystery boyfriend liked to buy her lingerie. And that he flew her down to Florida."

Sinclair shook her head. "We found lingerie in her room. One piece still had the tags on it. It was purchased from an exclusive store in the District. The clerk did not have sales records and promised to have the store owner check when she got back into town tomorrow."

"Did you show the clerk a picture of Dixon?" Malcolm asked.

"I did. He's not been in the store." Sinclair frowned. "We've all been so focused on Dixon, who I might add has an airtight alibi for the days Sierra went missing. I think we need to cast our net farther afield. Our tunnel vision could very well be allowing another killer to go free."

Malcolm rubbed the back of his neck. The muscles had tightened like bowstrings. He'd begun to worry about that as well. "You could be right, but I'm just not ready to cut Dixon loose."

Sinclair shook her head. "Sierra's lover Marty Gold had assault charges filed against him last year. Maybe we need to squeeze him a little bit."

"Sure, follow up on that." It felt like the wrong path, but Malcolm just couldn't prove it yet. "We also are exploring another angle. Garrison and I spent the better part of the morning looking for Lulu Sweet." He quickly reviewed her connection to Dixon and Angie.

Garrison, who sat to the right of Malcolm, added, "We've found no trace of her."

"Lulu's purse vanished from the bar, and a Maureen White who works at ZZ's found Lulu's shoe in the alley behind the bar. According to Maureen, Lulu went to the alley to hook up with a drug dealer named Tony."

"Maybe it's as simple as her overdosing," Sinclair said.

Malcolm nodded. "I visited with her mother. She's not seen Lulu."

"Or maybe someone's going after Carlson's clients?" Rokov said. "She's made her share of enemies in the courtroom. I can't say I'm her number-one fan."

Sinclair flipped pages in her file. "Carlson is good at what she does. And I do respect that. But that could have made enemies."

Malcolm too had gained a begrudging admiration for Carlson. Love her or hate her, she was smart and dedicated. And the idea that she'd been targeted did not sit well with him. "Sierra's roommate mentioned she'd received notes. What about them?"

"Forensics found them in a magazine in her room," Rokov said. "They were hand-written on plain paper. The writing is distinctive and does not match samples we have of Dixon's. And without something to compare it to, we don't have much of a lead. Paulie did say something about having it analyzed by an expert, but that will take time."

"Okay," Malcolm said.

Sinclair cleared her throat. "I had a ViCAP hit about an hour ago. It's a stretch, but the case has similar characteristics." ViCAP wasn't a perfect system, but from time to time it did match current violent crimes in other jurisdictions.

Malcolm shifted his attention to her and waited. "Let's hear it."

Sinclair pulled an old police file out from under her notepad. "Seems like a fairly remote link."

"If remote equates to a lead then I am all for it," Malcolm said.

"I haven't had much time to read the file," she said. "I just got it from archives a few minutes before the meeting."

"Let's have it."

She flipped over a page and read the investigating detectives' notes. "Thirty years ago, bones were found deposited at a construction site. These bones should have ended up buried under a ton of concrete, but a scheduling conflict with a cement contractor delayed the job. A couple of kids poking around the site found clean bones that had been dumped in a hole."

Malcolm leaned forward. "How were the bones stripped?"

"Investigating cops didn't know."

"Did they identify the victim?"

"Yes." She flipped over a page and read. "Just like us, they dug into their missing persons file. Long story short, they determined that their victim was Fay Willow. She was thirty-one and employed as a secretary."

"What about the notes?"

"The lead detective interviewed her roommate, who commented she'd received notes at home and work before she vanished. *I love you. Always together.* Endearing if you like the sender, creepy if you don't know the sender."

"Where did she work?" Malcolm asked.

Sinclair scanned the page. "The Talbot Museum."

Malcolm sat straighter. "That was the

museum that Angie Carlson's father managed."

"How do you know that?" Sinclair asked.

"Made it a point to know all I could about her during the Dixon trial."

Sinclair nodded and sat back. "Interesting coincidence."

"Is it?" Malcolm challenged. "What can you tell us about Willow?"

Sinclair dug out a picture of a young woman wearing a turquoise ruffled blouse and blond hair curled back off her face. She was smiling, and blue eyes sparked as if she knew a secret. "Who did she work for at the museum?"

She scanned the page. "Wow. Frank Carlson. She was his secretary for two years."

Malcolm's heart raced faster. "What does the file say about Fay Willow?"

"She was a smart, efficient woman with ambition. She liked the finer things. Months before she vanished, coworkers said she traded in her old car for a much nicer one. She also started wearing fancy jewelry and clothes. Friends figured she was sleeping with her boss, Frank."

"Could his wife have gotten wind of what was going on?" Garrison said. "Maybe that's why she left him."

Sinclair flipped through more pages. "According to this, police interviewed Frank, who had great alibis, but they never talked to his wife. The officer did note that Carlson looked agitated. Carlson mentioned that his wife had just left him."

Garrison drummed his fingers on the table. "Any mention of a Blue Rayburn in the file?"

She flipped through pages. "He was the museum's head of security. He was interviewed but said nothing of real help to the detectives."

"Were any of her bones missing?" Malcolm asked.

She pulled the autopsy report and quickly read through it. "Several bones were missing. But because she was found outside, it was assumed animals carried them off." Sinclair flipped through a few more pages. "Guess who else was mentioned?"

"All ears, Sinclair," Malcolm said.

"Darius Cross." She smiled, pleased with herself as she scanned the page. "He was seen with Willow a couple of weeks before she vanished. The museum was holding a big party, and Darius was seen flirting with Willow. Rumor had it they were having an affair. Cross was briefly interviewed, but nothing came of it."

"Interesting." Malcolm shrugged. Louise

Cross, Darius's wife, might well have known Fay Willow. Mrs. Cross was serving three life sentences in prison for killing three women last year. "Mrs. Cross probably knew her."

"She's been mute since her arrest," Garrison said.

"What if we enlisted the help of her son Micah?" Rokov said. "He was helpful last year."

"As I remember, she refused to see him as well," Garrison said.

"She has requested interviews with Eva," Malcolm said.

"No." Garrison shook his head. "Eva is not going to talk to that woman. She's been through enough."

Malcolm glanced at his partner, wondering whether the dark circles under his eyes suggested that he and Eva had made up or not. Whatever their situation, the tenor of Garrison's voice spoke of his love for the woman he was protecting.

"Well, we know Mrs. Cross couldn't have killed Sierra Day," Malcolm said. "But she did know Ms. Willow, a woman who'd been flirting with her husband." He rubbed the tension from the back of his neck.

"Louise Cross very well could have known the woman," Rokov offered. "Might have some insight."

"There've got to be other people who knew Fay Willow," Malcolm said.

"Want me to reopen Willow's case?" Sinclair said. "I could try and track down the old witnesses."

"It's worth a try."

"Another detail," Rokov said. "Day's husband is pushing to get the remains of his wife returned. He wants to bury her."

Malcolm shook his head. "Why would he suddenly care about her? He had nothing nice to say about her when we spoke to him."

"He's the grieving widower now," Sinclair said.

"What is his insurance payout on the wife?" Garrison said.

"Zip," said Malcolm. "Her death does save him a costly payout when the divorce is final."

"He's got the flair for the dramatic like his late wife," Garrison said. "Maybe killing his wife just wasn't dramatic enough."

Malcolm thought about the actor's smooth hands and his clean desk. "It's messy work stripping bones. I don't see Humphrey doing it."

"Then why worry about giving his wife a proper burial?"

"He cares about appearances." He'd seen this often enough when he'd interviewed people. "Better to play the part of the grieving widower than the angry ex-husband."

"Has Dr. Henson released the remains?" Garrison asked.

"No. I asked her to hold on to them."

"Good. Let the guy stew."

CHAPTER 17

Friday, October 7, 6 p.m.
The Cross mansion was located just north of Mount Vernon and sandwiched between Route One and the Potomac River. The rolling riverfront land in this area was premium and beyond expensive. A half acre could run millions. The Cross family owned six acres along the river. *If you have to ask about the land's cost, then you can't afford it,* Malcolm mused.

Garrison drove down a gravel driveway lined with cypress. "Easy to imagine we've left the real world."

Malcolm shook his head. "I know the rich put their pants on just like me, but they are a different breed of cat. They live in a rarified league of their own."

"They make their own rules." Hostility rarely crept into Garrison's voice as it did now.

"I guess from your tone you and Eva are

307

still on the outs?"

"She won't talk to me."

"Go by King's and see her."

"I did. She wasn't there. King said she took a couple of days off to finish a paper. She'll be in tonight."

"And?"

"And one way or another she's going to tell me what's eating her."

"Just like that?"

"Damn right."

"Best of luck."

Garrison parked the car at the top of a circular drive behind two construction vehicles. The name on the truck doors read LANE CONSTRUCTION.

Black lacquer covered the front doors and reflected the afternoon light. The house was constructed of an ancient brick, and the windows had the wavy appearance of hand-blown glass. The house screamed old money, but the Cross family was anything but. Darius Cross had grown up poor and had clawed and scraped his way to the top. It was often said of him, "He'd drive a pike in his mother's back to get ahead."

No truer words had been spoken. Cross had locked up his homicidal wife in a home for the mentally ill. She'd languished there almost twenty years. And then when Cross realized he was dying, he had turned his wife free so she could kill and maim the last of his enemies.

Garrison tightened his hands on the wheel. "I hate this guy."

His partner rarely spoke so frankly. "Micah's been nothing but helpful."

"I know. But he has a way of worming under my skin."

"You're tense about Eva. Why don't you let me do the talking?"

Garrison rattled change in his pocket. "I'll be fine. I won't blow this."

"Let me do the talking."

Garrison's jawline tightened and then released. "Sure, fine."

Seconds after they rang the front bell it opened. A woman dressed in a maid's uniform greeted them. They showed her their badges; she nodded and invited them in to the foyer.

Inside the house, the sound of hammers clanged and banged from the upstairs. The scent of fresh paint wafted through the house. "Doing a bit of work?" Malcolm said.

The woman nodded. "Mr. Cross is redoing the house top to bottom. Said it's time for a change."

So the new head of the clan was feeling his oats and was ready to make his mark.

The maid escorted them into a side room. When they'd been here a year ago the room had been filled with heavy mission-style furniture, and the walls had been papered in a heavy green pattern. Now a light beige coated the walls, and the antique furniture had been replaced with Scandinavian-style furniture that gave the room a more modern feel.

A fire crackled in a large stone hearth as it had a year ago, but above the mantel the portrait of Darius had been replaced with an impressionistic painting that featured light blues and hints of red. The photos of Micah and his twin Josiah were also gone.

"Doing his best to erase all traces of the old man," Malcolm said.

"Can't blame me, can you?" The response came from behind them.

The detectives turned and found Micah Cross standing on the threshold. He wore jeans, a black turtleneck, loafers, and horn-rimmed glasses. His hair was slicked back.

Malcolm opted not to respond to the comment. "Thank you for seeing us."

"I'm a friend to the police. I am here to serve." He held out his hand, indicating the two should sit. "What can I help you with today?"

"We're investigating a current murder that

matches an older killing that took place almost thirty years ago. The victim's name was Fay Willow. Rumor had it she was having an affair with your father."

Micah raised a brow. "I was two then, and I have no memory of this woman. But it wouldn't be a stretch to say my father had a mistress. He had many."

"Would your mother have known Fay?" Malcolm asked.

Micah frowned. "Hard to tell what Mother knows and doesn't know."

"Would you be willing to visit her with us and ask her a few questions about the woman?"

"She's refused my last six visits. And I doubt she'd speak to either of you. She would talk to Eva."

Garrison's jaw tightened, and a small muscle pulsed. "No."

Micah smiled and shifted his gaze to Garrison. "How is Eva doing? I think about her a lot. I worry about her."

Garrison looked relaxed, but Malcolm knew tension rippled through his partner's limbs. "No need to worry."

If Micah sensed the tension, he didn't care. "You two are still together, I assume?"

Garrison grinned, a sign of danger. "So you won't visit your mother with us?"

"It would be a waste of time." Micah's eyes narrowed barely a fraction.

"Do you have any papers, records, or diaries that might have belonged to your father? Something that might have referenced Fay?"

"My father burned all his personal papers before he died." Micah shifted his attention back to Eva. "Is Eva still working at King's? I've been meaning to visit her. She's come so far. I hear she graduates in the spring."

Garrison's grin did not waver. "Have a nice day, Mr. Cross."

"Can't you answer a few simple questions about Eva? Deep connections run between us."

For a split second, fury blazed in Garrison's eyes. "No, they do not."

I'll meet you at King's. Seven o'clock.

The text Olivia had sent Malcolm had been uncharacteristically brief.

Normally, Olivia sent chatty texts that highlighted tidbits from her day.

The kids had music today, and their winter-program songs sound great.

Had a faculty meeting at lunch . . . so boring.

After bus duty, I'm off to the gym.

But not today.

This text sounded like an order.

Malcolm had been back in town for three days, and he'd yet to see his girlfriend Olivia. They had spoken on the phone a couple of times, but with the Day investigation going full throttle, he'd not been able to break away. This terse text reminded him he owed her a meal and a visit.

When she'd chosen King's he'd almost said no. They'd never eaten there as a couple. King's was where he ate with cops. And until this moment he'd been careful to keep his personal and private lives separate. But she'd been complaining that he compartmentalized too much, so he'd said yes.

He had arrived on King Street a few minutes early, found a great parking spot, and realized he had time for a quick shower and shave. So he'd jogged across the street to the deco building and climbed the steps to his third-floor apartment.

He pulled off clothes as he crossed the large Spartan room, furnished with a huge couch and a wide-screen television. He jumped in the shower and ducked his head under the hot spray. It felt good to get the grime of the day off him.

Ten minutes later he had showered, changed into khakis and a dark turtleneck, and shrugged on his leather jacket over his brown leather gun holster.

He paused at the kitchen bar, flipped through his mail, and then glanced through the picture window toward King's. There was a time when seeing Olivia sent a thrill of excitement through him. Not tonight. And that surprised him. He liked Olivia. She'd done nothing wrong.

"Fatigue," he muttered.

He saw Olivia push through the front door of King's.

Malcolm dashed down the steps and shoved through the pub's front door just after seven. The place was packed, each table and booth filled with a variety of customers: tourists, squeezing in the last of the fall-season tours; folks who worked in the shops nearby; and a handful of cops.

Olivia had gotten a booth in the back. She raised her hand to catch his attention.

Smiling, he nodded and moved toward her, leaned in, and kissed her on the cheek. Her dark hair smelled of roses and crayons; her pale skin felt so soft to the touch. "You smell like an art project."

She kissed him back. "Hazard of being a kindergarten teacher. We began our section on Halloween and the letter T today."

He liked hearing about the kids in her classroom. He slid into the seat across from her. "So is that towheaded kid learning to stay in the classroom?"

"Andy. He and I drew a line across the threshold yesterday. We discussed that it's the line he's not supposed to cross." Kindergarten had been Andy's first experience with formal school. For the last few weeks he'd taken to running out of the classroom and down the hall when the mood struck.

Malcolm laughed. "And that worked?"

"He's very proud of his line. In fact he showed it to his mom today."

He traced circles on the table with his thumb. "I got to feel for the little guy. He's got a lifetime of rules waiting for him."

She feigned sadness. "Look who's talking; the man who never met a rule he liked. You're the worst for following rules."

"I follow them."

"When you make them."

He shrugged, no hint of apology in his demeanor.

A waitress, a cool blonde with a perky face, arrived at the table and laid menus in front of them. "What can I start you folks off with?"

Malcolm sat back in the booth, dearly

wishing he could order a beer and knowing he had too much work in front of him to allow the luxury. "Coffee."

Olivia smiled. "White wine."

"Mind if I go ahead and place my order? I've got to get back to work soon," Malcolm said.

Olivia, ever calm, smiled. "Sure."

"Number six," he said without opening the menu. "Mustard on the side."

Olivia glanced at the waitress. "Give me the same."

"You don't like red meat," Malcolm said.

"Oh, well, that's what I get for hurrying things along. Just a salad then."

As Malcolm watched the waitress walk away he couldn't help but scan the room for Angie. She came in here for dinner a lot. But not tonight. Disappointment tweaked.

"You must eat here more than I realized," Olivia said.

"Food is good. And you know Garrison dates a gal that works here." He still wasn't sure how he felt about sharing this part of his life with her.

The waitress reappeared and served Malcolm his coffee and Olivia her wine. He sipped, grateful to have something to do. A coworker had once told him he had ice water in his veins. He wished now that were so.

Olivia sipped her wine. "Look, Malcolm, I'm not one to beat around the bush."

And he'd appreciated that about her. "Sounds ominous."

"Not really. It's time we talked."

"About what?" *Damn. The M-word.*

She sat back in her seat, a frustrated sigh escaping her lips. "It just seems like if we were really that close, we would talk more about what you do."

"I like to keep you away from that kind of stuff. It's not nice or pretty, and I don't want that hanging between us."

"But I don't mind hearing your problems."

"That doesn't mean I want to talk about them."

She stared at him as if trying to peel away his skull and peer into his brain. "Where do you see us going?"

He wished he'd ordered that beer now. "I see us together down the road."

" 'Down the road.' Is that code for, *I see us getting married one day?*" She enunciated each word, and he had the sense that she'd used the same tone with Andy when she'd drawn the line over the threshold.

He met her gaze. "I still haven't thought

that far."

"Well, I have. I love you, Malcolm. I've told you that often enough. I know you're not a hearts-and-flowers kind of guy, so I've not worried so much that you never say it back. But we've been together nine months. And I still remember the panic in your eyes when I mentioned marriage a couple of weeks ago."

He arched a brow.

She pressed her palms on the table. "Nine months is long enough for me to know I want marriage, Malcolm. A family. A home. I want more than to just be your girlfriend."

Tension rippled through his body. He did not want to have this conversation any more than he had wanted to have it the last time. "Your timing is really bad, Olivia."

"I know. You're on a case. But the fact is that you're on a case most days. Cases are a fact of life for you. So now is as good a time as any."

"What are you asking?"

She laid her hand on his. "I'm saying I want marriage. And I want you to think long and hard about what you want. If you don't want marriage you need to tell me."

"I just haven't thought that far ahead."

"You know where this is headed whether you realize it or not."

He felt backed into a corner. "And if I don't want marriage?"

"Then we move on with our lives. We find people that will give us what we really want. I'm not trying to be a bitch, Malcolm. I just want more."

More. A lumbering heaviness settled in his limbs. "I can't do more now."

"When then?" Her voice was whisper soft and full of sadness.

"I don't know." And he really didn't. All he knew now was that he had a killer to catch.

She took a healthy gulp of wine before she set the glass down. "I don't want to wait anymore."

He couldn't summon any anger. She'd been clear about what she'd wanted from the beginning, and he'd loved that about her. He'd thought he'd wanted her and all the traditional things she represented. But now he wasn't so sure. "How long do I have?"

"I turn thirty in two weeks. Two weeks should be enough time for you to figure it out."

A huge decision and she gave him two weeks. It seemed like the blink of an eye. But when he had a suspect in his sights he could make life-or-death decisions in seconds. "Olivia, I'm not going to be much smarter about life in two weeks."

She hesitated as if she'd half expected him to reconsider the whole conversation and ask her to marry him. But when he didn't speak, she nodded. "Okay."

"I'm sorry."

She rose and kissed him on the cheek. "Take care of yourself."

He could have grabbed her forearm but didn't. "You don't have to leave. Stay and eat your dinner."

Olivia's smile was tight and controlled, and he had the sense she might cry. She never cried. He felt like a schmuck. "I'll take a pass."

He rose, a little annoyed. "So when did it become so black and white between us, Olivia?"

"When you went to the cabin without me."

"You hate the cabin."

"Because it's just another slice of your life where I don't fit."

"I thought I was doing you a favor by not asking you to come."

"It would have been nice to be asked."

He ran fingers over his short hair. The truth was he'd really wanted to go alone. He'd not wanted her with him. He leaned forward and kissed her on the cheek. "If you need anything."

"I'll be fine." She walked across the pub, calmly, quietly, with no drama. Even Olivia could make a breakup seem sensible. She opened the pub's front door, waited for another to enter, and then left.

Angie entered the pub, her gaze tracking the room for Eva. The day's grind had kept her on the go, and after her first call to Eva she'd not had spare time. And of course, Eva had not called her back. No doubt her sister hadn't even checked her messages.

Angie didn't bother to take her place at the bar. Instead she moved around it and shoved the door open to the kitchen. King stood at the stove mixing a pot of stew. Brenda, his other waitress, frowned over an order pad as if trying to remember who ordered what. And King's newly adopted son Bobby, now eleven, sat at a side table doing what looked like math homework. The kid wore a Redskins football T-shirt and jeans. Freckles peppered the bridge of his nose, and his hair was slung over his eyes.

Bobby glanced up, his frown vanishing when he saw Angie. "Hey, Angie!" He got up.

"Sit," King said without tossing the boy a glance. "Homework first."

"Yeah, but Angie is here."

King shook his head. "Yeah, but you should have done your homework two hours ago. Sit. Finish. Then play."

The boy grumbled but sat back down. He didn't look all that distraught, and Angie guessed if she pushed, the kid would have told her it felt good to have a caring dad in charge of his life now.

She rumpled Bobby's hair. "Hey, kid."

He grinned. "Hey, yourself."

"Eva should be up in a minute," King said. "She just went to get a bushel of potatoes from the basement."

An image of her pregnant sister struggling up the stairs with a loaded basket had her moving to the basement stairs. She might be in heels and a skirt, but better she did the heavy lifting than Eva. As she opened the basement door, she found Eva poised on the top step with her bundle.

"Give it to me," Angie said. She took the basket, wobbled a bit on her heels, and then carried her load into the kitchen. "Where do you want it?"

"On the counter." King glanced over his shoulder and saw that it was Angie who'd spoken. Frowning, he looked at Eva but didn't comment.

Angie set the potatoes on the stainless-steel worktable in the center of the kitchen.

Eva said in a low voice, "I could have done that."

"Yeah, well, you shouldn't. We need to talk."

"I've got to work."

"It can wait," King said without glancing up from his stew. "See if you can talk some sense into her while you're at it, Angie. She's been in a foul mood for a couple of days now."

Angie took Eva by the elbow. "That is my intention."

Eva pulled her arm free. "You can talk, but I'm going to bartend. Brenda can't hold down the fort alone."

King opened his mouth to argue but then closed it as if hearing the wisdom. "Okay, but I can break from the stove in a half hour if you need help."

"I can do both," Eva said.

Angie pushed out into the bar area and took her regular corner seat. Eva set about mixing and filling several orders before she found her way back to Angie. "So what gives? And if it's about what I told you, I don't want to talk about it."

She lightly drummed long fingers on the

bar. "Oh, we'll get to that gem soon enough. I've come bearing different news."

She grimaced. "I don't know if I want any more news."

"I hired a private investigator to find your dad."

Eva blinked several times slowly. "You went looking for Blue?"

"I did." She held her breath, waiting for an explosion.

"Why?"

"Because I can't keep my nose out of other people's business."

"So I see." A weight of silence settled between them as Eva seemed to teeter between anger and curiosity. Curiosity won out. "And did you find him?"

Angie rattled off the facts of Blue Rayburn's life and eventual disappearance. Eva listened, her gaze never wavering from her sister. "And here's the real kicker. Do you know who one of the biggest contributors to the Talbot Museum was?" Angie held up her hand. "Don't bother to guess. I'll tell. Cross Industries."

Eva leaned forward, her pale fingers splaying on the bar. "As in Darius Cross?"

Angie didn't feel so pleased with herself for unearthing the detail. "The one and only."

Eva looked sick. "Why the hell would he give your father money?"

Angie shrugged. "It made him look like a big deal in the community? The perfect image was very important to Darius."

She shook her head. "Darius made lots of contributions to lots of different organizations. He sat on countless boards. He didn't need the Talbot."

"Just another feather in his cap."

"I promise you, Darius Cross had a very specific reason for tossing money at your father. He never did anything without a string attached."

Drumming fingers moved faster. "I called my private detective and told him to dig deeper. I want to know more about the Cross/Talbot connection. We'll see what he discovers."

"I don't believe in coincidences, Angie. Cross was using the museum for something."

"You sound like Garrison," Angie said.

Eva shrugged.

"Speaking of which, don't tell Garrison what I've found. Let's really understand what we have here before we tell anyone."

A frown furrowed Eva's brow. "Why? It's ancient history."

"Like you said, Darius only gave money

when it suited him. I'm afraid he pulled Dad into something." She sighed. "About all Dad had when he died was his reputation. His wife was gone. His museum had closed. I just don't want to taint his memory."

"He had you, Angie."

I wasn't enough. The unspoken words tightened around her chest.

Frank Carlson glanced down at the term paper that had a bold red *A* written on the top. She'd been a junior in high school and was in the top five percent of her class.

Her father frowned and laid the paper back down on his desk. "Why wasn't it an *A*-plus?"

Angie blinked, her pride exploding like a balloon that had been pricked. She fumbled with the cuff of her school uniform jacket, balancing on a tightrope above anger and pain. "The teacher said it was the best in the class."

"I can promise you, Angelina, that the world is far bigger than that classroom. You better learn that only the perfect survive." He glanced up at her. "Tuck in your blouse. Your shirttail is out."

She tucked in the blouse and picked up her paper. She hesitated, waiting for some kind word or bit of praise.

Frank glanced up at her, his gray eyes

impatient. "Was there something else?"

Outrage and anger bubbled inside her, and before she thought, she said, "Did Mom leave you because you weren't perfect?" She was hurt, and she wanted to jab into a wound she'd known he could not heal.

His face paled. "What did you say?"

She'd hit her mark. She'd just spent last Saturday with her mother and Eva. Her mother and sister had seemed so close to each other. Eva spoke about teachers and friends that her mother knew so well, whereas Angie didn't recognize a single name. She'd felt like the interloper.

"Why did Mom leave you?"

He cleared his throat. "There's a lot you don't understand."

"Was it because you weren't perfect?"

He rose. "That's enough. Leave my study."

She stalked over the threshold, her paper clutched in her hand. "You are so intent on making me perfect because you know you're not. You are trying to fix in me what you can't fix in yourself!"

He moved toward the door, staring at her with a mixture of anger and pain, and then without another word closed the door in her face.

Anger churned in her, and she stood outside the door debating whether or not to storm in.

And then she heard a sound she'd never heard before.

Her father was weeping.

Needing a distraction from the memory, Angie sat straighter and glanced in the mirror behind the bar. She spotted Kier in a booth. "I see only half of the dynamic duo. Where's Garrison?"

The mention of Garrison darkened Eva's eyes. "I'm not so sure he'll be coming around for a while."

"Why not?"

She shrugged. "I broke up with him."

Angie blinked. "You did what? Why?"

"I kind of freaked out. He wanted to know what was going on with me, and I felt backed into a corner. You know I can dig my heels in when I feel trapped."

Angie blew out a breath. "You have got to talk to him. Now."

"I know. I know. I just haven't found the right words."

"You've got an IQ of a million, and you can't find the right words?"

"Math and computers I get. The rest is just as confusing to me as the rest of the world."

The door to the pub opened and shut with

a rush of energy. Eva's gaze rose. She paled. "Crap."

Angie glanced over her shoulder. Garrison stood in the doorway. He didn't look angry, but a grim determination deepened the lines on his face.

Her respect for Garrison grew by leaps and bounds. "He's not so easy to get rid of, and looks like you might be having that talk now."

She raised her chin. "What if I'm not ready?"

It would be easier to stop a freight train than Deacon Garrison. "I don't think that much matters."

As Garrison approached, his gaze remained locked on Eva. "Angie, can you give us a moment?"

She didn't feel snubbed, understanding that he was focused like a laser.

Angie rose. "Detective Kier looks lonely and could use the company. Excuse me."

She didn't bother to glance back as she moved across the bar and took the seat across from Kier. "Don't worry, I'm not here to hassle you. I just need a place to park while Garrison and Eva talk."

He kept his gaze on her, not bothering with a fleeting look toward the bar. "I doubt

he'll leave here this evening without answers."

"Good. Eva needs him to be the rock and
tell her it will be all right."

"What's wrong?"

She pushed Olivia's wine aside. "Not
wrong as much as there is a bit of a complication. Nothing that can't be worked out."

"Complication. Is she sick?"

"No. Don't worry. They'll be fine." She
looked toward the bar and saw Garrison
leading Eva to the kitchen. Seconds later
King appeared to tend bar. "So whom does
the wine belong to? Hot date?"

"Olivia. My girlfriend."

She glanced at the glass. "Is she hiding in
the bathroom?"

"Funny you should put it that way. She
just broke up with me and left."

Angie stared at him, wondering if this was
one of his jokes. His lips didn't rise to a
grin, nor did his eyes spark as they did when
he was jerking her chain. Damn. She kinda
felt sorry for him.

Brenda arrived with Kier's order and Olivia's salad. "Will there be anything else?"

Angie smiled. "Soda, twist of lime. And a
roast beef sandwich."

Brenda frowned as if the dots just connected. "Where's the other lady?"

"Won't be coming back," Kier said. He reached for the mustard and loaded it on his sandwich.

Brenda looked at the salad. "Want me to take that?"

"I'll eat it," Angie said.

Brenda nodded and left.

Kier raised a brow. "Why does it not surprise me that you like red meat?"

She grinned and drove a fork into the green, crunchy lettuce. "I never know how anyone can make a meal out of food meant for a rabbit." She enjoyed the taste of the salad. "You don't look that torn up."

"I probably will be tomorrow. She's a great gal."

"But." The word dangled in the air like laundry from a clothesline.

"She wants to get married."

"It's not unreasonable."

"It's not. But I can't right now."

Angie nodded, accepted the soda that Brenda brought, and finished her salad while he ate his sandwich in silence. "I've officially sworn off the institution of marriage."

"Because of Donovan?"

"In part. Hard to get your guts ripped out and not worry that it could happen again."

"You're stronger than him."

331

"I didn't say I wasn't. In fact, I'm a good bit wiser because of him. All I'm saying is I understand why you don't want to get married."

"Olivia is not like Donovan. She's a great gal. I have a lot of respect for her. Any man would be a fool to let her go."

She arched an eyebrow. "Did you just call yourself a fool?"

"I did. Shit. I know that I am."

He was anything but a fool. Malcolm Kier was many things. He was domineering, stubborn, and pigheaded. But he was no fool. He knew his own mind. "So why don't you go after her? Do what your partner is doing with my sister right now."

"Garrison is different. He knows Eva is the one for him."

She could read between the lines. "And you know Olivia is not for you."

He shook his head and rested his hands in his lap. "She should be. She really should be. I want kids. She wants kids. She'd be a great wife and mother."

Kids. Natural that he'd want children. Most men did. She'd never be able to give any man a child. The lightness in her mood plummeted as if someone had dropped an anvil.

"So what did I just say?" Malcolm said.

She refocused on him and realized she'd drifted. "What?"

He was totally focused on her. "I feel like I just said something that hurt you."

"No. No, you didn't." It amazed her when she heard herself say, "Talk of kids always hits hard."

"Why?"

She traced her fingertip in circles on the table. "I had cancer seven years ago. I can't have children." Nervous laughter bubbled. "And why I just told you that I have no idea."

Genuine concern, something he'd never directed her way, darkened his eyes. "You're cancer free?"

"I am. In fact, I just got the annual all clear. Doc thinks the chances are one in a billion that I'll ever relapse. But the price is no kids." She traced her finger over the rim of her glass. "In the long run, I come out ahead."

"How about a beer?"

Angie laughed. "I don't drink. Had an issue with that as well." She sat back, just amazed that she'd just told Kier her two darkest secrets. "Let's face it, Kier, I am nobody's rose."

He grunted and then chuckled. "Join the club."

CHAPTER 18

Friday, October 7, 8:45 p.m.

"You can't just drag me away from the bar like a caveman," Eva said through gritted teeth.

Garrison didn't break stride. "Sure, I can."

He shoved open the door to the back room off the kitchen. "King said he'd cover the bar."

"We do not need to chat," Eva countered. "I need to work so King can cook."

"That's why he told you to lance whatever is festering and me to let him know what it was when I figured it out."

Eva raised a hand. "Yeah, well I never got a vote."

"Tough."

Alone in the back room there was only the hum of a large refrigerator and the distant murmur of conversation and music from the bar. Her skin had paled more since they'd spoken two days ago. As tough as

Eva talked, whatever was happening between them was taking its toll. "Tell me
what's eating you."

"Nothing is eating me."

He smiled, knowing it was more effective
than ranting, which was all he wanted to do
right now. "I know you, Eva. I know when
you are worried or tired or happy or sad. I
know you. What's eating you?"

She tried to move past him, but he stopped
her.

"Did you get any more letters from that
lunatic in prison?"

The killer that had stalked her and nearly
claimed her life last year had recently been
sentenced to three life sentences. From the
moment the judge had rendered his guilty
verdict, the killer sent notes to Eva. Nothing had been outwardly threatening. In fact
it had all seemed innocent. *Please, please
forgive me. I'm sorry.*

At first she'd not told him about the notes
because she'd not wanted to upset him. But
when the last note had arrived, he'd happened to be present.

He'd watched the color drain from her
face and watched her hands tremble. He'd
read the note and immediately called the
Department of Corrections. They'd agreed
to suspend delivery.

"Do you swear there have been no other notes?"

"Yes."

And then came the question that had gnawed at him at two a.m. "Is it another guy?" He'd always worried that when she really found her power and saw her potential she'd leave him. He was, after all, associated with a dark past that any sane person would flee.

Shock blazed in her gaze. "No."

The bands of tension around his chest eased a fraction. "What is it, Eva?" He released her, stepped back, and ran a hand over his short hair. "What the hell is it?"

The edge of desperation in his voice triggered a well of tears in her eyes. One tear fell down her cheek, and she brushed it away. "I've messed things up."

Oddly, hope flickered. She seemed ready to open up. He could slay dragons for her, but he had to know what those dragons were first. "What could you have messed up?"

"I'd never planned to do this."

"I can see that." The edge in his voice softened.

She closed her eyes, drew in a deep breath, and faced him. "I'm pregnant."

"What?"

"I'm pregnant."

"Honey, that's not possible."

"It is very possible." Color flooded her cheeks.

He frowned. "We were very careful, Eva."

His sister had died of cystic fibrosis, a genetic disease. The illness had viciously attacked his sister over her short lifetime. He'd remembered all the pain and suffering and had sworn he'd never put a kid of his own through that kind of life.

"That's why I waited so long to go to the doctor. I figured it was the flu." She shoved out a sigh. "And when he told me I was expecting I made him run the test a second time."

"You're sure you're pregnant?"

"I told you, the doctor ran the test twice. And there was that one time a few months ago when we weren't so careful."

Garrison rubbed his hand over his jaw. She was right. There had been that one night when they'd been so excited to see each other. They'd not thought it all through.

Shit.

"Eva, I should not have biological children. The risk is too high for CF." Silence hovered between them.

"I'm not getting rid of it," she said. "I'm not."

"You've never seen what the disease can really do."

She shook her head. "I'm not giving this baby up."

A myriad of disaster scenarios pummeled his brain. He thought about the endless hospitals and tests and medicines his sister had endured. And then through the darkness the image of Eva holding his child flashed, bright and clear.

Emotion choked his voice. "Eva."

She shook her head. "I've been online and done a good bit of reading. There's a twenty-five percent chance the baby will be sick. Seventy-five percent chance it'll be fine. Either way, I'll figure it out."

He closed the distance between them and laid his hands on her shoulders. "You don't know what you're signing up for."

Another tear trickled down her cheek. "It won't be the first time."

Her shoulders felt small and fragile under his hands. He knew her well enough to know that she would keep the baby. God help her if this child was sick. Her life would be an endless stream of doctors.

Garrison didn't want to bring a sick kid into the world. He didn't want to remember the smell of the pediatric wing of the hospital or see the painfully cheerful wallpaper that decorated the rooms. He didn't want to worry about pills or ventilators.

He didn't want any of it.

But he'd deal.

"We're getting married," he said, his voice gruff.

"What?"

"I've been wanting to ask you for months but didn't because it's not fair to you."

More tears welled in her eyes. He cupped her face in his hands and kissed her on the lips. She held him tight and for the first time in days let go of her grip on the tension.

He kissed her on the forehead. "We can get married in a few days."

"There's no real rush. The baby's not due for seven months."

Baby. Due. Seven months. Shit.

His hand slid to her belly. He'd hoped to feel a flicker of movement, but there was nothing. "You're really sure?"

"Yes." She pulled a thread from his jacket. "I know the timing sucks."

Garrison and Eva were going to have a baby.

The idea quickly took root and overtook every sense in his body. A protective urge welled inside of him. "Mom's going to be thrilled."

"She'll be worried like you."

"She's more optimistic than me. She won't borrow trouble. She'll be too excited."

"I told Angie."

"And?"

"She was excited. Told me to tell you."

He grunted. "Points for her."

"The timing was a bit serendipitous."

"How so?"

"She hired a detective to find my father."

He frowned. "And?"

"She did find him, or at least information on him. And you'll never guess who he knew back in the day."

After Angie dumped way too much personal information on Kier, she felt foolish and embarrassed, so she'd paid for their dinner, despite his protests, and spouted excuses about work and deadlines. She left King's without waiting to hear what had happened between Eva and Garrison, figuring they were still talking so that had to be a good sign.

It made sense to return to the office. Work always waited for her. But she couldn't stomach the idea of staring at legal briefs for the next few hours. Too much restless energy hummed in her body. Sleep wasn't going to come easily tonight.

She drove, not sure where she'd go. The gym was closed. It wasn't like she had a huge number of friends. She worked, worked out, and spent time with her sister. Her life had become fairly limited in the last few years — a fact she could ignore until quiet, in-between moments like this.

She kept driving until she'd ventured into the lower-middle-class neighborhood of Vivian Sweet. She'd memorized the address after they'd spoken in court.

It was past eight and not the best time to pay a visit. And yet she slowed in front of Vivian's address. A light was on in the front room, and though shades where drawn, she could see a shadowed figure pass in front.

Angie parked and got out of the car. She rang the front bell.

Footsteps moved to the door, and from the other side Vivian said, "Who is it?"

"It's Angie Carlson. From the courtroom the other day."

Chains scraped across locks, and the door opened. Vivian stood in the doorway, with a sleepy David laying his head on her shoulder. His eyes were half open, his thumb in his mouth, but he looked as if he fought sleep like it were a deadly sin.

Vivian's face reflected her confusion. "Ms.

341

Carlson?"

Angie curled and uncurled her fingers wishing she had pockets or something to hold. Rarely did she scramble for words as she did now. "I was driving around. I thought I'd stop and see if you'd heard from Lulu."

The baby roused at the sound of her voice. He raised his head and looked at Angie, presenting her with a sloppy grin. Something tightened and twisted inside of her as she stared at the boy.

"No, I haven't heard from her," Vivian said. "If you got a minute, would you mind coming in?"

"Sure."

Vivian moved aside, holding the door open for Angie. The woman's pale, frail arm stretched out from the cuff of her housecoat. Blue veins skimmed just under the surface of her skin. "Have a seat."

Angie glanced toward a couch covered with a faded flowered slipcover. On the far end was a pile of neatly folded baby clothes. She perched on the edge closest to the chair where Vivian took her seat.

David was now fully awake and staring at Angie with bold curiosity. Clearly the last thing on the boy's mind now was sleep.

"I've messed up your evening schedule,"

Angie said. "He would be asleep now if not for me."

Vivian patted the baby on his back. "It's okay. I needed to talk to someone anyway about an issue that's been preying on my mind."

"Sure."

For a moment she was silent as if wrestling with her thoughts. "I never banked on being a mother again," Vivian said. "I was over forty when Lulu was born, and I'll be sixty-three on my next birthday."

Angie tried to keep her gaze on Vivian, but her attention remained on the baby. She wanted to hold him, but asking didn't feel right. "He looks happy and healthy."

"It's all I can do to take care of him now. And I really worry about what will happen when he is older. I'll be close to seventy when he goes to kindergarten."

The baby thrust out his arms to Angie and tipped his weight toward her. She reached out for him to steady him. Vivian released her hold on the boy and let him tumble into Angie's embrace.

He possessed surprising strength in his little body. She imagined when he grew up he'd be a big man. He'd have a body for football or soccer, not track or swimming. "Where is David's father?"

"Lulu doesn't know who his father is. She was mighty confused around the time he was conceived and made a lot of very bad choices."

"Is there anyone who can help you?"

"My husband died fifteen years ago, and I've no brothers or sisters. Ms. Carlson, I'm worried. What if Lulu doesn't come back? And if she does, what kind of shape will she be in?"

Angie couldn't scramble any words of encouragement. "I don't know."

"I don't want him going to the state. I don't want him with strangers."

"Is there a neighbor or someone that you know who could act as his guardian?"

"Can I even do that? I have custody, but I don't know if I have the right to make decisions on his future."

"I'm not an expert in family law, but I can ask around and see what your options are."

"I don't have the money to pay you or any attorney."

David's shirt rode up on his back, and Angie tugged it back in place. "No charge. It's important to me that he's taken care of. I owe that much to Lulu."

"I appreciate that." Vivian shook her head. "Two years ago when I sat in that courtroom and watched you tear into Lulu, I never figured you'd ever give me a reason to smile."

Angie patted David's back. He burped. She didn't always enjoy the demands of her job. "I had a job to do."

Vivian nodded. "We don't always like what we have to do. I sure never figured I'd be suing my kid for her child."

The older woman stiffened and closed her eyes. Her expression froze, and her skin lightened two shades. She leaned forward as if she was going to be sick.

"Are you all right?" Angie said. She wrapped one hand around the baby's midsection and reached out to Vivian with the other. The woman's skin felt like ice.

Vivian took long deep breaths. "Ever had that feeling that something bad has happened?"

"Sure."

"Well, I'm feeling it now." She raised her watery gaze to Angie. "I got the terrible sense that Lulu is dying."

Lulu searched the dark eyes of the new guy. She prayed he'd set her free, but feared he'd use her like his partner.

The last hours with the other guy had been an endless tumble of violence and sex.

He'd enjoyed hurting her and telling her she was getting exactly what she deserved. Now her body was so bruised and battered she doubted she could run even if this new guy flung the door wide open.

The man held up a syringe and squeezed the plunger until a faint stream of liquid squirted out.

She sensed without being told that the needle would take her pain away forever. She'd never have to struggle with sobriety or crappy jobs. She'd never again lay awake at night chewed up with guilt and ticking through the list of her screwups. She'd never have any more dreams about David being taken away from her. The needle offered freedom.

But it was the kind of freedom she didn't want.

"Where is the other man?" she said.

"Gone."

"Why?"

"He's finished with you. Now it's my turn."

"Are you going to hurt me too?"

"No. I'm not going to hurt you."

"I want to live," she said. Her bruised throat felt dry and scratchy. "I don't want to die."

The man's eyes remained cold and dead.

"You don't get a vote."

She raised her hand up to his and wrapped her fingers around his wrist. Surprising strength coursed through her fingers as she dug her nails into his skin. "Get the fuck away from me."

He jerked away and slapped her hand down. "Be nice."

"Nice. Drop dead."

"That's your move, not mine." In one easy move, he drove the needle roughly into her neck and pushed the plunger.

Liquid burned into her skin, sending death through her body. Her heart beat faster and faster, as if fighting against the attack. A vein in her neck throbbed.

She drew in a breath, but her lungs wouldn't accept any air. She pulled a second time, but her body refused the command.

The eyes that stared down at her now fired with excitement and life.

Like a vampire, he fed on her death.

Oh, God, I don't want to die!

Panic exploded as death stole the last bit of life from her body.

It was past nine when Detective Sinclair checked the address, glanced at the green tri-level, and got out of her police-issue car. The neighborhood was mid-income but nicely kept. The houses were older, smaller, but the lawns were large. The extra land was a real luxury in Alexandria, where nearly all the available land was developed with closely placed homes, condos, and high rises.

She crossed the lawn and rang the front bell. A dog barked inside the house, and she could hear the hum of a vacuum cleaner. When she didn't get an answer, she rang the bell again and knocked. The dog barked louder and the vacuum stopped. Seconds later footsteps moved toward the door, and after a pause, the door opened.

Standing behind the screened door was a neatly dressed woman who'd pulled back her graying hair into a neat ponytail. She wore minimal makeup, which softened the lines around her eyes and mouth. "Can I help you?"

Sinclair pulled out her badge. "I'm Detective Jennifer Sinclair with Alexandria Police. Are you Flora Redman Knight?"

"Yes."

"I was hoping you could answer some questions for me about Fay Willow."

She straightened. "Fay? She died almost thirty years ago."

"Yes, ma'am. We're looking into her case."

"Why now?"

The neighbor next door came out on his front porch and glanced toward her. He stared without shame.

Sinclair stared back until he shifted his gaze and retreated back into the house. "Would you mind if I came inside?"

"Sure." She pushed the screen door open wider.

Sinclair was greeted by the scent of pine cleaner. The living room was decorated in soft greens and was showroom clean. A baby gate between the kitchen and the living room kept a barking Pomeranian at bay. The dog yapped as if its home had been invaded.

"Tootsie, stop!" Mrs. Redman said. She moved to the gate, pulled a treat from her pocket, and fed it to the dog. "She'll calm down. She's been nervous around strangers since my husband died last year."

"Yes, ma'am." Sinclair never considered herself a dog person. Cats were more to her tastes. They were quiet, independent, and not emotionally needy.

"You wanted to ask me about Fay."

"Yes, ma'am. The original police file listed you as her roommate at the time of her death."

"Yes. We shared an apartment for about a year."

"Can you tell me about her?"

"Beautiful. Ambitious. She liked men and they liked her. When she went missing I knew something was wrong. We'd been scheduled to travel to New York for the weekend, and she loved New York. I knew when she didn't come home to pack her bag that something was wrong."

"Any idea who might have killed her?"

"You know she was sleeping with Darius Cross?"

"There was a brief mention of it in the police file."

She adjusted the pearl stud on her ear. "Darius never would have admitted to the affair, of course, but I knew. Fay couldn't keep a secret so well."

"How did the two meet?"

"At a party for the Talbot Museum. She was in charge of inviting the rich and famous to an opening. She delivered an invitation to Cross personally. I guess he took one look at her and decided to follow. Shortly after, he made a big donation to the Talbot."

"How long did the affair last?"

"Six months. Up until about a month before her death. She and Darius got into a fight."

"About?"

"She wanted marriage, and he of course did not. She was so sure that she had him wrapped around her finger. It was almost as if she had some kind of leverage. And don't ask me what. For once in her life she was very quiet about juicy details. I can tell you when she left Darius, she jumped into another man's bed within days."

"Who?"

She folded her arms. "I don't know his name. But he made deliveries to the museum. She never brought him around, and I was planning my wedding at that point and wasn't so worried about her dramas."

He stared down at the woman's lifeless eyes, savoring death's stillness. He brushed knuckles against her warm skin, knowing her temperature had already dropped a few degrees. In an hour she'd feel cold to the touch, her limbs would stiffen, and she'd be harder to manage. He'd have to get her into the melting vat soon so that the liquid could strip the flesh from her bones and erase all traces of evidence linked to her death.

His father had always said, "Cover your tracks. If you're smart enough you'll never be caught."

And he didn't want to be caught. The idea of living the rest of his life in a small gray cell conjured nightmares for him. So he would do as his father had once advised and erase the evidence from her body.

If only he could erase his own evidence from his body. The scars and mutilated skin, such a source of bitterness, would be with him until he died, and his flesh decayed away from the undamaged bone beneath.

He stroked her pale skin. He didn't have to take her right at this moment. He had a little time to savor the quiet stillness — the way her chest did not rise and fall with breath, the way her gaze did not judge or recoil from his naked body.

Death brought its own special beauty to a woman that nothing in life could match.

For so long, he'd denied his taste and dark yearnings to kill. He'd put all his energy and power into blending in and simply disappearing.

But that had changed a couple of years ago. He'd met his partner. Seen the dark need in his eyes and known together they would be invincible. Together, they'd taken a hooker. When his partner had finished with her, the creature inside of him, hungry after its long slumber, would not be denied. It no longer whispered that he kill. It shouted and demanded that he kill.

And so he'd answered the call. One, two,

three, four, and now five times.

Killing the hookers had been satisfying for a time. But then he'd grown bored. What was the point of genius if no one knew about it?

So, they'd agreed upon the actress. And now the hooker turned good girl. He wasn't afraid of the cops at all now. He was smarter than they were.

He stared at her a long moment and then leaned forward and pressed his cheek to hers, inhaling the growing scent of death. He cupped her face, stared into the vacant eyes, and kissed her on her lips, savoring the chilled, still softness. With his fingertips he traced her jawline, her collarbone, and then he circled her nipple. He grew hard.

Other women intrigued him far more than this one ever would. Soon he'd find them and release them from their frantic holds on life. Their limbs would still, and the heat would evaporate from their bodies. They too would become perfect.

But until then, he had this one. He slipped his hand under her torn blouse, squeezed her breast, and slid his hand down her flat belly. There'd still be warmth inside of her to welcome him. He smiled.

For the next few moments, she was the perfect woman.

CHAPTER 19

Saturday, October 8, 8 a.m.

Angie had dreamed of Kier. She was not sure where last night's dreams had come from. They'd been dark and erotic, and they'd stirred her from slumber well before dawn. It had been a long time since she'd felt desire, and she'd missed it. Craved it.

She had always had a healthy sexual appetite. There'd only been a few men in her life, but she'd enjoyed them all. That had all changed with Donovan. His sweet, soft words had set her up so perfectly for the cutting betrayal that had left her so wounded and fearful.

Now as she stared down at the morning paper and Donovan's byline on the front page, she wondered why she'd given that creep so much power. Why was she denying herself because he'd been such a shit? She'd never been afraid of risk before, and yet he'd turned her into a risk-phobic ninny.

Donovan's article was an artful blend of fantasy and fact. He'd turned Sierra into a saint. He'd taken jabs at Angie and the cops, namely Kier and Garrison, questioning why there'd been no leads since the body had been found five days ago.

Five days. Kier and Garrison had worked almost around the clock in that time. She knew cops well enough to know that they barely had time to shower during an investigation. And to top it off, Kier's girlfriend had broken up with him.

Her mind skipped to Kier's face last night. Dark circles had hung under his eyes, and fatigue had softened his rough edges. He would hardly want or expect her pity. In fact he'd likely resent it. But she found a tender spot for the man.

Maybe that moment of tenderness is what had stirred the dreams.

Angie's cell phone rang. The shrill tone yanked her attention from the morning paper. She glanced at the caller identification. Eva.

She flipped it open. "It's good to see you know where your phone is."

"Yeah. Sorry. I saw the missed calls."

She picked up a steaming mug of coffee, raised it to her lips, and paused. "You drive me crazy when you don't answer."

"I can only hope my winning charm makes up for it."

Angie laughed. "You sound like you're in a good mood today."

"I am."

"So, I assume you worked out your issues with the good detective."

"I did."

"Any salacious details you can share with the lonely lawyer?"

Eva laughed. "Sorry, no."

"Too bad. So what prompts this call?"

"Remember when you said not to tell Garrison about our family connection to the Cross family?"

Angie set down her cup. "You did."

"I did."

She pressed fingertips to her temple. "And?"

"He wants to talk to you. So does Kier."

Heat rushed in her face. "When?"

"One hour. At headquarters."

"That sounds ominous."

"Garrison says it's a friendly chat."

"What about Kier?"

She dropped her voice a notch. "Kinda pissed."

Angie's laugh had a nervous edge. "Great."

"But you'll come?"

"See you in an hour."

Malcolm stood at the dry-erase board in the conference room, staring at Sierra Day's name. He'd drawn a circle around it and from it lines that extended to the names of those who'd wanted to kill her. Her husband. Her lover. Dixon?

And then there was Fay. Dead twenty-eight years. An employee of the Talbot. Darius Cross's mistress.

And then there was Lulu. Missing. From her name he had only one line, and it extended to Dixon's name. He knew Sierra, and he sure as hell had a reason to kill Lulu.

Malcolm wrote another name. *Angie.* He circled it three times, and then drew lines to Sierra, Fay, Lulu, and Dixon.

Right now the only common denominator was Angie.

Malcolm's cell phone buzzed. "Yeah."

"It's Garrison. Eva and I are here."

"I'm in the conference room."

In a few minutes, Garrison and Eva appeared in the doorway. Both looked tired but in a good way. Eva had a glow, and Garrison had lost the angry edge that had left him so sharp and brittle last night. They were holding hands.

He didn't resent their happiness, but it

357

sure as hell didn't improve his mood. "You two look chipper. Work out the kinks?"

Garrison nodded. "We did."

"Good for you." He looked at Eva and managed to soften the gruffness in his voice. "So where is that sister of yours?"

Her cheeks held a glow. "She's on her way."

"I'm very curious to hear what she's found out about your family."

"She gave me some of the highlights last night, but I was a little distracted. She can give you the full report."

"Can't wait." Angie had sat with him last night, and for just a few moments he'd felt a strong tangible connection to her. His attraction to The Barracuda hadn't shocked him as much as it had the first time. In fact, he was getting used to it. Maybe that was what bothered him now. He felt a connection. And she didn't.

And to top it off, he'd dreamed about the counselor last night. They'd been in his bedroom. There'd been a candle flickering and casting a soft glow on her pale skin. He'd reached for her shirt and slowly unfastened pearl buttons that trailed between her breasts. When he'd peeled back the silk he'd discovered a red push-up bra that made her breasts so sinfully beautiful he'd been unable to resist suckling them through the lace.

He shoved out a breath. The counselor had secrets, but it wasn't naughty underwear. It was a big-ass skeleton in her closet that involved the Cross family.

The elevator in the hallway dinged, and he tensed, just knowing it was Carlson. Seconds later she appeared in the doorway. She carried her worn briefcase, but her hair was free around her shoulders, and she wore a soft blue turtleneck. Jeans hugged her hips, and black boots gave her an inch of height that brought them eye-to-eye.

"Looks like a party," Angie said.

"And it seems you're the guest of honor," Malcolm said.

"Really?" She moved into the room and set down the briefcase on the conference table. She tossed a quick glance toward Eva, then lobbed it right back at him.

"Seems you've done a little digging, discovered a few gems, but chosen not to share."

She leveled her gaze. "I've never been good at sharing, Detective. I guess I just don't play well with others."

"Maybe you'd better learn."

Her eyes narrowed, and he suspected she was calculating all the pros and cons of working with the police. "You worked with us last year and helped us in a murder investigation."

A former client of hers had asked her to broker a deal with the cops. He would trade info on a murder if he could walk on breaking-and-entering charges. She'd agreed to the deal but had been clear she'd do nothing to impede the murder investigation.

"I thought I was investigating a family matter," she said. "I didn't realize it had anything to do with the police."

He folded his arms. "You dug up a juicy gem. I want to know what it is."

"Why? I don't see what the connection could possibly be between my family history and your current investigations."

Garrison cleared his throat. "We had a ViCAP hit on Sierra Day's case. A similar crime occurred almost thirty years ago. The woman who was murdered, Fay Willow, worked for your father, and we suspect was also having an affair with Darius Cross."

The look of shock on her face gave Malcolm a moment of satisfaction. Nice to know she could be thrown off balance. But she was too practiced and careful to reveal too much emotion. He'd have bet she was one hell of a poker player. "Okay."

He felt a muscle tighten in the back of his neck. "I can appreciate that you did not know this when you discovered your family connection to the Cross family. But now that Garrison has told it to you, it would be nice if you shared."

"I haven't made sense of what I have found, so I really don't want to discuss it."

He crossed his arms over his chest and leaned against the conference table. "What connection did you discover between your father and the Cross family?"

"Like I said, I've not fully analyzed it. And, to make my position clear, Wellington and James now represents Micah Cross. So for me to discuss anything related to him with the police would not be appropriate."

"You've taken Micah Cross on as a client?" Disgust bled through each word.

She raised her chin. "Not me personally but the firm. We're representing his charitable foundation."

Garrison glanced at Eva. "Did you know about this?"

"Yes. She told me before she accepted him as a client." Eva cleared her throat. "I have no ethical bounds in this matter."

Angie shrugged but didn't look upset or ready to silence her sister. "No, you do not."

"So I can tell them what you told me?"

Angie shrugged.

"My father, Blue, worked for the Talbot Museum as the security director. Angie's dad was the museum director. Shortly after my father arrived at the museum, he began an affair with my mother. As you know, that affair ruined the Carlsons' marriage."

"Counselor, can you tell us what your father did during his time at the museum? I mean, I doubt that would raise any conflicts of interests," Malcolm said.

Angie absently traced the FCT initials on her briefcase. "He was the director. Administrative, membership, ticket sales, exhibits. He *was* the museum."

"What kind of exhibits?"

"The Talbot Museum wasn't large, or widely known beyond academic circles. It was dedicated to the Talbot family. My grandfather served with the senior Mr. Talbot in World War II. I'm not sure of the details, but after the war my grandfather went to work for the family. The Talbot family was wealthy and had ties that went back in this country a couple hundred years. Long story short, the family decided to set up its own museum. My grandfather was put in charge. And when he died my father took over."

"What did the museum display?"

"Memorabilia and souvenirs from the family's extensive trips to Africa and Russia. As I said, the family has a long history so the collection was quite extensive."

"What kind of memorabilia?"

"Portraits. Clothes. Furniture. Muskets. You name it. Whatever was collected was processed and displayed by my father and grandfather."

Eva cleared her throat. "Darius Cross made a large donation to the Talbot. I argued that Darius never did anything without good reason."

Malcolm frowned. "If this old family was so rich, why did Cross make a donation?"

Angie folded her arms. "Every pot has its bottom. The younger Talbot generation wasn't so wise when it came to money. A lot was lost in the stock market. They cut way back on museum funding. My father, out of loyalty to the family, tried to keep the museum alive and healthy."

Garrison grunted. "It would have appealed to Darius to 'save' a rich old family. It would have made him feel superior."

Eva nodded. "Darius would have expected a favor in return for the donation."

Angie frowned. "Dad wouldn't have done anything illegal."

Eva shook her head. "Darius made good

363

people do awful things. I've seen pictures of the Talbot's collection. Your father displayed animal skeletons."

Angie's lips flattened. "Look, if you're saying that Dad had something to do with this Fay Willow's death, you are way off base."

"Maybe not her death," Malcolm said. "But maybe Darius needed help disposing of her body. Your father must have understood how bones were stripped if he managed animal bone collections."

"That's one hell of a leap," Angie said.

"Not when you consider the way the bodies were handled after death. The manner is almost identical."

"And you think the guy that killed Fay killed Sierra?"

"I don't know," Malcolm said. "But I've got a correlation, and I can't ignore it." She didn't speak, her mind clearly trying to regroup. An attack on her father was the last thing she'd expected today.

He eased up his tone, knowing he'd get more from her if she wasn't so defensive. "According to Fay's roommate, Fay had been having an affair with Darius Cross. I'm willing to bet that old Darius never intended to marry her, and that when she got a little out of hand, he killed her."

Garrison nodded. "Reasonable to assume

that he turned to Frank Carlson, called in a favor, and asked him to help dispose of the body."

"No," Angie said. "No."

"Darius was a bit like the mob, Angie. You know that," Eva said quietly. "Darius would think nothing of calling in a favor from your father."

Angie's fingers furled and unfurled as if grasping for a lifeline. "I can't believe my father would be involved in a murder cover-up. He was a gentle man. Flawed, sure. But he'd never hurt anybody."

Eva looked at her. "You remember how Darius was. He forced me to plead guilty. I lost ten years of my life because of him."

Angie seemed to be the type that turned to logic when emotions got out of hand. "Eva, Darius has been dead two years. He wasn't around to kill Sierra."

"His son was," Malcolm said.

Angie raised her hands. "Stop right there. I am not having this kind of discussion with you regarding my client."

"Apple might not fall far from that very rotten tree," Malcolm said.

Angie leveled her gaze on Malcolm. "If your apple theory holds true, Detective, then Eva and I are just as guilty as our fathers. Are you saying we are guilty?"

He leaned toward her, lowering his voice a notch. "Don't play word games with me, Counselor."

Color warmed her cheeks. "I will not let you crucify my father when he's not here to defend himself."

"Right now your father's reputation means nothing to me. Nothing. I have a killer to catch. And if you find out something that can help me with this case, and you keep it from me, I promise I will make your life a living hell."

She snatched up her briefcase. "Legally, you can't compel me to say anything, Detective. And I don't scare easy. Take your best shot."

Some of the fire left his belly. "I'm not trying to win a debate, Counselor. I'm trying to solve a murder, maybe two or three. If you can help, you should."

"I won't let you ruin my father's memory."

"I'll do whatever it takes to catch this killer."

"And I'll do whatever it takes to protect my father."

He leaned forward. "What happened to the museum? I've never seen it."

"It burned to the ground seven years ago," she said.

"Where was it?"

"In Alexandria."

"Everything was destroyed?"

She hesitated. "The museum was completely destroyed."

"Museums have outbuildings and storage facilities for collections they can't show. Any place like that remain?"

Again she didn't answer.

"You can delay. We can play games. But, Counselor, I will find it."

Still she didn't speak.

"One way or another we have to find out what happened between your father and Darius. Better me looking into this. Someone else finds out about it first . . . someone like Donovan . . . and there will be no saving your father." Mention of Donovan's name was a low blow, but it had the desired effect.

"There's a place in western Fairfax. I found out about it after my father died. But I've never been there." Her voice sounded so even and cool, a sign she'd fallen back behind the ice wall. "A storage unit."

"Do I need to get a warrant? Or are you going to take me there?"

Dr. Dixon sat in his study staring at the scrapbook he'd so carefully kept for years. He'd gently and lovingly cut out each

367

article, paying close attention to creating neat, even edges. Clear lines. A surgeon's touch.

He smoothed soft hands over the pages of an entry made a year ago. The headline read: CARLSON DEFENDS SISTER'S DECISION.

Angie Carlson.

He studied the grainy newspaper photo of her. He smiled. She had such a determined gaze as she stared into the camera's lens. She was the type of woman who could bring a man to his knees. She was a fighter, a modern-day Athena, and a woman warrior.

For the last couple of years he'd been content to watch. And as much as he wanted more from her, he needed to be careful. He'd been charged with attempted murder once, and he never wanted to go through that again.

He'd never intended to kill that whore. He'd simply been getting his money's worth. She'd promised rough sex, and that's what he'd paid for. It wasn't his fault that she freaked out.

It was just his damn luck that the woman's screams had caught the attention of Kier and Garrison. The detectives had been dogs with a bone. They'd believed that he had killed the missing prostitutes. They'd tried

368

to bully him into a confession. That's when he'd sought out Angie, his Athena, and she'd come to his rescue.

He knew having a woman defending him would pay off in the court of public relations. And in the courtroom, Angie had been brilliant. She'd made the prosecution's star witness look foolish enough that the jury had dismissed the charges. There'd been no more talk about him having killed those other women.

And he'd not killed them. That had been the work of The Other. He'd done the killing.

He'd also suggested they change the game. He wanted different women. More challenging kills.

And in all honesty, Dixon wanted more too. He'd grown tired of whores. So they'd chosen Sierra and then Lulu.

The Other had been clear who would be next. He wanted Angie.

She was no great beauty. Pleasant looking to be sure, but not anywhere close to the beauty she could be if he had time to really work on her. He'd once suggested during his trial that he could straighten out her nose and add a bit of fullness to her cheeks. She'd tossed back a quick but polite no.

That had been the first time she'd said

no, and he'd felt the rush of anger. But they'd been in the midst of his murder trial so he'd been careful to hide his feelings. Their time would come. It would just have to be later.

After his trial, he'd come to her a second time. Their professional relationship had ended, and he'd felt free to suggest that they spend personal time together. He believed they were perfectly matched and destined to be together.

Again, she'd told him no. However this time the veil of politeness had dropped, and he glimpsed her disgust for him. She'd taken up his cause not because she believed in him but for the money he'd paid her. She was no different from the whores he'd paid and used for sex.

That's when he'd begun to plan and dream of the day he'd have his Athena all to himself. Then, she could satisfy his sexual appetites.

He had to be careful. The Other would not appreciate his rebellion. He expected Dixon to do as he was told. But Dixon didn't want to share her with The Other. He wanted her for himself. He wanted to hide her away and use her over and over again.

Dixon knew he'd have to move quickly, before The Other realized what he planned.

CHAPTER 20

Saturday, October 8, 3 p.m.

"Hey, would you wait up," Malcolm said as he got out of the police car. Angie had driven her car to Liddell's Storage, and he had followed. He'd offered to drive her, but she'd refused. Eva had begged off the trip, and Garrison had remained behind to search for more connections between the families.

Angie had seemed almost relieved that Eva wasn't coming. Malcolm could see she was worried over what they'd find in the storage unit.

Liddell's wasn't the typical metal-box storage place where people stowed excess furniture. It was a large warehouse with climate-controlled areas.

He opened the trunk of his car. "There is no race, Carlson."

She didn't glance back or slow her pace. "Keep up. Move faster."

Malcolm stared at Angie's straight-back posture and clipped steps. Despite brave talk, she was scared of Daddy Dearest's secrets.

He grabbed a crowbar from the trunk, which he figured might come in handy with a storage shed full of crated boxes. He slammed the trunk closed. Parking-lot gravel crunched under his boots as they crossed to the front office.

He pushed through the door and found Carlson standing in front of a plain desk. Behind it sat a kid with long hair, a white T-shirt, and jeans. A television with rabbit ears resting on a crate by the desk broadcast the afternoon football game.

Malcolm shut the door behind him, catching up to Angie as she showed her Virginia driver's license to the kid behind the counter.

"The name is Carlson. No, I don't know the unit's number."

The kid glanced briefly at Malcolm, then pulled out a big black spiral notebook, opened it, and searched the pages. "Number Nine. Go through the doors behind me, and then go all the way down the center hall. It'll be on the right."

"Do you have a spare?"

"For this account, yes." He flipped the

book to the back, where several keys were taped. He grabbed the one with a nine on the tab and handed it to her.

She held the key in her hands as if it were a foreign object. "How long have you been working here?"

"Six months."

"Not exactly a lifetime," she said. The kid barely looked old enough to drive.

"Yeah. I guess this kind of business doesn't make for long-timers. Nobody stays more than a year."

"What about the facility's owner?" she said.

"I hear the place has been sold three or four times."

"What do you do if someone doesn't pay rent on a unit?" Angie asked.

"We notify them, and if they don't respond within two weeks we haul the contents away to the dump."

"You can just throw people's stuff out?" she said.

"Hey, we tell them our terms and conditions when they take on the space."

"What about the Talbot Museum?" Kier said.

"They are paid up. So there's no reason to call or write until the bill is due, which is thirteen years and two months from now."

"What about visitors?" Malcolm pressed. "People visit storage units all the time."

The kid glanced back at his big black book. "According to this, there's been no activity since the stuff was first put here."

The kid manager glanced back at the television and back at Malcolm. "You need anything else from me?"

Malcolm shook his head. "Nope."

"Great. I want to catch the last of the game."

"Hey, if Alabama scores let me know," Malcolm said.

The kid laughed. "No way, man. I'm Florida State."

Malcolm glowered. "Great."

The kid pressed a button under the desk, and the door behind him buzzed. "You can go in."

Malcolm opened the door for Angie and waited as she passed. They walked silently down the hallway.

"I made some calls on the way out here about the fire that destroyed the museum," he said.

She glanced at him. "Why?"

"Gut feeling, I guess. And let's face it. Fires have a way of happening when a Cross family member is involved."

"So what did fire investigators say?" Angie said.

"The fire department determined that a short in the museum's electrical wires caused the blaze. They never proved arson."

"It was just a fire."

"Maybe. The lieutenant said the fire might have been contained, but the sprinkler system malfunctioned. The fire spread very quickly and destroyed the building in half an hour."

"I remember when it burned. It was just days after Dad died. Nothing survived the fire."

"That had to be rough."

She shook her head. "I'm glad he didn't live to see it."

"Was your father the kind of guy who missed critical details like maintenance on a sprinkler system?"

"I never knew him to ever take a shortcut with the museum." She sighed. "But maybe he was planning to get it fixed. His heart attack was very sudden."

"I wonder why he rented and prepaid twenty years for this space."

Angie tensed. "I don't know."

When they reached the unit she opened the big heavy lock with the key. Her hands didn't tremble, but there was tension in her body. The chain dropped free and clanged against the door.

Malcolm reached around her, pushed the door open, and flipped the light switch on. Overhead fluorescent lights flickered on and cast a hard glow on a series of wooden crates. Each box was marked with stenciled letters.

VALENTINE EXHIBIT. NEWMAN ROOM. BANNER ROOM.

Malcolm's gaze skimmed the boxes. "So where do we start?"

Angie rested her hands on her hips. "I don't know."

"You have no idea what's here?"

"None."

"You've known about this place for seven years, and you've never been curious?"

"I wasn't fond of the museum." She shook her head. "That's not true. I hated that place."

"Why?"

"The museum had my father's heart. I knew it, and I think my mother did as well."

He shook his head. "Then why keep this place?"

"I don't know. There was a lot I didn't understand about my father. I guess I hoped one day I might have the strength to see what was so important to him."

"Let's start front to back."

"Right." There had to be forty crates of varying sizes. Their search would take the better part of the afternoon.

Malcolm hefted his crowbar and wedged it under the lip of the first box. With a quick jerk of his wrists, the nails securing the corners came free and the top opened. Foam padding stuffed the box. A little digging and they found vases wrapped in the foam.

"This is going to be a long afternoon," she said.

"Welcome to the world of a cop. We dig through a lot of hay to find that golden needle."

The next several boxes revealed much of the same: a dusty collection of spears, a collection of muskets, paintings, and shards of pottery. Finally, they opened a box that held lots of pictures. They weren't arranged in any kind of order, but each had been marked on the back with a brief description of the scene.

The odd collection appeared to have been taken thirty-plus years ago. Angie discovered an image of her parents.

"That your mother?" Malcolm stared over her shoulder.

"Yes."

"You look like her."

"That's what Eva says, but I don't remember her from her younger days. She was always tired and worn in my memories."

"You have pictures, don't you?"

"No. Father never allowed pictures of Mother in the house. Bad memories for him."

"What about you?" No missing the anger in his voice. "A kid has a right to a picture of her mother."

"Once when I visited her, I took pictures. Dad found them and tossed them. She must have shattered his heart."

"That didn't give him the right to rob you."

She traced the outline of her mother's smiling face. "She was so happy. And young. And Dad never smiled like this."

"Why save the pictures?"

"Who knows? He never even told me about this unit."

There was another picture of Angie as a small child. She had a bright, wide grin as she held both her parents' hands. "This is like staring at an alternate universe. These people look like people I knew, but they sure don't seem to act like them."

"What do you remember about the time your parents were together?"

"Mom stayed out a lot. Dad finally got mad about it. They fought more and more."

"Where was he?"

"Always at the museum. He loved that place."

"What happened after they fought the last time?"

"Mom said she was going to the drug store. She said she'd be right back. But she never did return. It was another five months before I saw her again."

"How old were you?"

"Four. I figured out later that Mom must have been pregnant with Eva. She left Dad and went to live with Blue. After that, I only saw her once in a while."

She studied the pictures taken of her parents. She went silent.

Malcolm shoved the crowbar under the lip of another box and rammed his arm up with brutal force. Wood splintered and cracked. He dug into the box, pushing the batting aside. "Look what we have here."

"What?"

"Looks like employee records."

"Really?"

He thumbed through a file. "A list of anyone who ever worked at the place. The board members are all listed."

"Dad knew all the employees by their first

names. He even remembered the names of wives and children."

Malcolm frowned.

"What?"

"Your father can recite chapter and verse on an employee but can't keep a few lousy pictures of his kid's mother."

"He did the best he could." She set the pictures aside and picked up the crowbar and shoved it under the lip of another box.

"Right." Malcolm glanced at the names.

Her face tight with growing anger and frustration, she drove the tip under another box lip. This time she wrenched so hard the wood on the top of the box splintered.

"Shit," he said.

"What?"

"Louise Cross was a board member at the Talbot."

The edge of the crowbar skipped, and she stumbled forward. She'd have fallen forward if she'd not had the box to steady herself. Her hand slipped into the crate. Immediately, her hand recoiled. "Oh, God."

Malcolm looked up from another journal.

Her face paled. "It's a box of bones."

Inside the storage unit a lightbulb flashed. Paulie Sommers snapped pictures. "Kier, you have radar."

Malcolm pushed away from the wall inside the unit and moved toward the door. Finding the bones had triggered calls to forensics and Garrison.

"How so?"

"My ass hits a soft chair, and you call. No other cop has that talent."

Malcolm grinned. "I do try."

He glanced down the hall to Angie, who stood silent, her arms folded over her chest. They had barely spoken since the bones had been discovered. He'd tried to strike up a conversation, but she'd been too tightly controlled to speak. She'd sunk into a sullen silence that bothered him. She was afraid, and he had the sense she clung to her composure with a death grip.

Dr. Henson appeared at the end of the hallway, ducked under the yellow tape, and strode toward them. She was dressed in jeans and a sweatshirt, both of which were covered in splashes of robin's-egg-blue paint. She'd swept her auburn hair into a ponytail.

The doctor paused when she reached Angie. "Ms. Carlson. What brings you here?"

Angie straightened and let her arms fall to her sides. "The contents of the unit belonged to my father."

The doctor's brow wrinkled. "Memory

serves, he passed away about seven years ago."

Angie nodded. "You've got a good memory."

"I visited his museum several times. Quite interesting. You spend much time there as a kid?"

"No," Angie said. "My father didn't want me around the place."

Dr. Henson let the comment pass. "So let me have a look." In the unit, she extended her hand to Malcolm. "Two crime scenes in a week. We're setting some records here, Detective."

He shook her hand. "Sorry to say, yes. What did we pull you away from?" Malcolm said. He wasn't sure why, but he wanted to lighten the mood for Carlson's sake.

"Painting my library."

"I heard you moved in to a new house."

"I did."

"Got a lot of books?"

She shrugged. "A couple thousand."

"A couple thousand. Really?"

"Sure."

"Anyone else and I'd have called bullshit on them, but you, Doc, I'd believe it. A couple thousand books. Damn."

A frown creased her forehead. "I don't see the humor. Everyone has books."

Angie arched a brow as she came up behind the doctor. "I bet Detective Kier has three and the first two have pictures."

Paulie grunted out a laugh.

Dr. Henson smiled.

Malcolm let the quip pass. Good to see some of Angie's fire return.

The doctor moved past him into the room and went directly to the crate. She glanced into the box.

Squatting, she studied the bones for less than a minute. "Detective Kier."

He came into the room. "Yeah?"

"The bones aren't human."

"Say that again?"

She rose and stripped off her gloves. "Not human. I'd say a bear's hind claw."

"What?"

Paulie snorted his laughter.

"Don't feel bad," the doctor said smoothly. "It has the distinct appearance of a human hand when stripped of the flesh."

Malcolm rubbed the back of his neck with his hand. "Shit."

"What about the other bones?" Angie said.

"Appear to be animal."

"Why have the bones?"

"From what I remember from my trip to the museum, Mr. Talbot was an avid hunter. This likely was one of his kills."

Garrison appeared in the doorway of the unit. Malcolm had faxed museum employee files as well as the names of the board members. It had surprised Malcolm to see that Louise Cross served on the board of the Talbot for a brief time. "You found Gentle Ben?"

"It was his little brother." Malcolm figured he'd never hear the end of it. He'd learned long ago to let the jabs of other cops roll off his back. The more defensive he got, the more they circled, like sharks around blood. "You find anyone of interest?"

Garrison motioned him out into the hallway. "So far, I contacted eight of the thirty names, and all had either died or moved out of the D.C. metro area. Starting to feel like I'm chasing ghosts. Sinclair is running down the last names."

Malcolm glanced back into the room at Angie. He dropped his voice a notch when he asked, "What about Louise Cross?"

Garrison pulled a pack of gum from his pocket. "Her position on the board would have meant she knew the players of that time. But she and the boys were in Europe for that entire summer."

"But she knew Blue, Frank, and Darius. And I'll bet money she knew Fay."

"Do you really believe she'd talk to us?"

385

Garrison said.

"No," Malcolm said. "But she would talk to Eva."

"We've been through this. I won't put her through that."

"She's a big girl," Malcolm said.

"I see what no one else sees," Garrison said. "Louise Cross left her with emotional scars that will never heal. And now that she's pregnant . . ."

"She's pregnant?"

Garrison let some tension ease. "Yeah. We're getting married as soon as we can arrange it."

Malcolm nodded. "I didn't think you had it in you, old man."

"I manage from time to time." Garrison's mood darkened. "I want her to have no contact with that woman."

"Garrison is right," Angie said as she approached.

"What, do you have dog ears?" Malcolm said.

"Just about," she said. "Eva is to be kept out of this." The steel in her voice promised one hell of a fight if anyone tried to do otherwise.

"We need to talk to Louise," Malcolm said.

"She might settle for the next best thing,"

Angie said. "Me."

Malcolm shifted. "You?"

"I'll talk to Louise and ask her any questions you want. Set it up."

It was Malcolm's turn to worry. "It won't be easy for you. I promise if she knows something about your father she will use it against you."

Angie shook her head. "Let her try."

"So I can set it up?" Garrison said.

"As soon as I talk to Micah," Angie countered.

"Him? Why?" Malcolm didn't hide his frustration.

"I need to offer full disclosure. Besides, Micah cooperated fully with police last year. I doubt he'll have an issue with the visit."

"And if he does?"

Her lips flattened. "We'll cross that bridge when we come to it."

"I don't like it."

"Detective Kier, if it was your mother you'd want to know."

"My mother runs a restaurant. She isn't a serial killer serving three consecutive life sentences."

"You'd care even if your mother had three heads. You're the kind of guy who built his world around family."

"Maybe." *Yes.*

"Nearly thirty years is a long time for a killer to remain dormant."

"It's rare but not unlikely." He stared at her, searching for any trepidation. "You aren't afraid to see her?"

"Please. I am the master of mind games. I've interviewed my share of prisoners."

"She's different." He leaned forward and dropped his voice a notch. "We both know it. She might be the key to an active murder case, and you are the key to her."

"So, I play into her fantasies about Eva and then see if I can get her to open up. We have nothing to lose."

He had to agree. "Right now I got nothing on this case. Nothing. I need to take the chance that she will talk."

She shoved out a sigh, turned, and crossed the room to a desk by the window where she'd left her BlackBerry. She checked her calendar. "When do you want to go?"

He crossed, keeping the distance between them at a minimum. "It's a two-hour drive. Would Monday morning work?"

"I've got a seven p.m. meeting with Cross this evening. That will give me the chance to get his approval. You a morning person?"

"I'm any kind of person I need to be."

"How about six a.m. on Monday? I'm not

in court and can make up the work at night."

"Okay."

"You look surprised, Detective."

"I'm used to you throwing up road blocks, not solving problems."

"Believe it or not I do have a soul."

His laugh rang genuine this time. "That's what all the Children of the Night say."

Charlotte arrived at the offices of Wellington and James at six-fifteen. She and Angie were scheduled to have a seven p.m. meeting with Micah Cross to discuss the contract she'd drawn up.

Charlotte liked to arrive early. It gave her time to prepare and run through her check-list. Doors locked? Windows secured? Closets bad-guy free? She could refrain from the routine when Iris or Angie were here, but when she was alone she checked all the places bad guys could hide.

Stupid. Illogical.

In fact her therapist would encourage her to have a "conversation" with the empty spaces and ask *them* why *they* scared her so much.

"Well," she muttered, "because three years ago a lunatic had slipped into my office and shot me in my gut."

The absurdity of her train of thought would have made her smile if it all wasn't so pathetic. She raised her finger to the keypad on the front door, a grocery sack filled with cookies and fruits dangling from her arm. She'd ventured into the grocery and bought a few refreshments for today's meeting.

It was a good and polite thing to offer guests refreshments. It was something she'd never done naturally — sharing always went against her grain. But she'd learned that refined women offered tea and cookies.

She pushed open the door. The alarm dinged its countdown as she moved across the room to the keypad and punched in the code: *Mariah.*

Setting her bags down, she turned to re-lock the front door and get ready for her meeting. To her surprise, Micah Cross stood in the doorway. He wore a camel coat that cut him mid-calf, a dark suit, and a white turtleneck. His highly polished shoes reflected the porch light.

In one fluid move, Charlotte jumped, screamed, and dropped her grocery bag. The sound of glass breaking signaled that the bottle of honey she'd bought had broken. "Micah!"

He held up his smooth hands in surrender. "I didn't mean to scare you. I thought you heard me call your name from across the street."

Her heart pounded so hard she feared it would crack through her chest. "I didn't hear."

Breathe. Breathe. Shit!

"I scared you."

"No. Just startled me." She kept her fears in close check. But right now they ran rampant like marauding Huns, laying waste to all good sense.

He maintained his distance as if sensing her fear. "We have a meeting."

"Yes. Yes. I know." She glanced at the bag crumpled around her feet but couldn't quite take her gaze off of Micah. This was so not like her. She got rattled all the time, but she could function. Now she felt like a deer caught in a hunter's sites.

"The meeting was for six-thirty."

"I had seven on my calendar." She sighed. He was just early.

"God, no wonder I scared you."

"Not scared." And to prove it she gritted her teeth and gathered the strawberries that had rolled out on the carpet. "Just startled. But I'm fine." Right now if she had a moment she'd talk to her fear and ask it, *What the fuck gives? Stop rattling me!*

She rose, clutching her bag in a white-knuckle grip. "We just got our wires crossed. Happens all the time."

He jabbed his thumb toward the door. "I can leave and come back. We can do this at seven."

"No. No. This is silly. I've got the contracts all drawn up and ready to sign." She offered a weary smile. "I planned to offer you strawberries, but I'm afraid they're bruised now."

"I appreciate the gesture." He clasped his hands together. "Could we head to the back and sign the contracts? That really would suit. I've got a meeting with my marketing department at eight."

"Sure. Sure. Let's go." She glanced toward the darkened hallway that cut through the center of her office. She hated the dark. But to show weakness would ruin her reputation. Ball busters didn't worry about what went bump in the night.

Squaring her shoulders, she moved to the hallway and flipped on the light. She expected her nerves to settle once the fluorescents kicked in, but her nerves still danced and tweaked.

She smiled at Micah. "Have a seat in the conference room. I'll get those contracts."

"Sounds like a plan."

She hurried to her office, dumped her bag in a chair, and pressed trembling hands to her flushed face. "God, this is such bullshit." Her doctor had suggested medication, but she'd flatly refused. Now that she stood at the edge of a major panic attack she questioned the decision not to take meds.

The chime covering the front door dinged. To Charlotte's relief she heard Angie say, "I'm here! Is everything all right? The door wasn't locked."

Charlotte wasn't alone. She would be fine. She shrugged off her coat and smoothed her hands over her waist. "In here. Mr. Cross and I were just about to review the contracts."

Angie ducked into Charlotte's office. "He's here? Did I mess up the time?"

Charlotte shook her head. "No. He did," she whispered. "He startled me, and I forgot to lock the door. So stupid."

Angie gripped the handle of her briefcase. "You okay?"

"Great. And I'm ready to sign some papers."

"All right." Angie studied her. "You sure you're okay?"

"Right as rain."

They found Micah standing in the conference room, his hands clasped behind his back as he studied a painting on the wall. They all exchanged pleasantries, took seats at the table, and reviewed the contracts. As they were ready to sign, Angie cleared her throat.

"In the interest of full disclosure I want to tell you that the police asked me to travel to Statesville and visit your mother."

Micah sat back in his chair. "My mother? Why? Has she been writing Eva again?"

"No. This has to do with a case that goes back nearly thirty years." She explained where she'd been most of the day.

Charlotte's fragile control ebbed as she listened to Angie explain the situation. *What the hell?*

Her mind skipped from the odd announcement to the billable hours that would fly out on Monday while Angie gallivanted around the countryside playing junior detective. But with Micah present, she didn't air her thoughts.

"Of course you should go," Micah said. "And let me know if I can be of any help."

Angie smiled. "Thanks."

It was all very civilized and normal, and yet Charlotte could not shake the sense that something was wrong.

Intellectually she knew her fears linked directly to her post-traumatic stress, but on an emotional level she simply sensed danger that was as real to her as the breeze that blew outside or the table and chairs in the room.

As the clock chimed in midnight, he rose from the bed and stared down at his angel of death.

He'd spent almost twenty hours with her. Too much time. He had to let her go.

Now he warmed the water to one hundred and ten degrees. Too warm and the heat would scar and discolor the bones. Too cool and the flesh-stripping process took too long.

And he wanted the bones stripped and ready to present soon.

He knelt down and lifted the woman's body. Lifeless, her frame felt heavy, unwieldy, and stiff as he lifted her and laid her into the water. She floated for just an instant before sinking, her face slowly descending below the muddy surface. Blond hair skimmed the surface as if clinging to the light, but the weight of her body slowly sucked all traces of hair and bone below the surface.

He checked his watch. It would take thirty-six hours before most of the flesh fell from the bones. He'd bleach the bones, and then he'd find the perfect place to display them.

He dipped his fingertips in the water and swirled them around in circles.

He wanted Kier and Garrison to find his work of art and to wonder and search. He wanted to see the fear and concern as they all tried to guess if there would be more victims.

And of course, there would be more.

He'd been careful to cover all his tracks. He'd created so many fail-safe scenarios that no one would ever find him.

He had finally escaped the shackles of fear.

No one would ever catch him.

And he was free to kill for years to come.

CHAPTER 21

Monday, October 10, 9 a.m.

The ride south to the correctional facility took just under two hours. Kier drove, dodging in and out of the morning rush of traffic with a lightning quickness that took Angie's breath away. A couple of times she gripped the door when he skittered behind an eighteen-wheeler, but she said nothing. Several times she caught the hint of a smile on his lips. He was enjoying this. He liked the speed and the fast pace. And the fact that she was on edge was icing on the cake.

But worrying about traffic and near misses was preferable to obsessing about the woman they were about to visit.

Louise Cross was a true sociopath. The world, as far as she was concerned, revolved around her.

She'd justified her killing spree last year by crying revenge. She'd killed to avenge her dead son Josiah, who had been murdered. However, her vengeance had taken on a life unto itself. Once she'd killed those she'd believed were guilty of her son's death, she'd gone after Eva, the one person who'd had nothing to do with the crime.

Angie believed if Louise had not been stopped she'd have continued to kill. The taste of blood, once she'd savored her first sip, was too sweet to forget. She craved death and killing like an addict.

As they pulled up in front of the stone and barbwired gates of the prison, she let a sigh of relief seep out through her clenched teeth. "I'd say you set a land-speed record today, Detective."

He shut off the engine and faced her. "Sorry, no records today."

She brushed imaginary lint from her lap. "You're joking?"

"The traffic slowed me down. I'll bet I shave twenty minutes on the return trip."

"Please don't rush on my account. Really." She got out of the car, savoring the crunch of steady, solid ground under her feet.

"Ah, come on, Counselor, where's your sense of adventure?" He closed his door and came around to her side of the car.

"I save it for vacations." She glanced up at the prison's gray walls, swallowing the tightness in her throat.

"So what is your idea of a good vacation? And please tell me you're not one of those people who like to lie on the beach and bake."

She appreciated his attempts to distract her, even if they didn't quite work. "No, that's not for me."

They moved toward the central office, where Kier checked his gun. They passed through a metal detector, and the guards searched Angie's purse.

"I don't see you on vacation," he said. "I see you toiling away twenty-four/seven, three hundred and sixty-five days a year."

She thought back to her last vacation. Was it three years ago? Or four? "I dance on the wild side occasionally."

He laughed. "Like one of those cruises where they feed you all day while you sit in deck chairs?"

"On my last vacation I hiked Kilimanjaro."

He raised a brow. "You're kidding?"

"Nope. I love the outdoors. I spend so much time inside for the job that I get out whenever I can."

"Never would have figured that of you."

Their banter carried her through security and down the hallway to the visiting center. Because Louise was high risk, Angie would speak to her through a thick glass pane using a telephone. But of course that was assuming Louise showed. She was within her rights to refuse the interview.

Angie took her seat in the hard plastic chair in front of the viewing window. Kier clasped his hands behind his back and stood with his feet braced, a silent sentry. He'd not told her he'd be there for her if things got rough, but she knew he would.

Her back ramrod straight, Angie did her best to shove her nerves aside. Louise would latch on to any visible weakness and use it against her.

"It'll be fine," Kier said softly, clearly.

She caught his reflection in the glass. He stared at her. "I know."

"Relax your shoulders."

She shrugged them up and down. "They are relaxed."

A hint of a smile tipped the edge of his lips. "Your spine looks ready to snap. Louise will see your fear and use it."

"I'm not afraid." How could he see her fear? She'd buried it deep below the surface.

He held her gaze in the reflection. "It will be fine."

The door on the other side of the glass opened. The movement made Angie flinch. She recovered quickly and folded her hands in her lap.

In the next instant Louise Cross entered the interview cell. She wore an oversized orange jumpsuit. Her gray curly hair hung wild and untamed around her face. Louise Cross might be an unfeeling monster, but the added lines around her eyes and mouth proved that prison had taken a toll on her.

Louise's eyes, dark as a bottomless pit, flickered and sparked to life when she saw Angie. Through her narrowed gaze, she studied Angie for long, tense seconds before taking a seat and lifting the phone to her ear.

Angie raised the phone and glimpsed the reflection of Kier doing the same. "Thank you for seeing me, Mrs. Cross."

The woman brightened, clearly savoring Angie's respectful tone. Sociopaths believed they were the center of the universe and expected others to believe the same. Likely, Louise hadn't got much kid-glove treatment since she'd arrived here.

"This is a surprise, Miss Carlson." Louise's voice telegraphed delight. "Have you come about your sister?"

"I was hoping you could help me with background on an old murder."

"An old murder? That is intriguing." Louise grabbed a tendril of gray hair and twisted it between her fingertips. "Who?"

"Fay Willow. She worked for my father at the Talbot Museum."

Louise nodded. "I remember Fay from my days on the museum board. She was a lovely young girl. She was having an affair with my husband. Darius enjoyed his lovely young girls."

"Darius was sleeping with Fay?"

"You didn't know?"

"I suspected but wasn't sure."

"Rest assured, Darius was sleeping with her."

Angie studied Louise's face closely. "Fay was murdered."

"Yes. It took a while to identify her, as I remember. Reduced to bones." Louise smiled as if she'd just remembered a private joke.

Angie eased forward on her seat a fraction. "Do you know who killed her?"

Louise sat back in her chair, her shoulders relaxed. She liked playing games, especially when she had the upper hand. "If I talk, I want him to leave." Louise's gaze remained on Angie.

In the glass's reflection she saw Kier shift his stance as if bracing for a fight. He wasn't going anywhere.

Angie, like Kier, understood power plays.

And it was important to establish which person really was in charge of the interview. "Kier stays."

Louise smiled. "He leaves. Or I don't talk."

Angie shrugged. "Then don't talk." She hung up her phone, rose, and turned. Her posture was rigid just as it was when she faced a jury or judge.

Kier hung up his phone, no trace of dispute in his expression.

Angie crossed the small room in a handful of strides and wrapped long fingers around the door handle. She was betting Louise was starved for information and would compromise to get it.

A rap on the glass had Angie hesitating and smiling. Another more forceful rap had her losing the smile and turning.

Louise motioned for her to pick up her phone.

Kier's face remained turned from the viewing window as he whispered, "Bingo."

In no real rush Angie moved back to the phone. She picked up the receiver but did not sit down. Kier raised his receiver to his ear.

"He can stay," Louise said. "But he doesn't ask the questions."

"It's my interview," Angie said. "Not his."

403

"Okay. I'll chat with you about Fay, but first I want to know how Eva is doing."

Louise went right for Angie's weakest spot, a favorite courtroom tactic of her own. However, recognizing Louise's tactic didn't diminish the stab of apprehension. Louise Cross had developed a fan following since her arrest, and Angie didn't want to expose her sister to any danger.

"She's doing well, Mrs. Cross."

Dark eyes glistened. "Does she talk about me often?"

Angie understood how this game was played. Give Louise a little of what she wanted, and maybe she'd get what she needed. "She mentioned you the other day."

Louise leaned toward the glass a fraction. "What did she say about me?"

"She admires your intelligence." That wasn't untrue. But Angie had carefully omitted Eva's utter disgust for the brutal woman who'd slaughtered women and branded Eva.

"She admires my brains." Louise sounded pleased. "That's saying a lot. She's a genius."

"Tell me about Fay," Angie said.

"I want to hear more about Eva."

"Not yet."

Louise narrowed her gaze as if she was

clearly wondering how much she could push. "Fay Willow worked for your father for two years. I saw her from time to time when I sat on the board."

"Who do you think might have killed her?"

Louise laughed. "You mean you can't figure that one out?"

Angie said nothing, just stared at Louise.

Louise ran gnarled hands through her coarse gray hair. "Darius killed her."

"You know that for certain?"

"Oh, I can't prove it. But I know. Fay had dreams of being the next Mrs. Cross. I heard them arguing once. Darius of course was not going to let a little whore dictate what he did or did not do. No matter what she did for him in or out of bed." She smiled. "And I was in Europe with the boys when she died. So you won't be able to pin that one on me."

"As you said, her bones were stripped. Someone must have been helping Darius. He didn't dirty his hands."

Louise shook her head. "Is Eva still dating Garrison?"

Angie hesitated. "They broke up six months ago."

The lies tripped off her tongue without effort or hesitation. She sensed Kier's gaze and could almost hear him reminding her

405

that Louise couldn't be trusted.

Louise nodded. "I didn't think they'd make it. There is too much darkness in her. She's a lot like her father."

Angie swallowed her rebut. "You knew Blue Rayburn?"

"Sure. Is Eva still in school?"

"Yes."

Louise twisted a strand of hair between her fingers. "She should be graduating soon."

"Blue was head of security for my father at the museum."

"Head of security. Is that what your father told you?" Amusement sparked. "Make no mistake, my dear girl, Blue worked for Darius, not your father."

"Darius? No, he worked for my father."

"Darius called the shots from the moment he gave your father that big fat donation check."

Hadn't Eva said that Darius always had a hidden agenda? "What did Darius have to do with the museum?"

Louise shook her head. "My turn. Does Eva still have the scar?"

Frustration mingled with fury. "Yes."

"She'll always remember me."

Bitch. "What interest did Blue and Darius have in the museum?"

Louise leaned forward, pleasure deepening the lines on her face. "I'll tell Eva. Have her come and ask me."

"Eva is not coming here."

"Why? I only want to talk." She raised her hands, the shackles dangling and clanking together. "I can't hurt anyone."

"Tell me what Blue and Darius's connection was to the museum, and I'll talk to Eva about writing you a letter."

"I want the letter first."

"No."

Louise moistened her lips. For long, tense seconds she didn't answer, and then: "Darius said once he'd strip Fay of all her humanity if she ever went up against him."

And then it hit Angie. "They stripped her bones using the museum's facility."

"Not they, my dear — your father. Frank Carlson stripped the flesh from Fay's bones, just as he stripped the flesh from the animals in his museum."

"My father wouldn't do that."

"Of course he would. He loved you. Knowing Darius, my husband promised to do awful things to you if your father didn't play along."

All the years her father had pushed her away and kept her from the museum . . . he had been protecting her.

"Why not just bury her?"

"Darius wanted a memento of his time with Fay. My guess is that he saved one of the bones. Human bone can look like ivory when it's carved and polished."

Angie thought about the walking stick that Darius had always carried. It had been crowned with an ivory figurine. Oh, God. "Blue was involved as well?"

"Like I said, Blue did a lot of things for Darius. Taking care of Fay was just one job of many." Louise picked at the chains linking her arms.

"There was another recent killing. Bones stripped like Fay's were found."

"Interesting. I didn't think Fay's death was of real interest to you. You're here to solve that case."

"Yes."

"Now that is a puzzle. Who would want to kill this woman and then strip the flesh from her bones as your father once did for Darius? No one on my side could have done it. Josiah is dead, and Micah is too weak to kill a fly, let alone a woman. Maybe it was you."

"What?"

"Maybe you killed the woman, and maybe you're here to keep the good detective guessing."

When Angie didn't react to the bait, Louise added, "It broke your father's heart when your mother left him."

In that moment she didn't have the strength to stand and walk away.

"But Blue Rayburn was a hard man to resist. And Marian wanted so much more excitement than her dull little life offered. Blue was hard competition for a man who loved his books and specimens." Louise licked her lips. "But to be fair to your mother, I can see a woman leaving her husband for Blue. God knows I wanted to leave Darius at times, and Blue would have been the man to tempt me."

Angie said nothing, not really trusting her voice now.

"But to leave you, her child," Louise said. "Now, that is a different kind of woman altogether. I never would have willingly left my boys. But I guess you were just too much of a reminder of Marian's lackluster marriage."

Angie hesitated. "You misjudge my mother."

"I remember seeing you at museum functions when you were two or three. You were a happy child. Later, after the divorce, you were quite sullen."

The sharp edge of Louise's words sliced

through her strength. All she wanted to do was run from this room. "Fay also had a boyfriend, other than Darius. What was his name?"

"I don't know. Let your detective friend figure that one out. Get me a letter from Eva and maybe I might remember more. Like what Darius and Blue were really doing at the museum."

Angie had reached the end of the interview. Louise had given all she was going to until she received communication from Eva.

Angie would not beg or plead with Louise Cross, nor would she ever involve Eva. She could only hope this visit had piqued the old woman's interest so that she could return and ask more questions. "Thank you, Mrs. Cross, for your time."

She set the phone down. When she faced Kier, she could see the anger brewing below the stony surface. She walked stiffly toward the door.

A rap on the glass had Angie turning. Louise stood at the glass, laughing so hard that tears ran down her cheeks.

Angie could barely breathe as she hurried toward the security checkpoint. She wanted to get the hell out of this prison. Her hands trembled as she collected her purse from the guards and moved back through the scanner.

Kier was on her heels, shoving his gun in its holster and collecting his badge. He caught up to her but said nothing as they walked outside. The morning sun had warmed, and she tipped her head back to absorb the heat and energy.

"Do you remember the cane Darius used?" Angie asked.

"He was before my time."

"It's a piece of Fay."

"We don't know that."

A shiver burned through her limbs. "We locked gazes during the trial. He raised the head of that cane at me during Eva's trial." She smoothed her hand over her hair. "I can't believe my father would have helped Darius hide a murder."

"I don't completely trust anything she said."

She shoved out a sigh. "I hope you're right."

"What else do you remember about Darius?"

"He liked ivory. He had cuff links. A tie clip. I remember them all from Eva's trial years ago. Dear God."

"Don't get ahead of yourself. Louise is a master at jabbing old wounds," Kier said.

"I knew that going into the interview." A

breeze blew across the parking lot, teasing wisps of hair that had escaped her bun.

"Knowing and feeling are two different things."

"Don't feel sorry for me. I'm a big girl, and I can take it." She checked her watch, wishing she could teleport back to Alexandria and put this whole scene behind her. "What's your driving record for the trip north?"

"One hour forty-five."

"Let's see if you can break it."

When Connor Donovan's contact in the prison had told him Angie had scheduled a last-minute visit with Louise Cross, his interest had been stirred. He'd watched as Kier had picked her up at her house and quickly merged on I-95 South. He'd been unable to match Kier's pace, but knowing where they were going had allowed him to hold back.

Now as he sat in his car, parked across from the women's detention facility, and watched them leave, he wondered why she'd bothered to visit.

The Sorority House Murders were closed. And Kier's most active investigation was Sierra Day, a woman who likely didn't know Louise Cross existed.

So why did Carlson and Kier travel the two hours south? He picked up his phone and dialed. When his call was answered on the third ring he said, "Robert, I have another job for you."

Minutes after Malcolm dropped Angie off at her house, his phone rang. He maneuvered into traffic as he flipped it open. "Detective Kier."

"How did it go at the prison?" Garrison said.

"I'll fill you in when I see you. What's up?"

"We've found more bones."

Shit. "Where?"

"In an alley off of Temple."

"Give me the address. I'll be right there."

He arrived in the alley ten minutes later. Ten squad cars flanked the alley and the street around it. Yellow crime-scene tape roped off the alley. Forensics was on scene, and he saw the flash of a camera.

He found Garrison, who stood at the lip of the alley, his hands on his hips. "The trash man found her bones piled by the Dumpster. These bones aren't as clean as the others. The killer might have felt rushed."

"He's anxious for our attention?"

"Could be."

"You said 'her.' " The alley smelled of rotting food and urine.

Garrison shoved his hands into his pockets. "A guess by forensics."

Malcolm glanced around, searching for surveillance cameras. He didn't see any. "Witnesses?"

"The alley serves a grocery store on one side and a liquor store on the other side. Both were closed at midnight last night, and both proprietors did not see the bones at that time."

"They were brought here last night?"

"Or very early this morning."

"Any bones missing?"

Garrison nodded. "The femur bone."

He relayed what Louise had said about Darius's fascination with bones. "Whoever is killing these women is keeping their bones as trophies, maybe even making them into things he likes to carry or display."

Garrison shoved out a breath. "Darius Cross is dead."

"Fay's old boyfriend has got to be in his fifties."

"At least," Garrison said. "Whoever is behind this was a player then and now."

"Or knew someone that was."

"Like Angie Carlson?"

Malcolm shook his head. "She looked

414

pretty shaken when Louise told her Frank Carlson helped dispose of a body."

"I'll bet." Garrison shook his head. "She's the common denominator for all the victims."

"We know who this victim is?"

"Contact Lulu Sweet's mother and see if she has dental records on file. I'll bet money we found Angie's missing client."

Malcolm thought about that gooey kid with the sloppy grin. "Will do."

CHAPTER 22

Tuesday, October 11, 6 a.m.

The cool waters of the pool did little to soothe Angie's ragged nerves. All night she'd tossed and turned and thought of her parents: her stern father, her vivacious mother, and the marriage that had imploded. She imagined her father relenting to Darius Cross's demands. Could he really have helped dispose of Fay's body?

Her father had never once spoken of his work at the museum and the dark tasks Darius had required of him. Was Fay the only woman Darius had killed, stripped of flesh, and turned into a trophy?

Angie dug deeper into the water, pulling against it as if the exercise could drive all the frustration and sadness from her body.

She paused at the wall, her lungs screaming for air. Her muscles demanded a respite. She pulled her goggles from her head and set them on the concrete lip of the pool.

"You're tearing that water up."

She glanced to the lane beside her and saw that swimmer guy. What was his name? Martin.

Water clung to his dark hair. "How goes it? You look a bit driven today."

She pulled her goggles up. "It's been one of those weeks."

This close she could see that he had blue, blue eyes that made her want to stare. No doubt he'd heard a million comments about his eyes, and she did not wish to join the legion of women who likely followed him. Had her mother once looked into Blue Rayburn's eyes and felt the same tingle of excitement?

"I haven't seen you here for a couple of days," he said. He swam faster than she did, even today, and he was barely winded.

"Work. Gets in the way of life."

He laughed, flashing even white teeth. Her spirits lifted just being near him.

"So what's on your agenda today?"

"Paperwork. Lots of it." She never discussed work with anyone except Eva. Donovan had planted that seed of distrust.

In one fluid move Martin hoisted himself out of the pool and sat on the edge. "Well, if you can ever tear yourself away, Angie, we can grab coffee one morning."

"Thanks, Martin. I'll see how the work goes."

He cocked a brow. "Remember, Angie, there's always work to be done. But the moments when we can really enjoy our lives aren't so frequent."

Her name sounded sexy when he spoke it. "I'll keep that in mind."

He stood and walked toward the steam room. She liked the shape of his body and the way he filled out his suit. It had been a long time since she'd had sex. Suddenly she was painfully aware of it.

"That dirty look could get you arrested in half the world."

Kier's voice startled her and had her turning to face him. Dark circles hung under his eyes, and he wore the clothes he'd had on yesterday.

Heat burned her face. "It wasn't that kind of look."

He grinned. "Of course it was."

"Fine. You caught me. What can I say? I really do have blood in my veins."

"Hey, no need to be defensive. Nice to know there's fire in your belly."

She pushed out of the water and stood. The cold air brushed her skin. Her nipples hardened. Kier's gaze dropped, lingered, and then rose to her eyes. He slid his hand into his pocket, managing to look relaxed and powerful all in an instant.

"You didn't just come here to harass me." She slipped on her flip-flops and reached for her towel.

Everything about Kier had to do with purpose and reason. "No."

In the open air, her skin chilled. Goosebumps puckered her flesh as she dried her skin. "Why are you here?"

All traces of desire vanished from his gaze. "We've found another body."

"Lulu." The word was a faint whisper.

"For now it's a body. But Dr. Henson has Lulu's dental records and promises a confirmation soon."

She clutched her towel. Oh, God. She'd barely known the girl, but that didn't stem the sharp pang of sadness. She thought about David. Did he feel alone and abandoned? She hoped not. "Have you said anything to her mother?"

"Not yet."

"If the body is Lulu I'd like to go with you when you talk to Vivian."

"Death notices aren't nice, Counselor."

"No, I don't suppose they are."

"I'll call you when we have a confirmation."

"Thanks. Does Eva know?"

"Garrison is telling her."

"Good."

"We released Sierra Day's body for burial. Her husband has scheduled the funeral for Tuesday of next week. Says he wants it all behind him."

"Right."

His phone vibrated. He glanced down at a text message. The lines in his face deepened. He appeared to age ten years in seconds. "Dr. Henson has identified the body. It's Lulu Sweet."

"If you give me ten minutes, I'll change and go with you to see Mrs. Sweet."

"Sure."

Donovan stood at the back entrance to the restaurant waiting for his contact to emerge. She was late. Impatient, he took a long pull on his cigarette and let the smoke seep slowly from his mouth and nostrils. He'd never been a smoker until last year, and then after the stabbing and the nightmares he'd found smokes calmed his nerves, especially when he had to hang out in alleys waiting for nitwits from the medical examiner's office.

They'd agreed that meeting at the medical center would be too obvious. Since last year's coverage, Donovan's much-guarded anonymity had been destroyed, and too many people, especially in cop circles, knew his face.

A thin woman peeked her head out of the back of the door and quickly spotted him leaning against the wall. "Let's make this quick," she said.

Donovan inhaled from his cigarette. "Fast or slow. Doesn't matter to me."

She rolled her eyes and dug a folded piece of paper from her pocket. "You said to call if we got more bones in the medical examiner's office."

His senses perked. "That's right, babe. What do you have?"

"We had a Jane Doe delivered early this morning. Nothing but bones, stripped almost as clean as the last."

He lifted a brow. "Really."

A grin tugged at the end of thin lips. "And for an extra hundred, I'll tell you her name."

"The cops have her name already?"

She glanced from side to side to make sure no one had spotted them. "Apparently they've been looking for a chick."

He snapped his fingers. "Name. Give me the name."

"The hundred first, pal."

He dug five twenties out of his pocket and handed them to her. "Now."

"Lulu Sweet."

"Lulu Sweet? The hooker in the Dixon case?"

"Yep."

Angie Carlson had torn her apart. Another connection to Carlson. On some days life didn't get much better.

"How did you ID her so fast?"

"Dental records."

"How'd she die?"

"Anybody's guess."

"Where was she found?"

"Laid out by a Dumpster near Temple and Redemption Streets."

"Redemption? That's interesting." He pulled in a lungful of smoke. "Who called in her missing persons report?"

"From what I hear on the grapevine it was her attorney. Carlson someone."

"Carlson was representing Sweet?"

"Custody thing, I hear."

He pulled an extra fifty from his pocket. "You hear Carlson's name come up at all again, you call."

"Why do you care about her?"

"I'm going to nail her to the cross."

Dr. Dixon studied the picture of Angie Carlson. He'd taken it a couple of weeks ago when she'd been walking out of King's.

Hair the color of ripened wheat brushed her shoulders as a light breeze teased the edges upward. Frowning, she'd looked both ways before she crossed the street toward her car.

He traced the lines creasing her forehead. "You need to relax. You need to stop worrying. You need someone who can look after you."

His phone buzzed. He lifted his gaze to the receiver as he carefully tucked the picture in his middle drawer. "Dixon."

"Your next appointment is here."

"Right. Thank you."

He rose, tugged the edge of his sweater vest down, and adjusted the collar of his white lab jacket. The door opened, and his secretary extended her arm. "You can go right in."

Dr. Dixon tensed as he came around the desk and extended his hand. Aware that his nurse was watching, he smiled. "Welcome."

The man smiled. "Thank you, Doctor."

When his nurse shut the door, he pulled his hand free and backed up a step. "What are you doing here?"

The man sat back and folded his arms together. "I need some professional advice."

Dixon glanced toward the door, wondering if he should lock it. He opted not to turn the dead bolt for fear his nurse would hear and wonder. Just play this smooth and easy. Normal.

"What kind of professional advice do you want?"

"Plastic surgery of course." His smooth, even voice had the power to shred Dixon's nerves.

As tempted as Dixon was to sit behind his desk, he took the chair next to his newest patient. "Do you want to change your face?"

"Good God, no. I'm fairly fond of my face."

"Then what?" His gaze roamed over the man, who kept his body trim and his muscles sculpted.

The man stared at him, hesitating. "I have a few scars I'd like removed."

"Scars?" In all the time Dixon had spent with this man they'd never discussed scars. But then their relationship wasn't built on trust but dark murderous tastes begging to be fed. Dixon recognized that he was a sexual sadist, and his friend liked to kill. Dixon found his release when a woman screamed in pain. His partner found satisfaction when the light drained from her eyes.

Each was smart enough to know their individual desires would eventually draw the attention of the police. However, together, they could be unstoppable.

Dixon wanted to ask about Lulu Sweet. Was she dead? Had he discarded the bones? But that had been their number-one rule after their initial agreement. No talking shop. Ever. And so they'd maintained an oddly impersonal relationship. Barely a word was spoken when his partner would deliver a woman to Dixon, and even less was said when Dixon handed her back for the final act.

"How old are the scars?" Dixon pulled a pen from his front coat pocket and clicked the tip.

"No notes. No records, please."

Dixon set the pen and paper down on the desk. "Yes, of course."

"Thank you." He pulled an imaginary piece of lint from his pant leg. "The scars are old. I've had them since I was a teenager."

"What caused the scars?"

"Does it matter?"

"Yes. It will help me determine treatment."

"I was burned."

Dixon made several notes. "I've had some success with laser treatment."

"I don't want surgery. Anesthesia can dull

the mind and make people say things they should not."

"There are ways to numb your skin so that you would be fully awake and fully conscious."

"Perfect."

"Mind if I examine the scars?"

"Sure." He rose and moved through the connecting door into an exam room. He sat on the table and pulled off his shirt. He had a well-muscled flat stomach and a sprinkle of hair on his chest, but the lower part of his belly was disfigured with puckered, pink flesh.

Dixon nodded. "This must have been terribly painful."

"It was."

"These are deep. It could take quite a few laser treatments, and even then it won't be perfect. The skin will never be like it was."

"I'm hoping you can get rid of it all."

"I don't know."

"It's important that you try. They link me to a past that I want to release completely."

"Sure."

He pulled his shirt back on. "When can we start?"

"I can schedule you next Tuesday."

"Any time after two would work. I have a one o'clock appointment."

The obits page in the paper had listed Sierra Day's funeral for Tuesday of next week. Dixon had sense enough to stay away from the event, which would be crawling with cops. He prayed his friend had the same kind of sense.

"Tell me you are not going to her funeral." He lifted his gaze. "I *need* to know. Are you going?"

The man raised an index finger to his lips. "It's none of your business if I do or don't."

Dixon lowered his voice a notch. "We agreed to stay away."

"I know what we agreed to."

"So what are you doing?"

He shrugged. "I wasn't the first to break the rules."

"What do you mean?"

He leaned forward and flashed even white teeth. "You want to keep her all to yourself, don't you?"

"What are you talking about?"

"You've been following Ms. Carlson."

"I've not been following Angie."

A thick eyebrow arched. "So it's Angie now?"

"It's always been Angie. She was my attorney. And I went to see her because the cops came to see me. I needed legal advice."

"Please, you did not need advice. You

wanted to see her, to smell her." His eyes danced with glee. "Don't feel bad — I've thought about her too." He leaned forward and whispered, "I've thought about the warmth draining from her skin as I choke the life out of her lungs."

Dixon's tension ratcheted up. He'd often thought about keeping Angie all to himself. "I don't want her to die."

"That's the deal. You play. I kill."

"I know. But she's different."

The man shook his head as he hopped off the table. "She's not different. She's just like the others. She's a whore. Willing to sell her soul for fame, relief, or power. You fill in the blank."

Dixon's anger simmered below the surface. "I want her."

"I can see that." He leaned forward. "But you can't have her for yourself. We share. That's the deal."

Dixon fisted his fingers. "I can stop you. I can stop you from killing her."

Lightning-quick reflexes sent the man's hand shooting up to Dixon's throat. He tightened his hold, choking the breath. "You cannot stop me. No one can stop me."

Dixon clawed at the hands around his throat. "Let me go."

"Say it. Say that you can't stop me." He

428

squeezed his fingers, bending cartilage and bone to the point of breaking. "Say it."

Dixon twisted his neck trying to break free. His lungs screamed for air. "Fine. I can't stop you."

The pressure eased just a fraction to allow him to speak but not really to breathe. "And?"

"I'll do what you say."

He released Dixon's neck. Instantly Dixon sucked in air. He'd only been afraid three times in his life. When he'd found his girlfriend's killer leaning over her dead body all those years ago. The second time had been when Garrison had arrested him for attempted murder. Garrison questioned Dixon for hours about Lulu and the missing prostitutes. The cop had sworn to link Dixon to all the women. But he'd kept quiet, knowing silence would serve him as it had in the past.

The third time was now. Now he was afraid of this partner he had brought into his life. He hoped silence would be enough to save him this time.

The ride to Vivian Sweet's house was solemn and quiet. A heaviness had settled on Angie's shoulders, and she found emotions kept jabbing her.

Malcolm pulled up in front of the small house and waited for her as she walked around the front of the car. He followed her up the front walk. She rang the bell.

Vivian appeared seconds later. The lines on her face deepened when she saw them. Her eyes were bloodshot, and her face pale. "I dreamed about her last night. I dreamed that she'd died."

Malcolm drew in a breath.

But it was Angie that spoke. "Her body was identified early this morning."

"Identified this morning. You couldn't tell it was her just by looking at her?" Her knees buckled, and Angie pushed forward and caught her under the arm. She guided Vivian inside and helped her sit on the couch.

"I'm so sorry, Mrs. Sweet."

"How did she die?"

"We've yet to determine that," Malcolm said. His voice held a tenderness she'd never heard before.

The silence in the house tweaked Angie's senses. "Where is the baby? Where is David?"

"In his bed asleep. He's been cranky all morning. He must sense that his mama is gone."

"Do you have someone who can stay with you?" Angie said. "Someone who can help you with the baby?"

"Got a neighbor who said she'd come by. Should be here soon."

"Good. You shouldn't be alone." Vivian needed care, but so did the baby. And Vivian, her body so fragile and worn as it was, didn't have the strength to care for him now.

"I can call social services," Malcolm said.

"That's not necessary," Angie said. "Vivian and her neighbor can watch out for him today."

Malcolm shifted his weight as if wrestling with a new frustration. "Right. But what about tomorrow?"

Vivian looked up at Angie, her eyes watery and red. "He's right about tomorrow. I don't have it in me to take care of him. I was barely holding on, hoping Lulu would return. Now I just don't know what I'm going to do."

The idea of turning the boy over to strangers or social services made her sick. "I'll help you figure out something. I promise."

"Did she suffer?" Vivian said. "Did my girl suffer?"

Angie did not want to lie, but the truth could not be good. Her killer had stripped the flesh from her bones for a reason. "She's at peace now."

Vivian dropped her face to her hands and

cried. For long, tense minutes Malcolm stood over them while Angie patted the woman on the back. And then in a split second the front doorbell rang, and the baby wailed.

"I'll get the door," Malcolm said.

Angie nodded and rose, knowing she'd take care of David. She found the boy standing in his crib holding on to the railing. His eyes were watery, and he clutched a pacifier in his mouth. He smiled when he saw Angie. She grinned and picked him up. The weight of his diaper told her he needed a change. She'd never changed a diaper before, but how hard could it be? She carried him to the changing table.

"Hey, guy," she said.

He raised his hands and grabbed her lip.

She laughed, pulled his hand away, and kissed his palm. "I don't know much about diapers, but I can manage."

He kicked and squirmed as she unsnapped his pants. She stared at the diaper, not quite sure what to do first. She smiled at the boy, who kicked his feet harder.

"The neighbor is here," Malcolm said. He stood in the doorway.

"Great."

"Are you changing him?" No missing the amazement in his voice.

She blew a wisp of hair from her eyes. "That's the plan."

"And you've never done it before."

"Not even once."

He moved beside her and grabbed a diaper from the shelf below. He made quick work of stripping the soiled diaper and replacing it with a fresh one.

"I'm impressed, Detective."

"Niece and nephew. I babysit from time to time." He handed her the baby.

Emotion hitched her throat. "You'll be a great dad."

Angie hadn't dwelled too much on the fact that she couldn't have children. It was what it was. But for the first time in seven years, a well of sadness rose up in her. She simply wanted to cry.

The visit to Vivian Sweet's house weighed heavily on Angie's mind as she parked illegally on the city street corner near a newsstand. She dug in her handbag and fished out her change purse, and locking her car, dashed to the newsstand. She counted out a handful of quarters and glanced up at the news guy, a black fellow who wore a red knit hat and a blue scarf wrapped three times around his neck.

"A paper to go with a diet soda," she said.

433

"You're usually my magazine junkie." He grabbed a cold soda from a small refrigerator and a paper.

"What?"

"You show up the third week of every month and clean me out of magazines. You never buy a paper."

He was yet another person who noticed her habits. "My paper never showed up this morning."

"You are a news junky." He pulled a paper, folded it, and handed it to her.

"Am I that obvious?" She never considered that he'd noticed her buying habits.

"I know most of my regulars' habits."

She wondered who else noticed her habits. Maybe the time had come to mix things up a bit. "How much do I owe you?"

"Five dollars."

She dropped the money in his hand, replaced her change purse, and grabbed the soda and paper. "If I don't get back to my car I'm going to get another ticket."

"Get going then."

She smiled, turned suddenly in a rush to get to her car, and smacked right into a man who felt more like a wall than flesh and bone. Her gaze darted up as she uttered an apology.

Her words halted before they were uttered. "I know you."

"From group." He wore a dark turtleneck, a blazer, and jeans. He'd chosen a relaxed style, and yet his aura possessed a formality better suited for a military uniform.

She'd never run into anyone from group before, and it unnerved her a little bit to have that world collide with this one. "Hey."

"Angie, right?" He held out his hand, and she hesitated before taking it.

"Right." Warm, strong fingers wrapped around her hand, igniting a jolt of energy. She pulled her hand free. "Good to see you."

He nodded to the paper. "Hear about that woman they found?"

"It's in the paper?"

"On the radio this morning. Weird, isn't it? Another chick reduced to bones."

Her senses tensed. "Why would you bring that up?"

He shrugged. "Just making conversation. News reports say you were her attorney."

She shoved out a breath. "I've got to go."

He followed. "Do you work in this area?"

She stopped and stared at him. "Who are you?"

"I'm Robert. From group."

Angie shook her head, studying his face. "What do you really want?"

"How about that cup of coffee?"

"Sorry, no time."

The last thing she wanted was to spend more time with him. She just wanted to keep moving. No reason not to like this guy, but she didn't.

"Maybe I'll see you around. Seeing as we work in the same area."

"Yeah. Sure." She glanced past him to her car. A police car was making its way down the block. "I've got to go."

He looked frustrated. "Yeah, sure."

Angie didn't look back as she ran to her car, but she sensed that he stared at her.

Dr. Dixon had to work quickly. After the visit from his partner he needed to act soon if he was going to save Angie. He slumped low in a parked car in the darkened parking garage, sipping coffee, watching her empty parking space. He'd been following Angie for months, standing in the shadows learning all her habits.

One thing he had learned was that her boss, Charlotte Wellington, had a thing for security, so getting a hold of Angie in her offices would be hard. Not impossible, but hard.

Her black BMW pulled into her spot, and she burst from her car, briefcase in hand.

Long legs carried her across the deck to the elevator. Quickly, she punched the button.

He rubbed his hands on the steering wheel, anticipating what it would feel like to touch her bare flesh. He couldn't wait for the day.

Dixon would have to work quickly. His partner would not appreciate him changing their arrangement. But as soon as Dixon had Angie, he'd have her out of the country in less than an hour, and then they'd have a lifetime together.

The elevator doors opened, and she vanished into the car.

His body hardened at the prospect of having her. A restless energy stirred. The raw sexual energy inside him was so powerful it made his skin crawl. He had to exorcise the demons clawing at his insides.

He shouldn't be out in public now trolling the streets for a whore, but he needed the release or he'd never be able to concentrate on taking Angie.

"I found whores before *him* and didn't get caught. I'll do fine without *him*." He'd learned his lesson when Garrison had arrested him. Have your fun, pay your money, but just don't get too rough.

Holding back would be hard — he so enjoyed a woman when she cried and begged him to stop — but he would find a way not to be too rough. A little pain would have to suffice.

He put his car in drive and headed toward his favorite street corner.

CHAPTER 23

Tuesday, October 11, 5 p.m.

Malcolm strode into ZZ's and spotted Margo standing behind the bar. She wore a sleeveless shirt that accentuated toned arms covered with tattoos. She glanced up at him. His scowl deepened.

He showed her his badge. "Margo."

"Cop."

"Got a few questions."

She set the glass down and leaned into the bar. "You were here the other night."

"That's right."

"That chick with Eva was a cop."

"Nope. Attorney."

She shrugged. "Just as bad. What do you want? I told all the cops that I haven't seen Lulu."

"Lulu Sweet is dead."

For a moment, granite features softened. "Sorry to hear that."

"I've got a few questions."

"I don't have many answers."

Malcolm leaned into the bar. "I got friends in Vice that would like nothing better than to camp their asses on your barstools and chat with your customers."

"I ain't got nothing to hide."

"Then don't worry." He pushed away. "When you are ready to scramble for answers could you let me know? I'll call the bloodhounds off then."

Margo cursed under her breath. "Ass."

"That a yes?"

"What do you want to know?"

"Anybody seen Tony?"

"Nope. He split right after Lulu vanished."

"Anybody hanging around Lulu or talking to or hassling her?"

"Not more than usual. She was cute and bubbly, and the dudes liked that."

"What about her purse?"

She hesitated. "I don't know."

"Really? I smell bloodhounds."

"Shit. Behind the bar."

He didn't mention that she'd told the other cops the purse had been nowhere to be found. "Thanks."

It was a satchel fashioned out of blue-jean material with brightly colored patches on the side. He fished through it. Comb, wallet with no cash in it, gum, crackers, and in the

440

very bottom a wad of paper. He set the purse on the bar and unfurled the paper. It was a handwritten note.

Love watching you. You are the best.

"Any idea who might have given this to her?"

She read the note. "No, I really don't. If anybody was bugging her, she never said."

He handed her one of his business cards. "If you think of anything or see Tony, call me."

"Got you on speed dial, sport."

Malcolm's head pounded as he pushed through the front door of King's. He saw Angie sitting at the bar. She was talking to Eva and doing something he didn't see often. She was smiling.

Whatever was coiled inside of him eased, and tension melted from his shoulders. She'd been in his thoughts the better part of the day. Seeing her standing over the baby not knowing how to change a diaper. The way she'd watched him with that kid, her eyes sad and reflective. It must sting like hell to hold a kid and know you'd never have one of your own.

As he moved toward the bar, Eva looked

up and spotted him. She nodded and mentioned to Angie that he'd arrived. She turned. The smile faded from her face. In an instant, the light vanished. The *serious* Angie had returned, and he was sorry for it.

He sat beside her and grabbed a handful of nuts from the bowl on the bar. "Eva, I could use a beer, but give me a soda."

"Sure."

She poured a tall soda and set it in front of him. "You want what you ordered the other night?"

"I don't remember what I had."

"Chili, crackers, extra hot sauce."

He jostled peanuts in his hand. "How do you remember that?"

"She has a photographic memory," Angie said. "She could tell you what you wore two months ago. Or what you ate that day."

"Garrison said something about you having a good memory. I didn't realize it was that extreme."

Eva shrugged. "Sometimes. Remembering isn't always the best." She punched his order into the computer.

"What do you remember about your father?" Malcolm asked.

She arched a brow. "Where did that come from?"

"I've been chewing on this Fay Willow

case on and off all day. Has your sister told you about our visit to the women's prison?"

Angie faced him. "I didn't supply many details because she doesn't need to know."

He shrugged. "Back off, Mama Bear. I'm just asking."

Eva refilled Angie's water glass. "I've been after her to tell me, but she won't. She and Garrison think I'm made of glass."

He faced Angie. "She won't break if I ask her questions about her father."

"She doesn't need the stress."

Eva laughed. "She can talk for herself, Angie. And *she* does remember a little about her father."

He shifted his gaze back to Eva. "What do you remember?"

"He was fun. He made me laugh. Always had a magic trick. But the more I dig back to the past, I remember that he and Mom were never really happy. He would be out a lot at night, and when he came back she'd argue with him. She cried often."

"Why did he leave?"

"I don't know. One day he was there, and then one day he was gone."

"Louise said that Darius forced Frank to hire Blue."

Eva shrugged. "I don't know. It all went over my head."

Garrison pushed through the front door of the bar. He came around the bar, took Eva in his arms, and kissed her. Several customers whooped and hollered, but he didn't seem to care.

Color rose in Angie's face as she watched the two embrace.

Malcolm's phone rang, and he was relieved to answer it. "Kier." He lifted his gaze, growing darker and slowly shifting to Angie. "Are you very sure?" He listened and then nodded. "Thanks."

"What was that about?" Angie said.

Garrison picked up on her tone and shifted his gaze while keeping his arm around Eva.

"An undercover cop working the streets called in. Dixon is back on the prowl. He's talking to hookers."

"He's not done that since his trial," Garrison said.

"He understands that keeping his nose clean is part of staying out of jail," Angie said.

"Yeah, but why now?" Kier said. "What has changed?"

"Maybe he was just biding his time," Eva offered.

Angie shook her head. "He was interviewed by the cops only a week ago. He'd

444

have to be a fool to solicit sex. It's what got him into trouble in the first place."

"He was so careful, and now he's taking risks. Why?" Malcolm turned to Angie. "You need to be very careful."

"Me? Why?"

"He has a thing for you. I could see it in the way he looked at you in the courtroom."

"We *had* a strictly professional relationship." She wasn't sure why she needed to say that to Malcolm.

"I'm not saying you didn't. But I'm not so sure about him. You said he'd came around last week."

"He wanted legal advice."

"And when you said no?"

"He wasn't happy, but he dealt with it."

Kier shook his head. "Be very, very careful, Counselor. If he's taking small risks, he could be getting ready to take big risks."

"I can take care of myself."

"I know you're a big girl." Sarcasm rattled around the words. "But you may have a lunatic that's got you in his sights."

Eva reached across the bar and laid her hand on Angie's. "Be careful. I know firsthand how clever they can be."

Dixon had tied the woman to the hotel bed. Tear streaks and mascara trailed down the side of her face. She wasn't bleeding. He'd been careful not to make her bleed. And when the bruises darkened her pale skin, a shirt and pants would cover them easily. He'd only bitten her once on the underside of her breast.

He pulled up his pants, fastened the top button, and zipped up. He liked watching her twist at her bindings and try to hold off the tears. Given a little more time, she'd have been weeping and begging. But he didn't dare risk it.

He pulled two hundred dollars from his pocket and tossed it on the nightstand. He sat on the edge of the bed, and the cheap mattress sunk under his weight. Humming, he reached for her bindings and slowly untied them.

The woman quickly sat up and rubbed the red raw bands around her wrists.

He grabbed her by the chin and held her face. "You and I are going to keep this little date private, aren't we?"

Her agreement came quick and sure. "Yes."

"Good. I don't need trouble, and you don't need trouble from me." He pulled a small camera from his pocket and snapped several photos. "Got it?"

Her head bobbed up and down. "I get it.

I get it."

His desire satisfied, he was anxious to get rid of her. "Get your clothes and get out of here."

She scrambled off the bed and quickly pulled on a short jean miniskirt and tank top. She grabbed her purse and snatched the money off the nightstand.

"Maybe I'll call you again."

"Yeah, sure."

She hurried out of the room. Dixon sat on the bed for a moment, savoring the total sense of relaxation. His thoughts were clear now. He could plan his escape with Angie.

The motel door opened, but he didn't bother a glance up. "What did you forget?"

A heavy silence hung in the room, sending a sting of fear through his limbs. He rose and turned, his fingers fisted.

The whore stood in the doorway, but she wasn't alone. His partner was with her. The Other held the woman's neck in his hands, squeezing so hard she couldn't move.

His expression was as dark as Satan's and made him seem all the more frightening and imposing.

"What are you doing?" he said in a cool, even voice as he pushed the door closed behind him.

"Just having a little fun."

"I told you, no more fun. Not now." He shoved hard, and the woman tumbled forward onto the carpeted floor. She wept and crawled toward Dixon as if he would somehow save her.

Dixon ran a shaky hand through his hair. "I just needed to release some tension."

"That's what you said when you picked up Lulu Sweet the first time. That led to one hell of a mess."

"I kept quiet, just as we agreed. I never implicated you."

"No, but you put a crimp in my fun. We had to lay low for a year because you couldn't control yourself."

"I didn't get rough with her like I did with Lulu the first time."

"You've created a loose end who will talk to someone sooner or later."

The woman glanced up at him. "I won't talk. I swear."

The man pulled a knife from his back pocket. The woman gasped and screamed. The customers who came to this motel heard screams often and didn't call the cops unless it became really annoying. "No, you will not."

"Shit!" Dixon gasped.

He held out the knife to Dixon. "Clean up your mess."

Dixon held up his hands. "Me? I don't like that part."

"You made the mess — now you have to tidy it up."

He shrank away as the woman wailed. "No."

A smile twisted his partner's face, and he stepped forward and in one smooth move grabbed the woman by the hair and sliced her neck. Instantly she collapsed to the floor. Her blood pooled around her head as the air gurgled from her lungs.

"Shit!" Dixon wailed. "What have you done? My fingerprints and DNA are all over this room." He backed up a step so that the whore's blood didn't touch his shoes. "I'm not going to jail for this."

"No, you won't go to jail for this."

Dixon wanted to run in the bathroom and vomit. "Then what the hell was the point of killing her?"

The Other shrugged as he tossed the knife on the floor beside the woman. "Fun. Entertainment. Boredom."

"I can't do this anymore with you. I can't."

"I understand." His smile was warm and forgiving. "It's too much."

Dixon's breathing slowed just a fraction. "You'll let me go."

"Of course. But I need you to do a favor

for me."

Dixon's hands trembled, and it was all he could do not to piss on himself. "I'm going to be sick."

"Suit yourself."

Dixon dashed to the bathroom and threw up in the toilet. His eyes watered. The muscles in his stomach ached. Finally, he swiped his hand over his mouth and rose.

"Now about that favor."

"What do you need from me?"

"The cops need someone to blame these murders on. I've got the perfect person to give them. Let's go to my car."

"Your car? Why?"

"The less people who see you now, the better. Let's go."

Dixon grabbed his coat and tie and wobbled out the door to the dark sedan. He slid into the front seat, his nerves and body dancing with illness and adrenaline.

He laid his head back against the soft seat. "Why do you like to kill so much?"

"It's a dark hobby, I'll admit."

"How long have you been killing?"

He shrugged. "I killed my first woman when I was sixteen."

"Shit."

The Other nodded, amazed by his own admission. "Something, isn't it?"

Dixon opened his eyes to say something else but felt the prick of a needle in the side of his neck. His head immediately spun. His gaze grew hazy.

"You're killing me," he choked.

"Never make a deal with the scorpion. They'll sting you every time."

The call on the prostitute came in around midnight. The hotel owner had rented the room for five hours, and time had come up and customers were waiting. He'd found the woman and called the cops.

Now Kier and Garrison stood by the body, staring down at the woman who lay on her stomach, blood pooling around her head.

"Is she the one who left with Dixon?" Malcolm said.

"Yeah." The woman that answered was dressed like a hooker — tight pants, a tube top, and a gold belt — but she had a badge slung around her neck. Her name was Officer Julian. "Her name is Foxy. She's been in town a couple of months. Not more than twenty years old."

Malcolm studied the body, noting the bruising around her throat and the bite mark on her shoulder. "The bruising and bites are classic Dixon."

"No doubt the medical examiner will find bruising on the inside of her legs and signs of very rough sex," Garrison said.

Julian's bright red lips flattened. "The girls in the area were surprised to see him. They told Foxy not to go with him, but he was paying two hundred for an hour. She decided the money was worth it."

Foxy lay on her belly, her hands splayed out in front of her. One blue high heel was half off and the other wedged on tight. Her sack purse lay beside her.

"Foxy's neck was sliced with a sharp blade, and that is not like Dixon at all," Malcolm said.

"Killers evolve," Garrison said.

Thin silver bracelets jangled on Officer Julian's arm as she moved her hand to her hips. "Maybe he didn't want word getting back to the streets about this 'date.' He had enough trouble coaxing Foxy into his car."

"I'll bet we find his DNA all over this room," Malcolm said. "Killing her doesn't make sense. Are there any cuts on her body?"

The forensic tech continued to snap photos as he shook his head. "No cuts. Lots of bruises. Track marks. But no cuts."

"None of this feels right," Malcolm said.

Garrison nodded. "Dixon likes to hurt

women, not kill them."

"Exactly."

"You think he's working with someone else?"

"It wouldn't be a huge stretch. One killer is in it for the violence and sex, and the other is in it for the kill. Not the first time that's happened."

"Where's the motel manager?"

"Outside," Officer Julian said. "His name is Kline. Sammie Kline."

Malcolm and Garrison found the short, troll-like man hovering by one of the police cars. A bright red shirt covered a round belly. He held the remains of a cigarette between his thin lips.

Malcolm held up his badge. "Sammie Kline. You manage this place?"

The man sniffed. "I work the desk at nights."

"So everyone has got to go through you to get a room."

"Yeah."

"You see who rented room number twelve?"

"It pays not to pay too close attention."

Garrison grinned. "It's going to pay big dividends if you did pay attention."

Sammie sniffed, dropped his butt to the ground, and twisted his foot on it until it extinguished. "I didn't do nothing wrong."

Malcolm planted his hands on his hips. "Do us both a favor. Think hard about who rented room twelve."

He studied Malcolm, realizing that he'd come out farther ahead if he dug deep into his memory. "The chick's name was Foxy. She paid cash and said she needed the room for a couple of hours. That's longer than normal. Most girls don't book the room for more than a half hour."

"Who was with her?"

"He didn't come inside, but I saw him. He's not been in here in a long time, but I recognized him. It was Dixon. I remember his trial."

"You're certain?"

"Positive."

"Anyone with him?"

"Nope. He was alone."

Malcolm studied the parking lot. "Did he leave alone?"

"I don't know," Sammie said.

"Do you have security cameras?" Garrison said.

"No one wants any record of any comings or goings. There's a gas station a half block away. It might have picked up someone driving to the motel."

Malcolm shoved out a breath. "Time to

start knocking on doors and figuring out who saw what."

"Right."

They spent the better part of the next hour doing just that. Getting people to answer had been difficult. Several times they'd had Sammie use his pass key to open doors. In the end, no one had seen Dixon leave. If anyone had seen them leave they'd long since left. "Let's put Officer Julian to work. Let her ask around. One of the girls might have been working at the time and seen someone leave with Dixon."

"Will anyone talk?"

"It's in their best interest. Either Dixon or someone else had some very nasty, violent tastes."

CHAPTER 24

Wednesday, October 12, 3 a.m.

Court order in hand, Malcolm and Kier arrived at Dixon's house ready to search for any signs of the doctor or the murder weapon. The small brick home was located in an upscale neighborhood. The home's exterior was perfectly maintained. This time of year leaves fell daily, but there wasn't a leaf or stick on Dixon's lush green lawn, which looked so smooth in the moonlight. Whoever maintained the yard came several times a week.

They rang the bell, and when no one answered, they pounded on the front door. "Dr. Dixon," Malcolm shouted. "This is Alexandria Police. We have a warrant."

When the house remained stoically silent, Malcolm tried the front door. "Locked."

"No surprise."

"What about the garage door?" Garrison offered.

They moved around the side of the house to the side door illuminated by a light. They peered inside and saw that Dixon's car was not parked in the space. The door beside the garage was also locked.

Malcolm found a small landscape rock by a flowerbed and broke the glass on the door. He reached between the shards and unlocked it. The detectives moved inside the house, flipped on the garage light, and made their way into the house.

The garage, like the house, was neat and clean.

Flipping on lights, they moved through a kitchen and den. All of the rooms were as neat and organized as the front yard, but unlike the exterior the interior was Spartan.

By the looks, pictures had been stripped from some of the walls, and it seemed quite a few pieces of furniture were missing. Dixon had a taste for antiques. The only room that remained fully decorated and intact was a front parlor.

"He wants the world to believe he's doing fine, but he's selling his precious antiques to pay the bills," Malcolm said.

They moved upstairs, taking their time to determine that the house was indeed empty. Dixon's bedroom was furnished with just a mattress and box spring. The nightstands were cheap plastic pieces. The bureau looked like it was from a box store.

Down the hallway, the first two rooms were stripped bare. "Sinclair is having a look at his financials as we speak."

"It still galls me that he's walking the streets," Garrison said.

"Not for long." They reached the back bedroom. Malcolm flipped on the light. "Shit."

The walls in the room were plastered with pictures of women. The pictures were arranged in groups, and all followed a progressive pattern.

The first in a grouping showed the women smiling and seductive, clear participants in whatever was happening. But then the images changed. Smiles vanished and were replaced by looks of terror. Tear-streaked mascara ran down their faces. Some had bloodied lips. Others had bruises around their necks. But in each and every photo the women were alive.

"The pictures appear to go back decades." Garrison's voice was tight with anger.

Malcolm's fury burned in the pit of his stomach. "He's been at this for a long time." He pointed to the wall. "Look, that's Lulu Sweet on the far right. Other than Foxy, she must have been his most recent." He let his gaze roam to the next woman. "Sierra Day."

The next two pictures were of two prostitutes who'd vanished this past summer. "We never found their bodies."

"No."

"And before them is Lulu again." But she was a couple of years younger. She wore her hair short with spiky pink tips as she had during Dixon's trial.

"And before Lulu, the other three missing prostitutes."

"If these pictures are an accurate time line, it looks like he took a couple of years off between his trial and his next victim."

"The murder trial must have scared him enough to stop for a while." Garrison studied the images that went back decades. Neither of them recognized any of the women.

"It's going to take legwork to find these women."

"Yeah." Garrison's gaze settled on the first image. "Shit. Look at the first one."

The picture was at least thirty years old, but he recognized the face. "Fay Willow. She was his first."

"Dixon was the boyfriend?" Garrison said.

"He could have been. He would have been in his early twenties when she died."

"Fay's roommate said the boyfriend made

deliveries to the museum."

"A little digging will confirm his employment records."

Malcolm moved to a table on the far end of the room.

It appeared to be a workstation where Dixon cropped and arranged his pictures. He glanced down, and instantly his blood turned to ice. "Garrison, look at this."

Garrison moved and studied the images of the woman. The pictures were snapped when she was selecting produce in the grocery store, walking in Old Town Alexandria, and standing on the steps of the courthouse. "His next victim."

Malcolm fisted his fingers. "Angie Carlson."

It was nearly four in the morning when Angie arrived at Dr. Dixon's house after receiving a call from Kier. Kier's normally abrupt tone had been sharp like a razor, cutting into her deep slumber. Curt and direct, he'd told her she had to come immediately. She pulled on jeans and a sweatshirt. She pushed her feet into loafers.

Police cars surrounded the home, their lights flashing in the darkness. The forensics van blocked half the neighborhood road.

She found a place to park several houses

down and walked toward the chaos. The front yard was roped off with yellow crime-scene tape. She moved toward a uniformed officer.

"My name is Angie Carlson. I received a call from Detective Kier." She moved to pull her driver's license from her wallet to prove her identity.

He held up his hand. "I know who you are." He handed her a set of plastic gloves. "He's on the second floor."

She ducked under the tape, pulling the gloves on as she moved across the yard. When she reached the front door another uniformed policeman greeted her and directed her up the stairs to the second floor. The house hummed with the snap of cameras, conversations, and officers moving around as they searched all the rooms.

She found Malcolm in the back bedroom. He and Garrison leaned over a table of photos, and both seemed deep in thought.

Her greeting died on her lips when she looked at the pictures on the wall. The women's pain-filled eyes stared back at her, sending a haunting appeal for help. The sharp, crisp images were so vivid she could almost hear their cries. For a moment she thought she'd be ill.

Dear God, she'd defended this monster.

She'd used all her legal know-how to put him back on the streets.

"Carlson." Malcolm's deep voice startled her from her thoughts.

She squared her shoulders. "Detective."

"Interesting glimpse into your client's mind, isn't it?"

"He's no longer my client." Her voice wasn't as strong as she'd have liked.

"But when he was, you did a bang-up job of defending him. You put him back on the streets." Bitterness laced the words.

Guilt mingled with anger. "I did my job very well, Detective. And if you'd done yours better we wouldn't be here."

His jaw hardened.

She tightened her hand around her purse strap. "Did you call me here to argue?"

"No."

"Then why?" The grotesque images behind him taunted her. She didn't want to see the damage Dixon had done.

"Your client killed another woman."

He was baiting her, directing his anger at her. A part of her knew she deserved his ire. "He's not my client."

Kier arched a brow as if he didn't quite believe her. "I want to make damn sure you have no information about him that might help us."

"I've not spoken to him in over a week."

"He's not contacted you in any way?"

"No."

"You're sure?"

She leaned in so close she could smell his scent. "Call me a bitch. Call me a barracuda. Hell, call me the Queen of the Night. I don't care. But do not call me a liar, Detective. I've gone out of my way to help you with this case."

He held his ground, maintaining the close proximity. He stared at her so hard; she suspected he was trying to read her thoughts. "There's something else you need to see."

She didn't want to see any more. She wanted to leave. She wanted to slip into a dark bar and drink wine until her mind was numb. "Show me."

He guided her across the room to the table. "Have a look."

She braced and glanced down. Immediately, her insides constricted. The images were all of her. "These are all recent. Taken in the last couple of months." She didn't dare touch the images. "I never once saw him."

"He may have taken the pictures himself or hired someone. But it's clear he has a real obsession with you."

She moistened her lips, praying she didn't get sick to her stomach now. "I was his next victim."

"I think so."

"You said he killed another woman?"

"He cut her throat."

"Cut her throat? That doesn't sound like Dixon."

"Why?"

"Dixon is so fastidious. And he wouldn't be so bold."

Malcolm considered her closely. "Why do you say that?"

"He was truly terrified at the prospect of going to jail. He said many times that he'd never survive in prison. Killing a woman like this is messy, and his DNA would be all over the room. He'd be too easy to track after a killing like that."

"Maybe he got lost in the heat of the moment."

"Dixon? Doubtful. I never ever saw him once relinquish control. Control is critical for him. I just don't believe he'd be so foolish."

She studied a photo taken of her entering King's. Eva was at her side, and they were laughing. She remembered the spring day clearly. They'd gone shopping, and for the first time in a long time she felt as if they

464

were sisters. To realize Dixon had been lurking and snapping pictures of that moment made her feel dirty.

"I want you to look at another picture." His tone had lost some of the harder edges.

Unshed tears burned her throat. Numbly she nodded and followed him to the end of the photos. She glanced up. "Who is this?"

"Fay. We think she might have been his first."

"Was Dixon her boyfriend?"

"He could have been. He would have been in his early twenties. She was twenty-nine when she died. Not an impossible arrangement."

"He killed her and stripped her bones?" She shook her head.

"I don't know. That's why we're searching for him." He cupped his hand under her elbow and guided her away from the picture. "Could he be working with someone?"

"A partner? I doubt it. He liked things done his way."

"Maybe he changed his mind?"

She nodded. "What can I do to help you?"

"Is there anyone whom he would have worked with?"

"None that I know. He had no family that he ever told me about. Whatever friends or acquaintances he had before his trial abandoned him. I got the sense he was quite alone in the world."

"What was his social life like?"

"I can't speak for his recent activities, but in the past he was a patron of the arts."

"The theater."

"And the ballet and the art museums. He loved that world."

"Okay." He tightened his jaw. "Call Eva. See if you can stay at King's for a few days. Until we find Dixon or his possible partner you are not safe."

She didn't want to surrender her life to scum like Dixon. But she had to be practical. "Sure."

Her agreement seemed to strip away some of his stress. "Good. I'll have a uniform follow you to your office and then to King's."

"Thanks."

"Angie, be very, very careful. For whatever reason, Dixon has not killed you, but he's got something planned."

Dixon's head pounded. His mouth felt as if it had been stuffed with cotton. In a pitch-black room, he tried to pull his arm to his mouth but discovered it was tied above his head. Not only were his hands tied, but his feet were tied as well. "Hey!"

Immediately, an overhead light clicked on,

blinding him. Shutting his eyes, he turned his head. "What the hell is going on?"

"Now you of all people should know what is going to happen." The familiar voice echoed out from the darkness.

Dixon's heart slammed fast and hard against his chest wall. "Why are you doing this? We're partners."

"Let's say I'm tired of playing the game with you. I'm ready to play alone."

"But it's been going well." He wanted to keep his voice calm, but a shrill of panic twisted its way around the words.

"It suited for a while. I did have a lot to learn from you after all." The voice circled around the table, but the blinding light made it impossible for him to focus.

"It can still be great. Look, I know I got a little over the top today. I see that now. But we can take it back to the way things were."

"You can never go back. You said so yourself."

"I wasn't thinking straight. I was frustrated. But I'm not frustrated anymore."

"Neither am I. And I had been for a very long time. I ached to be who I once was and to regain what I'd had before, but I was afraid. You gave me the courage to take what I craved. And for that I want to thank you."

The cool tip of a knife blade traced his

eyebrow, making him flinch. "We're partners!"

The Other smiled. "It is never wise to
trust a scorpion."

"You are not a scorpion. You are a man.
You can reason and see beyond this moment. You know this does not have to happen."

The knife lip pricked the top of his scalp.
Within seconds warm blood oozed from the
spot.

Dixon screamed. "You need me."

"I do?"

"You said you needed me to make a call."

The Other snapped his fingers. "That is
right. That is right." He pulled a phone from
his pocket. "And I have your phone." He
started to type a text.

"What are you saying?"

"I'm telling him to meet you at the corner
of West Braddock and Route Seven in the
basement of the burger joint that went out
of business."

"Is that where we are?"

"Yes." The Other hit send. "Good."

"So you're letting me go?"

The Other snapped the phone closed and
tucked it in his pocket. "No. I'm not."

"Shit! Don't do this!" Dixon pissed on
himself.

The Other wrinkled his nose. "I wish I had time to strip all your bones. They'd make a nice addition to the chess set. I was thinking the bishop."

"Don't!" Dixon twisted at his bindings.

"I wanted a memento of our partnership. But your body needs to be found by the cops."

Dixon yanked at his bindings. They didn't budge. "Why?"

"They need someone to pin these murders on, and I'm going to give them you."

"If you kill me they'll know there is someone else."

"You just texted your 'accomplice' and told him to meet you here. You both will go down for this."

"You don't have to do this! Let me live, and I will help you."

"Help me? You tried to steal Angie from me. And you know how much I've wanted her."

Dixon rattled against his bindings as his partner moved behind him and set down his knife. "You can still have her. We both can. Let me help you!"

His warm breath brushed Dixon's ear. "I promise to take extra time with her bones and fashion them into the finest queen."

He picked up an ax and walked to the foot

of the table. Before Dixon could scream, blinding pain sliced across his calf as an ax cut through his anklebone. Dixon screamed, railing against his bindings.

"I can clean these bones later and make them into something special."

The pain overwhelmed Dixon's senses, blinding him to his desires for Angie, his anger, or reason. His partner unstrapped his hands and foot. But he didn't care. There was only the pain.

And then a knife blade sliced across his throat, severing his jugular.

"Good-bye, James."

As the blood drained from Dixon's body, the strong scent of gasoline grew. "I do want to thank you. I'd still be asleep now if it wasn't for you. You've showed me just how wonderful and full my life could be again."

The Other lit a match and stared at the flame before blowing it out. "As soon as our friend gets here, it'll be a party."

Angie spent a long tedious Wednesday at the office, and by the time she was ready to quit she was exhausted. She'd promised that as soon as she finished her work, she'd call for an escort and head to King's, where her sister waited.

Angie rubbed her eyes and glanced at the

clock. It was ten o'clock. "I've got to get out of here."

Charlotte also worked late, and when Angie heard Charlotte move down the hallway to the back door, she realized the time to wrap things up had arrived.

She rose, listening to Charlotte clicking the back door's dead bolt back and forth, back and forth. It was Charlotte's custom to do this several times until it sunk into her mind that the door was truly locked.

Angie had been aware of Charlotte's quirks for a long time, but in the last week, with the deaths of Sierra and Lulu, they'd grown worse.

Angie shut off the light at her desk, grabbed her purse and coat. She found Charlotte standing by the back door, frowning. "It's okay. It's locked."

Charlotte startled and turned. "I know. It's locked." A hint of panic wove around the words.

"Do you want me to check it for you?"

Charlotte glanced at the door. "No, no. It's fine."

"It's been a hard week for us all. All our nerves are on edge." She'd not told Charlotte about the photos. "It's okay to be scared."

Charlotte frowned. "I'm not scared."

Angie shook her head. "Charlotte, I'm scared too."

Her boss stared at her a long moment and then sighed. "I guess all that's happened has made me remember. And when I remember I start to obsess about things."

"You and me both."

She arched a brow. "You don't seem to worry about much."

A crooked smile tipped the edges of her lips. "I'm great at faking it."

Charlotte laughed. "Welcome to the club."

"Hang tough."

"It's the only option." She drew in a breath. "I've got to get a little sleep. Tomorrow's a long day. Are you leaving soon?"

"I'm right behind you."

"I can wait."

"Don't." Angie didn't want to mention the police escort she was supposed to summon before she left. "I'll be fine. I'm parked right out front."

"And you've got the mace I gave you for Christmas?"

"Yes."

After Charlotte left the office, the rooms grew so quiet she could hear the air flowing through the ducts. Outside a horn blared. Suddenly she felt so alone, as if she were the only person in the world. At King's there would be plenty of noise and conversation there for hours to come.

The idea of crowds didn't appeal, but what she wanted didn't really matter. Dixon was on the prowl, and she had to be practical. Better to go to King's.

She called the number Kier had given her for an escort and waited until a marked car pulled up in front of the office. She grabbed her purse, shut off the last of the office lights, and headed out the front door. She waved to the waiting police car, set the alarm on the office, and climbed into her car.

The drive from her office to King's only took ten minutes. She found a spot down the street from the pub under a street lamp, waved to her escort, and hurried down the uneven brick sidewalks to the front door. Her hand on the front door, she glanced up toward Kier's place. His lights burned bright. His muscular frame passed in front of a shaded window.

The ache of loneliness grew stronger. Suddenly she dreaded the crowd inside the pub. She stepped inside and watched her escort drive away.

The music, laughter, and conversation blared and grated her nerves. She glanced

473

up again through the front window at Kier's.

On impulse Angie gripped her purse, pushed out the front door, and crossed the street. She climbed the side staircase to his apartment. Sweat pooled at the base of her spine. Her stomach fisted tighter with each new step.

What the devil was she doing? Leave the man alone. His day had to have been longer than hers.

As logic nagged her, she kept climbing until she reached his apartment door. Just ask him about the case and leave. Maybe he'd have a few reassuring words.

Immediately, she feared if she took one more moment to think, she'd dash down the stairs.

Heavy footsteps echoed down a hallway, and after a brief hesitation the door opened.

Kier stood in the doorway, his hair damp and his shirt-tail out. His face was hard with suspicion. She glanced down and noted he had his gun in hand at his side.

CHAPTER 25

Wednesday, October 12, 11 p.m.

"Sorry to bother you. I know this is unexpected." She felt silly now and wished she'd stayed at King's.

"Angie. What are you doing here? Everything all right?" No missing the confusion and concern.

"Oh, yeah. I'm fine. Really. Impulse drove me up here. I thought I'd ask about the investigation. And I can see that I caught you at a bad time." She wanted to dash down the stairs and forget this lapse in judgment.

"Timing's not bad. Come on in. I just put a pot of coffee on."

In the courtroom she was in her element. She was in control. But standing here right now, she felt gawky and silly. "Honestly, I shouldn't have come."

He stepped aside. He was barefooted. "Come in."

If he'd hesitated an instant, she'd have run. But his voice was clear and firm, and it drew her inside the apartment. She entered, moving past him, drinking in the scent of his soap.

The apartment was loft style, open with no walls. He'd fashioned rooms by grouping a couch and television in one corner and a large four-poster bed in another. The bed caught her off guard. Somehow she expected sleek and modern from him, not traditional antiques.

The kitchen was galley style and ran along the edge of the south wall. There was a large table with six chairs by the kitchen that looked like it doubled as work and eating space. Right now it was covered with files and boxes.

As he'd said, a coffeepot perked. She could smell something cooking in the oven.

"Great space," she said.

He closed the door behind her and put his gun in the holster hanging on a peg by the door. "Did you have a patrolman escort you here?"

She let her purse slide from her shoulder onto the table. "Yes. Even carried mace."

"Good." He moved into the kitchen and pulled a couple of black oversized mugs from the cabinet. "Keep using one until this is over. That's what we're here for, Angie."

That was the second time he'd used her first name. Not Carlson. Not Queen of the Dammed. Just Angie. And it sounded nice when he said it.

"I know." She flexed her fingers, wishing she had pockets or something to do with her hands. "How goes the case?"

"Slow. No sign of Dixon. His credit cards and bank show no activity, so we're hoping he's not gone far yet." He pursed his lips. "I'm sorry about earlier today. I was frustrated and took it out on you."

"I get that. It's okay." A weighty stillness settled between them. She cleared her throat. "Have you learned any more about Dixon's connection to Fay?"

"No. We just know he was in this area at that time. He worked for Gregg's Shipping, which did a lot of work for the Talbot. He'd been accepted to medical school, but had deferred entrance to make money. Then suddenly after Fay's death, he contacted the school and told them he could attend. He left and didn't return to the metro area for a decade."

"Do you think Darius paid him off?"

"It's possible. But we might not ever know what happened between the three."

"Do you have any theories?"

"Sure. Plenty." He turned and lifted the full pot from the burner and filled each cup. "How do you take your coffee?"

"Black."

He grimaced as he handed her the cup. "I've got to have milk. Stuff is too harsh for me."

She sipped, knowing the brew would keep her up half the night. "What can I say? I'm bitter."

He laughed as he pulled an organic milk bottle from the refrigerator. "Not so bitter."

"What about Darius and the museum? What did Darius want with the Talbot?"

"I don't know for sure, but the museum had so many boxes coming into the country, and they had a stellar reputation. It would have made sense for Darius to capitalize on that in some way. Dixon might have even figured it out."

She cupped her hands around the warm cup, not sure if he'd just tossed a compliment her way or not. "So what are your theories about Dixon, Darius, and Fay?"

"It's one of the oldest in the books. She's dating Dixon, a younger man, to make her older rich lover jealous. One of the two men got angry and killed her. My guess is that it was Darius that killed her. He never seemed like the kind of guy who liked to share.

Dixon found out and got paid off to keep quiet."

"Dixon must have been involved in disposing of her body."

Kier nodded. "Likely."

She traced the rim of her cup. "But he had alibis for the nights that Sierra and Lulu vanished."

"Which just supports my belief that he has a partner."

"Two of them out there."

He stared at her over the rim of his cup. "All the more reason for you to be very, very careful."

"I might not even know this other partner."

"Or you just might."

She held her cup close, trying to ward off the sudden chill. "Oh, great."

He studied her. "I've got a frozen pizza in the oven. Hungry?"

She set down her cup. "I've barged in here, drank your coffee, and complained. You don't have to feed me."

"I want to feed you."

"Why?"

"You look like you could use a good meal."

She chuckled. "I'm not sure if that's a good thing or bad."

He opened the oven and pulled out a pizza

that smelled great and looked pretty good. "My parents own a restaurant. I grew up working in their place and feeding people. All second nature."

"Did that come out of a box?"

"No. My mother would weep if she knew I ate anything out of a box. She makes the pizzas and ships them up to me. I put them in the freezer."

"That's nice." The tomato and basil smells made her mouth water.

"I'm spoiled. And I appreciate that."

"Your family is in Richmond?"

"Yeah."

"You seem close. Why the move up here?"

"The job in Alexandria opened, and I wanted to move to homicide." He sliced into the pizza with a chef's knife.

"You get home much?"

"Not as much as I'd like."

He plated her pizza and his own and carried both plates to the table. "Push aside the papers."

She sat down and cleared a spot for them both. He set a stack of paper napkins between them. She felt oddly relaxed as they sat and ate in silence.

Her stomach rumbled as she raised a slice to her mouth. She'd not realized how hungry she'd become. She bit into the slice and savored the fresh cheese, tomato, and basil flavors. "This tastes wonderful."

He nodded, pleased. "I'll pass it on to Mom."

She wiped the edge of her mouth with a napkin. "Ask her if she's willing to start a mail-order business. I'll be her first paying customer."

He laughed. "I'll mention it to her." Carefully he wiped his hands with a napkin. "Did you read Donovan's article in the paper today?"

"I go out of my way not to read his stuff. As you might have noticed in the courthouse, we are not on the best of terms."

He balled up his napkin in his fist. "You've been the focus of his articles this week."

"So I've heard. He's still pissed because I sued him last year and was able to prevent some of his book from being published."

"I'd heard something about that."

"He's just looking for his pound of flesh."

"That doesn't bother you?"

"Honestly, it gives me a little pleasure to know I've gotten under his skin."

He dropped his gaze. "You still have feelings for him?"

Laughter burst free. "You mean like romantic?" He didn't answer but raised his gaze to hers. The intensity made her skin tingle.

"Donovan has a talent for spotting the lonely. He charms them, and he uses them. I played right into his hands." She picked at the edge of the crust. "Where he is concerned, I feel foolish and angry but never romantic."

"Good. To the 'never romantic' part." He was staring at her as if he wanted to touch her.

She felt as if an invisible force reached out and stole her breath. Her gaze dipped to the *V* of his shirt and the dark hair curling out. Thoughts of touching him overwhelmed her before she caught herself.

She rose. "I've imposed enough."

He stood, but he appeared to be in no rush to show her the door. "It would be a big stretch, wouldn't it?"

"What?"

"Us. Sleeping together. Not something I'd have pictured a year ago."

Nervous laughter bubbled. She wanted to pretend like she didn't know what he was saying. "I guess you were about the last guy I'd ever have gotten into bed with."

He arched a brow and took a half step toward her. "The last guy?"

She moistened her lips. "Just about."

He tucked a stray strand of hair behind her ear and traced the line of her jaw with his fingertip. A riot of sensations burned through her body.

"How about now?" he said softly. "Am I still almost last on the list?"

Emotion tightened her throat. For a moment she wasn't sure her voice would work. "You've jumped ahead in the line."

Malcolm traced the bottom edge of her lips. "Getting closer to first?"

She closed her eyes, wishing she didn't want him so much. "This probably isn't a good idea."

"Nope." The word was as rough as sandpaper. "Probably one of the dumbest ideas I've ever had."

She cleared her throat. "What about Olivia?"

"We broke up, remember?"

"I thought one of you would change your mind."

"No."

He closed the gap between them and, cupping her face, kissed her softly on the lips. He tasted vaguely of salt and coffee. The feel of his lips . . . soft . . . willing . . . inviting . . . overrode all things rational.

She leaned into the kiss and wrapped her arms around his neck. His hard chest pressed against her as his arms banded around her and pulled her close. He deepened the kiss.

The senses in her body exploded, and for a moment time simply stopped. She was aware only of him and the energy pulsing between them.

"I want you," he whispered.

"Me too."

Malcolm took her by the hand and guided her over to the large bed. He shut off the overhead light.

Using only the moonlight trailing in through the window to guide him, he unbuttoned her blouse, lingering when he reached the pearl buttons between her breasts. He leaned forward and kissed her right breast. He kissed her left breast. Her nipples hardened.

She unfastened the remaining buttons, shrugged off the blouse, and let it fall to the floor. Kier smiled, removed his own shirt, and smoothed his hands over her shoulders. The calluses made her soft skin tingle. He reached for the bra snap between her breasts. He flicked the clasp open with practiced ease. He cupped her breasts, teasing her nipples to hard peaks before he pushed her back against the mattress. The down comforter sagged under their weight

484

as he climbed on top of her.

She stared up at him, realizing she'd never wanted a man as much as she wanted him.

Malcolm pushed up her skirt and smoothed his hand over her flat belly. She reached for the zipper of his pants, anxious now to feel him inside of her.

Tomorrow they'd likely look at each other and wonder why this had happened, but right now it was all that she wanted. She cupped his erection, savoring the silky feel.

He lowered and kissed her. Her skirt slid up her hips and hugged her waist. She wriggled out of her panties. He shed his pants. The instant they were free of their clothes, he pushed inside of her.

Angie sucked in a breath, savoring the invasion. Raising her hips, she deepened his entry. Soon he began to move inside her quickly and urgently, stoking the heat between them.

She'd never been more aware of her body. She wanted to hold off on her release and savor every sensation, but her body wouldn't listen. She'd never wanted as much as she did now.

The tempo built, and she arched back and gave in to the storm. He moved faster and faster, catching up to her so that they came together.

■ ■ ■ ■

Connor parked his car across the street from the burger house. It was boarded up, and CLOSED signs plastered the front window. He'd gotten the text from Dixon in the early hours of the day. But the doctor had instructed him to arrive at eleven. So he'd waited, writing his story and chomping at the bit. His latest article was mostly conjecture, but if Dixon could prove a connection between Angie and the dead women, then he would have something he could really run with.

A flicker of movement in the rearview mirror had him reaching for his tape recorder. "Showtime," he muttered.

He got out of the car, wincing as the skin on his belly pinched. The skin always ached more when it was cold. He pressed his hand to his belly, wondering if he'd ever be whole again.

The pain distracted him for just a split second, but that was all it took. He raised his gaze in time to see a man lunge at him with a syringe. The needle plunged into the side of his neck. Hot liquid burned his veins, and within seconds he dropped to his knees. He glanced up and processed what he saw.

"Fucking figures." He dropped to the ground out cold.

By the time fire engines reached the burger house and turned their hoses onto the structure it was so deeply engulfed crews did not dare enter. All they could do was shoot water onto the blaze and contain it until it died.

Fire department Lieutenant Macy LaPorta stood on the sidelines staring at the inferno. She was a tall woman with dark hair pulled back in a tight ponytail. Her father had been an arson investigator, and she'd been hanging around firehouses since she could walk. She'd joined the department right out of college.

Around her firemen yelled for more water pressure as they pulled and tugged the hoses into position. The initial moments at a fire were controlled chaos.

The flames swayed and danced in front of her, so hot and furious. It almost seemed to laugh and taunt as it consumed the structure so rapidly. Lieutenant LaPorta would wait for the embers to cool so that she could investigate the cause of the blaze, but experience told her this was arson.

She hoped no one had been in the abandoned structure. If anyone had, recovery crews would be lucky just to find fragments.

CHAPTER 26

Thursday, October 13, 6 a.m.
Angie found herself alone when the sun rose and shone its brilliant red and orange lights into the apartment.

At one a.m., Malcolm's pager had gone off, and he'd called in to headquarters. When he'd returned to bed, he'd kissed her on the head and told her to sleep. He'd see her in the morning. Immediately, she'd missed his warmth.

Angie had slept hard, called Eva and told her she was with a "friend," and then not stirred until just before dawn. She'd not slept so well in a very long time. When she'd risen, she'd made coffee and grabbed the morning paper from outside Malcolm's door.

She opened the paper and poured her coffee. The front page headline nearly took her breath away. ATTORNEY'S SECOND CLIENT MURDERED.

Shit. She thought about her clients. They'd all read this. They'd be justifiably terrified. Charlotte would be furious.

As Angie moved through the article her anger burned hotter at the half-truths and innuendos. Her fear for those she represented also grew. Even if Donovan had distorted the facts to suit himself, the reality was that someone might be targeting her clients.

The front door opened, and she glanced up to see Malcolm. Dark circles hung under his eyes, and she had the urge to cross to him and hug him close. But somehow that felt more intimate than what they'd shared.

"Hey." She poured him a cup of coffee and retrieved milk from the refrigerator. She set both on the table, watching as he shrugged off his jacket. His holstered gun, phone, and handcuffs hugged his belt.

He poured milk in the coffee, tossing her a quick smile. He took a sip. "Thanks."

Concern for him swirled inside her. "You must be exhausted."

He leaned forward and kissed her on the lips. "I'm not complaining."

She forgot about her own unease. "What pulled you away last night?"

"A fire. Two bodies were found."

"Who were the victims?"

"Dixon's car was found across the street. We think one of the bodies, or at least what's left of it, is his."

"What about the other body?"

"We found Donovan's car as well. There was a body found by the back door. Fire crews theorize that Donovan set the fire and was trying to get out of the building, but the fire got to him before he could get out."

"Dixon and Donovan?"

"We need to wait on confirmation."

"So they're both dead?" She glanced at the paper. "I was just reading Donovan's article. He must have filed it yesterday."

He glanced at the open paper. "I was hoping I could grab that before you read it."

"No such luck. I got to read all of Donovan's lovely words." She managed a smile. "Whether he's dead or not, I might be looking for a job sooner than later."

"Angie, you are good at what you do. Your clients aren't going to drop you over this."

"Donovan hates me so much."

"I put a few calls into the paper. No one has seen him."

"I don't believe he has the nerve to kill."

"Maybe not alone, but with Dixon he might have had plenty of nerve. Alexandria is a big small town. They could have crossed paths at a hundred different times."

"It all feels like it's closing in a bit."

He set his cup down and took her into his arms as if he'd done it a million times. "We'll figure this out. But until we have proof I want you to be careful."

God, this man would be too easy to love. She kissed him on the lips. Last night had awakened something inside her. For the first time in a long time, she wanted more.

But a small, very insistent voice in the back of her head cautioned against loving him. Whatever they were feeling now might be burning hot, but one day life's pressures and conflicting priorities would collide and extinguish it.

Malcolm took her by the hand and guided her to the rumpled sheets of the bed. She followed, knowing this would be the last time they made love.

Angie's office phone buzzed at ten sharp. She hit the intercom button as she continued to type on her laptop. "What is it, Iris?"

"Mr. Micah Cross is here to see you." Iris dropped her voice. "And he doesn't look happy."

Angie picked up her phone. "Thanks, Iris. Is he in the conference room?"

"Yes."

"Where's Charlotte?"

"Court."

"Thanks."

She rose. She'd fielded a few calls this morning from clients and knew a client visit was inevitable from someone. Still, she didn't relish the meeting. Smoothing out her blouse, she pulled down the jacket hanging on the back of her door and slid it on.

She'd learned long ago that you could be afraid, but you could never show fear. With her best courtroom persona in place, she relaxed her shoulders and straightened her spine.

Smiling, she moved into the conference room as if she owned the world. Extending her hand, she smiled at Micah Cross. "Good morning."

"I don't have much time. I'm on my way to a ribbon-cutting at the hospital. The new Cross pediatric wing opens today."

"I read about that. It's very generous of you."

He waved his hand. "You read the morning paper." Cross stood at the head of the conference table. He wore a dark, handmade suit that fit his lean body perfectly. Cuff links glinted from the cuffs of his hand-tailored shirt. A red silk tie completed the look of the successful man.

"I won't deny that the article is disturbing."

"Disturbing? Ms. Carlson, Donovan suggests that there is a serial killer murdering your clients."

Even as anger radiated from her gut she kept her smile relaxed and intact. "You may not be aware of this, but Mr. Donovan and I have a personal history."

He frowned. "Really?"

"It goes back to last year." She hated drawing her personal life into her professional world. "Long story short, we broke up and now he is doing his best to take a few scattered facts and turn them into a story."

"You have had two clients murdered."

"True. But I don't believe I'm the common factor that links these women."

"What is the common factor?"

"I don't know. But I can assure you that the police are working hard to figure that out."

"Have they made any progress?"

"I know they are working around the clock."

"That's a no?"

"Give them a bit more time, and they will solve this." She smiled. "Mr. Cross, you are in no danger."

He arched a brow. "Are you sure about that?"

She hesitated and then sighed. "I'm not totally sure of anything in life. But I can see that you do not fit this killer's profile."

"And what is that profile?" His interest sharpened.

"Young, vulnerable women. Attractive. Blond. Looking to make changes in their lives. Maybe they took shortcuts that they shouldn't have." She held out her hands, palms open. "Mr. Cross, you are safe. And Wellington and James is the right firm to represent you."

He nodded.

She'd avoided all mention of Darius but knew their association needed to be addressed. "Our families have had a complicated past. I know you aren't responsible for what happened."

A wry smile lifted the edge of his lips. "It's the elephant in the room for us, isn't it?"

"Yes. But I want you to know I do not believe the child should be saddled with the sins of the father or mother."

"Mother. Yes, that's right, you went to see Mother. Did she agree to see you?"

"Yes. She spoke of your father's affair with a woman that worked for my father. But she gave just enough information to leave more unanswered questions than answered questions."

"That's my mother. A game player to the end." Absently, he twisted an onyx pinky ring on his right hand. "The police asked me about the connection between our fathers. Like you, I was a toddler when our fathers conducted their business. Did Mother give you anything else?"

"No."

He nodded. "The past has nothing to do with us, Ms. Carlson. It's only the present that I worry about now."

"I can assure you that what is happening now will not affect you."

He studied her a long moment, then nodded. "I'm trusting you with my life that it won't."

Malcolm and Garrison stood by the chrome table in the medical examiner's autopsy room, staring at the charred remains pulled from the restaurant-warehouse fire. The intense blaze had all but melted the bodies. Little more than charred bones and flesh remained.

"Can you make an identification?" Malcolm asked Dr. Henson.

The doctor's blue eyes stared at him through the clear plastic facemask she wore during autopsies. "It's going to take some time. I've got bits and pieces here."

"Can you tell us anything about the bodies?" Garrison asked.

"It would be conjecture at this point."

"We'll take what you have," Malcolm said.

"Based on what I've seen of the skull, I'd say that the first victim was male. The growth lines on the top of the skull suggest our victim was older than forty. By that age the lines are completely fused."

"Could he be older than that?"

"Sure. But I can't say for certain at this point. I have requested dental records for Dixon so we shall see if the bones are his."

"Do you have enough teeth?"

"A few, and one molar has a very distinct crack. If that crack shows then we can assume the remains are likely his. And there is some DNA evidence that I can extract. But DNA will take weeks."

"Do you know how he died?"

"I might know that." She moved to the head of the table. "This is his spinal cord. See this slice in the vertebrae?"

Both leaned in and saw the faint slice in the bone. "Yeah?"

She lifted her gaze. "It appears his throat was cut."

"Really?"

"Death usually leaves a mark on the bones in some way. In this case it's a knife mark. He was also tortured before he died."

"What?"

"His right foot was cut off."

Malcolm stared at the bones. "Was the foot found?"

Dr. Henson shook her head. "Not yet."

"What about the second body?"

"There's more of that to examine. It's charred but more intact. Whoever he was, he was six feet tall, had broad shoulders, and was in his late thirties."

"Like Donovan?"

"Again, waiting on dental records."

Garrison rested his hand on his hip. "Are the markings on victim number one similar to the prostitute whose throat was cut?"

She nodded. "I've not had a great deal of time to examine her body yet, but the knife wounds are in similar locations."

Two killers made sense. Could it be as simple as Donovan killing Dixon and then getting trapped in the fire he set? It could.

But for reasons Malcolm could not explain, he felt as if someone had handed him a nice wrapped gift filled with shit.

Malcolm's day was spent talking to anyone who might have known Dixon. His secretary, his neighbors, even a couple of patients. As they had learned two years ago, he possessed a Jekyll-and-Hyde persona. To neighbors and friends, he was the model citizen. Charming. Witty. Funny. To the people that worked for him — people he considered beneath him — he could be dark, moody, and very controlling. No one had ever seen him with Donovan . . . ever.

Donovan had few friends. He'd become isolated and withdrawn in the last year. At the paper he still worked with one other reporter named Robert Farmer.

Malcolm found Farmer at his desk just after lunch. He sat in the middle of a busy newsroom at his desk eating a sandwich. The room buzzed with conversation, phones, and faxes.

"Robert Farmer?" Malcolm said.

Farmer was a tall guy with broad shoulders and short hair. He dressed in khakis and a sport shirt. "Yeah?"

Malcolm held up his badge. "Detective Malcolm Kier."

Farmer wiped his hands on a napkin. "Yeah."

"I'm looking for Connor Donovan."

"I haven't seen him in a day or two."

"Know where he might be?"

"Nope."

"You know anything about the articles he's been writing?"

Robert leaned back in his chair. "I was working with him on them."

He thought about the crap they'd spun about Angie. "Really?"

"We were looking for a connection between Carlson and the killer."

Malcolm was tempted to kick the guy's chair and watch him pitch over on his back. "You find anything?"

"Not really, but it wasn't for lack of trying."

"The articles spin a lot of theories, but they were short on facts."

"Believe me, I dug deep. But I came up empty handed."

By seven Malcolm was bone tired and needing food and a break. He'd thought about Angie several times over the day, and each time he did, his sense of urgency for the case ramped. They'd not made plans or agreed to see each other again. This morning he'd kissed her and told her to be safe. But that had been it.

Now as he parked across the street from King's he realized he wanted to see her. Not just to assure himself that she was okay, but because he wanted time with her. Around her, he could be himself. He could show her all the darkness and ugliness of his job and know she wouldn't be afraid to listen. An encounter with her always left him juiced and ready to tackle the next hurdle.

He pushed through the front door and found her sitting at the bar talking to Eva. Their heads were bent close. He could see they were lost in conversation. His sisters were like that. They had some kind of code talk that only they got. Like all sisters, his sisters fought, laughed, and would defend the other to the world in a heartbeat.

He didn't want to intrude on their vibe so he took a booth table. Just seeing Angie calmed his worries and allowed him to relax if only for a few minutes.

He ordered his meal and was on his second coffee when Angie slid into the seat across from him.

"So were you going to say hello?" she said.

With Angie it was right to the point. That's what he liked about her. "You had your sister thing going. I didn't want to interrupt."

"You could have interrupted."

"Naw. I learned long ago not to get between sisters."

She raised a brow. "You have sisters?"

"Two. Eleanor and Tess." He pretended to

shudder. "Getting between them is like putting your hand in a shark tank."

A smile tipped the edge of her lips. "I promise not to bite."

"That's saying a lot."

"I may be the Queen of the Dammed, but I can restrain myself."

God, but it felt good sitting here with her. He knew that whatever he tossed Angie's way she'd give it right back.

"How many Kiers are there?"

"Some would say too many. I'm number three of four."

"Good to know."

His meal arrived. "You eating?"

"Eva said she'd send it over."

"Good." He was hungry, but he'd wait.

She sat back in the booth. "Go ahead. Don't let your meal grow cold."

"No rush."

The lull gave her an opening to ask about the case. "I'm trying not to obsess, but . . . did you get an identification on those bodies?"

"No word yet. But assume that it was not Dixon or Donovan. Could be a couple of vagrants fighting over shoes or drug dealers. Don't let your guard down."

"I've been careful. Has anyone seen either?"

"No. I spoke to many of Dixon's acquaintances and came up empty. Also spoke to a guy at the paper named Robert Farmer. He's one of the few at the paper who will still work with Donovan."

"Robert? Tall guy, short hair, nicely dressed?"

"Yeah. How'd you know?"

A wry smile twisted her lips. "A guy joined my AA meeting last week. His name was Robert. He was nosy and didn't seem to fit." She shook her head. "Typical Donovan."

He shoved out a breath. "I wish I'd known when I was talking to the guy."

The waitress arrived with Angie's salmon cakes, and they both held back comments until she moved away. "One fire victim appears to have been killed like the girl in the motel. His throat was cut."

"Which means?"

"Could mean a lot of things. Just keep your eyes open and your mace in hand."

"Sure."

They ate in silence for several minutes. "We should talk about last night," he said.

"We don't have to." The truth was she didn't want to. She just wanted to cling to the glow.

"Like it or not, last night changed a lot."

She raised her gaze, her shock clear. "Please, you don't have to."

He cocked his head. "Don't have to what?"

"Make more of it. I mean, it was great. Really great in fact. But . . ."

Malcolm shoved out a breath. "Are you running scared, Carlson?"

Her gaze steady, she shook her head. "No. I'm not scared. I'm practical."

"Maybe I'm not." What the hell had gotten into him? "Maybe, I'd like to see more of you."

"Why?"

That made him laugh. "Gosh, Carlson, I don't know. Maybe it is the way you ride your broom or cast spells."

She set her fork down. "The thing is, Malcolm, I could really learn to like you. I don't know why, but I could get attached."

That pleased him. "And that's a bad thing because?"

"Oh, it would be great in the short run. It would be really great. But in the long run we'd hit the wall."

"Why do you say that?"

"You want things in life that I can't give you."

"You're kind of jumping ahead, aren't you?"

"Yes. I am. But that is one of my strengths. I can look ahead and see the problems. It's what makes me a great attorney."

"So you don't want to spend more time together?"

"I would. But I'd always be wondering when you would finally realize I wasn't enough."

"You're enough."

"For now." Bitterness tightened her voice. "But not in the long run."

"Why don't we just take it a day at a time? Hell, you might wake up one morning, look at me, and decide I'm not worth the effort. I mean, I work like a demon and I'm moody as hell when the case goes poorly."

She chuckled. "You, moody? Never."

He leaned toward her. "My point is neither of us knows what will happen, so for now let's let it ride."

"I've never been good at letting anything ride."

"Try it. You might like it."

She sighed. "Can you tell me if we got serious that it would not be an issue for you that I can't have children?"

"Carlson, you are just too many steps ahead of me."

A sad, knowing smile tipped the edge of her lips. "I might be able to let it ride with someone else. I can't do that with you." She leaned forward and laid a warm hand on his forearm. "Let's end it now while we're still friends."

He shook his head. "You're dumping me."

"Just preventing us a lot of pain."

Angie's head pounded with the final image she had had of Malcolm Kier. He'd been sitting in the booth, staring at her. The hard lines of his face were deep with frustration and annoyance. She'd have loved to get to know him better, but the facts were plain. He wanted children, and she could never give him that. Unshed tears burned in her throat as she got out of the car and grabbed the grocery bag from the backseat.

"I am not going to cry. This is silly. I don't need him. I don't."

She parked her car in front of Vivian Sweet's house. She wasn't sure why she'd slipped down the back staircase at King's and driven without an escort here. She walked up the sidewalk and rang the front bell. She'd called minutes ago from her cell, and Vivian had agreed to see her.

The front door opened with a whoosh. Vivian's expression was sober. "What brings you here so late?"

"I was in the grocery and passed by the

formula and diapers. I thought you could use them." It seemed a paltry offering in light of what the woman was enduring.

Vivian accepted the bag, but didn't invite Angie inside. "Every little bit helps."

She searched beyond Vivian into the living room for the baby. She was disappointed he wasn't anywhere to be seen. "How is David?"

Vivian shifted so Angie couldn't see into the house. "Doing fine. He's sleeping now. Had a bad day. Fussy."

"He's not sick, is he?"

"He's cutting teeth."

Angie didn't know the first thing about baby timetables. "Is it normal to cut teeth at his age?"

"He's a bit late, but he'll catch up."

"Does he see a doctor?"

Vivian's eyes narrowed. "Lulu took him when he was little. He's been healthy since I had him so I haven't taken him."

That didn't sound right. "So he's current on all that he needs?"

"Close enough for now." Defensiveness crept into her tone.

Angie wanted to say that wasn't good enough. But the boy wasn't hers. "How are you feeling?"

She raised her shoulders. "I'm doing just

fine. Don't worry."

"I can't help but worry."

Vivian frowned. "The paper said today that Lulu died because of you. The paper said whoever is killing these women is killing the ones that know you."

"The writer made some terrible assumptions that are not based in fact."

"It's got to be true or it wouldn't be in the paper."

Resentment burned. "The papers don't always get it right."

"Sounded convincing to me." She stared down at the bag in her hand. "It's better you stay away from us. I don't want nothing to happen to David."

"I would never do anything to bring harm to that boy."

"I can't take that chance. Now if you don't mind, you'd better leave."

"What about the legal work?"

"I'll find another attorney."

He followed Angie from King's to Vivian Sweet's house and then back to the pub. As he stood in the shadows across the street from the pub, he watched the top attic light turn on and then finally off. He imagined her sliding off her clothes before slipping under the cool sheets of her bed.

Absently, he rubbed his hands together, anticipating what it would feel like to take his knife and drag it across the tender flesh of her neck.

"Sleep tight, Angie Carlson. We have a big day ahead of us tomorrow."

CHAPTER 27

Thursday, October 13, 7 a.m.

Briefcase in hand, Angie disarmed the alarm
at the office and pushed through the front
door. She'd not called for a police escort
this morning. She should have. But after
last night with Malcolm, she'd simply not
wanted to deal with anyone — especially a
cop.

She'd spent a restless night at Eva's. Her
mind had tossed between Malcolm and David, and no matter how much she tried to
distract her mind with other thoughts the
two haunted her.

She savored the silence of the office and
kicked the door closed. The phones weren't
ringing, the fax machines weren't buzzing,
and Charlotte or Iris wouldn't be standing
in her doorway with a question. She crossed
to Iris's desk and set down her briefcase.

She heard the door settle into the frame
but didn't hear the lock click closed. Turn-

ing to close the door, she watched the door push open. A tall man, his face obscured by a hoodie, stood in the doorway.

She screamed and backed up until she bumped into Iris's desk. Thoughts scrambled to the mace buried on the bottom of her purse and the phone behind her. But she didn't dare move her gaze from this man. "Get the hell out or I'm calling the cops."

How could she have been so stupid and careless?

The man raised his hands and pushed the hoodie from his face. "Angie, stop. I just want to talk."

Martin!

"Stay away from me!"

"I don't want to hurt you. I just want to talk."

Her hands trembled, and she fumbled for the phone receiver behind her. "If you want to talk, come back later when there are people here."

"I need to talk to you. In private."

Her fingers blindly skimmed the desk and grazed over the top of the receiver. She held it up to her ear. "Later today, Martin."

He remained in the doorway, seemingly more afraid than her. "My last name is Rayburn. I'm Blue's son."

Angie held the receiver so tightly her knuckles whitened. "What?"

"I'm Blue's son. Eva's half brother?"

The information stunned her. "Why are you here now?"

"I finally screwed up the courage to talk to you."

They'd first spoken days ago, and yet he waited until now when she was alone. "I don't believe you. How long have you been stalking Eva and me?"

"I'm not stalking you. When you didn't show up at the gym I figured you were here. I'd hoped we could talk at the gym this morning."

Every nerve in her body tightened to the point of snapping. "Where is your father?"

"Please, I'll tell you everything. Just relax."

"Relax! Have you read the papers lately?"

"Yeah."

"Where is your father?"

He rubbed his hands over his worn jeans. "Dead. He died a couple of years ago."

"I'm supposed to believe that?"

"Yes."

She moistened her lips. "Why not just contact me the normal way? Why are you here now?"

"I was afraid. I want to meet Eva. She's my sister. And I want your help."

Angie's protective urge rose up strong. "There are better ways, Martin. You've handled this badly."

A heavy silence followed, and for a second she thought he'd leave. "I'm not so good with words or the conventional approaches."

"No shit. Come back later, Martin."

Another pause. "When?"

"After eight."

"Okay. I'm going to leave a book on the front steps. It's Blue's diary. It will explain a lot."

"Come back later, Martin."

She watched him leave and close the door behind him. She heard the soft footfalls of his feet on the steps, and then utter silence followed. She waited, held her breath, and then shoved out the air trapped in her lungs.

She waited several more tense minutes before she slammed down the receiver and crossed to the front door. She opened it. There was no sign of Martin, but as he'd said a slim red book rested on the top step. She picked it up and thumbed through the pages. Blue's scratchy handwriting would take time to decipher, but immediately she recognized her father's name. Would Blue be able to tell her what had happened so long ago?

Shoving out another breath, she tried to

regain her composure. Martin was gone, and yet . . . she sensed something, someone.

Abruptly she turned to her right. A man raced out of the darkness and up the steps. She turned to run back into the office, but as she turned to slam the door he shoved a large, booted foot into the doorjamb. He quickly used his weight and jerked the door open.

The man's familiar features were almost rendered unrecognizable by the dark menace burning in his eyes.

She screamed. He lunged and shoved a needle into her belly, pushing the plunger with a violent force that radiated through her body.

"Bitch."

Immediately, her strong muscles turned to jelly. Her mind spun as if she were on a merry-go-round. She dropped to her knees, and the book slid from her fingers. She hit the floor, but fought to stay conscious as she looked up at him.

"Why?" she whispered.

"I've been dreaming about this moment for a very long time."

"No."

He knelt beside her and grabbed her chin, straightening her face so that she was forced to look at him with her dimming gaze.

"Now the fun starts."

Charlotte had always considered her super paranoia to be a curse. She'd grown tired of the worrying, the double-checking. and the sleepless nights. She was a woman ruled by logic, and needless worrying was beyond any reasonable logic.

But when she realized the front door to Wellington and James was unlocked, her mind tripped from fear of an intruder, to anger that her office manager had forgotten to lock the door, and back to fear that something was terribly wrong.

She dug her cell phone out of her purse and put her finger on the speed dial for 911. "Angie! Iris!"

Instinct told her to call the cops, but she'd overreacted in the past, and her terrified calls had earned her annoyed and angry glares from the responding officers. She'd made great strides in the last couple of months, and she didn't want to lose ground now.

"Analyze and look before you call," she muttered. The front office appeared fine. There were no signs of trouble, and yet . . .

"Angie! Iris!"

A heavy silence hung in the air.

She spotted Angie's briefcase and purse

on Iris's desk. Damn. Angie had left the front door open. Not good. She lowered her cell. "Angie!"

But the lingering silence nagged. Angie was good about locking up and being a calming force. She spotted the slim red book on the floor. It was old, faded, and the edges were beat up from wear and tear.

The book was a journal, written in a thick, scrawling handwriting that grew shakier with each new entry. On the last page, written in a clear firm handwriting, was the name Martin Rayburn.

Rayburn. That was Eva's last name.

Charlotte quickly swept the offices, bathroom, and conference room in search of Angie or Iris. She found neither.

Her nerves kicked up into such a high alert that no calming mantra would ease it. She called 911.

Malcolm and Garrison arrived at the medical examiner's office just as Dr. Henson was pulling into her parking spot. Dr. Henson worked long hours, and even on a regular day she arrived early.

"Doc," Malcolm called out.

She carried a small cooler for her lunch, a large black purse, and a workout bag. Turning, she looked a bit harried. "Detectives.

I'm just heading to my office now."

"So you left a message for me," Malcolm said. "You have something?"

"I am ninety-five percent sure the body in that facility is Dixon. His dental x-rays showed a pronounced crack on his back tooth and so did my John Doe. There were also fillings in the left molars, which was also consistent."

"Ninety-five percent sure?"

"Won't be one hundred until I get the DNA tests back, but I'd say it's him."

Garrison opened the front door for her. "Has the foot been recovered?"

"No."

"And the other guy?"

"No identification yet. Mr. Donovan did not see a dentist, so we have no records to compare. I'm going to do DNA on the marrow."

Shit. "Thanks, Doc."

"If the second man was the one that tortured and killed Dixon, it would stand to reason the foot would still be on site."

"Maybe he took it somewhere and then returned."

"And leave Dixon alive and risk discovery?"

Malcolm nodded. "It's all feeling like a stage production."

"Yeah."

They turned and moved back toward their car. "Let's talk to Dixon's nurse again. Maybe she saw Donovan or someone else."

They arrived at the medical offices. Dixon's nurse was on her phone. "I'm not sure when we will be able to reschedule, Mr. Marcel. I will call you as soon as I speak to the doctor." She listened. "No, no. He's fine. He just had to go out of town on a family emergency."

She hung up and looked at the detectives. "Detective Kier, back again?"

"I show up like a bad penny."

She rose. Her body was stiff and nervous. "He tells me to tell the clients he's out of town when he doesn't show. Did you find him?"

"We did," Malcolm said.

"Where is he?" she said. No missing the annoyance in her voice.

"He's dead."

She blinked several times as if her brain could not compute what she'd heard. "Dead? How?"

"We're still piecing it together. Do you have that list of the people he saw in the last few weeks?"

"Yes." She turned to the computer on her desk and hit print. The printer under her desk spit out pages.

Malcolm studied the print out. No name jumped out at him. "Did he see anyone else?"

"It's funny you should mention that. When you came by yesterday it just didn't register. But he had a patient stop by. He didn't have an appointment, but Dixon said he didn't need one."

"Who was it?"

"He never gave his name."

"What did he look like?"

"Tall. Dark hair. I didn't get a good look at his face. He breezed past me while I was on the telephone."

"Why was he here?"

"Dr. Dixon didn't say, but later when I was in his office I saw his notes on the patient. I shouldn't have looked, but I was curious."

"Good for you."

She folded her arms. "He was here to have burns removed."

"Burns. What kind?"

"I don't know. Dr. Dixon just noted he had a large patch of scarring."

Malcolm pulled several DMV photos from his pocket. "Is it this guy?" He showed her the picture of Sierra Day's husband.

"No."

He then showed her pictures of Terry Burgess and Marty Gold.

"No."

He flipped over a picture of Connor Donovan.

"No."

The last picture in his stack had been an afterthought for Garrison. It was a picture of Micah Cross.

Her eyes widened. "That might be him."

Malcolm's heart kicked up a notch. "Are you sure?"

"Pretty sure. I just saw the side of his face."

Eyewitness testimony could be the worst. Human memory could be faulty at best. "Thanks."

When they got outside, Garrison's face was a tight drawn mask. "I want to talk to Cross."

"You and me both."

He shook his head. "Louise Cross announced her 'arrival' with a fire. And now there's another fire."

"So why is Micah Cross trying to hide burns? I don't remember him ever being in a fire."

"His twin brother Josiah died in a fire."

Garrison nodded. "According to eye witnesses Micah Cross was in the District the night of that fire."

He grunted. "Eyewitnesses. His father could have paid for eyewitnesses."

"Do you think Micah could have been with Josiah the night of the sorority house fire?"

"I don't know. But the burns make me wonder."

As Malcolm pulled into traffic, his phone buzzed. "Kier." He listened as the dispatcher relayed the message. "Shit. There's been a 911 call at Wellington and James."

"What happened?"

"Charlotte Wellington has reported Angie missing."

"No, it is not normal for her just to take off!" Charlotte's loud angry voice drifted from the reception area as Malcolm and Garrison arrived.

Malcolm had been holding on tight to his temper and fears as they'd raced across town, but he nearly lost control when he heard the panic in the attorney's voice. He moved past the uniformed officers and went directly to Charlotte.

She stood in front of the receptionist desk, her hands clenched and her face pale and drawn. She looked as if she'd aged ten years. "She would not leave her briefcase or just take off."

"Ms. Wellington," Malcolm said.

She pushed past the officer. "Thank God. I told them to call you."

"What happened?"

"Angie is missing. And I found this on the floor." She held up the little red book. "I told them that this guy must have taken her."

Malcolm shoved aside his own fears and glanced at the book. He flipped through the pages. "Martin Rayburn."

Garrison tensed. "Rayburn? As in Blue, Eva's father?"

Charlotte nodded. "The journal is written by a guy named Blue who was dying of cancer. I guess this other guy is his son. There's a boy named Martin mentioned in the journal."

"Eva has a half brother?" Garrison said.

"What would he want with Angie?" Malcolm said. "Technically, they aren't related at all."

Charlotte pointed to the book. "If you read the journal, you'll understand why Blue was positioned at the museum."

"Positioned?"

"Darius ran guns through the museum. He used the exhibit crates to stash weapons that he sold all over the world. It was Blue's job to pack the guns and see that they got shipped. He was also there to make sure Frank didn't go to the feds. Blue makes it clear that he hated Frank because Frank made Blue feel like a cheap thug."

"That's why Blue stole Frank's wife?"

"It is. Blue could bully Frank, but he wanted to be accepted on Frank's level. Marian Carlson's attention gave him validation."

Malcolm sucked in a breath. "So is he here to finish off the Carlson family?"

The uniformed officer cleared his throat. "We ran Martin Rayburn's name. He's got a warrant out for his arrest in Colorado."

"For what?" Malcolm said.

"Assault."

CHAPTER 28

Thursday, October 13, 2 p.m.

The stench pulled Angie out of a deep sleep. When she reached consciousness she recoiled, wishing she'd not awoken. Her limbs were stiff, and her head pounded with a force that took her breath away. She raised trembling fingers to her head and tried to open her eyes. The faint light in the room made the pounding worse, forcing her to lower her lids.

Where was she?

Headache or no, she had to find out where she was and get out of here. Pressing her hand to her head, she rolled on her side. Her fingers brushed concrete, and she realized she was on a cold floor. The slight movement made her sick to her stomach, and she curled her bare feet up.

As the putrid smells swirled around her, fear bit at her and stirred terrifying scenarios in her head. God, what was he going to do to her? She thought about Lulu and Sierra. Had they found themselves in this same place, scared and alone?

She pushed up on her arm, bracing as her head spun, and her stomach churned. She opened her eyes again and watched as the room spun. It would be easy to just drop back and let the maelstrom wash over her. But there was no telling how long it would take for her mind to clear and she'd bet anything she didn't have much time.

Pressing her fingers into her stomach, she pushed up onto her knees. The room was very basic, a utilitarian workroom that sported a large tub and a workbench with all kinds of tools. There was a plastic case that appeared to be filled with bugs.

The sight of the creeping insects crawling over a mound of flesh set her off. She turned to the side and vomited what little she had in her stomach. She wiped her mouth with the back of her hand. God, where was she?

Tears stung her eyes as she stared at cinder-block walls. This windowless room could be anywhere, and no one was likely to find her.

"Don't do this to yourself, Angie. You're a survivor."

"We are a great deal alike, you and me."

The man's voice radiated from a shadowed corner. He'd been watching her struggle and retch.

"How are we alike?" Disgust dripped from the words.

"Survivors. Near-death experiences. You and your cancer. Me and . . ." He abandoned the edge of the shadow and moved toward her.

Micah appeared.

"You?"

"Yes."

"I don't understand. Why me?"

He turned and knelt in front of her. "Because your sister took my family from me, and now I'm going to take her family from her."

"Eva didn't take your family."

"Mother said she was the dark temptress and she needed to be stopped. Eva is like her father. Soulless. A taker." He traced her hairline.

She jerked away. "None of this makes sense."

He rose, awry smile tipping his lips. "It will very soon."

"Where are you going?"

"I've a few toys to fetch before we begin to play."

■ ■ ■ ■

Setting up a direct feed between the police and the state prison didn't happen often. But Malcolm had called in favors, bullied, and begged to get Louise Cross to a computer screen so that they could talk. He'd have driven down to the prison but feared Angie didn't have the four hours it would take for the round trip.

Louise had agreed to talk, but her condition had been non-negotiable. Only Eva could ask the questions.

Garrison had sworn when Malcolm had told him. But after the wave of temper had passed he'd seen what needed to be done. When he told Eva the situation she'd only been annoyed that he'd waited so long to bring her into the mix.

Now Eva sat in front of the computer screen in the police department's conference room. It was a plain, simple room awash in tired beiges. A drop ceiling and conference table and chairs dated back to the eighties.

She smoothed shaking hands over her thighs. Garrison stood to her right, his arms folded but his body braced for a fight. "When will she appear?"

"It should be any minute," Malcolm said. "No matter what she says to rattle you, don't rise to the bait. We need answers about Micah and where he might have taken Angie. He wasn't at his home, and the family has dozens of properties. We need it narrowed quickly."

She nodded, then glanced up at Garrison. She smiled. "It will be fine. I'll play any part to satisfy that bitch and save my sister."

Garrison smiled. "That's my gal."

The monitor clicked on, and the prison warden appeared on screen. A tall, thin man with a pointed chin, he had owlish eyes magnified by the lenses of his thick glasses. "Detective Kier, are you ready?"

Malcolm leaned over Eva's shoulder. "Ready."

They watched as the warden moved from the screen and the door behind him opened. Louise Cross, dressed in an orange jumpsuit and shackles, made her way to the screen. She sat and stared directly into the camera. Her eyes, bright with excitement and insanity, glistened.

Malcolm stepped back, and Eva leaned forward.

Louise couldn't see Eva's hands or the way she'd twisted them so tightly together that her knuckles were white with stress.

"Hello, Louise," Eva said. Her voice didn't project the usual strength, but it was steady.

Louise's gaze narrowed and she smiled. "Eva. It's good to see you. You look well."

"Thank you."

"You've put on weight. It suits you." She looked almost gleeful. "Do you think of me often?"

"Yes."

"I hope the burn is healing."

"I'll always have a scar."

Louise seemed pleased as she said, "I am sorry for that. I didn't mean to hurt you."

Eva swallowed. "I know."

"Do you?" Louise leaned into the camera. "I didn't think you did. You haven't responded to my letters."

Eva hesitated as if searching for the right words. What did you say to the woman who'd tortured and nearly killed you? "Louise, you know I'm here to talk about Micah."

Louise's brows knitted. "Why do you want to talk about Micah?"

"We think he has Angie."

Louise sat back in her chair, her jaw tightening. "Why would he take her?"

"He's suspected of killing a couple of women."

Louise muttered an oath. "I told him not to take any unnecessary chances. Fool."

Eva tensed, knowing she'd hit a hot button. "He's taken a lot of chances. The police are hunting him."

She nodded her head. "He's my last child. I wanted him to stay safe. That's why I wanted him to keep his secrets."

Malcolm's jaw tightened. *Secrets?* What the hell was Louise talking about? As much as he wanted to shout the question into the screen, he held steady.

Eva held her composure. "We need to find him, Louise. If Kier and Garrison can get him, they are going to do their best to keep him alive. Other law enforcement officers might not really understand him. They could hurt him."

"He's my only child."

"And I don't want you to lose him."

Tears glistened in the old woman's eyes, and Malcolm didn't know if they were real or not. He never imagined that Louise loved anyone more than herself and her own dark needs.

"Help Kier and Garrison find him, Louise. We need to save him. Where would he go that is safe? Where would he hide?"

For several seconds she didn't say anything. Her body swayed as she drummed her fingers on her thigh and chewed her lip. Seconds ticked. It seemed she had dipped into another world.

"Louise. Tell me. Where is Micah?" Eva said.

Louise refocused her gaze. "Kier is there, and so is Garrison?"

"Yes."

"You won't hurt him," she said to the detectives.

"No," Malcolm answered with a clear voice, knowing he'd do what needed to be done to save Angie.

"There's a house in Alexandria. It's on the river. His father bought it years ago."

"His home is on the river. Are you talking about the same one?" Eva said.

She shook her head. "Yes."

"We sent a patrol car to that house," Malcolm said. "No one has seen him."

A prideful smile tipped the corner of her lips. "His father had a half dozen ways of getting into that house so that no one would see him. There are rooms off the basement that his father built. Both my boys loved those rooms."

Malcolm straightened, ready to bring down the force of the city on that house.

Eva touched the screen as if for a moment she saw the woman she'd once thought of as a second mother. "Thank you."

An odd flicker of tenderness flashed in

Louise's gaze. "There is something I need to tell you about Micah. It's a secret only I know."

Angie wasn't sure how much time passed when she heard the sound of a door scraping open. After Micah had left she'd wanted to search the room and find her escape, but she could barely stand, let alone walk. She'd been sick several more times before she'd rolled on her side and fallen into a fitful sleep.

Now, thankfully, her stomach was calm and her mind clear. Her body still felt shaky, but she could sit up without the world spinning. She rose slowly, steadying herself with one hand on the cinder-block wall.

The room wasn't as large as she'd first imagined. The stainless-steel table in the middle of the room had a drain underneath and a light overhead. It also came equipped with leather straps at the head and feet.

Water sloshed gently in the tub. The oddly soothing sound drew her closer. She staggered toward it and stared into murky, oily depths that smelled foul. She covered her nose and stared deeper. In the swirling water, she saw something floating in the current. The current caught the object and pulled it briefly to the surface. It was a foot.

Angie staggered back. The bones in water. The beetles in the cage. The police had found three bodies that had been stripped of flesh. "My God, Dad, how could you be a part of something like this?"

The door opened to the room, and she whirled around. Micah Cross had returned. With her mind clear, this time she could see that his entire demeanor had shifted. Meekness had been replaced by an intense energy that reminded her of a lion on the hunt.

She did remember that he'd promised to return with toys. Bracing, she took a step back.

His gaze locked on hers. He smiled. "You can see the difference, can't you?"

"You've changed."

"Not changed. Returned to my true self."

"I don't understand."

Manicured fingers reached for the buttons on his shirt. He slowly unfastened each button.

"What are you doing?"

He laughed. "Don't flatter yourself. I've no interest in you sexually."

"You said something earlier about stealing Eva's family."

"There is that. But I feel the need to tell you the whole truth. I don't get the chance to tell the truth to anyone, and I need to say the words out loud."

"What words?"

He shrugged off his shirt and revealed a chest and back covered with pink, puckered flesh. The deformity covered nearly his entire upper body.

"I laid in bed for months. The pain was so terrible that I thought I'd go insane."

"What happened to you?"

"You can't recognize burn scars when you see them?"

The pieces of this dark puzzle connected. Her sister Eva had nearly died in the fire that had killed her rapist Josiah Cross. Micah's brother. "You were at the fire that nearly killed Eva."

His eyes brightened with appreciation. "I was. But there is more."

Eva had spoken of Micah years ago. Gentle. Soft. Nothing like his violent twin. "Eva never saw you there."

"No, I arrived just as the blaze started to eat through the house. After my brother was dead."

"You tried to save Josiah?"

He tapped the edge of his nose with his fingertip. "You've got it half right." He leaned forward a fraction. "There's a big secret that I've been keeping for a very, very long time."

The intensity of his gaze had sharpened to razor points.

She raised her hand to her throat. "You escaped the fire."

Appreciation gleamed as he waited for her to guess the rest of the story. "I did."

"I read all the reports until I memorized them. They found your body."

"Not mine."

The dark truth dawned. "They found Micah's body."

Josiah had been in so much trouble with the law, but Micah had not. Darius Cross wanted to keep his troubled, surviving son out of jail. Josiah Cross might not have been able to weather a trial and avoid jail time, but Micah could. Darius had changed other evidence in the case. It made sense that he'd alter autopsy reports.

"You're Josiah?"

Laughter rumbled from his chest. "Bingo."

"Josiah Cross is alive!" Garrison barely controlled the rage burning through his body.

Malcolm wove in and out of traffic, the lights of the marked cars flashing. "I always thought that guy was too good to be true."

Garrison fisted his fingers. The woman he'd loved had been savagely raped by

535

Josiah Cross and suffered at the hands of his family for it. And now he had the chance to right a wrong. "Drive faster."

Malcolm prayed they would be in time to prevent another tragedy.

"You're Josiah," Angie said. Terror knifed at her insides, but she kept her voice calm. *Keep him talking. He wants to talk about himself.* And she intended to use that fact to buy as much time as possible.

"Surprise!"

"How? What happened?"

"Micah and I liked to play games with people. Often we'd switch places. It was a rush to know we could fool anyone. We did that a couple of times with his girlfriend in college."

"Her name was Kristen?"

"Good memory."

"Why did you go to the sorority house that night?"

"Your sister fascinated and angered me. I wanted her, and she'd have nothing to do with me. Here she was the daughter of that lowlife Blue Rayburn, and she turned me down. I wanted to teach her a lesson."

Angie remembered what a bright and motivated kid Eva had been in high school. She'd been making herself into a success despite the fact that she'd lost so much. And these monsters wanted to strip her of her successes.

She could barely keep her rage contained. "How did Micah figure into your plan?"

"He was along for the ride. He wanted to watch." Josiah shook his head. "He and I had always been a team, and I was willing to share."

Tears choked her throat. "What happened?"

"You know what I did to your sister? After I burned her, she passed out from the pain. Micah came inside and, we switched. It was his turn. I went out the front door for a smoke. I had no idea Kristen had come in the back door. She struck and killed Micah and set the house on fire. I tried to go in and save my brother, but when I looked at him on the floor I knew he was dead. The place was already in flames, so I ran."

He'd left Eva to die.

"The curtains were on fire and fell on me. That's how I got my burns." He shook his head. "But your Eva found her way out the other door. She's a survivor. Like me."

"Your father sent you to Europe during Eva's trial so no one would guess."

"It wouldn't have taken any guessing. I was burned and in pain. There was no hiding it. Father had lost one son, and knew if the truth was discovered he'd lose his other one. Josiah attended Price University so the cops assumed it was Josiah."

"And you became Micah."

"Unfortunately, yes."

"You got off."

"Not really. Father kept me heavily medicated for years. When he got sick, I tossed away the pills. But it took over a year to get back to my old self." Anger hardened his features. "So much time lost because of your sister."

"She had nothing to do with Micah's death."

"She is the dark temptress. She drew me to her. If she'd not done that I never would have been at that damn house."

He grew silent, and she panicked. Keep him talking. "What about Dixon?"

"He and my father crossed paths years ago. Under very similar circumstances as a matter of fact."

"Dixon killed Fay for your father?"

"No. Dixon never had a taste for killing. His dark appetites were sexual. He and my father shared a woman once."

"What happened?"

He seemed relaxed, happy to talk. "Fay thought she could manipulate my father into marriage. She knew he and Blue were running guns through the museum, and she tried to blackmail him. When that didn't work, she took up with Dixon. He was young and weak. When Father approached Dixon, he threatened to kill him. Dixon confessed that he and Fay had cheated. Dixon said he wished he'd not been so gentle with Fay. Father suggested that they could both get revenge and have a bit of fun if they worked together. Dixon agreed. Dixon took Fay, and when he was finished with her, Father brought her here and killed her."

Her heart tightened. "Did my father help him?"

For a moment he hesitated. "I could lie but what's the point? The truth is so much more interesting. Darius learned of the process from your father. The idea of stripping the flesh from his mistress's bones appealed. When Fay's body was found later, your father put the pieces together. He confronted Darius and threatened to go to the police. Father simply reminded Mr. Carlson that he had your safety to consider. After that, your father kept his mouth shut."

That's why her father had kept her from the museum and why he'd grown so distant. *You'll never be vulnerable.* Those had been the words he'd uttered after her surgery. Oh, God. He had been protecting her.

Josiah leaned toward her as if they were best friends. "You're lucky, you know. If Dixon and I were still working together you'd be in fairly rough shape by now."

She was at the mercy of a killer and oddly grateful that she'd not had to face Dixon. "What happened with you two?"

"We met at a charity function a couple of years ago. I could see the dark need in him hadn't faded with the years. I suggested we team up. He'd been excited. We killed three prostitutes. And then he got bored. He hired Lulu. Got sloppy. Said too much. She ran, and you know the rest."

"What happened after the trial?"

"I demanded he stop and he did. Then this past summer he contacted me. He swore he'd be careful. So we started hunting again. But the whores were like shooting fish in a barrel. I wanted more challenging prey. I saw Sierra on stage and knew she'd be the next one. I told Dixon about her and could see the delight in his gaze. The things he wanted to do to her . . ."

"You could each work it so that you had alibis when women vanished."

"Exactly. When Dixon finished with a woman, it was my turn. But then he broke the rules a second time." He shook his head. "I forgave him once, and then he went against me again."

"What did he do?"

"He wanted to keep you all to himself. He didn't want me to kill you." A grin tipped the edge of his mouth. "My father taught me well. . . . If someone crosses you, you take everything from them."

"Your father took Fay's beauty. And you were smart, so he drugged you and took your ability to think."

He frowned, pensive. "Yes."

"Did Dixon tell you about Fay?" Her words sounded rough, like sandpaper.

"Father told me about Fay before he died. He thought I'd not remember because of the drugs. But I remembered. I suppose Daddy needed to cleanse his soul."

"Did Blue know?"

"Blue ran the guns. He knew about Darius's affair with Fay, but he wasn't involved in the murder. Blue was so worried about being respectable and getting one over on your father. Poor dumb Blue wanted the reputable life. And he had a thing for your mother."

The download of information had her brain reeling. She couldn't talk any more about her parents or the destruction of their lives.

"Who is your next partner?"

"I don't want another partner. There's a certain pleasure in doing things by yourself."

There was nothing left for him to tell her. Nothing left to talk about, and still she scrambled through her memory searching for something to talk about. "What's next for you?"

"I don't know, long term. I'll lay low for a while. Maybe a trip to Europe. But in the short term you and I have unfinished business. The time for talking has ended." He grinned. "I must say, though, I've enjoyed it. You are smarter than the others, and your quickness is refreshing."

Desperation coiled in her gut. "Then keep talking to me."

He shook his head. "Time to play, Angie Carlson."

Malcolm, Garrison, and three other squad cars pulled up in front of the Cross house. They'd cut the sirens several blocks back, fearing that Josiah would hear their approach and kill Angie.

Guns drawn, they moved to the front door and rang it. A maid answered.

Malcolm raised his finger to his lips, telling her to be silent. "Where is the basement access?"

She pointed toward the kitchen. He and Garrison moved through the house and down the stairs. They could see the outline of a secret door illuminated by an interior light.

They rushed the door.

Josiah lifted Angie to her feet. "So how do you want to die? I have many ways I can steal the breath from you. I'm feeling generous, so you can choose."

Her legs wobbled, but she tightened her gut and straightened. "How did you kill the others?"

"More talk. You were wise to choose law as your profession."

He dragged her toward a metal table. "I'll cut your wrists and watch the blood drain. I was nervous with Sierra and rushed. With Lulu, I had a bit more time. But with you, I've been careful to clear my entire night. If I do this right, it'll take all night for you to die."

Angie jerked free of his hold. She whirled, ready to run for the door, but the drugs in her system made her dizzy. The sudden movements made the room spin, and she fell to her knees.

Josiah laughed. "It's why I drugged you. You're awake enough to know what is happening but not mobile enough to run. Great combination, if I do say."

He wrapped his fingers around her arm. Thoughts of Malcolm, Eva, even David swirled in her head. So much love had come into her life. So much she should have embraced but didn't.

She should have grabbed the chance with Malcolm and loved him despite the risk of loss. She should have tried harder at life after her second chance.

"You monster." She reached around and raked her fingernails over the back of his hand. "I might die, but I want you to carry scars from me forever."

"Bitch." He drew back his hand and slapped her hard across the face. She fell back to the floor. Her brain rattled against her skull. He grabbed a knife from the workbench.

And then in the next moment the world exploded.

The door burst open and Malcolm appeared. His face a mask of anger and fury he shouted, "Back off, Josiah!"

Hearing his real name threw Josiah off for an instant before he rallied and raised his knife to stab Angie.

She braced for pain.

Malcolm fired his weapon. The bullet struck Cross in the chest. The man stumbled back. He hit the wall and slid to the ground, a plume of blood exploding on his scarred chest. He dropped the knife clutched in his hand, and his head slumped forward. Malcolm moved forward and kicked the knife far away from Josiah.

Garrison moved into the room, his gun trained on Cross as his gaze swept the room for any other threats. When both detectives were satisfied Josiah worked alone, Malcolm holstered his weapon.

With Garrison still alert, Malcolm knelt beside Angie. "Are you okay?"

"Yes." Her voice was a raw whisper.

Garrison loomed over Cross as the uniforms arrived.

Angie glanced at Josiah. Wincing, she looked away and up at Malcolm. "I can't stand so well. He drugged me."

"It's okay, Angie." Malcolm cradled his hand under her elbow. "I'm here. I'm here."

She leaned into him, savoring his scent and the feel of his body against her.

"Everything is going to be okay, Angie." His voice was low and rough. His grip was firm and tight and so very soothing. "I swear."

Angie gripped his arm. "I believe you."

EPILOGUE

Three months later

Angie glanced down at the dried milk stain marking the shoulder of her silk blouse. "More dry cleaning. Great. At the rate I'm going, I'm going to be wearing a raincoat every time I hold you."

One-year-old David gurgled up from his car seat secured in Angie's backseat. He grabbed his sock, pulled it off, and tossed it on the floor. It was a game they played a lot. She'd put a hat on him. He'd toss it away. It had gotten to the point where he had only one hat left and most of his socks didn't match.

"Kid, you are going to break me," she said softly.

He laughed. When she leaned forward to unhook his seat he grabbed a handful of her hair. David was strong and had a grip that could be hard to break.

"Hey, mister. That hurts."

Angie laughed, tickled him under his shirt until he released her. She hefted him out of the back of the car and glanced toward King's.

So much had happened in the three months since Josiah had nearly killed her.

The diary Martin had given Angie had confirmed what Josiah had told her about Darius and her father. Darius's donation to the museum had been his foot in the door — the leverage he'd needed to get Frank to do just one favor. That favor had led to a decade worth of arms dealing.

The cops had searched for Martin. They'd found him in Kentucky several weeks ago and he'd been extradited back to Colorado to face the pending charges against him.

The second body had then been identified as Donovan's. The man who'd called in the missing persons report, Robert, had been trailing Angie. He'd been the one at group and the one at the newsstand. Donovan had hoped she'd reveal personal information that he could use in his story. The police had also tracked down the drug dealer Tony who had identified Lulu's abductor as Micah, a.k.a. Josiah Cross. When the cops had asked why he'd done nothing, Tony had simply shrugged and said, "It wasn't my business."

In Josiah's house they'd found so many pieces that appeared to be ivory but were in fact human bone. He'd been working on a chess set. The pawns were in place, and he'd left notes to himself that next he'd carve the queen. He'd planned to make Angie his queen.

With Josiah's death so many questions had been answered. Louise had been enraged when she'd heard about her son's death, and she'd threatened to kill both Angie and Eva. Garrison and Malcolm had made calls to the prison bureau and had Louise transferred to an out-of-state prison. They'd also severed all her contact with Angie, Eva, or anyone else they knew.

Angie had been shell-shocked by the entire scenario but as her mind cleared, she'd begun to question the course of her life. She'd gone into law to prevent injustice, and yet all her efforts had brought so much pain and heartache.

Eva and Garrison had married ten weeks ago in a quiet ceremony. Garrison's folks had been present and so had Angie and Malcolm.

Through it all Malcolm had been at her side. They'd spent quiet evenings together, making love and trying to build upon the foundation that they'd created. However, she'd never wrestled free of her worries that one day Malcolm would leave her.

And then Vivian had contacted Angie nine weeks ago seeking advice. The older woman knew she couldn't raise David in the face of her own health issues and wanted help making an adoption plan for the boy. Angie hadn't hesitated before saying, "I'll take him."

Vivian had been shocked by Angie's offer. But as they talked and discussed the boy's future Vivian had seen that if Angie adopted the boy, Vivian could still remain a part of his life.

Through tears, Vivian had whispered, "I want to be his grandmother. Not his mother."

And so, Angie had hired an adoption attorney to draw up an agreement. They signed the final papers two months ago. Though Angie loved David as her own from the moment she'd held him, he'd legally become hers yesterday when the judge had signed the final decree.

Without the stress of raising David, Vivian had had the time to grieve for her daughter. Slowly, her health had begun to return.

Angie had visited Lulu's grave several times. She prayed for the girl who had made so many mistakes but had desperately wanted to change her life. She'd vowed that she'd tell David about his birth mother often.

Malcolm had been supportive, but the adoption had created a space between them that seemed to grow by the day. She'd assumed he wasn't ready or willing to parent David. She'd let him go, knowing her path was first and foremost with David. They'd not seen each other in a month, and as much as she adored her son, she missed Malcolm.

"Now we get to go see Aunt Eva and see if she's gotten the test results back."

Angie glanced through the picture window into King's. There appeared to be a crowd. "David, we are going to have some company."

She'd taken leave from Wellington and James and had spent the last nine weeks learning to be a mom.

A cold wind rushed down the street, whipping up the edges of her coat. Balancing a diaper bag, she kicked the car door closed and, cupping her hand over David's head, rushed into the heat of the pub.

She'd not taken two steps inside when the crowd turned in unison and shouted, "Surprise!"

Angie startled. David flinched and looked

up at Angie waiting for his cue to cry or laugh. Angie smiled and the baby relaxed.

Her entire group of friends had gathered. Charlotte, Iris, King, Bobby, Garrison, and Eva. She searched briefly for Malcolm but didn't see him.

Eva cut away from the crowd and moved toward Angie. Her slightly rounded belly and fuller face made her look lovely. "We wanted to throw a party for the new mom."

Angie saw the sign that read, WELCOME, DAVID. "Honey, this is so wonderful. You have enough going on and did not have to do this."

"I wanted to do it." She squeezed Angie's arm and whispered, "The CF test was negative. My daughter is fine."

The words took a moment to penetrate. *Daughter. Fine.* Tears pooled and ran down her face. "Honey, I am so glad."

Garrison moved toward them. For the first time in weeks she sensed his grin was heartfelt. "We both slept like the dead last night. First night with no real worries."

Angie had had a nightmare the other night. She'd dreamed of Louise stealing into her house and taking David. "You owe me a son," the old woman had cackled. Angie had awoken with a start and gone to the baby's crib. She'd been so relieved to see him sleeping, she'd wept.

When she'd returned to her bed, it had grown cold. She thought about Malcolm and how good his body had felt next to hers. She missed him and wished she could have both him and her son in her life.

Eva tickled David's stomach. "Put your bags behind the bar, Angie, and let me hold my nephew."

Releasing David didn't come easy to her. She loved David so much that it frightened her. The little guy had opened her heart so wide. But she needed to let the fear go and enjoy her life. She smiled and let the boy go to her sister.

I will always keep you safe, no matter what.

Garrison touched the top of the boy's head, now covered with thick brown hair. "We promise to take good care of him and will have him back in a minute. My sister Carrie wants to meet him, and my mom is itching to hold a baby."

Angie watched as her sister moved through the crowd introducing her new nephew to everyone.

She'd grown so accustomed to carrying the boy around she felt oddly lost without the weight of his body in her arms. But this moment alone gave her the chance to scan the crowd again for Malcolm. There was no sign of him.

Irritated and disappointed, she moved to the bar, where King had laid out a feast. She reached for a square of cheese. It had been weeks since she'd eaten a meal without David in her arms.

"He's a great-looking kid," Malcolm said. His deep voice glided down her spine, making her skin tingle.

She turned and faced him. He looked good wearing a flannel shirt, jeans, and hiking boots. His hair was brushed back, and despite the winter chill, he had a tan. He'd no doubt gone to his cabin in the woods.

"I'm so lucky," she said. It was all she could do not to touch him. "You look really good."

He nodded. "So do you."

If she'd learned anything during those horrific moments with Josiah it was not to hide her feelings. She spoke what was in her heart. "I've missed you."

He cocked his head. "Really?"

"Yeah."

He rubbed the back of his neck with his hand. "That's good."

"It is?"

"Makes it easier to say what I need to say."

"You look nervous, Detective."

"I am."

"Why?"

"Because I love you. And I've been trying for weeks to screw up the courage to tell you."

She closed her eyes, unable to bear his gaze.

"I needed to make sure I had it in me to be the man you and David needed." Tension rippled through his body. "When I make a commitment I don't back down." He grabbed her arm and pulled her through the crowd into the kitchen. King was at the stove. He raised his hand to speak, but when he caught Malcolm's expression he mumbled something about the bar and left them alone.

Malcolm turned Angie to face him. "I'm crazy about you, Angie. I want to make a go of it with you just like I did before."

"My life is a little more complicated than before."

"David's the kind of complication I like."

She wrapped her arms around his neck and kissed him. He hugged her, growing at her touch. He deepened the kiss.

She broke the kiss. "I don't want to jump ahead and borrow trouble, but it's what I do best. What if —"

"Stop with the what ifs. Please. For once."

She leaned her forehead against his. She

spoke softly, unable to not say the words. "I'm not going to be able to ever give you the perfect storybook kind of life you wanted. No mini-Malcolms running around."

Malcolm traced a strand of hair from her face. "My mother would tell you that one Malcolm is quite enough."

She laughed and kissed him. "I'm just so glad there is the one."

The kitchen door burst open, and Eva held a crying David. The instant he saw her, he held out his arms.

Eva handed him over to Angie. "I swear he was just fine, and then in the next instant he looked around the room and didn't see you and just started crying."

Angie kissed him on the head. "It's okay. I got him. The books say they start to tell the difference between Mom and the world at this age."

Eva patted the boy on the back. "Well, he sure does know who his mama is."

Angie's mind flashed to Lulu, the young woman who'd loved this kid to distraction. She would always make sure the boy knew he had two mothers.

When Eva left and David calmed, Angie faced Malcolm. "You two haven't seen much of each other lately."

Malcolm tickled the kid's belly. "Angie, why does the boy have one blue sock and one green sock?"

"He keeps tugging them off. This was all I could find today."

Malcolm laughed. "Kid, you are going to be a handful."

David shoved his thumb in his mouth, and then thrust his weight toward Malcolm. He caught the boy easily and hoisted him up.

The baby stared at Malcolm and then at Angie. He grinned, still managing to suck his thumb.

They all three laughed.